STOLEN SHROUD

STOLEN SHROUD

By Daniel Westlund

For the Win Publishing, LLC
 Author can be contacted about attending a book study or event either in person or over Skype.
For information, go to stolenshroud.com
Cover and interior design by Miblart

1. Literature & Fiction > Religious & Inspirational Fiction > Science Fiction & Fantasy
2. Literature & Fiction > Religious & Inspirational Fiction > Christian Fiction > Futuristic
3. Religion & Spirituality > Christian Books & Bibles > Theology > Apologetics
4. Literature & Fiction > Religious & Inspirational Fiction > Christian Fiction
5. Literature & Fiction > Religious & Inspirational Fiction > Christian Fiction > Mystery & Suspense
6. Literature & Fiction > Contemporary Fiction > Christian
7. Literature & Fiction > Religious & Inspirational Fiction > Christian Fiction > Historical

ISBN: 978-1-7334438-2-1 (Paperback)
ISBN: 978-1-7334438-1-4 (E-book)

Stolen Shroud is by far the best Christian thriller in recent memory. Nothing about the story is vanilla, shallow, or naive. This is a tour de force of very real and mature struggles with faith and skepticism packaged inside a gripping science fantasy rollercoaster. Magic, love, and gritty adventure are seamlessly interwoven into a high-tech, philosophical, far-reaching narrative that will keep you on the edge of your seat until the very last page. Not to be missed.

– Joshua David, author of Amazon bestseller *Seed: Judgement*

The book switches back and forth chapter by chapter [from present to past]. At first, I found this annoying. Why do I give a rip about this guy's childhood when I want to know what happened to the Shroud? However, as time went on, I found something happening.

While I came skeptical and at first was having a hard time getting into it, before too long, I found out that I was. I wanted to know what happened. I found, in the end, a story with many threads that weaved together in a wonderful way.

The villain of this story was one of the most diabolical ones that I have come across and it was fascinating how all of that came together. . . This was truly one of the great villains.

– Nick Peters, host of Deeper Waters apologetic podcast

Stolen Shroud is Christian literature at its finest. The fascinating mystery of the disappearance of the Shroud of Turin is complemented perfectly by issues about doubt and skepticism. Christians and non-Christians alike will agree that this perfect package of sci-fi, religion, and humanity is not like any other book out there. Its depth and personality sticks with you.

-Brandon Crowther, owner of AffordableEditors.com

This author has crafted an intriguing story filled with suspense, heart, humor, and wit. The premise is absolutely brilliant. Using scientific and technical details, he convincingly suggests that by manipulating quantum physics, humans truly could obtain superhuman powers, an aspect that makes a seemingly implausible story theoretically possible.

Clearly this author researched the subject of the Shroud of Turin thoroughly. Details concerning the Shroud are fascinating, many of which I was previously unaware of, even though I have studied the Shroud extensively. This novel also makes other compelling arguments for Christianity but doesn't shy away from telling both sides of the story.

Not only does this author tell the main story thread, but he also gives compelling backstories to explain the rationale for the characters' actions. I found the back stories just as compelling and suspenseful as the main story line.

Congratulations to the author for an outstanding debut novel. I look forward to reading more from him in the future.

– R.A. Williams, author of Amazon bestseller *Carbon-14: The Shroud of Turin*

PART 1

1

The Shroud

I stare at the figure of Christ, arm drawn back behind his head, poised to strike at the damned. I'm staring at one of the most famous paintings in the world, 'The Last Judgment' fresco, on the altar wall of the Sistine Chapel. Below Christ stands St. Bartholomew, holding his skin, since he achieved martyrdom by being flayed alive. I only notice this because yesterday when I toured the Vatican, the guide pointed out Michelangelo often made not-so-subtle statements in his paintings. In this case, he painted St. Bartholomew with his (Michelangelo's) own face to show how poorly he was being treated by the Pope. I know a thing or twelve about self-pity, but this seems extreme.

But now is not the time for self-pity. Here I sit in the Sistine Chapel among about two hundred of the world's Who's Who in the fields of science, journalism, and religion. What the hell am I doing here? I'm not a leader in any of those fields, though I do my best in two of the three. I'm sitting four rows back in an uncomfortable chair on the right side, fighting to understand the Pope read his remarks in English. I see him over the sea of heads in front of me, wearing his white suite along with a matching white beanie and a big silver crucifix around his neck. His backdrop is the Last Judgment fresco, and to his right is the real star of the night. Mounted vertically, it's more than twice as tall as his Grace: The Shroud of Turin.

From where I sit I can barely make out the faint sepia images of a man, the front-facing image on bottom and dorsal image on top. It doesn't look like the most remarkable artifact in human history. In fact, no one thought of it as such until one day, toward the end of the 19th century, when an amateur photographer named Secondo Pia took its picture, and what he saw in the negative image was so striking he almost dropped the photographic plate from shock: the detailed and vivid image of the man of the Shroud. I can relate to this as I almost dropped my phone when I received a call requesting I join the 'STURP 2' team to test the Shroud of Turin. In fact, I had recently become obsessed with this same artifact and was researching the Shroud the very moment they called. The original 'STURP' team (Shroud of Turin Research Project) was the group of researchers who were given access to conduct scientific tests on the Shroud for five days back in the 70s. The Vatican is conducting this ceremonial press conference the night before we (STURP 2) will perform our more modern tests.

I need to focus. "No matter what are the results from the tests of tomorrow, the Shroud of Turin will always be a source of wonder and reverence for the faithful," the Pope hedges. I don't blame the Pope for hedging in light of the 1988 carbon dating debacle–when the Catholic Church allowed the Shroud to be carbon dated, which ballooned into a media frenzy where that test alone became a binary for the authenticity of the Shroud, only for the results to indicate that it was a medieval forgery. In fact, last year when the Vatican announced new tests were going to be administered on the Shroud, the media was gobsmacked, and sneered accordingly, since in its collective mind the case was closed.

The man next to me is spilling over into my chair, and I'm trying not to touch him. I sneak a peek at the crowd to my left and try to guess why each person is here. The priests and the nuns are easy, dressed in their outfits. I peg the older, less attractive people as scientists or religious leaders, and the younger, better-looking ones as journalists. I'm sure there are some exceptions. Hopefully I'm one of them.

I zone back in on the Pope, looking down at his notes. "The Church does not condone the imbalance of wealth between the rich and poor of the world." Wow. Wonder how he transitioned to his soapbox so quickly? Everyone besides me is listening intently. I gaze up at the ceiling and find the iconic scene of God reaching out to touch Adam. Yikes. It has to be over 50 feet high. I can imagine poor Michelangelo perched up there on shaky scaffolding, paint dripping into his eyes. No wonder he felt sorry for himself.

Wait a minute. The Pope hasn't said anything for a few seconds. Longer than a pregnant pause. He has a blank expression on his face, and his mouth is stupidly opened. Is he panicking? Normally this would feel awkward, but I'm not picking up on an awkward vibe. I don't hear any whispers of concern or confusion from the crowd. In fact, they're completely silent. I wheel my head around and see rows of witless faces, with opened, vacant eyes staring ahead, and the same dumb opened mouth as the Pope.

What. The. Hell. Are they mimicking him? Everyone?

Behind the rows of people is the short marble wall with a screen on top that divides the Sistine Chapel into two sections, and perched above that on a platform is a TV camera, manned by a camerawoman. Can't see her face but she's perfectly still like everyone else. I turn and look at the guy next to me, with his big, shaved jowls. Same blank stare, mouth agape. At least I see his chest rising and falling with breath.

Again. What the hell is going on? Mass hypnosis? For everyone except me? Who else in this room is conscious?

Just before I stand and ask if anyone knows what's happening, I hear some commotion at the back of the room and turn my head. Through the holes in the screen I see two men enter the chapel through the back door, wearing black slacks and black long-sleeved shirts–with assault rifles strapped to their backs!

I freeze, barely keeping my wits about me enough to slowly turn my head forward to blend in with the mindless zombies. I even open my mouth like them.

I see them from the corner of my eye as they walk forward, up to the Shroud. They speak to each other in whispers that I can tell are not English. I can't get a good look at their faces but can tell they both have thick mustaches and dark complexions. They are standing in front of the case and I can't tell what they're doing.

Crash! One of them smashed the glass case, and the Shroud crumpled to the ground.

Holy balls. They're stealing the Shroud of Turin!

They fold it up and stuff it in a big leather bag one of them throws over his shoulder. They walk briskly, past the Pope, toward The Last Judgment fresco, and out the door underneath it on the right. The side of the damned. One of the Pope's Swiss Guards, in his blue and yellow court-jester-looking outfit, stands sentry by door, open-mouthed, inanimate.

This can't be happening, whatever it is.

I force myself to stand up on shaking legs. "Is anybody

there?" I shout. "Did anyone else see this?"

Nothing but my voice echoing around the great room. Everyone I see has an open mouth and lifeless eyes. If I'm on a hidden camera TV show, this is the best prank ever, complete with a performance by the Pope and the man-handling of the Shroud of Turin.

What to do? They took our phones for fear of us interrupting the ceremony. Not sure where they're being held. I could go to the back of the chapel, back through the door from which we entered, and try to find my phone, or someone lucid.

Or I could go the other way and singlehandedly give chase to armed terrorist thieves.

I walk out of my aisle, stepping over legs, and turn toward The Last Judgment, toward the door by which the criminals left. If it was anything other than the freaking Shroud of Turin, I wouldn't be going toward the guys with guns.

"Hello?" I try to address the Swiss Guard at the door. I wave my hand in front of his face. It feels like I'm at Buckingham Palace trying to get a reaction out of one of those British Guards. Nothing. I think I'm stalling.

Thud! I turn around. The door on the opposite side of the chapel bursts open and slams into the wall. A black blur streaks through it. A man, a priest it looks like, is running toward the front.

"Hey, over here," I yell. "Do you know what's going on?"

He passes the screen and heads toward my door. Toward me! Crap.

Slam!

I gulp for breath. He launched his body into me like a linebacker.

"What did you do with the Shroud?" He's standing over me now. He knocked me through the doorway and down a few stairs onto a little landing. A flight of stairs leads down to my right.

"What?" I suck in air. "Some guys came in and took it right–"

"You are different," he interrupts. "Hawk changed you?"

"What? Who?" Another breath. "I don't know what you're talking about." Breath. "I'm a researcher here to test the Shroud tomorrow..."

I stop talking because at the word 'test' he took off like a hound of hell, down the stairs, disappearing.

Now what? I pull in another breath and my ribs throb. I look down the marble stairs.

I find my legs giving chase after him. I'm skipping two stairs with each step. My pride that I'm running toward the conflict for once outweighs my fear of what awaits me at the bottom.

I reach the end of the three flights of stairs and I'm in the modern section of the Vatican museum. To my left is a long hallway. Not exactly a hallway, but a series of rooms connected to each other, and at the end of them I can see the priest as he disappears from view to the right.

I charge after him. I pass a Swiss Guard, standing like a statue. What is going *on*? My lungs scream at me. When I get to the end of the hallway, it opens up to a large room with a staircase on the left, and to the right and ahead I see a doorway. Must be the way the priest went since there is no other exit to the right. This is not really happening, I tell myself. No way.

"Wait up!" Someone calls from behind me. A female voice. I look behind and see her on the other side of the modern art gallery. No time to answer. I turn and bolt for the doorway ahead.

I have to jump over a red velvet keep-away rope blocking the doorway, and when I do, I find myself in one of the Raphael rooms. The Immaculate Conception, if I remember right. Less grand but as beautiful as the Sistine Chapel. No priest here. I run ahead to the main door that leads to another hallway. When I reach the doorway, I look down the hall but I still don't see the priest. I stop in the doorway to catch my breath, wondering which way to go.

"Wait!" The lady from earlier appears in the door on the other side of the Raphael room. As she runs toward me, I realize she's a knockout. No time for that now. I turn right and run down the hallway with her behind me.

"Where are we running?" she calls after me.

"I don't know," is all I can think to say. At the end of the hallway I have to turn left, and quickly left again, sending me back in the direction I came from down a parallel hallway. I see nobody ahead and use that, along with my burning lungs, as an excuse to slow down and wait for her.

"Who are you?" she asks. She's barefoot, in a shimmering silver dress. I imagine she's kicked off high heels. I start running again to keep up with her.

"Mark Eberhart. I'm supposed to be testing the Shroud tomorrow. Who are you?"

"Cora Byron. Journalist covering the ceremony."

Journalist. Figures. Wait, have I heard of her?

We reach the end of the hallway and can only turn right. I see an impossibly long corridor ahead of me but still no priest. I recognize it. The gallery of maps, with old maps of Italy on both sides.

I hear some commotion ahead. It's coming from a room off the hall on the left. We reach the doorway and I try to process the scene in front of me. The backdrop is a Vatican Museum room, I don't remember which from the tour, with busy frescoes on the walls and ceilings. The priest is standing over two men, dressed in all black and sprawled out on the ground, AK-47's lying next to them. The same guys who stole the Shroud.

"Did you just take down two armed gunmen?" I ask.

"Shhhh," he orders.

"Do you have the Shroud?" I whisper.

"They did not have it. Do not follow me." He has an accent, maybe Italian. He's past middle age, with a plump nose, salt and pepper hair, and age-lines creasing his olive skin. He turns to the altar behind him (I guess this is a chapel). I notice the altar is turned slightly askew from parallel to the wall. The priest pushes it further off-center and I see there's a hole in the ground underneath where the altar had been.

"We're coming with you and you can't stop us," replies Cora.

He looks at her. She goes limp and falls to the ground. Her head is facing my direction and I can see her eyes are dilated and her mouth is opened, like the people in the Sistine Chapel. I turn toward him and we lock eyes.

"What did Hawk do to you?"

"I don't know what that means."

"Do you want me to get the Shroud, so you can test?" he asks.

"Yes."

"Then stay here," he says, as he disappears down the hole.

2

Ditched

Mark
22 years earlier

"Let's stay here," Ronnie said to me. "We can play. Just us."

"No, Ronnie. Let's go play with our other friends."

"Ok, fine. But when we get back from Globals you have to come over to my house and spend the night? You can bring your Nintendo."

"Maybe. We'll see," I answered. Ronnie smiled, which turned his eyes into upside down smiley faces. It would be summer break when we got back home. I hoped Ronnie wouldn't find a way to track me down. Ronnie's real name wasn't Ronnie, but Stephen. At the beginning of the school year he showed up with a hand-me-down PE shirt with the name Ronnie embroidered on the front, presumably because his parents couldn't afford to get him a new PE uniform. He had pouted about his nickname at first, but finally gave up and embraced it.

I looked in the mirror to check my appearance before we left the room. I hoped, against all historical evidence to the contrary, that a situation would present itself where I would strike up a conversation with a cute girl from another school, charm her, and end up getting my first kiss. I've never figured out how girls determine what makes a guy cute. I think I'm good-looking enough. Tall, tan skin, dirty blonde skater hair. Although, my nose had recently gotten a little long for my face, and my braces didn't help either. At any rate, girls took no interest in me. Maybe because they sensed I was petrified of them. That's why all my friends were dudes, and I'd never said more than a few words to a girl I liked. "All right. Let's go."

Ronnie and I skipped down the eight flights of stairs between our dorm room and the main floor. Globals had been a blast so far. Our 'Destination Imagination' (DI) team was one of the two from our school that won Regionals, and the only one to win State and move on to Globals. Our Technical Team had to solve the problem of how to mechanically move a person up a ramp, without wheels, with only $25 to build our contraption, and no adult help. We had a dream team with Jay, who was a genius, leading the way. The next smartest kids in school were me and Abel. Then there was Shane, who wasn't traditionally smart, in fact he had been held back in elementary school (he might have been dyslexic), but he had what we called 'Shane logic,' which wasn't logical to anyone except Shane. Because he approached problems differently than the rest of us, he made more than his fair share of contributions. Ronnie was obviously the pity member of our team, put on it by the GT teacher, Mr. Kaluza, who was trying to give him a break for once in his life. However, the second day of Globals, Jay made sure to put Ronnie in his place, telling him he was only there to be our 'retarded mascot.' I pointed out to Ronnie he was the only one small enough for our ramp to support and so he was the MVP, bringing that familiar smile to his face.

I wish I was always that kind to Ronnie, though. That same night I saw a kid wearing a bolo tie and got the idea to gather various goofy items from the other guys in the dorm: a fedora, super baggy pants, the bolo tie, and convinced Ronnie he would look cool if he dressed up in the ensemble. I even found someone with a boom box, and on the way to the assembly I got a 'posse' together, blasted rap music, and started the chant, "Go Ronnie! Go Ronnie!" Right on cue Ronnie busted out some hilarious old dance moves like the running man and the cabbage patch, all to the cheers and laughter of the gathering crowd. His faux entourage ballooned up to about 100 people, and it got so out of control that during the assembly, a high-school kid from another school got his girlfriend (who was the prettiest girl at Globals and a full head taller than Ronnie), to sit by him and pretend she was his date for the evening. It was a rotten thing to do, but Ronnie didn't know any better, and hopefully he would never figure out everybody was laughing *at* him.

Presently, Ronnie and I reached the lobby of the dorm where Abel and Shane were standing awkwardly among the couches of squealing and posing and flirting teenagers. Abel was heavyset (he said he wasn't fat, but his body was a hoarder), medium height, and Hispanic, with deep sunken black eyes, and fluffy brown hair parted down the middle. Shane was tall and pale, with long, dull hair and a large helping of acne. I think a quick note on these guys would be helpful. Abel's read every sci-fi book ever, and Shane has watched every horror movie, and every weird, artsy-fartsy movie, which he claims to enjoy. We call them 'Shane movies.' Meanwhile I was kind of the sports guy of the group.

"Hey guys. We just barely got here," I said in an over the top Mexican accent, making fun of the one time Abel accidentally sounded like a Mexican American. Shane laughed.

"Butthole" said Abel.

"Hey, I'm just jokin'," I said, still with the accent. Then in my own voice, "Where's our beloved Jay?"

"He can't make it because he is meeting up with his fictional girlfriend," Abel dead-panned.

"Oh, you mean the one from Canada who we keep missing somehow?" I asked rhetorically. "I really should move to Canada. Apparently it's a land full of hot girls who are only interested in losers who can't get a girlfriend in the U.S. of A."

Abel shrugged his shoulders, "I'll come with you."

"Sad. Rather than hang out with us, he's going to hide all night and pretend he's getting with a girl just so he can tell us about it tomorrow."

"Yep," said Abel. A girl on the couch behind him shriek-laughed at something her friend said.

I changed the subject. "Last night here, boys. We need to do something epic. Not just have fake seizures in front of random girls again." We were without adult supervision for the first time in our lives, and our freedom manifested itself in the form of acting like idiots in front of strangers, with me as ringleader.

I leaned in close to Abel and Shane and whispered, "Meet me back at the cafeteria." Ronnie leaned in to hear the whisper but couldn't make it out. The four of us headed out from the chaos of the lobby and into the balmy, late-spring Tennessee night. "Any ideas, guys?" I asked. We approached a fountain in the quad.

"Actually, we could get on the public bus and try to get that crazy driver again," Abel suggested.

"Oh, you mean that time y'all freaking ditched everyone to go to the mall?" Shane asked in mock outrage. Partial mock outrage. I didn't intend to ditch even Shane that day, but

Abel and I started walking off campus and ended up on the other side of Knoxville, and had to take the bus to get back before the evening ceremony.

"Speaking of ditching," I answered. "Aaaannnnd now!" I took off in a sprint to the left of the quad and Abel and Shane ran to the right. Ronnie followed after me but was quickly losing ground.

"Mark, wait," Ronnie yelled after me, but I had doubled back behind the high-rise dorm and was heading toward a maze of apartments. "Where are you going?" he pleaded.

I zig-zagged through apartments. I could hear the tears in his voice and almost stopped out of pity, but I didn't. The promise of hanging out the last night with just the core three outweighed the guilt of ditching Ronnie. Once I lost him, I jogged back to the high rise and went inside to the cafeteria where Abel and Shane were waiting.

"Never gets old," I said. The other guys laughed.

"You're such a freaking jerk," Shane was smiling. He was half-serious again.

"Yeah, but at this point it's tradition." We'd been ditching Ronnie all week. When we met back up with him he would play along like it was a joke, but the last time we did it he acted pissed off the rest of the night.

We walked back outside. "I mean, really, he's kind of fun to have around," I said. "When it's just him and me, it's like I'm playing with a little brother. But when other people are around, I feel responsible for his dorkiness. But I'm not outright cruel to him like Jay. Now *he's* the jerk. Not sure what he gets out of being cruel to him."

Abel said, "My abuel–my grandma says that's what people do when they are insecure to make themselves look better, but I don't think that's it. Or not all of it, actually. Some people are just pricks."

"You know what? I'm gonna stand up to him," I said as we turned and headed toward the edge of campus. "I'm gonna tell him we don't believe all his B.S. stories about getting with girls, and we think he's ridiculous, and he needs to lay off Ronnie and Abel–"

"No, you're not," said Abel. "Because you're all talk."

"Yes, I will," I said, but I was taken aback by Abel's contradiction. Up to this point Abel had always been my 'yes man.' I felt my face flush.

"Actually, you're not much better than him," Abel continued. "You laugh along when he makes fun of me and Ronnie. You talk like you've had girlfriends like him, but I've known you since sixth grade and you haven't had one. The girlfriends you talk about at your old school would have been fifth graders. Have you seen how small fifth graders look now that we're in eighth grade?"

"I still have the rest of the night to find one," I said lamely.

We walked on in silence. We had run up against a busy street on the edge of campus and I could see a McDonalds up ahead. Everything Abel said was true, but it still stung that he called me on it. I thought he bought into my act. There was something about Abel that made me care about his opinion above everyone else's, and I would find myself trying to impress him. Maybe it was because Abel had such strong opinions himself.

"Dude, I'm sorry I snapped at you," Abel said. "I didn't actually mean it. Things are always more fun when you're around."

"Thanks," I said, not knowing what else to say. I changed the subject, "So, what are we thinking for tonight's prank? Panty raid?"

"Ha ha!" Shane laughed. "That's so freaking stupid. Like a freaking '80s teen movie."

"Yeah," jumped in Abel. "I've never actually understood the point of a panty raid."

"I guess if you take all their panties . . . they have to wear the same underwear the next day?" I speculated.

"We don't know any girls, so we'd just be creeps breaking into their room. Assaulting them," said Abel.

"Ok, not my best idea. How about this? We take tonight off, since we don't know anyone here anyway, and when we get back, we toilet paper the principal's house."

"I'm down," said Shane.

"Sounds stupid," said Abel.

We waited at the crosswalk for the light to change, and then crossed the street and walked up to the door of the McDonalds. I was sticky with sweat.

"I'm not even hungry," I said.

"Me neither," said Shane. "Let's go into the kid's play area. They let parents go in with their kids and we're smaller than some parents."

"Flawless logic," said Abel.

We walked through the door and headed back to the outside play area, where we climbed into the Hamburglar, which required ducking into the doorway and climbing up a ladder, and then awkwardly wedging our bodies around his 360 degree mouth, with a cage outlining his teeth. We were laughing and horse-playing, with our heads near the next guy's butt because the space was too small for the three of us, when Shane ripped one into Abel's face, or 'busted a grumpy' as Abel called it, and we died laughing. Abel worked his way back to the ladder to make his retreat and I followed. We got on the merry-go-round and rode it lazily around. Cars zipped by on the other side of the playground fence.

"Why don't you stand up to Jay?" I asked Abel. "It appears your testicles have finally come in."

"Why are y'all intimidated by Jay?" interrupted Shane. This was an honest question, as Shane wasn't scared of him. Every once in a while he would tell Jay he was full of crap, but Jay would laugh it off like he was kidding, and Shane let it go at that. And for some reason, Jay didn't make fun of Shane to his face, despite the ample material. They had a weird, symbiotic relationship.

"Because that's the normal human reaction to him," I said to Shane. "You're a cat. Most people are dogs because they form bonds and care what people think about them, but you just roam around and . . . crap in your litter box. Sorry, my analogy fizzled out, but you know what I mean."

"Why do y'all care about his stupid stories?" asked Shane. "I think they're freaking hilarious."

"I don't know," I said. "It's like he builds himself out to be this person who he's not, and then makes life hell for Ronnie and Abel because they are not as great as his fake persona. And I go along with it like a wuss and am Jay's best friend in his mind, when in reality I'm a hypocrite. If we knocked him off his high horse, it would change the whole dynamic."

"No, it wouldn't," said Abel. "Maybe you'd humiliate him. Maybe he would even cry and run away. But the next day, he'd come back and be all, 'What's up, guys?' like it never happened, and we'd fall into old habits and play our roles, because he has a stronger personality than us. And we actually won't have it in us to fight that battle every day."

"You're probably right," I said, realizing in fact he was exactly right. "Here's what I don't get about him. Like your grandma said, bullies make fun of people to make themselves feel better. It's the same for people who make up stories about 'doing it' with girls. They're insecure with themselves and want everyone to think they are impressive when they aren't. The thing about Jay is, he *is* impressive. He got a freaking

1600 on his SATs in seventh grade. That's impossible. Why doesn't he just rest on the fact that he's a genius?"

"Because being a genius is not enough for him," said Abel.

Shane was standing up now and pushing the merry-go-round faster, his flat white belly showing under his shirt. He said, "I don't know. It's just . . . he'll grow out of it. I have a cousin who was a genius and he screwed off at school and did drugs and failed out. Then one day, when he was like 20, he decided to turn his life around. He got his GED and went to Community College and then U.T. and now he's in law school at the top of his class. That's why I like Jay. Anyone can be a nice, regular guy. But he's special. I'd rather be friends with a guy like that than some freaking schmo any day of the week."

"Shane logic," Abel and I both said at the exact same time, followed by "Jinx." We both laughed.

After a few seconds of silence, I said, "Maybe he'll just move away."

Abel got off the merry-go-round. "Or die."

3

The Tunnel

I swear I don't have a death wish.

I'm looking around the room in the Vatican Museum. Two thugs and journalist Cora Byron are lying on the floor unconscious. I guess she'll be ok.

What should I do? Run and try to find some authority figure? If I found someone, they could get medical help for her, if that would help with this sort of thing, and they could get a security team to give chase to the Shroud of Turin down this magic hole. That would make sense. Assuming I could find someone. Or . . . I could ignore the priest's admonition and go after him myself.

Who is this priest? On the one hand, he apparently has telepathic powers, so he could be in league with the people who stole the Shroud. On the other hand, he seems to be legitimately trying to recover it, and the guys lying on the floor indicate he's not with them. He considers me more of a nuisance than anything else.

Screw it. I've come this far already. I'm going down the hole.

I walk over to the altar and stare down the hole. Blackness. I see at the top there are footholds carved into the wall, like a ladder. I lower myself into the hole, the colorful frescoes disappearing as my head goes beneath the floor level. I climb down, and down some more. I look up and see what is now a small opening of light into the room above. It reminds me of what I imagine it would be like to die, and walk into the light. My feet touch the ground, which feels like uneven, solid rock. I can make out a passageway about six feet tall (shorter than me anyway) and wide enough for about two people. It is angled slightly downward, and the air is stale and hot, and smells musty. I start walking slowly, crouching, waving my hands in front of me because I can't see ahead. My hand bumps into the side of the wall and I realize it's best to hold one hand along the side of the wall, and the other ahead of me. Soon it's total blackness. I close my eyes and it looks the same as when they're opened. The ground starts to feel soft, and the wall too. I can feel dirt falling off the wall as I run my hand along it.

Why am I doing this? I have always steered clear of conflict. It's my natural defense mechanism. At the same time, I'm a bit of an adrenaline junky (I know, I'm a regular walking contradiction). But this is different. Jumping out of an airplane with a parachute on my back is statistically safe. It's a way to trick my brain to think I'm risking my life to get a rush. Whereas whoever is at the other end of this tunnel probably intends to do me harm. What do I think I'm going to accomplish anyway? Find a bad guy and wrestle the Shroud of Turin from his hands? Again, if it was anything other than the Shroud of Turin–my obsession for the past two years–I would not be in this tunnel.

The tunnel is angling upward now. My steps feel heavier than before. Why the hell is this tunnel here? It's like something out of a Dan Brown novel. There must be a reason. It couldn't have been dug just for this heist. I toured the Vatican Grottoes and Vatican Necropolis yesterday, which are basically graveyards under Vatican City, but I think those developed because Vatican City was built on top of an old graveyard, the spot where they believed St. Peter was buried, rather than being manmade like whatever this is.

I touch something soft in front of me. *Whack!* Something hard hits my arm. I step back.

"Fool," someone whispers. The priest.

"I'll be quiet," I whisper.

No response from him, so I continue ahead slowly, still feeling the wall with one hand, and ahead of me with the other.

After a few minutes, I can make out his shape about ten feet ahead of me. There is a source of light up ahead somewhere and the tunnel is heading upward now. My hands are feeling cold, wet, solid rock again. The priest crouches down.

Thump. My head hits the ceiling. Duh. I see now he's crouching because while the path is angling up, the ceiling is level. It's getting brighter and I hear voices ahead. Now I see the source of the light. There is a two-foot gap in the ceiling on the right side, cut perfectly straight. The priest is on his hands and knees, crawling up the opposite side from the gap. I crawl up behind him and can barely make out some words.

"What do you mean you don't know where he is?"

"He's missing."

"I know he's missing. Who was supposed to be watching him?"

"I don't know, Sir. I'll find him."

"No, you won't. You'll secure the package. Then, and only then, you'll find him."

"Yes, Sir."

"Close that door."

I hear a loud, low rumble. It's the ceiling. It's moving smoothly to the right, closing the gap. It makes a boom sound and all light disappears.

A few seconds go by.

Then, the earth starts to shake and I hear the sound of wood cracking all around me. Suddenly, brightness pours in from above and I think I see the ceiling flip forward. *Crash!* There's a huge gap where the ceiling had been and light assaults my eyes. The priest jumps about four feet in the air, into the place above, where the voices came from. Now they're cussing, whoever they are.

I get on my feet, still crouching down, and raise up a bit and put my head above the hole to see where we are. My eyes adjust quickly. We're in someone's living quarters. Bed and door on the right, bookshelf on the left, fireplace straight ahead. Normally it would look kind of cozy, with the soft light from the fireplace. There's one stranger, an Arabic looking guy with a beard, on the bookshelf side, and another, a grey-haired white guy, on the side with the bed and door. The priest is in the middle of the room, standing higher than the other two, because he's on top of what must have been our ceiling seconds ago in the tunnel, but now is a big rectangular slab of cut rock or marble or something, lying on the floor.

What I see now is impossible. Something flies through the air, toward the guy on the left. A fire poker from the fireplace. It stabs him in the gut, and he howls in pain. A burning log leaps from the fireplace and whizzes toward the guy by the bed. Just before it reaches him, it stops in midair. He's staring at it, with a look of concentration rather than wonder.

The door bursts open. A big blonde guy enters the room, dressed in all black and holding a machine gun. Someone else comes in behind him. I drop down. The priest jumps down beside me. I hear shouting from the room.

"Run!" orders the priest.

I crouch and run forward as fast as I can. *Smash!* It's the same colossal crash from before, but even louder this time. The earth shakes and the light goes out.

I stand up straighter and run ahead as fast as I dare. Faster than I ever would have thought I could run in pitch blackness. I can hear his footsteps behind me.

Slam! I crash into something and fall down, arse over elbows.

"Dammit!" I hear another voice. "Get off of me." It's Cora again.

"Pardon me. Didn't see you there," I say overly casual.

"Go!" shouts the priest behind me.

I scramble up and run, ahead of both of them.

"What happened?" she asks. "What was that sound? Why are we running?"

"I don't know where to start." I'm jogging and waving my hand in front of me in case there is something else ahead.

"Did you find the guys who stole it? Did they set off a bomb or something?"

"I think so. I mean, I think we found the guys who stole it. But no, they didn't set off a bomb."

"What was that noise then?"

"Um, so this tunnel leads up to a room, like a bedroom. There were a couple of shady-looking guys in there, and the priest charged in and started to fight them, but some more of them burst in, with guns, and so he jumped back down into the tunnel. That sound was the priest closing the door to block their entrance."

"What? A bedroom? And how did he jump back into the tunnel and have time to close a giant door before they could shoot him?"

My steps are heavy. We are angling upward again, back up toward the chapel room.

"Well . . . I think he moved it with his mind."

"Oh, well that explains it," she says.

"I don't know what else to say. When he was fighting them, he was throwing crap around with his mind. Ask *him* about it."

Finally, I can make out some light up ahead. We're almost there.

"So these guys you fought, they stole the Shroud of Turin?" I can tell she's turned her head to ask the priest.

"Yes," he says.

"Who are they?"

"They are working for a man called Hawk."

I see something ahead in the light. Something that doesn't make sense.

Cora gasps. Guess she sees it too. We slow down and edge closer to it, or rather, him. Staring back at us, at the bottom of the ladder leading back up to the Vatican museum, eyes unflinching, is a young child. A boy.

From behind me, I hear the priest ask him "What are you doing here?"

"Father said to come."

4

Revenge

Ronnie
22 years earlier

"Stupid kid," Ronnie said to himself under his breath. "Stupid, stupid, stupid! Why are you so cotton-pickin' stupid?" Being stupid was the reason for all his problems. Tears welled up in his eyes again, for the million-billionth time. "Stop crying, you stupid head. You dumb, dumb, poopy head." Ronnie's cry suddenly changed to a laugh. "Poopy head." He laughed again. I may be stupid, he thought, but I am funny. Even Mark thinks I'm funny, when I say funny things. I know 'cause he laughs. Then he says something funny too. Like butt nuggets, or wiener head. Ronnie laughed again. He wiped his tears.

But when Mark goes with Abel and Shane, he turns all mean. I say a funny joke, and he says, "Shut up, Ronnie." My name's not Ronnie. It's not stinkin' Ronnie. It's Stephen. I hate Ronnie. Ronnie is the stupid one. Stephen is funny.

Ronnie was wandering around campus searching for Mark and Shane and Abel. His skin felt tight around his eyes where his tears had dried. He had been looking for them for forever. He went into the tall building they stayed in, and rode the elevator up to his room. Next, he went to the food place, and to the big place they sat when the grownups would talk and everybody would clap. He walked to the building with all the classrooms, where they did their DI show for the judges. And outside, he searched everywhere. Around the whole college. Twice. The only place he didn't go was outside of the college because he didn't want to get in trouble.

Ronnie loved Mark. Mark was the first big kid who was ever nice to him. His own big brother, Paul, was mean. Real mean. He called Ronnie stupid and ugly. And he beat him up all the time. Jay didn't beat him up, but he was super mean too. Jerk face. Everybody was mean. Except for some kids in his class. His special class, the grown-ups called it. Dummy class is what the other kids called it. But he never invited those kids to spend the night, because he knew Paul would beat them up and call them stupid. But not Mark. If Mark comes over, Paul will be nice to him. I know it. Cause Mark is smart. But maybe Mark would be mean to me when he got around Paul. Mark changes when he gets around different people.

If I wasn't so stupid, he would always be nice to me. He's mean because I'm stupid. I'm gonna try real hard in school next year. I'm gonna get smart. Then Mark will say, 'Ronnie, when did you get so smart? You're more smart than me. I'm gonna call you Stephen again.' And he'll spend the night at my house. No. I'll spend the night at his house. We'll play on his Nintendo 64. Mario Kart and James Bond. Shane and Abel will come over and we'll be best friends. Not Jay. He won't ever come over.

Ronnie was on the other side of campus from the big buildings where they slept. He was walking on a sidewalk around a big circle building. Ahead there were some trees and a grass field, and past them another busy street, with a

Taco Bell and on the other side.

Someone was walking toward him on the path, coming the other way. Jay. He had skinny, yellow hair that stuck to his head, and big eyes that stuck out. He was bigger than Ronnie, but smaller than the other guys.

"What's up, Jay?" Ronnie turned and tried to wipe his tears inconspicuously.

"Hey Ronnie. What are you doing over here?"

"Nothin'."

Jay stopped in front of him. "Tell me the truth, Ronnie."

"I don't know."

"Did Mark and those guys ditch you again?"

How did he know? Ronnie's lip started to quiver.

"Come on, let's find them." Jay started walking ahead and Ronnie turned and walked beside him. Why was Jay being nice? Maybe he's nice too when he's by himself.

"Do you know where I was, Ronnie?"

"No."

"I was behind the bushes with Melinda Nelson. She's the hottest girl at Globals."

That was the girl who sat by Ronnie the night he was cool. "Were you playing with her?"

"You could say that," Jay chuckled. "Tell me what you think I'm doing when I'm 'playing' with her."

"Hide and seek?"

"No Ronnie, not hide and seek."

"Mark said you were playing hide and seek with a girl tonight."

Jay stopped walking. "Do you remember exactly what he said?" He started walking again, and Ronnie started back with him.

"He said you would hide and play pretends with a girl from Canada."

They left the winding sidewalk and walked on the grass, making a straight path back toward the tall buildings. They came upon picnic tables. At one, a couple of college kids were kissing.

"See those two, Ronnie? That's what I was doing with Melinda Nelson."

"Oh. Kissing."

"Do you think that's yucky?"

"No," said Ronnie, even though he still kinda thought it was yucky. But he kinda thought it was good too. Either way, he knew that was the right answer for Jay.

They walked under some big, leafy trees, and were getting close again to the big building where they went every night with all the clapping.

"Ronnie, I didn't want to tell you this, but when you're not around, Mark is always making fun of you. The other day when you dressed up in those other peoples' clothes with the hat and the tie, and we were playing music for you and said you were the coolest guy here, it was just a big joke Mark thought up. I hate to say this, but you looked ridiculous, Ronnie. And afterwards Mark was saying, 'Did you see how stupid he looked? What an idiot.'"

Jay continued, "Everyone here, from all over America, even some from overseas, they were laughing at you. He even got Melinda Nelson to act like she liked you, but she was laughing at you too. She just told me. I'm sorry to tell you this, but you need to know so you don't fall for his jokes again. He is not a nice person, Ronnie."

Stupid! Stupid, stupid, stupid! Ronnie tried to fight the tears–not in front of Jay–but they forced themselves out of his eyes. Ronnie knew he wasn't smart, but he also knew deep down what was happening the other night was too good to be true. Everyone chanting his name. Well, Ronnie's name. He was dancing and acting funny, and everybody was laughing. Even the pretty girl liked him. It was just like he dreamed about happening every night when he lay in bed. But the day after that awesome night, everything was back to normal. Mark was nice/mean again. Abel and Shane ignored him, and Jay was mean/mean. That girl Melinda ignored him too. Mark's not really nice/mean. He's mean all the times. When he's nice, he's pretending so he can play tricks on me.

They were past the big building now. Ahead of them, a sidewalk ran directly across the path they were making.

"Look, there they are on that bench," Jay pointed them out. "What a bunch of queers. If I were you, I would walk up behind Mark and punch him in the face."

Ronnie saw them. Mark and Abel were on the sides, pushing against Shane in the center while they all laughed. He should be there with them, playing and having fun. *I want to hurt you.* It was less of a thought than a feeling. *I want to hurt you like you hurt me.*

He walked up behind Mark, brought his arm all the way back, and he punched him in the side of the face with a hook punch, like in 'Mike Tyson's Punch Out.'

Mark's head snapped toward Shane in the middle and then he fell to the ground.

"Owwwwww!! What the hell!?" Mark looked up at him, holding his jaw, eyes lit with fury. "Ronnie, what is your damn problem?!"

"Ohhhh. Mark got his ass kicked by Ronnie," laughed Jay.

Mark got up and walked slowly, deliberately, toward Ronnie. He faked a left, and punched him straight in the nose. It exploded in pain. Ronnie couldn't figure out why he felt water running down his nose to his mouth."

"Oh my God. You broke his freaking nose," said Shane.

"Dammit Ronnie, you stupid *retard*!" Mark cried the last

part, and sat back on the bench, facing the other direction, his body shaking in sobs.

Rage poured through Ronnie's body. He quaked with it. Every ounce of his body tingled with it. It was as if all the times that everyone had been mean to him, Mark, Jay, his brother, all the hurt from all those times was converted into raw anger. Ronnie turned his head and saw a rock the size of an orange two feet from his face. He grabbed it and stood up.

"I *hate* you!!" he screamed, and hurled the rock at Mark, with every bit of rage transferred from his body to the rock.

It struck its mark.

Mark collapsed to the ground.

He was still in a coma two weeks later when Ronnie, or Stephen as the paper said, got his dad's hunting rifle out of his unlocked gun rack, stuck it in his mouth, and pulled the trigger.

5

The Restaurant

Bang! The waiter behind me just dropped a plate and scared my balls off. I'm sitting here in the restaurant of the Parco dei Princi pi Grand Hotel in Rome. The lighting is low and the prices are high. The woodwork and light fixtures are ornate, in a classical way. The room is large and about half of the tables are occupied. How did I get here? Let me backtrack a bit.

After we found the boy in the tunnel, we climbed up the ladder back into the Vatican Museum. The two guys who stole the Shroud were gone, no longer lying on the floor unconscious. The priest said the boy was going with him and we were not to follow. Cora said 'like hell,' and she and the priest had a stare down. I was ready for her to collapse again, unconscious, but before that happened, she backed off a little, and asked him what the hell was going on. He said 'if you meet me at the Forum, I'll explain,' and I guess that was acceptable to her, because when he and the boy ran out of the room and down the hall of maps, she didn't try to follow.

We headed back to the Sistine Chapel the way we came and ran into some policemen who shouted questions at us in Italian, and when we didn't answer they switched their questions to broken English. From there we were taken to Vatican security for the rest of the night for questioning. I don't know what her experience was like after that, but as for me, I spent the next few days in various police offices and government buildings answering the same questions over and over. I told them about everything but the telekinesis and the boy. I didn't want to look more suspicious than I already did. White lies and all that.

They've finally given me permission to go home, and I have a flight back tomorrow. And fortunately they are keeping me out of the press. Not only my name, but also that there was someone who did what I did. This goes for the priest and Cora Byron too. The only details the world knows are that everyone at the ceremony was hypnotized, allowing two men to steal the Shroud of Turin. All the Islamic terrorist groups are taking credit for the crime.

I take a sip of water and see her out of the corner of my eye. Cora Byron, walking up to my table.

"I was starting to think this was a prank," I say.

"Why would I do that?" She pulls out the chair across from me and sits down.

"Why would you ask me to dinner in the first place?"

"Good question." She straightens her dress.

I know I'm overdue to give a description of Miss Cora Byron. Dark hair done up in a milkmaid braid around the front of her head. Skin so tan against her white, spaghetti strap dress it's almost mahogany. One shoulder has a tattoo of a white flower, which I don't recognize. Big, spring-green eyes, and a smattering of dark freckles on and around her nose. A smile that could melt your face. I'm obviously a fan.

"I wanted to discuss the story of the century with you before you leave town." She has a raspy voice, but not smoking-for-50-years raspy.

"Ok. Where do you want to start?"

She pulls out a yellow legal pad and a pen. Old school. "What's your theory on the mass trance?"

"I don't know any more than anyone else. I saw some interesting theories for the few minutes I caught the news: scientific device, alien technology, mass conspiracy, demons." Always demons. "My best guess–."

"May I take your order, Sir?" the waiter interrupts. I hate when they do that. She orders carbonara alla romana and a glass of red wine, which he pours for her right there. I chicken out and order a pizza with everything on it, and a coke.

"You were saying," she says.

"Well, you saw the priest. You felt it. He was doing it with his mind, just like he threw that stuff in the room with his mind. I don't know. The Force? You would know better than me. You experienced it."

"The trance? To me it was sort of like falling asleep, except I had no concept of the passing of time. I could have been out for a minute or a day." She takes a sip of wine. "If I may be more direct, my real question is, why do you think you were unaffected?"

"Now you sound like the cops. I don't know. The priest said he couldn't 'trance' me or whatever. He said something about 'Hawk' doing something to me." She's setting down her wine glass and it bobbles, but she saves it from spilling. "I don't know what 'Hawk' is, or anyone named Hawk."

"Your best guess, then, is that, for whatever reason, you're immune to whatever they did to the rest of us?"

"Exactly. I mean, whatever it was they did, you are pretty immune to it yourself. You woke up way sooner than anyone else but me."

People erupt in laughter at the bar. I think they're Englishmen.

"That must have been strange from your perspective too,"

I say. “How did you know to chase after us?”

“When I came to, I heard something happening outside of the chapel. I tried to get the people’s attention around me, and when I couldn’t, I followed the noise until I caught up to you. By the way, have you read anything about the tunnel?” she asks.

“No. But why did they need a secret tunnel in the first place? Couldn’t they have just frozen the minds of everyone they ran into on their escape and taken a normal exit?”

“Here’s my theory,” she leans her glamorous face in toward me. “These guys are limited in who and how they hypnotize people. Like you said, they can’t hypnotize you and can barely do it to me. I think the reason those two guys the priest knocked out didn’t have the Shroud is because they handed it off to someone in the tunnel, and they were planning to continue on above ground and send the chase for the Shroud in the wrong direction.”

“Weird, but ok. So why was there a tunnel in the first place? I’ve not had time to read, and the news story I watched mentioned it en passant, like everyone knew why it was there. I’m way behind on events but was planning to catch up on them tonight. Oh, I did see someone locally being interviewed speculate it was a secret entrance into the Vatican for the Illuminati, but that sounds like a fevered conspiracy theory to me.”

“Let me save you some reading time. You’re right, it’s not the Illuminati’s tunnel. They didn’t officially exist until the 1700s, although some date the true origin back to the 15th century before this tunnel was built. But that still makes no sense. How could the Illuminati sneak into the Vatican and dig a massive tunnel in secret? No, the room we found the tunnel in is the Apartment of Pope Pius V. He was a true believer, who oversaw the Catholic Counter Reformation, and kicked Queen Elizabeth out of the Catholic Church. What's that word?"

"Excommunicated."

"Yes. Anyway, in addition to being a true believer, he was also sort of paranoid. He feared he had enemies inside the College of Cardinals. It was only 50 years before him when Rome was sacked. At that time, the Swiss Guard was almost completely annihilated on the steps of St. Peter's Basilica, and Pope Clement VII narrowly escaped with his life via the secret Passetto di Borgo, to the Castel Sant'Angelo where he holed up until it was safe. The tunnel we were in goes from the Apartment of Pope Pius V to the current Papal residences, which are next to the entrance of the Passetto di Borgo. Even in the event of an internal coup, Pius V would have been able to escape from his chapel to the Castel Sant'Angelo, where he knew he had loyal men."

The best part of talking to Cora is it gives me an excuse to stare into her green, speckled eyes. They're mesmerizing, even to me. The worst part about it is I lose focus on what is being said. I'm getting the gist of it, though.

"You're very knowledgeable on this subject."

"Thank you, but you'll find this is sort of common knowledge now. The world is consumed with this story."

"And your job as a journalist is to feed their insatiable hunger?"

"Yes, but it's frustrating because I can't tell the whole story."

"The cops forbade you from telling it?"

"No one *forbade* me from doing anything. I'm torn between my impulse to tell a story and my desire to keep my life somewhat normal."

I've thought a lot about this. If this goes public, I will become famous. This is not how I want to become famous.

Shroud Boy. Shroud Man. The guy who tried to stop the crime of the millennium and failed.

"I can see that. Who do you write for anyway?"

"The Boston Globe."

"Really?" I ask, sounding more surprised than I mean to.

"I know it's sort of a dying media, but I did the blogging thing, and worked at The Huffington Post writing op-eds, and became a big fancy editor, but in my heart what I really want is to cover a story. I want to find a scandal, some onion I can unpeel, and this story is the motherlode."

"You don't really have a face for newsprint," I timidly throw out there. Her eyes flash. Uh-oh.

"You mean to say, why work so hard with your brain to get to the top? Why not simply use your looks?"

"No . . . I didn't mean . . . I don't know what I meant." I have a gift for putting my foot in my mouth.

The waiter brings out some bread and butter. I pour olive oil on my plate and dip the bread in it, and avoid making eye contact with her.

"I'm sorry," I tell her.

No response.

"So Boston," I bumble ahead. "You don't have an accent."

"I didn't grow up there." Good, we're moving on. "You don't have a Texas accent. What's your excuse?"

She's done her homework on me, "People my age don't have accents, except for the country people. I think we subconsciously lost it because we know it sounds ignorant to northerners. So you've read my file, then? Why do I have a file?"

"I don't know much," she dips a piece of bread in my olive oil. "Grew up in Texas. Associate Professor of Chemistry at Texas A&M. Sorry, I have to ask this. I know Texas A&M is a good school, but were you sort of surprised when you were chosen to test the Shroud of Turin?"

"Yes. I thought it was a mistake. When I finally believed it, I was flabbergasted."

"Why do you think you were chosen?"

"I don't know." I feel like I keep saying that. "It makes no sense. I'm an Associate Professor like you said. I do specialize in carbon dating, but I would be so far down a list of qualified people that I wouldn't make the list. But I wouldn't have been carbon dating the Shroud per se, well, not exactly."

"Right, because the first time that was tried, it proved the Shroud to be a medieval fake. So now the Vatican is trying something different to try to get a different result."

Salty. "Ok, hold on. Is it fair to say you think this entire event is a big joke because the previous carbon dating already proved all we need to know about the Shroud?"

"I will cover this story from an objective perspective because that's my job, but personally, of course I think it's a joke. You don't?"

All right. Here we go. "Looks like my file was pretty thin, then. You didn't see that I'm cautiously optimistic the Shroud is the real burial cloth of Christ."

"Really?" She makes a little patronizing lopsided smile.

"Sure," hopefully she doesn't notice me shaking. I get nervous when I talk about stuff like this.

"Make your case for me then."

"Ok. Um, where to start . . . first off, if this were a forgery, why is the image a negative? The image is not impressive to the naked eye, but the negative is amazingly detailed. How could the forger know photography would be invented, and leave an easter egg for moderns to discover? Besides that, the negative image is so detailed you can see his teeth through his face like an X-Ray, and you can count his ribs under his skin. The person in the Shroud is anatomically correct. His blood flows are consistent with gravity and having been crucified. The whip marks on his back were the result of being whipped by a Roman flagrum, which a medieval European would not have had access to. How could a forger in the Middle Ages have pulled this off? I mean, if you look at medieval paintings from the time this was supposedly created, they look like middle school kids painted them. There is no perspective. How could an artist from that time have created the negative image on the Shroud? There is even 3D holographic data encoded in it."

"Ohhhh kay."

"What?"

"It's just, you sound kind of . . . crazy."

"How so?" I ask, trying to sound confident.

"Ok, earlier you said the person being interviewed sounded like a fevered conspiracy theorist, but now you're talking about 3D holographic data on the Shroud of Turin."

"Well, it's there. It's real. No other two-dimensional negative has been found to contain 3D information that can be converted into a hologram. Is it impolite for me to mention it?"

"No, it's not impolite."

"How do you think the image was created then?" She's going to say it's a painting. That's what all the skeptics say.

"By the paint of a very skilled artist."

"It couldn't have been painted because the image is only on the outside of the cloth fibers and is 50 times thinner than a human hair. Paint would have bled into the fibers. It must have been burned on somehow."

"Let's hear your theory." She breaks a piece of bread.

I can feel her scorn building up, but I press ahead. "That the image was created by radiation from Christ's body at the moment of his resurrection."

She stops the bread short of her mouth. “What about the lack of distortion on the image?”

“The cloth would have been pulled taught on both sides, with the body in the middle.”

“What, floating in midair?”

“Yes.” I’ve found answering ‘yes’ directly when someone is trying to make you sound silly, rather than backing down, is the best strategy.

She smiles. It was not the snarky smile from before, but worse. It’s the smile of someone who thinks what I said was laughable and makes no attempt to hide it.

“I know that theory sounds fantastic, but that’s burying the lede as you journalists say. What’s fantastic is that the Shroud of Turin exists in the first place. There is an actual piece of fabric, I was about to say ‘in Turin’ but who knows where it is now, that has this impossible image on it. Think about it like this: there are many wacky theories for how the Shroud was stolen. These theories sound bizarre, but that’s not the strange part of this ordeal. The strange part is that everyone was hypnotized, and a priest was moving objects with his mind.”

“Let’s not conflate one with the other.”

“Fair enough. But it is still an impossible artifact.”

“Tell me what I’m missing here. The Shroud first showed up in history in the 1300’s, during a time when the Catholic Church was basically a cult of relics. Your church was only as good as your holy relic. Let’s see, there was the arm of Mary Magdalene, the breast milk of Virgin Mary. Every church made money by pilgrims travelling to see their relic and leaving a tribute. Suddenly this church in Lirey France hits the motherlode by finding the actual burial shroud of Christ. In France. 1300 years after the crucifixion. The church having an existential motive for this relic to exist. I admit what you said about the photograph negative 600 years later is interesting, and I imagine saints everywhere believed this was the one true relic, and they went so far as to try to use science to prove it. But alas, it gets carbon dated and guess what?" She makes a mock surprised face, "Three independent labs date it back to the 1300's. What a remarkable coincidence. Or was it a conspiracy?"

"No, I don't believe in conspiracies. As for showing up in the 1300's, there is a very plausible theory put forth by a writer named Ian Wilson, but as for the carbon dating–"

"Your food, sir." The waiter sets my pizza in front of me and gives Cora her pasta. I notice the tables around us have filled in and waiters and waitresses are scurrying about them. I take a bite. Buys me a little time to think of how to explain this.

"You were saying," she says.

"Ok, this gets a little esoteric, but I can tell you'll have no problem following along." I can see total focus in her eyes as she leans in to listen. "When you carbon date an item, you are telling how old it is by measuring how much carbon-14 is in the item. When a plant is alive, the ratio between regular carbon and carbon-14 remains constant, as it is constantly exchanging carbon-14 with its environment through photosynthesis. But when the plant dies, that exchange stops and the carbon-14 starts disappearing at the rate of half every 5, 730 years.

"Now, if you'll humor me, let's pretend the body of the man in the Shroud shot out a burst of radiation to form the image. There would have been protons and neutrons emanating from the body. The protons would be responsible for the body image. The neutrons would have mainly penetrated the Shroud and bounced off the walls in the tomb. Some neutrons would have also reacted to nitrogen-14 and created more carbon-14. It's possible the piece of the Shroud that was carbon dated had more carbon-14 than would be expected for a 2000-year-old item because the process that formed the image itself was responsible for creating the extra carbon-14."1

"Does that not strike you as very convenient?"

"Absolutely. The tragic part of the Shroud being stolen is that I was a day away from testing this, because if neutrons would have emanated from the body, they would have not only created more carbon-14, but other elements as well, some of which are so rare they are almost not found in nature. The existence of these elements would prove these neutrons caused the extra carbon-14 as well, and this would all have been settled."

"But the tests would have failed just like the first carbon dating attempt, and you guys would go back to the drawing board and come up with another elaborate theory for why this dates to the Dark Ages and not ancient Rome."

"Yeah, I can see that," I had to give her that one. There are multiple theories to try to explain away the carbon dating problem with the Shroud, and they can't all be true. I finally get to take a few bites of my pizza. She has the same idea. After a minute, the silence gets to me.

"So, when are you headed back home?"

"Not for a few days. I'm finally free from the police so tomorrow I'm heading to the Forum to see if that priest is still waiting for us, so I can find out who the hell that little boy in the tunnel was, and how he got there. You could come with if you want."

"I already have tickets to fly back tomorrow, but I'd love to know what you find out." Why did I say that? Go home to my boring life, or run around Rome with an attractive woman?

"Come on. This is a once in a lifetime story. Trust me on

this."

Wow. Why does she want me to come along? "You know what, why not? Flights can be rescheduled."

"Great. Just push it out a couple of days. That's how long I have anyway. I'm not scheduled to be back until then because I was supposed to be in Israel this week, before I became a police suspect on lock down."

"What's in Israel?"

"It would have been next assignment. I was supposed to cover the Lost Bones of Jesus tests as well."

Ah yes. The Lost Bones of Jesus. When the Vatican announced the Shroud of Turin was going to be retested, the anti-Christian crowd wanted to get in on the action as well and scheduled an event to piggyback on the publicity from the Shroud event, where they would test a secular relic, the supposed Lost Bones of Jesus.

"Sorry you missed it," I say.

"Are you?"

"Sure. I imagine it would have been a big deal for you to cover it."

"You have no idea."

Oh really. "Enlighten me."

"You know how I said I had blogged in the past. I used to blog about the Talpiot Tomb and the Lost Bones of Jesus."

Oh crap. Cora Byron. I knew I recognized that name. Crap crap crap. I mean, so she's skeptical of the Shroud of Turin. Who isn't? But a rabid, militant anti-Christian? I'm kind of wishing I would have not committed to stay in Rome with her now. Kind of.

"I knew I recognized your name. I read your blog back in the day."

"Really? No doubt you were working up counter arguments the whole time you read it."

"Something like that."

"Let's hear them."

I won't give a play by play of the conversation, but in a nutshell, the reason why this tomb, the Talpiot Tomb it's called, is thought by some to contain the bones of the real Jesus in the first place is because when it was discovered in 1980, the archeologist found an ossuary (a box containing a dead person's bones) with the name 'Yeshua son of Joseph' engraved on it. The other names in the tomb were Mary, Jose, Matthew, Judah son of Yeshua, and Mariamne. In 2007 a documentary aired on the Discovery Channel in which the archaeologist (and anti-Christian) Simcha Jacobovici arranged for a DNA test on the bones of Jesus and those of Mariamne, who some scholars believe to be Mary Magdalene. When the DNA results showed they weren't related (at least on their father's side), Jacobovici argued that Jesus in the tomb was probably married to Mariamne, and Judah was probably their son. The documentary makers attempted to calculate the odds of this being the real family of Jesus versus a random family with these names, based on how common these names were and the how well the names matched up with characters in the Gospels, or other theories about the historical Jesus. Their conclusion was the odds of this *not* being the real Jesus' family tomb are almost impossible, hence, there was no Resurrection. The crux of the case for these odds rests on the name Mariamne, which is a rare nickname for Mary, and there is an apocryphal book called the Acts of Philip with a character named Mariamene, who some think is Mary Magdalene. But there are many counter arguments to this claim. One being that Mary Magdalene is not associated with the name Mariamene until the 4th century, and even then the connection is dubious.[2] The large majority of academia remains unconvinced in Jacobovici's assertion.

But while Jacobovici's argument is inconclusive, the upcoming DNA tests would not be. They'll be testing Jesus' bones from the Talpiot Tomb against bones from an ossuary, engraved with the name 'James, son of Joseph, brother of Jesus.' The James' ossuary is thought to be authentic because one wouldn't have his brother listed in his epitaph unless he was an important figure, like the real Jesus. While the James ossuary was not found in the Talpiot Tomb, but by an antiques collector, there has been speculation it originally came from the Talpiot Tomb. If the tests come back positive and show them to be related, game over. The odds of them being two random guys named Yeshua son of Joseph, and James son of Joseph, brother of Jesus, and not be the real, historical Jesus and James would be just about impossible.

We finally finish our food and the discussion winds down. She says, "Like you said about your Shroud tests, soon this will be settled. The results from the DNA tests will be out any day now, and these arguments will all be moot."

"I'm looking forward to that."

"I don't think you are."

"I have the sneaking suspicion you are not a fan of Christianity."

"It's had a good run. Two thousand years of burning witches, torturing Jews, but all good things must end."

"You take the excesses of the medieval Catholic Church very personally."

"What about the modern Catholic Church? It is a factory and sanctuary for child molesters. But I have no special hatred of the Catholic Church over other denominations. Listen, I'm not going to open up about my childhood with a stranger, but I will say that I grew up in a Christian family, and there was a really bad person there, and his Christianity didn't make him better, but worse. And I know what you're thinking. Cora had a bad childhood in a Christian home and so she decided to become an atheist. That's not the case at all. I still loved Jesus after I got away, and I was devastated when I realized I didn't believe in him anymore. Maybe because of my experience I can see the facts more clearly than people like you who are hellbent on making the facts fit with their faith."

"Ba ha ha!" I can't stifle a laugh. Well, I guess I didn't try. "Sorry, I'm not laughing at you. It's just that, I've spent most of my life questioning and doubting my faith. It's kind of my thing." I never say things like, 'It's kind of my thing,' but it fits here. "I haven't attended church in years."

"That is not how you come across."

"Yeah, I sounded like I knew what I was talking about tonight. Don't know what got into me. If it makes you feel any better, I'm sure later tonight your arguments will play over and over in my head and a few of them will rattle me."

The waiter sets down the check and I snatch it before she does. She insists she can expense it, but there is no way I'm letting her pay. We exchange numbers so she can get in touch with me tomorrow.

She gets up and adjusts her dress. Forgot how tall she was.

I get up too and we walk side by side, wordless, over the marble floor, her heels clicking. We get in the elevator together and I hit number 4. "Nice," she says.

The elevator doors open and I let her off first. She lets me catch up to her. I reach my door and she continues walking. "See you tomorrow" she calls after me, without turning around.

"Goodnight."

Before I get in my room, I see her get out her keycard a few doors down. This is the hotel I've been at the whole time I've been in Rome. How long has she been here? What are the odds? Who is this Cora Byron and what is she up to?

6

Dad

Cora
22 years earlier

"The guys at our school are so gross," said Cora's friend, Avery. Both they and Cora's little sister, Madelyn, were leaning against the yellow bus, getting what little shade they could. It was parked on an asphalt parking lot next to the basketball goal where the boys were playing after lunch. Avery was small for a 14-year-old. She had dark brown hair, ivory-white skin, and a face covered in freckles. "They always smell like onions in the afternoon."

"It's not their fault," said Madelyn. She was 13, and Cora's blonde doppelganger. More accurately, she was the blonde doppelganger of Cora from last year, when Cora still looked like a girl and not a woman. "They have to go outside for recess and there's nothing for them to do but play basketball in the hot sun." Madelyn never said a bad word about anyone. She was so sweet Cora literally questioned the doctrine of Original Sin one time because of her.

"It's not only because they stink, " continued Avery. "They're not cute, and we're stuck with them."

The girls attended a Christian School, where the graduating class each year was around five kids. Junior High and High School was all in the same classroom, where each kid did their schoolwork in 'Paces,' 30-page booklets with a test at the end. They worked at their own pace while the teachers roamed around the room and worked with any kid who needed help. Cora and Madelyn's father was the pastor of the church that ran the school, and coach of the girls basketball team. A sense of dread poked Cora from the inside when she thought about her dad as her coach.

"They are a typical selection of 15 boys their ages," said Cora. "At a larger school, the talent pool to choose from is much larger. And more importantly, all these boys are extremely familiar to us. There's no mystery. At a big school, every guy doesn't feel like he's your brother."

"You had a crush on Noble when he went here," said Avery.

"He was older and didn't know I existed."

"Everyone knows you exist, Cora."

"You know, I think Connor will be handsome when he grows up," said Madelyn, looking at Cora with those big, glassy blue eyes.

"Yeah, Connor is a little cutie," said Avery gesturing towards a 12-year-old who was calling for the ball, but never got it.

A stray pass bounded toward the girls and Cora kicked it back to the boys. They were trying so hard to impress the girls, the Byron girls especially, but they were not succeeding.

"I wish I didn't have to go to this stupid school," said Avery.

"You wouldn't be friends with us if you didn't," said Cora.

"Why? You'd be too popular to be friends with me at public school?"

"I only meant, there'd be a lot of kids. We probably

wouldn't have become best friends there."

Avery crossed her arms and crinkled up her face, looking at Cora, trying to decide if she bought it or not.

"Doesn't matter, though. No chance of our dad letting us go to public school." Cora adjusted the tuck of her white, button-down shirt into her maroon plaid skirt, leaving enough slack in the shirt for her breasts.

"I like our school," said Madelyn. "My best friend and sister are here. We get to learn about God, and there's no drugs or anything like that."

"What about college?" Avery was looking up at Cora with her little brown eyes. "Will your dad make you go to college somewhere?"

"I'll have to go to a Christian college," said Cora. "He saw me wearing my Harvard sweatshirt and said I could go there over his dead body. I told him I wanted to be a journalist, and that the world needs to hear from someone with a Christian perspective, and the best way to get on at a good paper or website is to go to a respected university. He said it's too expensive and I'd turn into a liberal."

"I'm sure you'll become a famous journalist no matter where you go to school," said Madelyn. It was comical how positive she was. Cora tested her one time by telling Madelyn she was going to paint her own room blue. Madelyn went on and on about how blue was her favorite color and how perfect it would be. 'Did I say blue? I meant green.' Without missing a beat, Madelyn said 'That is so much better, because it would go with your eyes.'

The bell rang and they walked back to the classroom, the boys running ahead of them, passing the ball around and showing off. They had the rest of the afternoon to do their schoolwork, but she only pretended to work while she daydreamed. Avery got the thought of going to public school in Cora's head. It sounded like a dream. She could date hot guys, assuming her dad didn't catch her, but she wouldn't do anything bad anyway. No parties with drugs or alcohol. No sex. It would be fun, though. She would even bring her new friends, guys and girls, to church with her. Dad ought to love that. Best of all, her dad wouldn't be her basketball coach. She told herself not to think about it until it was game time and she was forced to.

"What's *he* doing here?!" Cora asked Madelyn, mortified. As if Madelyn would know.

It was halftime. They were at the rec center gym, getting pounded by a bigger school–at least big enough to not have to play junior high kids on the varsity team. And there was Noble Baines. He used to go to their school, but switched to public school so he could play football. He was tall and muscular, with blonde hair and dark eyebrows. In her mind he was just a silly fantasy, like having a crush on a Backstreet Boy, until a few weeks back at church when he started talking to her out of the blue. Now he was here, sitting in the stands with a few of his friends, dribbling a basketball on the bleachers.

"Cora. I. Need. You. To. Focus." Her dad paused after each word, like he was talking to a small child.

"Yes, Coach," she said. He stared at her, his mouth rigid, encircled by a dark mustache and goatee.

"Run number one."

"Yes, Coach." Number one, like all their plays, never worked. Her teammates didn't know how to set screens, and the other team knew their stupid plays.

The horn sounded. Her sister inbounded the ball to her. 'Go Cora,' she heard from the crowd. Was that Noble?

She dribbled the ball up.

"One!" she called out.

"Melanie's open!" her dad called out from the sidelines. She threw the ball toward Melanie the split second she heard him. The same time the other team heard him too. They stole the pass.

"You can't wait! You've got to throw it right away!" he shouted. She ran back to defend. She stopped the ball handler, who passed it to another girl, who shot, missed, grabbed her own rebound, and scored.

"Cora!" he clapped his hands, "You've got to *box out*."

There was no boxing that girl out. She was on the other side of the basket.

Madelyn threw the ball in, "It's ok, Cora," she said as she ran by.

Maybe for you. You're not dad's whipping boy. She dribbled the ball up the court.

"Three!" her dad yelled.

Cora faked left, which is where everyone knew three was supposed to go, dribbled right, pulled up, and hit the jump shot. Cheers from the crowd. Cheers from boys.

"Cora! Run the play!"

She ran back and they got in a box and one defense, her being the one, shadowing the other team's best player. She ran around a screen and put her hand in the face of the other girl as she shot. Off the rim. Rebound bounced right to Madelyn. Cora ran around and got the ball, pushing it up court. The other team wasn't set.

"One!" he screamed from the sidelines.

She kept pushing it. Two defenders closed in and she bounce passed the ball to one of her teammates, who missed the easy layup. The ball caromed out of bounds.

"Time out!" called her coach. He speared her with his

glare. She walked back, looking him in the eyes the whole way.

"Cora, would you like to coach this team?" he asked, way too loudly.

Yes, I would love to. "No, Coach."

"The plays will work if you'll run them correctly." No, they won't. They have never worked. Not once. "Tiffany, will you run the offense the *right* way?"

"Yes."

"Cora, you're sitting for the rest of the quarter."

Fine. Good, in fact.

The horn went off again. The other team scored easily. Over and over. Tiffany ran the plays, and the ball never made it further than one pass in. Her dad shouted at the team, but at no one specifically. He said to Cora, "This wouldn't be happening if you hadn't forced me to bench you."

Madelyn got a pass at the three-point line and shot. She made it *and* got fouled. The ref said the foul was before the shot and the shot didn't count, even though she shot it as soon as she caught it. Coach ran onto the court.

"Are you kidding me?! That shot counts."

"Coach, I need you to get off of the court."

"You're seriously not giving us those points? We're getting beat by 30." A vein bulged from the side of his neck.

"This is your last warning, Coach."

Coach walked to the scoring table. "I need you to put three points toward our score, *now*."

The grey-haired lady was flustered, looking between Coach and the ref.

"That's it! You're outta here." The ref threw his hand forward like he was pitching a ball, index finger sticking out, the motion ending with him pointing at the door.

Dad walked back to Madelyn, grabbed the ball out of her

hand, and launched it at the goal on the other side of the court. It hit the backboard with a thud.

"I won't forget this and I won't forget you," he said, pointing at the ref, a guy in his 20s.

"Get out of here!" said the ref.

Her dad turned and marched out, hitting the door so hard on his way out that he broke the handle.

Cora held onto the side of the pool and let the rest of her body float while she looked on at the tennis courts. Avery did the same. Avery's face was pink despite applying sunscreen every hour. Tonight it would be bright red with dark orange freckles. She had slept over at Avery's house last night and wasn't due home until dinner. Cora made sure even Avery's parents didn't know where they were.

"Rusty is so cute," said Avery of one of the tennis players they were watching. "And he's funny and sweet. You should go for him."

Cora watched Rusty playing tennis. Rusty was Noble's little brother, and he left their school at the same time Noble did. He had brown hair bleached blonde by the sun. Tan skin. Round face. He ran from side to side until a ball was out of his reach and he threw his racquet at it and laughed. "Everybody likes Rusty. He's a teddy bear. But think about this–he plays tennis and swims all day, and he's still a bit chubby. It looks good on him now, but imagine when he's an adult and he sits in his office all day. He'll balloon up to 250 pounds."

"Who cares about when he's an adult? He's cute and I want to make out with him."

"Then *you* should go for him," said Cora. "I'll see what I can do to make it happen."

"There's nothing you can do. Well, there's one thing. You could cease to exist. Because every guy has a crush on you, and to them I'm your annoying little friend."

"I love you, too."

"But no. Rusty is too easy for you. He's your age and you could snap your fingers and have him. No, you want his brother, because he's the only guy you couldn't get."

"You mean the same reason you want Rusty," she let slip. Whoops.

Avery shot her a look somewhere between pissed off and hurt. "Oh, you'll see what you can do to make it happen, huh?" Her eyes started moistening and she pushed herself under water.

Cora lunged down after her, got right in her face, grabbed it and mouthed 'sorry.' They swam back up.

Avery went back to her perch, gazing at the boys. "I know you're right. I have no shot."

"Yes, you do. You have a much better shot with him than I do with Noble."

Cora looked around the pool. Kids were splashing, old ladies were sun bathing. Her dad wouldn't let her be here without adult supervision, and he would especially flip out if he knew she was wearing a bikini . . .

Cora looked back at the courts. Rusty and Noble were playing doubles together against two guys she didn't know. She pushed off the side of the pool and swam lazily across the deep end toward the other side, just out of range of the landing area of the diving board. When she got to the other side she heard Avery call out, "They're coming!"

The boys were taking off their shirts as they ran across the grass toward the pool. This was part of their ritual to cool down between matches. As they got to the lawn chairs near the pool they pulled off their shoes and socks. Three of them dove in from the side while Noble waited in line to jump in from the diving board. When it was his turn, he jumped in with a flip. Then after some rough-housing they broke into a game of Marco Polo.

She saw Noble out of the corner of her eye, looking her way.

"Hey," he said. "Cora."

"Oh, hey."

"Come join in."

"Ok. Come on, Avery."

One of the boys from the other doubles team was calling out 'Marco.' She swam over to Rusty. He was yelling 'Polo' but was in the corner away from the action. She signaled to Avery to stay away.

"Hey Rusty, I have a strange request for you."

"Strange . . . in a good way?" he asked, raising an eyebrow.

"Would you swim right up to Avery and kiss her?"

He sighed, "Why is it always the hot girls who dare you to do stuff with their fugly friends and not the other way 'round?"

"She's not ugly. And I'm not asking you to French kiss her. Just a regular kiss."

He looked at Avery, who pretended like she wasn't watching them when he looked her way.

"I'll do it if *you* French kiss me later."

"No deal," she smiled.

"Ok. A regular, American kiss then."

"Maybe," she said, and his eyes widened. She turned horizontal in the water, bent her knees, put her feet against his chest, and pushed off him to swim away.

At this time, Avery swam up, "Whatever she told you, it's not true."

"I don't know what you're talking about," he replied.

"Marco!" Cora had lost track of the game, and Noble was within five feet of her.

"Polo," she called, and dove down to the bottom of the pool and swam under his feet, reemerging in the middle of the pool.

"Marco." He was a few feet away from her.

"Polo," she said, and stayed in the same spot, treading water. He reached out and touched her shoulder. "You got me," she admitted. He kept his eyes closed and said 'Marco' again, and latched onto her. Her heart banged against her chest.

"Marco," he said again, pulling her up against his chest. His fingers found the spaces between her ribs and he applied just enough pressure to tickle her. "Marco." She laughed and squirmed free.

"Cora!"

The shout came from an outraged voice at the side of the pool.

No. It couldn't be. Why *now*? The first thing she saw, since she was facing the opposite direction of the voice, was Noble looking toward him in pure fear. She turned and saw her dad's tall and broad-shouldered silhouette cut against the sun. Noble jumped out of the pool and ran.

"Let's go," he growled.

She started to cry and get out of the pool.

"No! This side!"

She looked up and saw he was holding a white towel. She got back in and swam across the pool, feeling every eye on her. She was halfway up the ladder when he grabbed her with the towel and picked her up with his iron grip. They walked toward the front gate, kids staring at them and adults acting like there was no spectacle to see, then past the front desk and into the parking lot. She climbed into his dark blue pickup truck and sat, feeling the hot nylon seat against the part of her legs the towel wasn't covering.

"I'm sorry, Dad." His expression had not softened. His forearms were flexed as he squeezed the steering wheel.

"Where did you get that two-piece?"

"I bought it with some birthday money. I walked to Walmart myself and bought it."

"Cora, you're a beautiful girl. You have no idea what that does to a man." He put his hand on her bare thigh and gave it a firm squeeze.

"They will look at you and only think of what they can get from you. They won't love you like I love you." He let go of her leg. They rode the rest of the way home in silence.

Cora lay awake in bed, thoughts jumping around too fast for her to fall asleep. Why did dad squeeze my leg so long? Was he trying to make a point and show me he loved me, like a leg-hug? That was a weird thing to say, 'they won't love you like I love you.' Of course they won't. They're not my dad. Something about it didn't feel right. The air felt tense, like he knew he was doing something wrong and was pretending not to know. Or maybe she was reading too much into it. Maybe he was trying to show her a lesson about how a boy would see her, and how he would act toward her.

Poor Noble. He was flirting big time. Sure, he took it too far, but now what? He would probably steer clear of her forever. He might even get out of going to church, or worse, dad might ask to speak with his parents about his behavior. A sense of dread started in her chest and worked its way through her body to her fingers and toes. Of course he will.

She was interrupted from her thoughts by her bedroom door creaking open. She could barely make out a dark figure in the doorway, and goose bumps sprang up all over her body. The figure walked slowly to the bed, and she felt her bed sag under his weight when he sat down, her body sinking down in his direction.

"Hi Dad."

She felt him tense up. "Oh you're awake, Sweetie?"

"Yeah. What's up?" she tried to act casual.

"Sometimes I like to check on you, to pray for you." He was quiet for a moment. Then he lay down on his back next to her, shoulder to shoulder. He continued, "I was thinking about what happened with you in the pool today."

"Dad, that wasn't what it looked like."

"What did it look like?"

"I don't know. Like he was groping me or something. But we were playing Marco Polo, and we got caught up together and he was just playing."

He rolled on his side to face her. "Cora," his breath smelled kind of rotten, "boys like that are after one thing. These," he propped himself up on his right elbow and grabbed both of her breasts through her night shirt. He slowly pulled his hands away until only his fingertips were making contact with her. "And this." He moved his left hand down below and squeezed her, and when he let go, he let his hand continue to rest on her.

Her thoughts became incoherent. This couldn't be happening. It can't happen. What can I do? God, help me.

"I'm gonna make sure he never touches you again."

She was drowning in a sea of panic. He put more pressure on her. She had a thought, foggy in the distance. She fought to bring it into focus.

He leaned against her. "Shhhh," she felt his hot breath whisper in her ear.

She reached down inside herself and drew every ounce of strength she could find. "Mom!!"

It was a guttural scream.

Her dad flinched and backed off just enough. She rolled out of bed to her feet, and looked across at him. In the dark, her eyes couldn't make out his real face and instead she saw what looked like a ghoul, or a demon.

"Sweetie, I don't know what you think–"

"I don't think. I know, Dad."

"I don't know what you think you know but whatever–"

"How about I tell the elders at church and they can decide?"

"Cora, don't be absurd."

"I will. If you ever do it again, I will. I swear to God."

"Don't you swear to God young lady–"

"Cora, what's the matter?" she heard from down the hallway. "What hap– Oh, Bill. You startled me."

"Sorry, Mom. I thought dad was a burglar or something."

Her dad walked past her mom, out of the room. Cora lay back down in her bed, wide awake.

7

The Attack

I'm lying in my bed, wide awake. Too much running through my mind. Thoughts of our discussion. Thoughts of her. Sure, she's beautiful, but that's just the packaging. She's a God hater. Why would I want to be involved with someone like that? I have a hard enough time talking myself into believing my faith without having a skeptic as a partner. Why am I pretending there is a chance of romance?

I took some melatonin to help with sleep but it's not helping. I had a late nap, which is always a bad idea for me. I almost cracked open my laptop earlier to read up on what the media was saying about everything, but I stopped short. It felt like homework. I had tried watching some soccer but turned it off, hoping to find sleep.

Knock knock knock. Nothing good ever came from a knock on the door after midnight.

"Who is it?"

"Cora." My pulse quickens.

I open the door and she's wearing one of those hotel robes. "Is something the matter?"

"No, and I'm sorry to wake you."

"You didn't wake me."

"You can lie back down. I couldn't sleep and wanted to

apologize to you."

"For what?" I sit down on the bed and lean back against the headboard. This isn't what I think it is. Surely not. She's standing in front of the desk, mirror behind her.

"For being dismissive of you tonight. I'm sure you picked up on it."

"You were a lot fairer than most people."

"It's nice of you to say that, but I wanted to tell you I'm sorry."

"Nothing to be sorry for, but I appreciate the sentiment. Your conscience wouldn't let you wait until morning?"

"Well, it could, but this couldn't," she pulls the belt on her robe. It crumples to the ground. This is really happening.

She's wearing a black lace bra and matching panties, and she's breathtaking. The only conceivable 'flaw' is either a C-section or appendix scar, I don't know the difference. I know I sound pleased with this situation but I'm not. Just painting the picture. On the inside, I'm freaking out, I'm disappointed in her, and I'm dreading what happens next. Is this behavior normal in her world?

"I'm sorry. You're beautiful, but I can't do this."

"I'm such an idiot," she scoops up her robe and walks to the door.

"Cora, stop." I call after her. I hear the door open.

"I mean that literally. I *can't*." I hear her close the door on her way out.

Greg McKinnon walked down the 4th floor hallway of the Parco dei Principi Grand Hotel. His heartbeat and adrenaline levels were normal. He was a former Navy SEAL. He had been on missions where his team was outnumbered 10 to 1, and he'd still achieved his objective. Tonight, the opponent he was up against was a sleeping, unsuspecting civilian. He ran his fingers along the edge of the keycard to Mark Eberhart's room. For some reason this guy could not be 'disabled, ' as he called it, but that made no difference to him. He had his gun, and his new intelligence.

His new intelligence, which he had dreamed of for so long. He had always struggled in school. His aptitude tests showed he was average. What an ugly word. The difference with him was he was one of the few average people who knew he was average. It shouldn't have been a big deal. By definition, the word means as many are below you as above, but it didn't seem that way. It was as though everyone else's scores were to the far right of the chart. The psychological self-protection mechanism most people have to shield them from disturbing truths about themselves was broken in Greg. Or maybe he never would have realized this about himself were it not for the kid who moved in next door when he was in high school. He was in the same grade as Greg, and he was *really* smart. Greg invited him over play video games and he would beat them in one sitting. Sometimes his neighbor would talk while he played, about philosophy or literature or science. Greg didn't understand what he said, but he was enchanted by it. He tried to study these things on his own, but when the subject became complicated, his thoughts became fuzzy and fizzled away.

After high school, Greg joined the military, and to his delight he found that he was a born soldier. He followed orders and had natural courage. He was content with this identity. Being smart was just a fun little fantasy he had. He never thought it could happen in real life.

Until his old neighbor tracked him down and made him an offer.

He reached the room of the target. He took a deep breath,

slipped in his keycard, and slowly opened the door.

I'm lying in my bed, still trying to find sleep after all these hours, when I hear my door click open. I freeze. Who the heck would have a key to my room? I hear the door close. I force myself to roll quietly off the bed, letting my body down onto the floor on the side nearest the door. There is barely room for me between the bed and the wall. Holy balls. I see a dark figure walk past where I lay, past the bed.

He's holding something in his hand that I can't make out.

A gun.

Phhhhht! Phhhhht! Phhhhht! Three shots go into the bed.

He pulls the comforter off the bed, and I have a micro-thought. It's now or never. I jump out of my spot, scramble over the bed, and dive headlong at him.

Smack! His head hits the dresser. I'm on top of him throwing punches. I feel one connect.

Oooph! He kicks me in the nuts so hard that it launches me forward, and he pushes me over the top of him. My head slams into something hard on the floor. I'm a ball of pain, lying there waiting for his next blow.

It doesn't come.

I look up and he's standing on the other side of the room, ten feet away from me. Why is he backing off?

Wham! Something strikes me in the head. It didn't come from the direction of my attacker, but from the other side of the room. The lamp. Oh crap.

Something moves in front of me and I turn to protect myself. *Thud.* The TV. He's throwing things at me with his mind.

My eyes focus on the ground and I realize what I'm staring at. His gun.

I grab it, turn, and fire. *Phhhhht* three times. I continue pulling the trigger but the sound has stopped.

He takes two steps at me and dives, slamming me against the wall. We fall to the ground and he's on me throwing punches as I try to deflect them. *Smack!* I take one to the ear. I block a few more, and struggle to get out from under him.

I land a punch on his ribs, but it feels weird. There's no resistance. Only give. I hit him again. Same. No punches or kicks are coming back at me.

I kneel there for a moment, still. My heart is pounding and my ribs, ear, and head are fiery slices of pain. A deep ache in my abdomen registers, from his kick to my groin earlier. He's still not moving.

I force myself up, walk to the door, and turn on the light. There on my floor lays a thick, well-muscled man, wearing all black. He has red hair, a red mustache, and a green dart is sticking out of his shoulder.

I walk over to him and kick him in the balls for good measure. It's like kicking a sack of flour. I feel for a pulse on his neck but I have never been able to do that. I can see he's still breathing, though.

I grab my wallet and phone, throw on my pants, and run down the hall to Cora's room.

Bang bang bang. "Cora, come here, quick!"

"What do *you* want?"

"Please, it's an emergency."

She opens the door. "Oh my God. What the hell happened to you?"

"I got attacked."

"What? Who–"

"I don't know. Some guy who's lying unconscious in my room."

"What?!"

"Come on, we'll talk on the way to the police."

"Do you have your phone?" she asks. She's wearing black yoga pants and a neon pink workout shirt, hair pulled pack in a ponytail.

"Yes."

"Lose it. They could be tracking you."

I fling it into her room. "Who could be tracking me?"

She exits her room and jogs down the hallway. I follow. "Whoever stole the Shroud. You know, we are witnesses to the greatest crime in history." She turns and heads down the stairs, "We can't go to the police station in case they're watching for that. First thing is to get out of the hotel."

Ok. She seems to know what she's doing. We exit the hotel, and cross a big street that's busy in the daytime but dead now, and run toward a small side street.

"Where are we going?"

"The Forum."

"You are obsessed with this story, aren't you?"

"Yes, but I also don't have any better ideas of where to go. We can call the police later and tell them about the guy in your room. So what, you knocked him out?"

"Can we slow down? My ribs are killing me."

She tapers her pace down to a fast walk. There is no one else on the street. I can hear some cars driving, but they sound distant.

"Well, what happened?"

"I shot him with his own gun. It was loaded with tranquilizer darts or something."

"What? How? What?"

"I'm more surprised than you are. It was a fluke."

"If I didn't know you better, I'd be suspicious of you, Mark Eberhart."

I like hearing her say my name.

"Are you going to be ok?" She turns down an alleyway

almost too narrow for cars. I see the back doors of businesses on both sides.

"What, do I look that bad?"

"You're bleeding," she touches my ear, then my hair.

"Don't worry. It feels much worse than it looks. No, it's fine. I'll be fine." We walk on.

"Elephant in the room," she says, "I'm sorry about last night. You cannot fathom how embarrassed I am."

"Don't be. I felt . . . flattered. How about we pretend it never happened?"

"Impossible, but I have no choice." We walk by a light. She's in workout clothes like I said. They're inappropriate for Rome, but she can pull it off as a tacky American tourist.

"So let's think about this," I say, "I know we were witnesses to the crime, but why would they want us now, after I've already told the FBI, INTERPOL, everyone, everything I know."

"I don't know. Do you have a better idea of who's after you? Angry colleague?"

"Probably. This happens a lot at the University. Bunch of drama queens."

The alley intersected with a two-lane street and Cora turned to the left. We're zig-zagging our way toward the old city. I notice a column to my right. It was for an ancient Roman aqueduct, providing the city with running water 2000 years ago. Rome is like that. It's a modern city, with ancient artifacts scattered about.

"So, if you don't mind me asking, what was the last straw that broke the back of your faith?" I ask. "We can compare notes."

She ignores me. We walk on, her slightly ahead of me. After a couple of minutes she starts in like I had just asked her the question.

"I finally saw the reality that the Jesus I prayed to and cried to and asked for help night after night, that he wasn't there. He never was. He was someone I wished existed and convinced myself was there and even spoke to me, but it was all a ruse. Something my dad had put in my head starting before I could remember. Brainwashing me. Sorry, but that's what it was. I know I said I wouldn't blab about my family to a stranger, but since you asked I'll tell you. My dad was a pastor when I was growing up, and he is the evilest man I've ever met. And I've met some bad ones."

"I'm very sorry, Cora."

"Honestly, if he had been a good man, my life would be completely different. I would be living for the Lord in some capacity, but that would have been based on lies. It would have been based on the belief that Jesus is what made him good, when I've seen first hand that Jesus didn't work on my dad."

"Cora, do you really believe your dad was interested in letting Jesus make him good? Or was he more interested in using God to manipulate those around him?" A car is driving toward us. Just act natural, I tell myself. It drives past us.

"It's not that simple." She's still keeping a little in front of me where I can't see her face. "Yes, he uses God however it's convenient for him, but he really believes he's doing God's work. He's obsessed with it. With building churches and getting people saved so he can get his gold star when he gets to heaven. Why would God make a system like that? I mean, if you follow the logic in the Bible, my dad's approach makes a kind of sense. Who cares about whether or not you're a good person in this life? God's grace is what saves you anyway. So all that matters is working to save people from hell."

"But that's not how the Bible reads," I keep walking ahead. Step step step. The pain is there but the conversation is helping take my mind off it. "I've wondered why it doesn't read more like that, following that logic, but it doesn't. I mean, if I were an apostle like Paul, I would have spent more time in my letters writing the arguments for why Jesus is the Messiah, and encouraging my readers to persuade others about these facts. Instead, the epistle writers spend more time encouraging their readers to live a pure and righteous life. Because Christianity isn't about getting people to say the 'sinner's prayer.' Yes I admit, you can't get into the club without getting saved through Christ, but the focus after that is giving God control of your life and dying to yourself. If you insist on keeping control of your life, and using God instead of letting him use you, you're doing it wrong."

"Ok, so he's doing it wrong. Still, if you believe the Bible, my dad's still saved. He's still going to heaven. Don't you agree?"

"I can't answer that question. Only God knows."

"Can't you see how stupid that is?" She laughs the last couple of words. "That a piece of scum like my dad can get in, but the Dalai Lama will burn in hell forever because he believes the faith he was born into. It's too ridiculous for words."

"What do you think should happen to them when they die?"

"They stay dead."

"But if there's a God and an afterlife, then what should happen?"

"We should all be rewarded based on our actions. My dad should suffer for the bad things he did, and the Dalai Lama should be rewarded for the good things he did."

We turn right down a one-way street. "That's hell, Cora. When you get judged based on what you deserve."

"You don't think the Dalai Lama has done some good

things that deserve to be rewarded?"

"Forget about the Dalai Lama. The best way to think about it is through your own eyes, because you don't know what's really going on with the Dalai Lama or anyone else. So what does Cora deserve when she dies?"

"I'd be happy to be rewarded for the good things I've done, and punished for the bad."

"So not heaven or hell, but someplace in between."

"Yes."

"Again, what you're describing is hell. Forget about the fire and the pitchforks. If you're spending eternity getting what you deserve based on what you did in this life, it might be ok, it might even be pretty good, but I bet it would get old after a few million years. That sure isn't heaven. Heaven is spending eternity going deeper and deeper inside the infinite layers of God, each one more thrilling than the last."

"So *that's* where my dad will be."

"Your dad doesn't deserve it, but neither do you or me or the freaking Dalai Lama. Only Jesus lived the kind of life to deserve such a reward. Salvation is facing up to who you are and what you deserve, and taking Jesus up on his offer to trade your reward with his. That's why he had to go to the cross. To deal with our 'reward.'"

We cross a two-lane street and get on an old stone path about the width of a sidewalk. It's the Appian way, which runs in fits and starts throughout Rome.

"That's such an arbitrary way to pick who gets to go to heaven," she says. "If you happen to hear about the gospel, and hear about it from a someone you love so you're more prone to believe it, and don't have an inquisitive mind so you don't go finding holes in it, why should that be how God determines who goes to heaven? Why not do what makes sense and let in the good people and keep out the bad?"

"There's no such thing as good people and bad people. There are only people. Sometimes I'm good and sometimes I'm bad. If you follow that logic, what you're left with is something like Islam, where there is a fine line separating good from bad, and on the razor's edge of this line you have two people who did the same amount of good and bad, but one of them stole a pack of gum when he was little, so the scale tips and he goes to eternal hell, but the other goes to eternal bliss. That's not how God sees us. From his perspectives, we're all his children, and we all screw up, but he wants us to get into heaven, so he sent Jesus."

"All right. Hitler is his child too. So he made a few mistakes? No big deal. As long as he had a moment of salvation right before he died, he gets into heaven. I got it."

"I'm glad we're on the same page," I agree, matching her sarcasm. Don't want to get sucked into the finer points of Hitler's hypothetical salvation. We've both said what we had to say. As for our trek, we walk on, silent again. Dawn is finally breaking, right over the Coliseum. I squint to try to picture what it must have looked like in its heyday.

Cora starts in again. "So, what do you do when you're not running for your life or chasing after the Shroud of Turin?"

"That covers most of my waking hours."

She turns her head toward me so I can see her roll her eyes.

"I teach class. I encourage students not to drop my class. I coach my grad students on how to teach my class. I write papers."

"I know you're a professor. What else do you do. Hobbies? Friends?"

"Um, well you know about my interest in the Shroud. I hate to admit it, but I've been trying to write a novel, and it sucks. My only friends are friends from high school, well, more junior high, or middle school I guess they'd call it now. But I never see them. I do have a dog."

"Family?"

"None who is speaking to me."

Guess she realizes her attempt to show interest in me is only revealing how pitiful I am, because she stops her line of questioning. Our road ends, and we turn onto another large street. There are five-story buildings on both sides. She says we should turn on a side street to look for a general store that's open. We can call the cops and grab some breakfast. After 10 minutes of searching, we find one with a couple of tables for customers. We both get sweet rolls. I get orange juice and she gets coffee. She has no choice but to let me pay because she doesn't have any money. She goes to call the police. When she comes back, she's holding a newspaper. She has a small, closed-mouthed grin. She wordlessly sets it down on the table. Ansa, an Italian newspaper, in English.

I read the frontpage headline: DNA Evidence Confirms Bones from Talpiot Tomb Belonged to Jesus. Resurrection Never Happened.

8

Six Flags

Mark
21 years earlier

I picked the last of the meat off the chicken bone as I stared out the bus window at nothing in particular. We were rolling over the flat, dry land of Texas, dotted occasionally with mesquite trees. My church youth group was making the four-hour trip to Six Flags. I'd invited Abel, who regularly came with me to youth group, and Shane, who didn't. My mom tried to guilt me into inviting Jay. He had a soul too, she said. I wasn't going to invite him and tell her I did, but on the last day of school Shane blabbed about the trip at the lunch table. When Jay asked what he was talking about, I invited him out of my natural instinct, which was to please everyone and do whatever it was they wanted, especially Jay.

There was a unique excitement to waking up while it's still dark out, with friends over who've spent the night, getting on a bus with a bunch of other kids, and watching the sun come up on the way to Six Flags. Unfortunately, I wasn't feeling it.

I had no memory of the coma. My first memory after it was waking up in a hospital bed and listening to my mom tell me what happened, my dad standing in the background, silent as usual. Later they told me this happened many times, but I only remember once. My mom said Stephen was a very troubled boy. Fortunately, he didn't have access to his dad's gun when we were at Globals, or he could have gone on a killing spree. But when he got back home, he used his dad's gun to end his life.

"What? He killed himself?!"

"Yes, dear. He did."

"No no no no no nooo," I began to sob.

"Mark, you have such a tender heart. I'm so proud you've already forgiven the boy who did this to you. But if he hadn't killed himself, who knows what the courts would have decided to do with him. You could have . . .," she paused, choked up with emotion, "died." Now *she* began to sob.

I lay in bed crying, glad that my mom stopped talking. Stopped saying ridiculous things like she was proud of me. *I* did this to Ronnie. Me. Every cheap little joke I made at his expense or trick I pulled on him, that was good for a few laughs, was killing him inside. And I punched him so hard . . . I started crying harder at the thought.

I mean, he shouldn't have hit me out of the blue, but I'm sure he had his reasons. The worst part was he probably killed himself out of guilt for what he did to me, his 'best friend.' He was such a sweet kid. Sweet and innocent. Worth 10 of me. The world treated him cruelly, and I had been the point of the spear. A friend can cause more pain than an enemy.

It took me all summer and the first half of the school year to recover well enough physically and mentally from my head injury that I could go back to school. But I still had a heaviness on my soul. I thought it would eventually wear off, whether I wanted it to or not, because that's the way bad feelings had always worked for me before. But this heaviness showed no signs of lifting. School was hard at first, and I worried I'd never get my mind back the way it used to be, but by the end of the year I was back to my usual spot, which was a distant second to Jay for the title of smartest kid in school. In truth, that title might belong to Abel, but he didn't have the reputation to go along with the brains. My friends who were with me that night treated me the same as before. Everyone else looked on me like I was a hero. A narrative had been spun that Stephen, or Ronnie to those who knew him, was mentally unstable and had irrationally attacked me, the kid who was the nicest to him, and then killed himself because he was scared of going to jail, or insane, or pick your awful reason.

"Are you going to mope all day at Six Flags?" asked Abel, snapping me out of my reverie. He was sitting next to me on the bus, staring straight ahead with his deep-set eyes even though he was talking to me. He had a wispy mustache, which was a recent development.

"Probably."

"Well this is going to suck ass."

"Probably."

"Dude, it's been almost a year. Time to move on."

"I know." But I didn't know how. It was like I'd lost my ability to be happy.

"Here's the deal. I'm actually going to try to be the fun guy today, like you used to be. All I'm asking is that you try to have fun."

"Ok."

"What would the old Mark do? Hmmm."

"No freaking clue." (I didn't say freaking. I've cleaned this up a lot.)

"You know," he said, "our cussing has gotten out of control. It's actually a miracle we haven't been busted yet. I have an idea. For the rest of the trip, every time I cuss you're gonna thump me, and every time you cuss I'm gonna thump you. Isn't that a stupid little game like the old you would have come up with?"

"Hell no," I said, trying to be funny.

"Ok, make a fist."

I presented my fist. *Thwwwack!*

"Ow! Son of a bitch. No fair. You have sausage fingers."

"That's another."

I made a fist and looked away. *Thaawack!*

"Ah! Son of a . . . gun. Ok, your turn."

"Ok, um, crap biscuit." (but again, he didn't say 'crap,' but a stronger word)

I thumped him with my thin middle finger. *Dink.* He smiled.

"Wait, this game is rigged," I said.

"Then don't cuss."

"I'm gonna shut up for a while."

After a bit, Jay turned around from the seat in front of us and looked at us with his big, bulgy eyes. "Bro, check out Melissa's ass."

I looked a few seats in front of us and saw the behind of a girl hanging off the seat. Melissa was a popular girl a few years older than us. She was asleep and wearing short shorts.

"She's next on my list," said Jay. "Today in the park, or on the way home."

"Whatever," said Abel.

"You don't think I can get that?"

"No, I actually don't, but what I'm talking about is, there's no list. You're full of crap."

Oh man. It was on now. I wanted to crawl into a hole to escape the tension.

"I realize it's hard for you to get your mind around the concept of being with a girl, but it does happen to some people, just not you. You know why, Abel? Because you smell like crap. Well, not crap exactly, but B.O. That time you came over to my house, when you left my mom said, 'Get the Lysol.' But we were out of it, so she drove to Walmart and that was the only thing she bought, and when she got back, she sprayed my room and the living room for ten minutes straight. It's simple, dude. De-o-dor-ant. Here, I have some in my bag."

Jay produced a stick of antiperspirant and held it out to Abel. Abel knocked it out of his hand and it hit the head of the girl sitting across from him.

"Ouch!" She grabbed her head.

"Sorry," said Jay, picking it up. "My friend here doesn't know how to use deodorant and I'm trying to teach him, but he's a little slow."

"I'm not your friend."

"No, you're not," said Jay, and turned to me. "Unbelievable."

I'm ashamed to admit this, but I smiled at Jay, as if to acknowledge he was right and Abel was the one who was out of line. Abel stared straight ahead as Jay turned around, staring holes into his seat. Hopefully he didn't notice my little betrayal, but he must have. Shane sat next to Jay against the window, with headphones on, oblivious. None of us said anything for a while.

"I see it," said a kid from the front. I looked up ahead and saw the bright colors and mountains of metal. A little off the road I saw the wooden maze that was the Texas Giant. I had never even ridden the Judge Roy Scream, the poor man's Texas Giant. I felt a little fear, but I liked it. I'd take feeling fear over depression any day.

When we got there, the youth pastor told everyone to break into small groups, so the four of us made a group. We started off with the Bobsled and the Viking Ship, then moved up to the Judge Roy Scream.

"Time for the Giant," said Jay.

"Not yet," said Abel. "We have to build up to it all day. Plus, it will actually be better at night."

"What do you want to do?"

"Kiddie swings," said Abel.

"I wasn't talking to you, fag. Mark, what do you want to do?"

"Kiddie swings." I wasn't about to take Jay's side over Abel again.

He stared at me, trying to read me. I had never bucked him before.

"Fine, y'all ride the swings and Shane and I will ride the Mine Train."

"I'm riding the swings too," said Shane. I figured he'd go on the Mine Train with his buddy Jay too, but you never knew what he was gonna do.

"I'm not riding the damn baby swings. I'll ride the Mine Train and meet you at the swings afterwards. Then we all ride the Cliffhanger. Deal?"

"Deal," I said.

Jay disappeared into the Mine Train line.

"Now I know what the old Mark would do in this situation. You have one more ditch in you?"

"Hell yeah," I answered.

"That's a thump," he said, and drilled me in the knuckles. We ran to the other side of the park without riding the swings. Abel tried his best to recreate our group's old mojo. He made us play a game that involved us acting like idiots in front of strangers. We had to convince strangers to do stupid stuff, like massage our calf muscles because we claimed to have a charley horse. There was other similar tomfoolery, which finally devolved into us hiding behind a corner and jumping out and screaming at kids and running away, scaring the crap out of them, until finally an elderly employee caught us and threatened to call security to throw us out of the park. Fortunately, I talked our way out of it. It was a good program by Abel, but I still couldn't shake my dark cloud. I tried to fake like I was into it, but I'm sure they could feel the magic wasn't there.

What did get my juices flowing were the big rides. The fear I used to avoid I now embraced. Too bad my acceptance of fear didn't carry over to my fear of confrontation. Abel was the opposite. He hated big rides but had no problem facing down anyone, a much more useful combination in life. At the end of the night, Shane and I persuaded/coerced Abel to ride the Texas Giant. The roller coaster roared as we dropped down the hill, and when got back to the top, it got quiet, and all I could hear was me and Abel cussing our hearts out. We were inventing cuss words. After the ride we gave each other 'Texas Giant Immunity' from the thumping game.

The park was almost closed now so we headed to the front gate. On the way I spotted Jay on my left heading straight for us. Oh crap.

"Where the hell were you guys?" His big eyes were moist but there were no tears.

"Us?" I answered. "We were looking for you?"

"I was only on the Mine Train for about ten minutes and when I got out you were gone."

"Oh, some guy let us cut to the front of the swings."

"Then why didn't you wait at the Mine Train?"

"We didn't see you and thought you were already gone." We'd scripted this out earlier in the day, and they nominated me to deliver the lines since I was the best talker out of the three of us.

We all walked through the gate and followed the crowd, turning off at bus parking. The youth pastor was waiting to reprimand the three of us who missed the meet up at supper, and all of us for being 30 minutes late for departure.

The bus got back on the highway and hummed some of the kids to sleep. I could feel the fumes coming off Jay from the seat in front of us. He knew he was on the outside.

He turned around. "I'm glad y'all ditched me. I ended up hanging out with Melissa's group and we rode every big ride at least once. When we were in line for the Freeze I casually touched her butt like it was an accident, and she smiled at me. I knew it was on and so I kept looking for a place where we could be alone, but there wasn't anywhere, so I said screw it, and started kissing her right there in line. She had gum in her mouth and when we stopped kissing, it was in my mouth, and I said, 'Watermelon,' and all her friends started laughing–"

"Stop!" said Abel. "I can't take it anymore. You are so full of crap. We all know it. Mark sits here and kisses your ass, but when you're not around, all we do is laugh at your stupid bullcrap stories."

"Listen you stinky Mexican, you can all go to hell and I'll hang out with Melissa and her friends rather than you dorks."

"Oh really? Is that what you'll do?" Abel turned his focus from Jay to a few rows ahead of him. "Hey Melissa, could you come here for a second?"

She turned her head, blonde ponytail whipping around, confusion on her face. She got up and walked back to us. I felt hot all over.

"Yeah?" she asked with a valley girl lilt.

"I was just wondering why you're not sitting here with Jay?" he indicated who he was talking about with an open hand.

"Who?"

"You know, Jay here. The guy who you were making out with today in the roller coaster lines."

She looked at Jay and burst out laughing. "Y'all are nasty." She turned and walked back to her seat. Shane, who I had thought was asleep, busted out laughing.

"I can't believe you made this so easy," said Abel. "I used to actually think you were smart, so I was planning out this moment. I asked my sister to ask Katie Coleman about you, and she had never heard of you and was pissed some kid was telling people he'd slept with her. And you've never hit a home run. Ever. I told Mikey Mulligan you said you've hit 10 home runs and he died laughing. You didn't even make the freaking majors as a 12-year-old."

The kids who were awake and sitting near us were watching the spectacle. Jay stood there quivering, determination on his face. Either he was trying to think of a comeback, or trying not to cry.

Abel continued, loud enough for everyone listening to hear, "Let's go through the list of every girl you claim you've has sex with. Becky McGraw." Laughter from the crowd. "Rachael Yarborough–"

"What's going on back here?" Some youth group volunteer in her 20s was walking down the aisle to see what everyone was looking at, mercifully interrupting the annihilation.

"Nothing," said Shane. "Everybody *sit* down and go to *sleep*."

The adult repeated what Shane said and went back to the front of the bus. Abel sat down, shaking from the adrenaline. Jay sat down and stared out the window past Shane. I saw tears running down his face, but he wasn't sobbing. If not for the tears, he would have simply looked resolute, his lower jaw set firm.

I turned to Abel, "That's four thumps."

9

The Forum

The Universe hit me. Right in the nuts. I'm sitting here waiting for the pain to kick in from the news about the bones of Jesus. I haven't felt this low since the early days after my injury. To her credit Cora has left me alone in my misery. When I was younger and read the Bible I would find apparent contradictions, which I resolved by reading Bible commentaries and going online to try to find answers. Eventually, I could work through any difficulty, even if I had to give a little on pristine fundamentalist purity. This time it's different.

The one non-negotiable belief of Christianity is the Resurrection of Christ. Fortunately for us this is the event in Christianity that has the most positive evidence. If you take away the Resurrection, our faith becomes a series of platitudes. Until now, the falsifiability of Christianity was the thing that made it different than other religions. It's the historical religion. No one can know whether or not Mohammed received the Koran from the angel Gabriel, but in the case of Jesus, he was executed publicly in front of thousands of people, in such a way that his death couldn't be in doubt except by the most unreasonable. Not only that, but his manner of death was prophesied in Psalms 22:15 – "They pierced My hands and My feet." So not only did Jesus happen to die in a public way that could be argued about by historians thousands of years later, but this manner of execution was predicted hundreds of years before that, before crucifixions were even a form of execution.

That he rose from the dead was not only testified to by his followers, but also by the empty tomb, which was prophesied in Isaiah 53:9 – "And they made His grave with the wicked–But with the rich at His death." In other words, at first the Romans were prepared to throw him in a mass grave for criminals (the wicked) as was normal with a crucifixion, but at his death, Joseph of Arimathea (the rich) intervened and had his body placed in his own tomb (although there are other interpretations of this verse). The reason the tomb is important is that secular historians generally admit the disciples themselves believed in the Resurrection. We can then ask, if the disciples believed in the Resurrection, what happened to Jesus' body? They couldn't have stolen it from the tomb if they believed he was resurrected. Non-believers must then do away with the tomb, or their theories get pretty convoluted, such as, the body was misplaced in the wrong tomb, accompanied by mass hallucinations from the disciples, etc. But again, like the public execution, not only is the tomb recorded unanimously among the early Gospel accounts, it was also prophesied hundreds of years earlier in Isaiah. How did the prophets know to predict the manner of burial such that it would make for lively arguments between Christians and skeptics thousands of years after the fact?

These are all well-worn paths for me. I first learned them when I was losing my faith, and these facts gave me a foothold whereby I could dig in, and I've become reacquainted with them as I've recently been trying to give my faith another chance. The Shroud was going to fix all my faith questions in one fell swoop. I would carbon date it, the results would come back showing it to be 2000 years old, and there would no longer be any reasonable doubt that The Shroud of Turin proved the resurrection of Christ. I'd start going to church again, along with millions of others. Now, with the DNA match between 'James, brother of Jesus,' and 'Jesus son of Joseph,' the results will be the reverse. There can be no denying these are the bones of the real Jesus. Unless there was foul play in the testing. I imagine this is the typical first reaction to faith-shattering news like this. In fact, when the Shroud of Turin was carbon-dated to the Middle Ages, many conspiracy theories rose up as to how nefarious scientists changed the samples to have the Shroud disproven and give science another victory over religion, mwa ha ha ha ha! Eventually, better scientific theories arose to 'explain away' the carbon testing, but maybe it was right all along. Probably it was, as things now stand.

"Ready to go find our friend the priest?" Cora interrupts me from my reverie.

I check the clock. 8 a.m. I've been lost in thought for a while. I stand up and stretch my legs, and then we head out into the warm Italian morning. The streets and sidewalks are full now. What are the odds we find him? What's the point anyway? To live for what purpose? I find myself wishing for the Rapture, which makes no sense–wishing for God to take me away from the world because *he* doesn't exist. Even if the priest does know who took the Shroud and how to recover it, who cares? I know what the tests would show. Even if they show the Shroud *is* authentic, the results would still be brushed aside because a DNA relationship to James is stronger evidence than the approximate date of the Shroud. And, the bones test came first. The narrative is in stone.

I trudge on, following Cora past the Coliseum, still standing strong after almost 2000 years. We walk by tourists, some laughing, some getting upset with their kids, as though the world is the same as it was yesterday. There are a couple of street performers dressed as Indian gurus. One is sitting on the ground with legs folded, balancing the other, who is sitting the same way a few feet above him, on a small stick that couldn't possible hold him, as though he's levitating. Neat trick. I see the Forum on my left, below the level of the street. There's not much to it. It's basically a big park, with grass fields littered with the white marble columns and other remains of antiquity here and there. We walk toward the center of it. Now what?

I spot a bench ahead. "I'm going to sit here and stew in my juices for a bit."

"Fine," she walks on.

So how will the church respond to this news? Billions of believers will get the rug pulled out from under them. Most of them won't take much notice of it. But I think what underpins the great mass of normal believers out there are the intellectual and spiritual leaders of past and present. One could always reason, 'well, I don't understand this but there are smarter people out there who believe the same as I do.' Those smarter people are intellectually honest for the most part. Some will come up with an explanation around the new findings, some will try to roll with a spiritual but not bodily Resurrection, but many will wave the white flag and give up the faith.

I probably should too. It's as though every time I try to get serious about my faith, one thing or another squashes my fire, but the challenge has never been this serious before. I guess it was wishful thinking all along, like Cora said. Placebo. The feelings I thought were God were merely good feelings from the hope that it all was true. The crazy thing is, if you follow the teachings of Jesus, they actually work. The man was the genius of all geniuses. The greatest man who ever lived. But the Resurrection was simply a story. An accident of history. Accidents upon accidents on top of each other, making it appear legitimate. Perhaps we don't know as much about early church history as we thought. If the historical Jesus' bones were put in an ossuary, it means they were treated by someone for two years to get the flesh off the bones. Who would have done this? His brother James, or one of the disciples? Then they'd know Jesus wasn't bodily raised from the dead. Perhaps they were able to maintain cognitive dissonance, knowing one thing but preaching another.

I feel a hard object shoved against my back!

"Don't turn around, Mr. Eberhart. Stand up slowly, or I'll blow you the hell away."

I want to stand up but my legs aren't working. He shoves it harder into my back and I stand up on quivering legs. Panic jumbles my thoughts into nonsense. He nudges me back in the direction I came from and we walk that way, his gun pressing into my back, compelling me forward. Oxygen is hard to come by.

He comes up beside me, gun poking into my side. My mind starts processing. It's the red-headed guy from my room. His right arm is draped around me, and his left must be inside his shirt, holding the gun against me. We're walking past tourists who are oblivious. Or maybe they're pretending not to notice. Maybe we look like a gay couple at a passing glance. That's what he's going for anyway. I lock eyes with Cora, who is 20 feet ahead on the path. She turns and walks ahead, pretending to be oblivious too.

We're halfway back to the street. Think. If all he wanted was to kill me, I'd be dead. He either wants to kill me somewhere without witnesses, or kidnap me and do who knows what. Torture? I've got to do something. Come on, Mark. We are closing in on the street.

In one move I turn toward him and punch at his gun as hard as I can. I feel it go free and at the same time I feel him punch me in the head with his free hand. I stumble back, but then swing at his face with my right fist and connect, because his left is still inside his shirt so he couldn't block me.

He swings at me again. I duck and jump back. He frees his left arm out his sleeve. "I was hoping you'd try something." He smiles and his teeth are covered in blood.

He steps back and bends down to pick up the gun. Points it at me. I see a family nearby scatter and hear a woman scream behind me.

He pulls the trigger.

Nothing.

He pulls it again.

Then he crumples to the ground.

Behind where he was standing, I now see a man running toward me. The priest, but he's in normal dress clothes.

"We must leave." The priest, or whoever he is, pulls me up and practically drags me in the same direction I was headed, back to the street. Onlookers are shouting at us in a foreign tongue. I see the back of Cora, walking briskly ahead of me.

"Cora!" I shout. She glances back at me and stays at her same pace until we catch up with her. We reach the street together and turn left. The back door of a black sedan in front of us opens–by itself.

"Get in." He half-shoves me into the back seat.

The priest and Cora jump in the front seats. He starts the car and floors it.

We tear ahead, in the wrong lane. He comes to a roundabout and goes the wrong way, honking at the oncoming cars, and then merges into traffic going the right direction.

"What the hell is happening?" I ask.

"We are driving away." He comes upon a slow car, and passes it by driving in the wrong lane. A car going the other way turns onto the sidewalk to avoid us, and the driver lays on his horn.

"From who? Who's that guy who keeps attacking me?"

"He is Stuart Hawk's man."

"What does he want with me?"

"I do not know. Maybe because you cannot be put in the trance." He comes to a line of cars waiting for a light. He lays on his horn and goes right, driving up the sidewalk. People scatter and curse at us. We get to the intersection and turn right.

"What is the trance?" asks Cora.

"A friend of mine made it by accident. He found how to make people very smart. When they are smart, they get, how do you say, side-effects?" He has a sing-song Italian accent.

"Yeah, side-effects," I say.

"But a man called Stuart Hawk stole his idea." We come to a red light and he doesn't slow down, but drives through cross-traffic and merges to the left. "He was my friend's boss at a company called Corpus Biotechnology."

"Your friend made you very smart and gave you the side-effects?" asks Cora.

"Yes," he whips around a corner to the right.

"Is one of the side-effects the ability to throw objects with your mind?" I ask. We're on a narrow road, with cars parked on both sides. No room for oncoming traffic.

"Yes. I can reach out to feel the object, like feeling with hands, but with my mind. I make it do what I want. It is this way I can put people in the trance. Except for you. It is like you are not there."

We get off the narrow street and turn left onto a two-lane road.

"Who was that boy in the tunnel at the Vatican?" asks Cora.

Crash! A car side-swipes us and spins us around. My world is spinning.

The car roars as the priest gives it gas, but the tires squeal and it goes nowhere.

"Get out! Stay behind the car."

I open the door and spill out of the car and scramble back behind it. Cora joins me. There are cars parked on both sides of the street, and tan three-story buildings lining the road. The car that hit us is sideways in the street, blocking one lane, and we're blocking the other. The priest is standing next to our car looking ahead.

I scoot to my left so I can peek out and see what he's looking at. There's a singular figure in the distance, walking down the center of the street. He's tall, wearing all black, with long blond hair covering his broad shoulders. He's aiming an AK-47 at the priest. In front of him a line of cars is forming on the right.

He casually waves his left hand, and at that moment a Vespa leaps from its parking spot and flies at the priest. The priest ducks and waves his hand up, and it just misses him and flies over our car and crashes into a building.

I stand up to check on the priest.

Poppop!

Explosion in my left arm! Otherworldly pain.

I fall down. Cora pulls me behind the car. I go to touch where the pain is coming from but can't bring myself to do it. Cora is now peering around the car where I had been.

"Get back here," I shout at her.

She doesn't. I look at my arm. There's a red hole in my bicep. I hear horns and shouting. I maneuver to a crouch and peek through the back window at the scene ahead. The blonde man is chewing up the road in large strides, about 50 feet ahead of us now. Our car starts shuddering, like giant invisible hands are shaking it. The priest faces the car and reaches out to it, barely touching it with both hands.

"Go to Holy Angels Monastery," he yells, face grimacing. "They will take care of you. Do not go to hospital. Go!"

The car is shaking violently now. I grab Cora and pull her back. We look on as the man in black approaches the priest, not slowing his pace. He pulls back his gun, and rams the business end into the priest's gut. At that moment, the car vaults from its position and strikes the two of them, launching them at the car parked on the other side of the road. The moment they crash against the parked car, our car smashes into it, crushing their bodies in between.

I run to them and look in between the cars. All I see is mangled gore. They're both dead.

I turn to Cora. "Let's get the hell out of here."

10

Truth or Dare

Cora
21 years earlier

"Are we just going to sit around and watch bad TV or what?" asked Rusty, his mop of hair almost covering his eyes.

"What do you have in mind?" returned Cora. She was wearing her most expensive pair of blue jeans, a white blouse, and had fixed her hair to look like she hadn't fixed it, but naturally woke up looking perfect.

"Sheila's like 18. Couldn't you get your hands on some beer? I've been meaning to start under-age drinking for a while now."

"No alcohol," said Cora. Her parents had gone to their church denomination's yearly meeting at headquarters. To babysit the girls for the weekend, her dad hired the most responsible girl in the church, Sheila, who'd been babysitting them off and on since she was 15, and was now a senior. What her parents didn't know was Sheila was *not* responsible–*at all*. Cora floated the idea of getting Noble Baines to come over and Sheila was game. To her surprise, her dad never confronted Noble's parents about the day at the pool.

Maybe he didn't want to upset good tithers. After missing the next week, Noble was back at church the following, and a few weeks after that he started flirting with her again.

Cora called Rusty and told him to come over the following night and bring his brother. The guys showed up around 11:00 p.m. and they sat down on the couch next to each other as they all watched Saturday Night Live. Cora and Sheila sat in recliners to one side, while Avery and Madelyn sat on the carpet in front of them.

"Are you sure your dad's not coming home tonight?" asked Noble. "No offense, but that guy is scary."

"Yes," answered Cora. "He has meetings all day tomorrow and won't be home until tomorrow night. And, he's not scary. He's just one of those guys who can't handle sports." This was not true. Sure, he was at his most intense and obnoxious when he was coaching. But it'd be more accurate to say he's one of those guys for who is never wrong, about anything. Or one of those guys who had to control every facet of his family's life. The house had to be spotless. The girls had to practice basketball two hours a day. Mom had to work out an hour every day. He'd accuse her of skipping workouts because she was 'getting fat,' even though she was skinnier than most moms. The only mercies were he was gone most of the day, and he usually directed his fire on Cora and her mom and left Madelyn alone. She could hardly remember the last time he'd been harsh with Madelyn.

"Or when he catches a guy tickling his daughter in the pool?" said Rusty.

"That goes for most dads," said Cora.

"Cora, they shouldn't be here," said Madelyn. Her big, blue eyes were almost in tears. She'd recently hit her growth spurt and looked like a woman now, but was still the same on the inside.

"It's ok, Maddie. We're just hanging out with friends. This is what normal kids do."

They got quiet and started watching TV again.

"No offense, but this party blows," said Noble.

Cora turned off the TV. "Truth or Dare?"

Rusty's eyes lit up. "I'm game."

"You go first," Avery said to Cora.

"Truth."

"Who do you have a crush on?" Avery shot her a 'gotcha' smile.

Cora gave her 'thanks a lot' look. "The closest thing to a crush would be Noble I guess."

"You're blushing!" said Rusty, and laughed his machine gun laugh.

"You're next, Rusty," said Cora.

"Why? What's the order here?"

"The order is you're next," said Noble.

"Fine. Dare."

"I dare you to kiss Avery," Cora smiled at him.

Rusty's face grew serious. He stood up from the couch, walked up to Avery, who looked terrified. He got down on his knees, and started kissing her. It took Avery a bit to kiss back, but when she did, it looked to Cora like a momma bird feeding a baby bird. She looked away and stifled a giggle, which was difficult as the awkwardness of the onlookers made it even funnier. She made eye-contact with Noble, and that was it. She fell on the floor cracking up. The kiss stopped. Avery's freckles shone bright orange. Now Rusty was the one who was blushing. "Remember our deal," he said to Cora.

"The statute of limitations is up."

"I don't know what that means, so our deal is still on."

"What? What deal?" asked Avery.

"Don't worry about it," said Cora. "Now it's Noble's turn,"

she said, changing the subject. "Truth or Dare?"

Avery put a pillow over her face to hide her permanent smile. Noble had a baseball hat on. His blonde hair showed under the bill of his hat, contrasting with his dark eyebrows. "Truth."

"Let's go with the classic. What is your worst fear?" asked Cora.

"Your dad," he said with a quick grin.

"No seriously. Think about it."

He sat there for a minute looking up at the bill of his cap. "Not starting at QB next year. Everyone knows I'm better, but Trey's dad is a business man and has the coaches in his pocket."

"Your dad's a business man too," said Cora.

"He owns a roofing company. It's not the same as owning convenience stores."

"Your deepest, darkest fear is *not* being the starting quarterback?" asked Cora, disappointed in his shallow answer.

"I can't stand injustice, especially when it screws up my whole life. My whole future."

The room got quiet and awkward.

"Mmmmoving on," said Rusty.

"Avery's turn," said Cora. "And please say 'dare'. You're an open book so truth is no fun with you."

"Sure. Dare." She looks over at Rusty.

"I dare you to run around the house in your underwear," said Noble.

"No way. That's nasty," answered Avery.

Rusty chimed in, "I dare you to drive around the block."

"No dude," said Cora. "Too risky."

"It's that or the underwear," said Rusty. "She's lucky we're giving her a second choice."

"The driving one," said Avery.

"It's not even illegal," said Noble. "You're 15, right? And Sheila's like 18."

Sheila, who was sitting silent and shy all night, blushed at the mention of her name.

"I've never taken Driver's Ed. I've never even driven a car for practice," said Avery.

"Then this is your practice," said Noble. He led the way outside and everyone else followed except for Madelyn. Avery and Sheila got into his small pickup. She backed out over the side of the driveway but fortunately it was the trashcan side and not the mailbox side. The trashcans looked no worse for wear. She stopped and started all the way down the road and out of sight, eventually coming back from the other side. When she got back to the driveway and turned in, they heard her scream as she ran over the curb, and floored it for a second before she slammed on the brakes, leaving the truck crooked in the driveway. She got out of the car laughing. Even Sheila was laughing. They all went back inside to their spots in the living room.

"You're up, Sheila. Truth or Dare?" said Cora.

"This is stupid."

"Come on, Sheila," said Noble. "We've all done it. It's your turn."

She sighed, "Truth, I guess."

"Who do you have the hots for?" asked Avery.

"No one. The guys at our school are idiots."

"Oh come on," said Avery, "there are a million guys at *your* school."

"A million idiots."

"Ouch," said Rusty.

"Some idiots are hot," said Avery.

"It's no one. I already told you."

"Sheila, you're under oath. You can't break the sacred

bonds of Truth or Dare," said Cora.

"That's stupid. This is stupid."

"How about this," offered Avery. "We're not saying you have the hots for this guy, but if you had a gun to your head, and you had to pick one guy at your school who wasn't disgusting, who would it be?"

"I guess Noble."

"Busy guy," said Rusty.

"I didn't say I liked him. He's just better than all of the other idiots at our school."

"Oh, we know what you mean, heh heh heh," said Rusty.

"Shut up, Buttmunch," said Noble.

Avery took over, "Cora, it's your turn again."

"Truth."

"What was the deal you made with Rusty to get him to kiss me?"

"Did I say truth? I meant to say dare."

"No," said Avery. "Too late. You can't change now. What was the deal?"

"I'll tell you when you're older. Now what's my dare?"

Avery gave Cora her patented scrunched up face that was supposed to look mad. "Fine, but keep in mind I'm a better friend than you. I dare you and Noble to go into your parents' room together and lock the door for 10 minutes."

She looked at Noble with a sheepish face. "That sounds like it's a dare for him too."

"I'm game if you are."

She got up, trying to hide a smile, and walked toward her parents' room. When he got up to follow, Rusty gave them a "Wooooo!" like a TV audience would do when somebody kissed, and Avery joined in. Cora opened the door. Her parents' queen bed with bedposts on the corners took up most of the room. Noble locked the door behind them and turned his hat backwards. She sat on the bed, a cluster of nerves. He sat down next to her.

"I wonder what they think we're doing?" asked Cora.

"What *should* they think?"

"That we're just talking for now."

"About what?"

"I don't know."

"You're scared."

"Maybe a little," she admitted.

He put his hand on the back of her head, gently pulled her close, and kissed her. She tried to act like she knew what she was doing. He leaned forward against her and she went with it and laid back on the bed, still kissing him. It was not like she'd imagined, kissing that is. He tasted hot and minty. There were no fireworks. It was kind of technical, tongues moving all around.

He put his weight on top of her and softly pushed her legs to the sides so he could get between them. She felt him pressed up against her. Was this going to happen? On her parents' bed in a stupid game of Truth or Dare?

She turned her head. "Noble, I'm sorry. I can't." She wiggled out from under him.

"Are you *serious*?"

"Sorry, it's just, it doesn't feel right."

He sat up. "You've got to be freaking kidding me." He walked to the side of the room and turned to look at her. She was sitting up now. "I haven't had a girlfriend in six months because I wanted you. I've been trying to figure out how to get some time with you. I was planning to ask you to prom but your dad would probably say no. Then you call and ask me over here and tell me you like me." He is quiet for a few seconds. "This is bullcrap."

Bang! Bang! Bang! Someone was pounding on the door.

"Get out of there!" It was Sheila. "Your parents just walked in."

"Oh hell," said Noble. "What do we do?"

Sheila overheard him. "You can make out if you hurry."

Noble unlocked the door and when he threw it open, there was Sheila, with Avery and Rusty behind them. Sheila started laughing.

"Not funny, Sheila," said Cora.

"I thought it was."

"Whatever. Avery, I blame you."

"I didn't do anything."

"What were you guys doing in there anyway?" asked Sheila.

"Absolutely nothing," said Noble, turning his hat back around.

"Sure," said Rusty.

Everyone filtered back into the living room.

"All right, who's next?" asked Sheila, who had perked up now.

"I'm done," said Cora.

"Wait, we skipped Madelyn," said Sheila. "Truth or Dare?"

Madelyn had never left her spot on the floor. She was looking down at her feet and didn't answer.

"Have you ever gone all the way with a guy?" asked Sheila.

Madelyn stood up, looked at Cora, and her face twisted into a cry. She turned and ran out of the room.

"Good going, Sheila. She's 14." Cora followed her to her room.

"Damn, I was just kidding around," Sheila called after them.

By the time Cora got to her room, Madelyn was sitting on

her bed, sobbing.

She sat down and put her hand on her shoulder. "I'm sorry Sheila said that, but it's not that big a deal."

"What if dad comes home?"

"He's not coming home tonight, and it's not like you'd get in trouble if he did."

They sat there quietly for a moment. Madelyn started to calm down a little.

"It's just . . . you're becoming a woman now. You're too old to flip out when somebody makes a joke about you having sex."

With that, Madelyn burst back into tears.

"What the hell? It's like . . ." a horrible thought popped into her mind. So horrible she tried to push it aside and continue as if the thought hadn't occurred to her. But it had, and she couldn't.

"Did Dad . . ." she wasn't sure what she was going to say after that, but she didn't need to say anything. At the mention of Dad, Madelyn's eyes locked with Cora's and the look of terror in them confirmed her worst fears.

Her vision blurred. "I'm going to kill that son of a bitch."

"Cora, you can't say anything."

"Like hell I can't."

"No one can know. Especially Mom. And he can't know that you know, or . . ." she trailed off.

"Or what?"

"I don't know. I just don't want him mad at me."

"Listen Madelyn, he has no right to be mad at *you*. You need to be mad at *him*."

"Cora!"

The horrible yell came from the other room. She'd heard it a million times, and always cowered, wondering what she had done this time. But not tonight. Tonight, it was his turn to cower.

She jumped up, boiling with fury, and stormed back to the living room. There stood her father in the far entrance, her mother behind him. The boys were huddled in the corner, petrified. Avery was on the floor, crying, and Sheila sat motionless. Cora stood across the room from him, shoulders square.

"What in God's name is going on here, Cora?"

"We're having a wild sex party, Dad. Do you want to join in?"

His brown eyes flashed with rage and he took half a step toward her. "I come into my house to find God knows what going on, with boys sleeping over, and you have the nerve to speak to me like that?"

"I have the nerve?" she shouted. "You're the one with the nerve. You stand up every Sunday before God and everybody telling us to do what Jesus would do, all the while you're raping your own DAUGHTER!" she screamed the last word.

"No!" her mother cried behind him.

Her dad swallowed, "I catch you throwing a wild party, and that's how you choose to respond? By trying to turn this on me?"

She was shuddering with rage. "You wanna screw one of your girls, Dad? Screw me. I know I told you if you ever touched me again I would tell. I take it back. Screw me all you want but leave Maddie *alone*!"

"Oh, now it's Maddie who's accusing me?"

"Maddie, come here. Now!" Cora called. She didn't remove her gaze from her dad

Madelyn walked up next to Cora, sobbing. "I'm. Sorry. Dad."

Her mom was wailing louder than Madelyn now.

"It's ok, Maddie," said her father. "You did nothing wrong."

"Dad, there are seven witnesses here. You need to let us leave, *now.*"

"You are not going to leave this house for the next month, young lady."

"Noble," said Cora, trying to sound calm, "would you please leave, and call the cops when you get home and tell them me and my sister are being held captive by a *rapist*?"

Noble looked at her, and looked at her dad, and didn't move.

"Why are you doing this to me, Honey?" her dad started to cry.

Cora gathered everybody up, all crying now, and pushed them past her dad and out the door. She was almost out when he grabbed her arm with his vise-like grip.

"You will regret this, Cora."

"Get your damn hands off me."

11

The Monastery

Pain radiates from the white-hot sun in my bicep. It's swallowed up all the other pain I was feeling from the fight. We run away from the bloody scene, people berating us in Italian out their car windows as they wait in traffic. We turn down a small road and no one follows us.

"We need to call you an ambulance," says Cora.

"The last thing he said before he died was *not* to go to the hospital."

"So you're going to bleed out then?"

"I'll be fine." I have no idea if I'll be fine or not.

"Hold it shut. I'll find something. Come on."

Hold it shut? I can't even touch it. I pull my sleeve down over the wound to soak up the blood.

We walk ahead. In addition to feeling like my arm is falling off, I'm feeling weak. I put one foot after the other, and every step sends a smidgen of extra pain to my arm. There's a little foot traffic coming the other way. Some people are staring but nobody says anything.

"There's one," says Cora. "Wait out here and I'll be right back."

She runs ahead and goes into a little store. I wait outside. Guess it would be rude for me to bleed on their floor. I turn and stand against the wall to hide my arm from onlookers. Why did he tell me not to go to the hospital? Would the guys after us know to wait for me there? Oh my God. This pain is unbearable. What are they going to do for me at a monastery? Fetch a doctor? He better have some good painkillers. Why is she taking forever?

I wiggle my fingers. Nice that I can still do that. How long do I wait before I go in after her? They won't have to take my arm off, will they? At least it's my left arm. I could type slowly. I could kind of play some sports. Maybe I'm being a big wuss. Come on, Cora.

"Cora!"

"One sec." At least she's still there.

I turn around and look inside. She's paying at the register. After a minute, she walks out with a bag of crap. "Had some shopping to do?"

She ignores my comment. "Here." She pulls a water bottle out of the bag and pours it over my wound, and then wraps a black towel around my arm above the bullet hole, like a tourniquet, and uses the loose part of the towel to clean off the blood and hide the wound. Then she gives me some aspirin.

"This will make me bleed more."

"And feel much better." She gets out four and gives me them along with what's left of the water bottle. I take them and she throws away the bag and heads back down the road, in the same direction we'd been walking before we stopped. I follow. There's a street ahead that intersects with ours. Before we get there, I see a white taxi parked on the side of the road.

"Holy Angels Monastery," she says as we approach the driver.

The driver looks at me, at my sleeve. "Hospital," he says.

"No, Holy Angels Monastery," she holds out her hand to me, and I grab my wallet with my left hand and give it to her.

She hands the driver a 50 Euro note, and he nods

On the way, the driver listens to a live recording of Toto, as if I'm not being tortured enough. There's no conversation in the car, thank God. Surely those guys who are after me have lost the scent. Why am I in Italy again, with a bullet in my arm, riding to a Monastery? Maybe the nuns are like nurses on that BBC show. Midwives can't extract a bullet, though. How can God let anyone endure pain like this? Yet the martyrs endured way more than this and were often peaceful through the ordeal, if the history is true. Either it's not true, or God gave them a special grace I clearly have not received.

Twenty minutes go by, my thoughts in a loop, my arm throbbing. We are out of downtown now. Not sure if we're still in Rome or not. I see a church ahead. The sign reads 'Chiesa della Santa Vergine.'

"What's that say?" I ask the driver.

"Is Church of Holy Virgin."

It's a tall, old, white building. The towers on the sides of the building are taller than the apex of the roof in the center. It practically looks like it's nestled in the rainforest. There is greenery everywhere. Palm trees. Other trees I can't identify. Shrubs. Gardens. To the right of the church is a matching building. It's the same color, but shorter and wider than the church. The driver parks as close as he can get to it. Must be the monastery.

We get out and take the sidewalk winding through the gardens toward the monastery. There's no door to it, only an open entrance into a courtyard in the middle, full of green hedges and more palm trees. Windows overlook the courtyard in every direction, both on the ground level and second story. The bone in my arm aches like a rotten tooth.

A young nun approaches us. "Are you to be staying with us today?" she asks in a British accent.

"Are you expecting us?" I ask.

"Your names please, and I'll check the reservations."

"Monasteries double as hostels," Cora explains. It sounded like she resisted tacking 'moron' onto the end of her sentence.

"Ruddy hell! Sorry, what's the matter with your arm, Sir?"

"I was shot. A priest told me you all could help me."

"*We* can help you?"

"He said to come to Holy Angels Monastery," says Cora.

"What priest?"

"Italian guy. Older. He could move things with his mind like a Jedi," I say.

Her eyes widen. "What do you mean, 'he could?'"

"He's dead," says Cora.

The nun reaches out and steadies herself on a tree next to her. Then after a minute, "Follow me."

She turns and scampers through the maze of hedges. She opens an old wooden door into the monastery and turns right, down a corridor with stone walls and no decoration except one wooden crucifix, with natural light coming in from the windows. At the end of the corridor we walk into a sparse room with two plain wooden tables, where three nuns sit, eating bread. They look up at us.

"What is it, Sister Mary Ellen?" asks a thin, black nun with a melodic African accent.

"They say Father Antonio is dead and he sent them here."

Her forehead creases and she looks at me, "Is this true?"

"I don't know his name, but yes I think so. He died protecting us, but before he did he said to come here, but I don't–"

"Did you kill him?"

"No. I was his friend . . . acquaintance. We were on the same side."

"And what side is that?"

"When he tried to recover the Shroud, I was with him . . .

in the Vatican."

She tilts her head sideways, like a dog trying to figure something out. "I believe you, Mr. . . ."

"Mark Eberhart."

"Mr. Mark. My name is Sister Miriam Francis, but you'll hear me called Mother Superior by the other nuns. Please forgive my suspicions. You have an honesty about you, but I do not know why Father Antonio told you to come here. He was to keep this place a secret."

"He didn't want us going to a hospital for Mark's arm," says Cora.

She squints her eyes, focusing on me. Suddenly her eyebrows shoot up.

"He's been shot," says Cora.

"Get the boy," Mother Superior orders.

"Boy?"

"Can you trust me, Mr. Mark?" she asks. The British nun leaves the room and walks back down the hall.

I do. Maybe it's her nun habit, but I don't think so. "I guess I don't have a choice."

"You will see."

Another nun at the table gets up and collects the dishes. I give Cora a 'what the hell' face, and she makes one back at me. My arm is killing me. Not sure if I mentioned that or not. A few silent moments pass before I see the British nun walking down the hallway holding a boy's hand. Of course. The boy from the tunnel. They walk past me and into the room. In the light I can see he looks about five, with olive skin, curly brown hair, and sparkling, striking blue eyes.

"Give him your arm," says Mother Superior. Huh? Her eyes implore me. The boy walks up to me. I hold out my arm to him and he grabs my hand. I feel a shock of electricity and reflexively pull back my hand.

"What the . . . ?"

"How does your arm feel, Mr. Mark?"

"Huh." The surprise of the jolt wears off and I realize my arm feels numb. No, better than that. I don't feel pain. I loosen the towel and take it off. I look at my wound, or rather, I look where it should be. There are blood stains on my arm, but where there should be a bullet hole, there is only smooth, tan skin.

Mother Superior sends me up to one of the lodging rooms. I shower and put on the button up shirt they gave me, which is tight but passable. There's a knock at the door. The pale British nun leads me back to the dining hall or whatever they call it. Only Mother Superior is at the table, sitting up straight as a rod.

"Have a seat, Mr. Mark," she points to a chair across from her.

"How did he do it?" I ask as I sit down.

"The boy has special abilities."

"Like the priest?"

"No, different than Father Antonio." I can see that. It's one thing to move a car with your mind, and another to create new flesh over a wound.

"How did you know about the boy's abilities?"

"Antonio told me."

"Who is he? How did he get in the tunnel in the Vatican?"

"I do not know. Father Antonio asked if I could watch the boy and I agreed."

A nun enters the room from the kitchen, bringing a plate with an Italian sandwich. A panino, I've learned since I've been in Rome. It has thick ciabatta bread and a few thin slices of salami in the middle.

"Thank you." I take a bite. Bread's a bit stale but it has a tasty zing. Not as much meat as I'm used to, but I imagine it's a prize delicacy in a convent. "It's delicious."

Cora walks in, still in her yoga clothes. Guess she wouldn't wear a habit. It'd probably burst into flames if she tried. She sits down next to me. "Sorry, I had to make a call."

"Tell me, Mr. Mark, how did you end up with Father Antonio in the Vatican?"

I relate the story to her as quickly as I can, not leaving out any details because I know she'll believe it. After I'm finally through, I say, "It's your turn. Tell me the story of how *you* ended up here."

She smiles a brilliant, large-toothed smile, "Why do you want to know?"

"Because I bet your story is better than mine."

"Ok, I will tell you. I was born and raised right here in Rome," she says in her lovely accent.

I raise my eyebrow at her. She lets out a full, mirthful laugh.

"I'm from the Sudan. South. My mother and father were shot and killed by soldiers from the North. Before they were shot, they told my brothers and I to flee from our home, while they stayed behind to fight the soldiers to give us time to escape. It did not work. We were captured and my brothers were turned into soldiers for the North and were forced to capture and kill our own people. I was kept as a sex slave. I was 11 years old."

"I'm so sorry," says Cora.

"Do you believe in signs, Mr. Mark, and Ms.–I'm sorry, what is your name, dear?"

"Cora."

"Ms. Cora?"

"No, I'm sorry, but I don't."

"I do," I say.

"Well, one day when I was 14, I was planning to take my life. I prayed to God and told him I was going to do it. I had stolen a guard's knife. I told God if he wanted to me to keep living, he needed to tell me. At that exact moment, a bird flew into my tent and started flying around in a panic when it couldn't get out. I held the door wide open and the bird flew out. God said, 'You are the bird. Today you will escape.'

"A soldier approached to check what was happening. I remembered my knife and ran back into my tent and hid it under my blanket. He asked what the trouble was and I told him a bird flew inside. He saw me lying on the blankets and got on top of me. I felt God give me an idea. After he finished and was still, I reached under the blanket and grabbed the knife and thrust it into his neck. He hit at my arm and pulled the knife out. He tried to come at me with the knife but I flew around the tent like the bird, until he dropped. I put my clothes on, grabbed the knife, and left the tent. He had been the guard on duty. I snuck past any other watching eyes and escaped the camp. A few days later, I was almost dead of thirst when I stumbled into a refugee camp."

"Wow! Your story *is* better than mine."

"God told you to kill a man?" asks Cora.

"*That's* your takeaway from her story?"

"Yes. I believe he did," answers Mother Superior.

"I mean, I'm all for it, but I thought your God didn't work that way."

"Once we try to pin down how God works, He will surprise us and do something different. He is not a predictable God."

"Is that why He let you suffer for three years?"

"No one knows the mysteries of God, but I've thanked him every day for 30 years that he saved me."

"I am really glad the bird flew into your tent, but I wonder if it was a coincidence. If it were me, I wouldn't have thought 'escape from camp' from a bird flying into my tent, but sometimes, when you're looking for a sign, whatever you find becomes one."

"Ms. Cora, it may have been a coincidence, but my life has been a series of such coincidences." While she speaks, she reaches across the table and holds Cora's hands. Cora lets her.

"You're obviously a remarkable person, and a person like you makes her own luck. Most people believe in God not because He rescued them out of a war camp, but because their parents believed in him before."

"May I take this one, Mother Superior?"

She beams at me. "By all means."

"One of the differences between true Christianity and religion by custom is that a true Christian is born again, or has a real encounter with God, usually not as dramatic as Sister Miriam's, er, Mother Superior's, but God comes into their world and touches them, and then they live their lives following where He leads, having more encounters with him. There are hundreds of millions of people with these 'coincidences.'"

"Well sorry," Cora turns to Mother Superior, "and again I don't mean offense Sister, but I don't know these people," she turns back to me, pulling her hands away from the nun, "but what I do know is people have a tendency to embellish stories to make them interesting. It's anecdotal evidence. And wait, why are we having this conversation? Did you forget about this morning's paper?"

I was wondering why she let me carry on like the world hadn't changed. I enjoyed going through the old motions, ignoring the cold ice in the pit of my stomach, still there from the 'Bones of Jesus' article. I address Mother Superior to change the subject, not wanting to drag her into *that* discussion.

"So you went from the refugee camp to the convent?"

"Yes, with some adventures in between. I was one of the few refugees who was placed in an American home. I joined a convent after high school, and here I am serving God in the Holy City."

"How did you know Father Antonio?" I ask.

"He worked at the Vatican overseeing many secondary schools, such as the school we run."

That's some superintendent. "Have you ever heard of a man named Stuart Hawk?"

"No, I have not."

"Do you know how Father Antonio acquired his special abilities?"

"No. I am sorry I am unable to satisfy your curiosity, Mr. Mark. I believe I have told you all that you would find interesting. And now, I believe you are due for a rest."

You're damn skippy. "Yes, that sounds great." We all stand up. Mother Superior beams another 120 watt smile at me, bows slightly and walks to the kitchen. Cora and I leave the room together.

"I have too much adrenaline to be tired. What am I supposed to do?" she asks.

"I just need a couple hours of sleep. Then I'll be able to think straight."

We enter the courtyard and there is the boy who healed me, sitting under a tree inspecting a leaf, while the British nun, Sister Mary Ellen I guess, leans against the same tree. "May I join the two of you?" asks Cora.

"Yes, please. Actually, would you mind if I used the loo?" asks the nun.

"Go ahead."

The nun walks back the way we came, and I walk through the courtyard, through a doorway, and up the stairs to my room. It overlooks the green gardens in front of the building, and the white serpentine sidewalks, and the street beyond. I need to use the 'loo' myself. After I do, I'm about to take off my shoes and crash into bed, when something catches my eye out the window.

It's Cora. Not just Cora. She's walking through the garden, and the little boy is with her, holding her hand. I see a white van come to a stop on the street in front of the church. Cora picks up her pace. She's running in the direction of the van, half dragging the boy. The side door opens. Inside the van is the red-headed man. She reaches the van and picks up the boy and hands him to the man. Then she jumps in after him and closes the door behind her as the van peels out.

PART 2

12

Red Light District

Raj
20 years earlier

"Amma, Tumi ki man kara–"

"In English, Raj."

Raj thought for a moment, "Do you think Uligamma's spirit enter you at night Amma?"

"From where did you hear that, Amar Shona?" Durgamma asked her darling son.

"I heard Uncle-ji telling man that your price is $100 Rupees because Uligamma's spirit enter you at night," said 10-year-old Raj. He sat beside his mother on the grubby floor, shirtless, as she washed his only shirt by hand.

"When I was a child, my father sold me to temple. Priest of Uligamma dedicated me to him. Some men believe that Uligamma's spirit enter me at night. At first I also believe because father told. I believed when I lived in my parents' house near temple, when I had many husbands, but then father sold me to Uncle-ji. . . I no longer believe."

"I don't believe. Uncle-ji wishes to charge more for sex."

Durgamma stopped scrubbing, "Raj you must not speak in this way."

"Tell me, Amma, in which way?"

"Means, of sex."

"I will obey, Amma, but why?" Raj looked up with his dark brown, almost black eyes.

"Little boys should not know this thing." Durgamma began to rub soap against his shirt again.

"Men are interested in sex only. Why is this, Amma?"

Durgamma sat still for a moment as two wrinkles formed between her eyebrows. "Man want women so much. He thinks about himself only and not about woman. You must not believe this when you are man, Raj. You must remember your Amma and remember other women are same."

"Women do not like sex," Raj said as a statement open for contradiction.

"You must stop talking this," she answered. Raj continued to question with his eyes. Durgamma dipped his shirt into the bucket of brown water and continued, "Women do, but needs man to love her."

Raj continued with his train of thought. "Amma, we should leave Red Light District itself."

"Where to go? I have no schooling. No way to earn money. If Uncle-ji caught me he would kill."

"Men in Red Light District do not love you, Amma."

Durgamma wrung out his shirt. "Maybe you go to school and leave Red Light District, Raj. Karma is there. I will be here and pay Karma. I will have good Karma in next life."

Raj remained silent. He would drop the conversation and silently disagree. He did agree with the part about himself getting an education. He dreamed of attending St. Mark's Boys School. But he did not believe the part about Karma. He did not believe everything that grownups told. To him, Karma was a larger version of the story of Uligamma's spirit entering his mother's body. A story adults told to get what they wanted. The high caste told this story to get the Untouchables to serve them. He determined he would get Amma out of the brothel, and he would get into a school. And . . . he had a plan.

When Raj was four he realized his friend Bhanu couldn't tell what color and shape each number inherently was. He thought Bhanu was an idiot, but as he took notice of other kids he realized no one else saw the color and shape of numbers either. They were empty, lifeless concepts with little meaning to them. Not full, beautiful objects with their own unique characteristics, even personalities, as they were to Raj.

When he was six, when his friends could not find a place to play cricket, he would watch a group of men playing cards in the street, carefully blending into the scenery to avoid an arbitrary kick or slap from a man who noticed him. At first he couldn't understand why the men were so bad at cards. He wondered if they would make bad plays for some reason unknown to him. Then he remembered the time when he was confused as to why his friends didn't understand numbers, and he put it together that the men were playing their best, but they didn't possess an ability to keep a record of the cards played and the cards that remained in the deck and which ones the other players held in their hands based on their previous plays, all of which was as basic to him as remembering the words to his favorite song.

Now, he would execute his plan. The next day, he chose the player who seemed the least violent and approached him after a game to explain his idea. After Raj received several smacks to the head for talking to an adult, the man finally heard him out. First, he got the man to agree to play him in a game of cards in exchange for five rupees he had stolen from his mom. After he beat the man, he challenged him again, this time for free. He won again. After five wins, he explained he had a special talent at cards, and he could help him earn 60 rupees every day, as long as he would pay Raj five, starting with giving the five back that he gave him to play. The man kicked him and said he was rubbish and told him to get out of there. The next day Raj showed up at the card game. When it was the man's turn to play, he held up the number of fingers for the card the man should play. At the end of the day, he followed the man home, and when he got out of sight of the other players, the man tossed Raj a five rupee coin. After a few weeks of winning, the man was kicked out of the game, and they had to find another game further away, where he was unknown.

"Amma, if you could leave Red Light District itself, would you leave?"

"Raj I already told few months back, I could get no other job, and Uncle-ji would kill me."

"But Amma, if you had money and didn't need job, and could leave where Uncle-ji couldn't find, would you do?"

"Why do you talk this? I have no money."

"But I *do* have," said Raj, looking up into his mother's incredulous eyes.

"Silly boy, only do dishes and do not talk."

"It is here, Amma." He got up from the floor where he was soaking the tin curry pan in a bucket of soapy water, and walked to the other side of the room, where his mildewed mattress sat on the floor. They were lucky Amma had her own room where Raj didn't have to see her work, although he always heard her work. He lifted up his mattress and saw his mom's eyes widen into moons. There, in five rupee coins, were over 1, 000 rupees.

"Raj, where did you get?"

"I help man play cards."

"What does this mean, you help man play cards?" she was now crouched down, inspecting the money.

"I'm very good at cards and found man I help to play. We could use money to leave Red Light District, and I could help different man play in new town."

Amma continued to question Raj and looked perplexed, the wrinkles forming between her eyes. Amma could not believe the story Raj was telling, but she would look back at the money that lay piled under Raj's mattress, testifying to the truth of his story, and ask again how he earned it. Eventually she accepted his explanation. After a couple more weeks of thinking about it and seeing Raj bring in money every day, she told Raj that they were leaving.

They made their exit early on a Saturday morning. It was early enough that if anyone saw them, they could play it off as though they were going to the store, but too early for any of the nosy neighbors or Uncle-ji to be awake. But, as they walked down the three flights of steps toward the street, one of their neighbors in the same building, a cantankerous old woman called Rani, went to pour dirty dish water down into the open concrete courtyard, if you could call it that, which was framed by the stairs. She asked what the stupid whore was doing up so early, but Durghamma told her 'none of your damn business,' and they kept walking. They took no possessions except a bag for the money that Durghamma held like a purse, and the clothes on their backs–for Durghamma a red sari with golden edges, and for Raj his only pair of clothes, grey slacks and a stained, white button-up shirt. Durghamma had spent the last week slowly changing Raj's coins into paper money, exchanging them at different shops in the market, giving an extra 5 rupee coin when the shop owner protested the pointless exchange.

They walked all seven kilometers from their house on Sonagachi Lane to the Calcutta train station, and from there took a train to Durgapur. Raj told his mother they should go to Delhi or Bombay and start a new life, but she was unwilling to leave West Bengal state. Raj had taught himself how to read. He got a map in a bookstore and studied it without the clerk noticing him. He found that Durgapur was the second largest city in West Bengal, and it was 170 kilometers from Calcutta. He tried to convince his mother to go to another state, but she would not relent.

Although Durgapur was the second largest city in West Bengal, it had only 500, 000 people, compared to over 10 million in Calcutta. They found a slum where they could blend in, and paid a slumlord an initial 200 rupees to move into a flat on the third level, similar to the one back in Calcutta. Raj found one card game but the men were not as regular about playing, and the version they played allowed for too much chance for Raj's abilities to be consistent. He could help someone win over a period of time, but he wouldn't be able to convince an adult of that. After a month, they were running out of money, Dughamma having bought necessities such as food, a flat skillet, mattresses, and dishes. Raj was lying awake contemplating how he could make money in Durgapur, when he saw his mother take a man into her room.

The next morning Raj told his mother he would devise a way to make money if she could only wait for one more week.

"It's not because of money, Raj. What can I do? I cook meals and stay home only. All I know is brothels."

"But Amma, you were going to meet nice man."

"How can I meet? I know no one. All men here are bad like Red Light district. How can I meet man with real job? I have no dowry."

"Amma you could get real job. I could help you, like I help man gamble," the idea hit Raj as he spoke it.

"It is too late, Raj. I already have man for protection."

Raj cursed to himself. Stupid pimps. He should have thought of this new plan sooner. He could find a job for his mom. She would buy nice clothes, and he would find a way to fake her education. The world of education and legitimate jobs remained a mystery to him, but he could steal what he needed from a bookstore and learn. He would find a job where he could stay with her and tell her what to do. Instead of using a dirty stranger as his adult proxy like he did with the card games, he could use his dear mother, and teach her along the way. He would only need to find a suitable vocation, one that women could work in, and convince her of his plan.

Raj lay awake in his bed. Often he could not sleep. If he tried to make plans as he lay in bed, there would be no hope of finding sleep. Making plans came natural to his mind, so he had to force himself to focus on other things, such as imagining attending a boarding school. This was not a simple thought, but because it was so vague to him, his thoughts would dissipate as he tried to imagine his life there, and he would be able to fall asleep.

Smash! He had just fallen asleep when their metal door

slammed open. A large figure filled the doorway. "Where are you, whore!?" It was Uncle-ji, with his broad face, thick mustache, and wide center. He was holding a container in his hand.

He walked over to Raj and kicked him viciously in the stomach with the point of his black shoes. He yelped in pain like a dog. Uncle-ji turned and walked to the door on the other side of the room. He kicked it opened. Raj heard his mother cry out in terror.

"You think I couldn't find you? You think I have no friends in Durgapur?"

His mother said through frantic tears, "I'm sorry. I made mistake. I will come back."

"No you will not, slut. I will teach you and all the girls a lesson." Raj tried to suck in air. He looked through the door. Uncle-ji was holding her down and pouring the contents of his container onto her."

"Noooo!" she shrieked.

Raj didn't know how but he knew Uncle-ji was killing her. He forced himself to walk over and grab the skillet from the floor and sneak back toward the door.

A light burst forth in the room, accompanied by the most horrible, unearthly scream of pain that Raj could never have imagined. As his mother twisted in agony, Uncle-ji turned around, Raj jumping out of view just in time.

As Uncle-ji walked through the doorway, Raj swung the skillet with all his might at Uncle-ji's knee, as though he were Sachin Tendulkar. He felt the knee give way to the frying pan and heard the crunch, like dropping a boiled egg. Uncle-ji cried out and plopped to the floor. He kicked his good leg in the direction of Raj but did not meet his mark.

"I will make you suffer, dog!" He yelled, and in one swift move he grabbed his container and flung it at Raj, striking him the head.

Raj fell to the floor. Stars filled his vision. The skillet was no longer in his hand. He saw Uncle-ji hop to where his container had landed, unscrew the spout, and hop back toward him. Raj's body was sluggish to respond to his mind's commands to run or find the skillet. He felt for it with his hands. Uncle-ji stood over him on one leg, malice in his face.

"I'm going to start with your knee, dog. Once I burn your legs, I will let you live."

A flame burst in from the bedroom and crashed into Uncle-ji.

It was Amma. When they hit the ground, the fire flared up so bright Raj had to close his eyes. Uncle-ji howled in pain. They struggled madly on the ground, looking like a flaming monster.

Uncle-ji broke free, still screaming and on fire. He scurried to his feet and ran out the front door, and then leapt over the guardrail. Raj heard the crunch as he hit the pavement. He jumped up and on top of his mom to try to put out the flames, but the pain was unbearable, so he ran and grabbed the water pot and poured the water over his mother, but she was no longer moving, her face a melted, ghoulish mask.

The pain from the burns on Raj's arms was all consuming. Still, he took their remaining money, 200 rupees, and managed to procure a train ride back to Calcutta. He had to pay a woman 50 rupees to pretend to be his mother, and another 50 for her to leave him alone at the train station.

When he got out of the station he made a bee line to St. Mark's Boys School. He watched the school from a distance for a few days. He was sleeping on the street away from the Red Light District. He thought if he showed up to play cards he might be recognized. After three days, he was out of money and after six days, his hunger was eating him alive from the inside. It was time to make his move.

In addition to the nuns who ran the school, there was also a priest, and Raj decided he was his best option. He waited by the gate for the priest, who would sometimes go to the market.

After one day, he emerged out of the gate. Raj ran up beside him.

"Uncle, I would like to go to your school."

The priest squinted at him with narrow brown eyes, looking him over. "Your parents can fill out the application and we will put you on waiting list," he said with an exotic accent.

"But I am orphan."

"We have orphanage in Howrah, but nephew, we do not have any openings. I am sorry, young man."

"I am not interested in orphanage, but school only."

"There are many children on waiting list. The line is too much long. Once again, I am sorry. Now I must go."

"But Uncle, I am different from the children on your list. I am smarter."

The teacher was nonplussed. "Most of my students would say the same. There are many bright children in India, and all think they are brightest one."

"But I can prove. Ask me any question of maths."

"A mathematician? Would you prefer differential calculus or trigonometry?"

"Multiplications only."

"Multiplication is easy."

"Ask for big numbers."

The priest sighed, "597 times 384."

Without missing a beat, Raj replied, "229, 248. Too easy. I asked for big numbers."

"How do I know that's right?"

"You're the teacher and you don't know?"

The priest was holding a notebook with a pen stuffed in the wiring. He pulled out the pen and worked it out. After a moment he looked down at Raj and sighed again. "Nephew, what's your good name?"

"Raj."

"Would you like to sleep in a warm bed tonight, Raj?"

13

The Plane

I wake up, sore and squashed, wishing I was in a warm bed. My nap was not restful. The knowledge of the DNA tests of Jesus bones is ever present, even in sleep. I look around to get my bearings. Oh yeah, I'm in an airplane. Where to, again? My stomach turns as I remember. Boston.

I think back to how I got here. When I saw the van leave with Cora and the boy, I ran downstairs and gave chase, but it was quickly out of view. I ran to the corner of the street and found a cab. 'Go to the police station. Policia,' I said in Spanish, like an idiot, but the driver understood. What would I tell the police? 'An American journalist kidnapped a boy.' 'What boy?' 'I don't know.' 'Was he her son?' 'No. I don't think so.' 'Hey, aren't you the guy we questioned about the Shroud of Turin?' They would think I'm suspicious. Rightfully so. They'd keep me there for days.

Forget that. I thought about the previous week. Was it the right move to go after the priest, both in the Vatican and at the Forum? Only time will tell, but I feel like it was, despite evidence to the contrary. I mean, I've always wished I was someone who could impose my will on the situation around me. That was my personal mantra for a while. 'Impose your will.' Didn't work. Whenever I ran into a stronger personality,

I backed down and did what I was expected to do. Played my role, but kicked myself afterwards. I wanted to be someone who wouldn't back down when the situation got too uncomfortable. Someone like Cora.

Cora. That's when a thought hit me. 'Driver, I'll give you 20 Euros if I can borrow your phone for one minute.' 'My phone? No Sir.' 'I just need to do one Google search. 100 Euros.' The driver pulls over. 'Show me Euros.' I gave him the money and he gave me the phone. 'I need it in English please.' He paused for a moment, and then switched the phone to English and handed it back. I searched for Corpus Biotech. CEO: Stuart Hawk. Location: Westborough, Massachusetts. 'Thank you, Sir. I'd like to change my destination to the Leonardo DaVinci Airport.'

I figured if nothing else, I'd rather be stuck answering police questions in America than Italy, in the place where both Cora *and* Stuart Hawk live. I know Boston is a big place and it's not much of a coincidence, but when my hunch panned out, it felt like a 'sign,' like we talked about this morning. I was able to change my flight. 5:30 p.m. to Boston, landing at 10 p.m. Longest day ever.

"Back from the dead?" asks a voice next to me.

"Excuse me?"

"You were asleep when I entered the plane six hours ago. I was wondering if you were still alive." She has a sweet voice. American accent but I can't place the region. I rub my eyes and look at her. She has strawberry blonde hair and pale blue eyes. She looks kind of familiar.

"Do I know you?"

"Do you ever hit the bars in Boston?"

"No I'm afraid not. Um, are you . . . famous or something?"

She snorts out a laugh. "Uh, no." And then, "Did you stay in Rome?"

"Yes."

"Did you hit any clubs while you were there?"

"Uh, no," I say, matching her tone, so she knows me going clubbing is as farfetched as her being famous. She looks like someone who would go clubbing. She's attractive, or am I drawn to her because she looks familiar? Her long, straight hair falls in front of her shoulders. She's wafer thin, wearing jeans and a touristy Rome t-shirt.

"You were there for business?" she asks.

"Yes."

"Oh, what did you do there?"

"Um," I don't want to get into it, but I also don't want to be rude or come up with a lie. "Did you hear about the Shroud of Turin getting stolen?"

"Of course. I don't quite know what that is, but it was apparently the biggest deal ever. Were you in town to steal it?"

"Yes, but please don't tell the authorities."

"Your secret is safe with me as long as I get a ten percent cut," her eyes twinkle.

"Seriously though, I was in Rome to perform scientific tests on it."

"Crikey. Were you there when everyone passed out?"

"Yes."

"What was it like?"

Now I *have* to make up a lie. I'll use Cora's line. "Not anything special. Just like falling asleep."

"The crime of the century and you slept through it. I'm unimpressed."

"Well, I've definitely done more unimpressive things than that."

The flight attendant interrupts. "Can I get you something to drink, sir?"

"Yes, water please."

"Ma'am?"

"Do you have Corona?"

She gets us our drinks. Ah yes, I lubricate my vocal cords.

"If you're free tonight," she says, "maybe you go bar hopping with me and impress me there."

What the heck? Another attractive girl coming onto me? It's not like I'm a beefcake. I've been told on more than one occasion that I would make a good character actor, or sidekick in a movie. Not leading man material. "I appreciate it, but since you haven't noticed, I feel the need to tell you: I'm old."

"What, mid-thirties?"

"Something like that."

"You're only as old as you feel."

"In that case, I'm in my mid-fifties," I take another swig of water.

"Oh, come on. You could pull it off."

"I've never been much of a partier."

"Really? Why not?"

"Hmmm. I'd have to think that through. I suppose mainly because I'm a Christian and that's not how we roll typically."

"How is it a Christian typically rolls?" Her face is close to mine. It feels too intimate for someone I just met.

"Um, no drugs. No illicit sex. Little to no drinking. Lots of family and church."

"Sounds like a blast," she says playfully.

"Well, I have a gift for embellishment. It's not as exciting as it sounds."

The conversation dies down. What will I do when I land? Get a car, find a hotel, and go to the police in the morning? Tell them what I know about Cora Byron? What if she simply denies knowing anything about the boy? I can't prove he exists. Should I look her up and confront her myself? Keep ignoring the authorities and pretending I'm James Bond?

The plane lands and I head for the rental cars. I have no bags. Only the clothes on my back, my wallet, and trusty credit card. I order the rental car at the desk. They don't understand why I didn't reserve it online beforehand, but eventually give me the paperwork and tell me the keys are in the car. I walk through the automatic doors into an anteroom with a show car on display, and out another set of automatic doors into the parking garage with the rental cars.

There's a black car idling on the roadway in front of the parked cars, like it's waiting for someone. The driver's side window rolls down. My legs lock. Staring back at me from inside the car is a red-headed man with a mustache. The same damn guy who attacked me in Rome.

I turn to run back into the airport. *Ooph!* I run into a huge guy. What? It's the long-haired blonde guy who the priest killed. His twin?

He grabs me and squeezes me to his chest.

"Don't. Move."

14

Vandalism

Jay
20 years earlier

Jay lay still on his sleeping bag on the floor across from Mark. Shane and Abel were in Shane's full-size bed, wrestling and playing grab-ass. Strange. He theorized that since it was taboo for men in western culture to show physical affection, because of homophobia, they were using wrestling as a thinly veiled excuse to do so. He felt no such need for physical bonding.

"I have an idea for a game," said Mark, his voice coming inches from Jay's ear. "Let's all come up with the most ridiculous 'Jay story' we can remember, and vote on whose is the best."

"Screw you," deadpanned Jay, and the others broke out laughing.

"Come on, Jay," said Mark. "It's good for you to laugh at yourself."

"I don't hear you guys laughing at *your* selves."

"There isn't as much to laugh about," added Abel from the bed.

"I was an idiot, ok. But I was not the first kid who ever

fabricated his junior high exploits."

"No, you weren't," agreed Mark, "but you were the most entertaining. How about you give us your favorite and we'll agree it's the best."

"And then you'll refrain from bringing it up again?"

"Agreed," said Mark.

"Guys. Guys," started in Jay, somehow doing an impression of Mark doing his impression of Jay as a frat boy, "last night, I couldn't sleep, so I walked down to the dam just to chill and look at the stars, and I'm just sitting there and I hear 'Hey Jay,' coming from the lake, and it's Mandy and Tiffany Yarborough, swimming. They ask if I want to come in, and I say, 'I don't have my suit,' and they say, 'neither do we.'

They all burst out laughing.

"Stop. Cannot. Take. Any. More." said Abel.

Their laughter waned, picked back up again, and finally died out. "Remember the first time Abel said he couldn't take it anymore, and meant it?" asked Mark. "The legendary showdown on the way home from Six Flags."

Jay inwardly winced. "How could I forget?" The day was a turning point for him.

"Once again, I'm sorry about that, man," said Abel. "We were buttholes ditching you that day, and I was ruthless. But you've got to understand, that was two years of frustration boiling out in one moment."

"Don't apologize. That was the best thing that ever happened to me, although I felt the opposite at the time. I wanted to kill you. Literally wanted to murder you. But, if that hadn't happened, we'd be sitting here and I would have told you that same story about the Yarborough sisters in the lake, but without irony."

"Actually, I would have sworn you would have bounced right back and kept on going with your act, but it was like I crushed your little spirit. You apologized, what, two weeks later? And two weeks after that you actually got a real girlfriend. And within a year you worked your way up to Katie freakin' Erikson."

"Like I said. The best thing that could have happened to me. Thank you for crushing my spirit, ass face."

"So what, you had a realization that everyone sees through my bullcrap, so I'll just be myself, and the bitches came flockin'?" asked Abel.

Jay sat up and leaned against the bed. "No. It was during the time my spirit was crushed and I was trying to figure out who I was. I couldn't go back to the old Jay. His shelf-life was well past expiration anyway. I already knew before Six Flags you guys didn't buy it, but I didn't know how to stop. Anyway, during my soul searching I had the revelation that girls want to be with us as much as we want to be with them."

"Well, yeah," said Mark.

"You don't get it. You're saying 'yeah,' but you don't really believe it. You believe girls are mystical creatures who are unattainable because everything else you truly desire is unattainable. Once you believe they want you as much as you want them, it starts to happen. I simply had to be patient enough to start from the bottom to find one who would go out with me, and work my way up from there. Didn't hurt that I have 'big puppy dog eyes,' or so I'm told."

Shane laughed a high-pitched laugh, "You're a genius with the ladies too."

"What I don't understand," said Abel, "is if you're willing to be socially mobile with girls, why are you actually still hanging around with us virgins as your male friends?"

"Old habits and whatnot." Jay thought about his journey from that night at Six Flags to tonight. He was so spurned, running around the park looking for his 'friends.' Knowing they were lying to him, to his face. And then he was humiliated in front of a crowd. How he later apologized to the group, and slowly, methodically, re-earned their trust.

"Well, are we going to do this or what?" he asked. His body tingled with excitement. He had never done anything like this before.

"Are you sure you're up for it?" asked Mark.

"*Hell* yeah."

He stood up, and the others followed. He had the perfect setup for the night. What had happened was, they were on the bus for a school field trip, talking about egging the principal's house. A girl told them they were full of crap and didn't have the balls to do it. Jay said he did not want to let Karina be proven right, and so they planned to spend tonight at Shane's to execute the plan.

They made a show of being stealthy when they sneaked out of Shane's house through the sliding glass door in his kitchen that led into the back yard, even though his parents were on the other side of the house and wouldn't have cared anyway. It was fun to feel like you were getting away with something. Jay stepped outside and felt the sharp November night air. A tremor of excitement shot through him.

"Where did you say his house was?" he asked Mark.

"In Santa Rita."

"That's four miles from here, on the other side of the highway. Not that it matters to me, but we won't get back here until morning," said Jay.

"Screw that," said Shane.

"Karina's going to rub it in our face that we're full of crap, and she'll be right," said Jay.

"Let's do something around here instead," said Mark.

"Perfect, let's go," said Jay. It *was* perfect. He didn't even have to be the one to insist they stayed around Shane's house.

"You realize what jerks we're being, hitting random people?" said Abel.

"Random *rich* people," said Jay.

"I especially don't get why you're into it, Mark," said Abel.

"Because it's fun, like riding the Texas Giant. You can tell your kids about it when you're older."

"Yeah. 'Hey kids, one time me and a bunch of my jerk friends ran around and vandalized innocent peoples' homes. It was hilarious, but you had better not do it.'"

It was a little strange how into this Mark was, and nice how he was playing right into Jay's hands. Before the injury Mark liked doing stupid things like acting idiotic in front of strangers. Now, it was like he was an adrenaline chaser. Abel was being a chicken like always, but he still went along with the majority. Even so, there was no denying Abel had taken over as the leader of their group ever since that night at Six Flags. Mark had lost whatever nuts he'd had the year before at Globals, and while Jay could always get them to do what he wanted and looked like the leader superficially, he never had their hearts. His blood surged when he thought about it. Mark, Shane, and Abel laughing at him behind his back. Abel humiliating him on the bus. He slowed down his breathing and tried to relax, telling himself it would *never* happen again.

They walked down Shane's winding block, with live oak trees hanging so far over the road they sometimes touched in the center. At the end of the block, Jay took out an egg, cracked it, and opened it onto the hood of a black Mercedes like he was making breakfast on it. They took off running up the street, Mark out ahead and fat ass Abel dragging up the rear.

They stopped after about a block and Abel caught up with them. "Dude, you could have warned me."

"The fun is the surprise, and the fear of getting caught,"

said Jay.

"You used to be the one who didn't like doing this kind of stuff," said Mark.

"I still don't like making a fool of myself in front of people for no reason. This is different."

"Crap," said Mark.

Jay looked ahead and saw a couple of men ahead on the opposite side of the road, walking in their direction. Hell. They could ruin *everything*.

"Just act like we're a gang of teenagers with good reasons to be wandering the streets at 1 a.m.," said Mark, always ready with a sarcastic comment.

The men walked past, ignoring their group.

"Dude, I'm done," said Abel. "They could have actually seen what you did."

"If you want to walk back home with those guys, go ahead. I still have some eggs," said Jay, hoping they bought his bluff. Praying they bought his bluff. He started walking. The rest of the guys followed him. He mentally exhaled.

They walked several blocks down the road, which curved back in the direction of Shane's house. Shane spoke up, "See that satellite dish? This one is mine." He grabbed a couple of eggs and missed his first throw, but on his second he hit the top of the massive structure, the yolk running down the length of the satellite. Mark grabbed a couple and threw them on the tennis court of the same house. They took off again, running a bit further down the road and cutting down an alley, which all the houses in this neighborhood had behind them, with driveways branching off. They slowed down, all sucking in wind, especially Abel.

After a moment Jay stopped. "Dude, I know this house. This is my old baseball coach. He's a piece of crap." There was a fully restored '60s Mustang in the garage, which could be made out by the lighted beer signs hanging on the walls. *Crack. Crack. Crack.* Three eggs–two from Jay, one from Mark–and they were off, down the alley, and in one block they were back to Shane's street. They stopped running, with about two blocks between them and Shane's house.

"Let's call it a night now," said Jay. "I'll just put the rest of these eggs back in the fridge."

"Thank God," said Abel. "I'm out on these in the future. I get it. I get the thrill. But at some point we're actually going to get caught, and my grandma would kill me."

"Hey! You!"

Jay looked back and saw a figure under the street light on the road they had just come from. A bulging figure, holding a baseball bat. It was really happening.

"Get back here!" he yelled.

"Oh crap! Oh crap! My coach has an older son who is the weight-lifting champion at the high school RUN!!!" Jay babbled as he started to run. Shane was already ahead, having taken off in a full sprint on the word 'hey.' Jay and Mark ran side-by-side and Abel fell behind. Jay stopped and looked back and saw the guy with the bat gaining on Abel. The guy caught up to Abel and tackled him to the ground.

"What the hell do you think you're doing, you little punk?!" He pummeled Abel with his fists. Abel cried that he was sorry and tried to protect his face. The guy picked up the bat and hit Abel on the side of the head. Abel stopped moving. The man dropped the bat and started walking around in a circle.

Jay ran back toward Abel and marched up to the assailant. "What the hell was that?" he asked defiantly.

"I'm sorry," said the man. "I didn't mean to go that far."

"Give me the bat," ordered Jay and held out his hand. The man looked at him, puzzled. "What?"

Jay grabbed the bat out of his hands, and with his foot he

pushed Abel over onto his stomach. Then he lifted the bat up over his head. And swung down with all his might. Connecting full force with Abel's spine. *Crack!*

Jay quaked with ecstasy. The moment was better than he imagined it would be.

"Oh my God! Oh my God! You broke his freaking back!"

"No I didn't. Look." For some reason, maybe panic, the man bent down to look, hoping to find evidence the spine wasn't broken. That he wasn't going to be charged with assault. But when he did, Jay pulled the bat back, and brought it down on the back of the man's skull. And then he did it again. And again.

15

The Nun

The blonde man in front of the airport doorway hits me in the skull with his fist for good measure. Then he bear-hugs me, squeezing my breath out. He's practically picking me up as he drags me toward the car. My ribs are bending, about to pop like toothpicks.

The next thing I know, he's falling to the ground and taking me with him, but his grip has loosened, so I spin free right before he lands on top of me. He's lying on the ground, struggling against nothing, intensity filling his eyes. It looks like he's having a seizure.

I hear the car door open. The red-haired man gets out and runs toward me. I scramble to my feet and turn to run back into the airport. There, standing in the doorway, hands outstretched toward me, is the young strawberry blonde lady who sat next to me on the plane.

"Get him," she orders me, nodding toward the man behind me.

"Huh?" I turn and see him, still coming at me, but it looks like he's running in slow motion. In quicksand. I charge toward him and dive into his chest. We tumble to the ground. I get on top of him, holding his arms down with my legs. I can see fury in his eyes.

"Get in a car and go," she says behind me.

I have no reason not to obey. I bounce up and run toward the rental cars. The engine of the black car roars to life. I try to run past it toward the rental cars, but when I do it lurches forward and rams into me. I fall down and look up to see it stop right before it runs over me. The engine is still revving, but it's not moving.

"Go!" she yells.

I scurry to my feet and dive between two of the rental cars. I jump into one and the keys are in the ignition. I put it in reverse and floor it, smashing into the black car.

I turn and have just enough space to go forward. I see her running toward me, with both men after her. I pull past the black car and throw open the passenger door. She jumps in and I hit the gas. The red-haired guy slams his body into the back door as I pull away.

I hear tires squealing behind me. I make a couple of left turns to get to the exit. There's a booth with a woman inside it on the phone, looking frazzled. She shouts something at me as I approach the down crossing arm blocking my exit. I speed up and it explodes when I strike it. I make another left turn to exit the garage, and merge onto the main airport road.

"Slow down," she says.

"What?"

"You heard me."

I slow down and look in my rearview mirror and see the dented black sedan merge onto the road. It's gaining ground on us quickly.

"Are you sure about this?" I ask. She doesn't answer.

It's about 100 feet away, about to pass a truck, when the truck jerks into the other lane, smashing into the car, pinning it against the guardrail.

"Speed up, please."

Wait a minute. She's speaking with a British accent.

"Holy balls. You're the nun from the monastery."

"Go for the Ted Williams tunnel. You can call me Amy, by the way."

"Not Sister Mary Ellen?"

"Amy was my name before I had my vows."

"What the hell is going on, Amy?"

"You are being chased by Stuart Hawk's men and I'm helping you escape. You should know the drill by now."

"How did you get the seat next to me on the plane?" I drive through an intersection and take the ramp into the tunnel.

"When I returned from the loo to get the boy from your friend and realized you all were gone, I told Mother Superior. She told me to look for you both at the airport. When I found you and realized you didn't have the boy, I listened to where you were going and bought a ticket on the same plane. When Hawk's mates attacked you in the airport I realized that you were, in fact, a stooge. By the way, did you quite like my American persona?"

"You're a pretty good actress," I'm passing cars.

"*I* thought so. I reckoned I should act the opposite of a nun so you'd be less likely to recognize me. I've found when I'm dressed in my habit, the only thing people see is some random nun anyway."

"I take it you have superpowers then?"

"Stay on I-90. Yes, you could say that, but your ability to resist our control is your superpower. Perhaps that's why Mr. Hawk is after you."

"If he's after me, why didn't he take me at the monastery?"

"I'm not sure. Perhaps he didn't want to deal with a bunch

of nuns with 'superpowers.' Reckon you didn't think you would hear that sentence today."

"Indeed."

"I daresay he thought it was easier for your friend to kidnap a boy than a grown man. Or he didn't know where his son was until you led him there. The boy is his son, you know?"

"No, I did not." That seems like a big deal, but I can't think how that makes this situation any more comprehensible. "So how did a monastery of priests and nuns come to acquire superpowers? I don't remember those as gifts of the Spirit."

There's a police car in the right lane. I slow down and get behind it, with a car in between us.

"On the night the Shroud was stolen, Father Antonio asked we hide the boy. Then he told us he'd appreciate our help protecting him and recovering the Shroud. He asked if we would be willing to receive a shot, and explained what the shot would do to us. The 'superpowers.' I was keen to take him up on his offer, and surprised Mother Superior was as well."

"What's it like?"

"Quite different from before. It's been less than a week, but it feels like years. I will catch myself on a train of thought, and find myself making an intuitive leap that connects it to some seemingly unrelated subject, and I discover there's an underlying law connecting the two, and I study more examples to test my new theory. As many mysteries as I've uncovered, I've created 10 times more, and if I keep down one of the rabbit holes, I get lost in thought for hours."

"That's right. The priest said the special abilities were a byproduct of intelligence."

"Yes, as I comprehend it. That's why I was able to overpower those two men back there."

"Huh?" I ask. "Explain."

"The more intelligence one has before receiving the shot, the more one will have proportionally after the shot. The more intelligence, the greater the other abilities. I believe those two men in the black car were rather stupid before their shot."

We emerge from the tunnel, Boston skyscrapers on the right, Fenway Park on the left. The cop takes an exit and I speed up.

"So what do you know about this Stuart Hawk guy? Why would he want the Shroud of Turin? Is he some kind of militant skeptic like his friend, Cora Byron?"

"No, I don't think so. Mark, what do you know about the Singularity?"

Whoa, where did that come from? "Well, I'm not a physicist, but the way I understand it is that inside a black hole the gravity is so strong that the rules of the Universe break down and we don't know what goes on inside, because the gravity doesn't let light out, or anything else for that matter. Don't tell me you figured out the mysteries of singularity over breakfast."

"Not quite. I'd need a couple of meals for that," she says. "When I say the Singularity, I'm talking about the way in which futurists stole that term from physics to mean what will happen when artificial intelligence surpasses human intelligence. Then the AI will create better AI at an exponential rate and leave human intelligence in the dust. Or when man figures out a way to merge his mind with a computer with the same effect. They use the term 'Singularity' because in the same way gravity is so strong in a black hole to change the rules of physics, the forces released from this exponential increase in intelligence will be so great it will change our reality in an unpredictable, fundamental way."

"And Stuart Hawk is developing this?"

"That is what I understood from Father Antonio."

"What does that have to do with the Shroud of Turin?"

"I don't quite know. But when I asked Father Antonio why he needed us, he started babbling about how we were necessary to stop Hawk from achieving the Singularity. I gathered Stuart Hawk's company was working on the project."

"How are you planning to stop him now?"

"Our best scheme is the simplest. You to go to the police tomorrow morning and tell them about your friend kidnapping the boy. Tell them who you are and that you believe Stuart Hawk was behind the theft of the Shroud of Turin."

"I was hoping you'd say that. I've had my fill of near-death experiences for a while."

"Take the exit to Newton," she points to the right.

There's a Marriott hotel that's built on top of the highway for some reason. I take the exit for Newton.

"We'll go a couple of miles to the right, and then ditch this stolen car and double back to where we're headed."

"Which is where exactly?"

"We nicked an address from Father Antonio's notebook. It appears it belongs to friends of his, and he lodged there when he visited the states."

I park at a gas station. After a few tries, she finds someone to call an Uber for us, to hide our tracks I guess. We pay him $40 in cash for an $8 ride. The Uber takes us back over the interstate and drops us off in front of a white, two-story New England style house, larger than average but not quite a mansion. No lights are on. We walk to the front door and she rings the doorbell. No answer.

She opens the door. "'ello?" Still no answer. We walk in.

We leave the lights off. We walk through a big, musty living room with a couch in the middle. She walks into the kitchen at the front of the house and I follow her. "Would you like a glass of water, Mark?"

"Yes, please." Food would be nice too, but I look and all that's in the fridge are condiments. I lean back against the sink and she leans against the counter. Her face is extra pale, lit only by the light filtering in from the street light out front.

"So . . . why become a nun?"

She takes a swig of water. "My origin story is not as good as Mother Superior's. My father's Catholic and we were raised as such. Mum's an Atheist but she attended Mass with the family, just didn't take communion. They were good parents, worked hard and gave us every advantage. I imagine they would strike you as decidedly unwarm and unloving based on the U.S. telly I've watched, but we thought nothing of it. I never saw any evidence they loved each other than mine and my brother's existence. I favor my Mum in my looks and personality, in every way really, including, at the time, her Atheism.

"After Secondary School I go off to University. I'm studying Environmental Science, I have a boyfriend, I have ambitions. One night my boyfriend and I are going out to meet up with some of our mates. The last thing I remember I'm sat on the bus, looking out the window at the passing buildings, when I find myself outside of time. I feel God intertwining himself with every atom of my being. Indescribable joy and love and energy roll through me. But what is me? All I know is infinite love for this other. This God."

She's opening and closing the silverware drawer with her hands as she talks. "My boyfriend rouses me and asks if I'm all right. I can't quite comprehend where I am. It comes back to me in bursts. I realize only a few minutes have passed, but that's impossible. I was with him forever.

"I finish the semester, drop out of University, and tell my

family I'm joining a convent. Mum is apoplectic. I tell her about my experience, and she makes a deal with me she will leave me be if I have an MRI on my brain. I agree, and there's no tumor. Also, no sign of epilepsy from the workup they did. She's convinced I'm schizophrenic. She keeps to her word and stops trying to talk me out of it, but I can see the heartbreak on her face. Dad was supportive. He said the thought of me becoming a nun never occurred to him, but he knew I would make a great one. He was still glum because I was essentially leaving their lives for good. My mates were more shocked than my mum. Just imagine what your mates would think if you told them you were to become a monk, and times it by 100. That's how much less accepted it is to take one's religion seriously in England."

She sits up on the counter and I lose her face in the darkness. "The convent was not what I expected. I suppose I imagined I would have all day to seek God with my mind and my spirit, and have the comradery of girlfriends during meals and at night. In reality, it's a lot of mindless work. Talking between the sisters is only allowed when necessary, and rigorous intellectual pursuits are not encouraged, though I managed to find books where I could pursue this on the sly. It comes back to the Benedictine motto, 'Ora and Labora,' which is 'Pray and Work.' There was plenty of time for prayer. Too much, at first. Transitioning from a 21st to a 6th century lifestyle is an arduous task, but once done, I was glad for it.

"In my prayer life, I followed the path of contemplation, which was the path of the Mystics. There is a step on this path we call 'kenosis,' which means 'empty' in Greek. I would empty myself in prayer, of my agendas, my frustrations with being called to monastic life, my pride, and once I was empty I'd invite God come dwell in me, and come in he did. The idea is not to hoard this presence for myself, but to immediately give it away by loving and serving others, which we would do with the drug addicts at the center in Bristol, and later with the children at the school in Rome. There's another Greek word, 'perichoresis,' which means 'mutual indwelling,' describing how each person of the Trinity abides in the other. It could be more literally translated as 'circle of the dance.' When I prayed, I felt like I was part of that sacred dance of the Trinity, with me dwelling in God, and God in me."

"Wow." Almost makes me want to become a nun.

Now she's opening the silverware drawer with her fingers and closing it with her calves. "And then one day it stopped. I would pray, but wouldn't feel his presence. This is what John of the Cross called 'the dark night of the soul.' When even the pleasure of spiritual experience must be surrendered to God. One doesn't seek after him because of the feelings his presence brings, but because he is worthy of it. It is easy to fall into the trap of loving the pleasure one takes in God rather than loving God for himself. If I had to praise him for eternity without ever feeling his presence, or enjoy his pleasures, I would be glad to, because of who he is."

"And I thought I was an ascetic," I say. "Glad that is not how the Bible describes heaven."

"Quite true," she hops back down to the floor and I see her face again. It's very pleasing. Big eyes, delicate features. Her strawberry blonde hair looks silver in this light. The freckles on her face look like stars. The cynical side of me thinks her looks are being wasted.

"How does the extra intelligence affect your contemplation or whatever?"

"It is much harder to quiet my mind now. I have not achieved it yet. But his grace is sufficient. Before the shot, I had already moved past the dark night of the soul, and God's presence and life have poured back into me during prayer. Since the shot, there are times when I'm lost deep in thought and God joins me even there."

She looks out the window. "I know you had a full night's rest on the plane, but I'm exhausted. I'd like to lay still and see if I can finally sleep before we get started on our day tomorrow."

"Of course. Good night then."

"I'll lie on the living room floor. I daresay the carpet will be rather soft compared to my bed at the convent."

I stay in the kitchen for a few minutes. I try to listen to her breathing to see if she's asleep, but I can't tell. I walk past her to the other side of the living room and plop down on the couch. I don't want to think about my plans for tomorrow, or any of the mind-bending ideas from our conversation, or that there's an attractive . . . *nun*, sleeping on the other side of the room. Instead I decide to pray, and after a few minutes, I realize I'm tired . . .

"Get up!" I open my eyes and Amy is looking at me, a foot away from my face, looking startled. It's morning.

Where am I again? "What?"

"He found us," she starts toward the kitchen. "We're surrounded."

16

Church Camp

Mark
19 years earlier

"We're surrounded by tools," I said to Abel. Outside our dorm room a water gun fight was raging. The door to our room opened, and Brett, some beefy senior from another church, shot a water gun into our room, onto my shirt.

"Dude, get out of here." I tried to close the door but Brett stopped it with his foot and pushed his way into the room.

"Come on, douchebags. The whole floor is having a water fight. I have extra guns. Last year some kids got kicked out for throwing water balloons off the balcony," he laughed his high-pitched laugh.

"We're not in the mood."

"Bro, it's your last night here. You should be into it by now like everyone else. If I were you, I'd sleep with one eye open tonight. I *might* have two huge cans of shaving cream in my suitcase with your names on them." He shot a couple more squirts at us and ran back into the hallway, laughing.

"What a dingleberry," I said.

Abel and I had our own dorm room for church camp,

which was good because other rooms either had three kids or two kids and a sponsor. Abel didn't want to come, but my mom had called Abel's grandma and told her it would be good for him to get out and the church would pay his way.

I had my own reasons for going to church camp. I was giving God one more shot. After a couple of years of depression, poor sleep, and low appetite, my parents took me to a neurology specialist. They ran tests and confirmed what they had feared. I had a damaged hypothalamus, the part of the brain that controls these functions. In fact, the neurologist was shocked I was as normal as I was, since my hypothalamus was essentially dead. She said the brain is very complex and the working parts can compensate for broken parts, but even so she did not have any reason to hope I would get any better. Then there's the whole sex thing. The hypothalamus has its fingers in that pie too. According to her, that wasn't in the cards for me either. I was still attracted to good-looking girls, but that would be as far as it'd ever go.

It was hard for me to compare what I felt like before and after my injury. I wasn't too far into puberty when it happened, and the memories from before were always getting foggier. The best way to describe the before and after was like a reverse Wizard of Oz. Before, my emotions were in living color, and afterwards I could still feel them, but they were in grayscale. I was prematurely living in the Elysian Fields of Greek mythology, which was a pleasant place, but bloodless.

It made me think about the hardware of the mind. If we are eternal spirits with free will, how could conditions like depression be controlled by defective machinery inside the skull? I explored the materialistic view of the world. We're all a bundle of cells trying to procreate to continue our species, but we don't admit that to ourselves because if we did, it would mean our lives were pointless, which is not a good mindset to be in when the goal is to forward the species. I had never considered this viewpoint before Ronnie hit me in the head with a rock.

But when I traveled down that road, I didn't like where it ended up. Thoughts of meaninglessness. If there is no higher power to observe man, and assign value to his life, his deeds, his struggles, then does life mean anything at all? Once the stars burned out and no one had any memory of man at all, all events would be rendered as pointless as though they had never happened. I compared it to professional sports. The only reason professional sports meant more than a pick-up game in the street was not because the sport was being played at a higher level, that's all relative, but because the pros played to an audience. That gives the games meaning, so that documentaries set to epic music could be made years later, with the players talking about these most important moments of their lives. If no one was in the forest to hear the tree fall, it would not make a sound.

Or maybe doing the right thing was enough, for example, sticking up for a special-needs kid getting verbally tortured by a bully. Would that have transcendent meaning even if there was no God to whom that meaning could transcend? If the stars burned out and there was no consciousness around to know that anything had ever happened, that moment in time still *would have happened*, and that special-needs kid for a brief moment in time was relieved of some suffering. Was that enough? I thought about such hypotheticals because I never did much to alleviate Ronnie's suffering, and more often than not, *I* was the bully.

Even with God, there was no hope of ever getting better, outside of a miracle. No matter how good my life became, I wouldn't have the receptors with which it could be appreciated.

"Sorry to interrupt your thoughts, but it's almost seven. Let's get this over with," said Abel.

"Sorry." I stood up and headed to the door as Abel rolled his wheel-chair after me. "You're the one who has a reason to silently brood after what Jay did to you."

"Don't say that name. Ever again."

"What about the letter of the alphabet?"

"That either."

"You're right. New rule. Anyone who speaks the name Jay forthwith and henceforth shall be thumped on the knuckles."

"No more stupid games."

"Come on. You're the one who once asked me if I was going to keep pouting forever."

He looked up at me out of the corner of his eye with no sign of relenting. I pushed him down the hall and thought back to the night he became paralyzed.

Shane and I were in his driveway, hiding behind his car, waiting to see if Jay and Abel would turn up. I saw Jay come into view as he reached the driveway.

"Jay, what happened?" asked Shane.

He jumped when he heard his name. Then he turned and walked toward us, and when he stepped into the light, I could see his shirt was covered in something dark. Blood?

"Shane, call 911. Abel is badly hurt, and . . . I think I just killed someone."

An ambulance came and got Abel. The police took us in for questioning. I told them everything about the vandalism. My game of pretending to be the perfect child to my parents was over. Normally I would have thought that was the end of the world, but now it was a trifle.

Jay's story was that the guy started punching Abel, then grabbed his bat and clubbed him on the head, and then smashed his spine. When Jay saw that, something inside him snapped. He wrestled the bat from the other guy and in the heat of the moment, Jay bashed in his head. I bought it because I couldn't think of any alternative, but it sounded a bit too much like one of the old Jay stories.

The rumor was the police took his story at face value, having no other witnesses. They were going to consider what Jay did as self-defense, and his blows to the man's head as his overzealous effort to subdue him. The assailant was a lowlife who had been arrested for drugs and assault before. But why was he there? At the time I had thought he was some high school kid whose car we had just egged. But after a couple of months, the rumor changed.

We later found out a detective did some digging and talked with the murdered man's friends, who claimed to have seen Jay come to the man's apartment a few days before. They said Jay gave him some money, which they thought was for drugs. Then the smoking gun. The police seized Jay's family's computer and found files he had deleted. He had been building websites for local companies and made over $5, 000, far more than the $2, 000 the police found bundled in a rubber band in the dead hitman's apartment.

A plea deal was eventually reached. Jay was charged with conspiracy to commit assault and battery in the second degree. He was not charged with murder; his defense attorney claimed when Jay saw the assailant break Abel's spine, he became so upset the hitman had gone too far that Jay attacked him, and killed him in self-defense. He was sentenced to juvenile detention for a year, and then probation until he became of age. His parents moved away to who knows where and we didn't hear where he ended up. Meanwhile, Abel was crippled for life.

If I had manned up and been the one who confronted Jay at Six Flags, I'd be the one in a wheel chair. In fact, I was probably still on his hit list. Crazy little bastard. I was the one who humored the old Jay and kept him at arm's length, out of the inner core of me, Shane, and Abel. Once he turned into the new Jay and was let into the core, he must have been seething every time we poked fun at the old Jay, as he pretended to laugh with us. No reason to think this seething was reserved only for Abel. I actually took up boxing for a while (I'd never seen my dad so proud of me), so I could know how to fight if Jay ever came for me. I was surprised I enjoyed it so much. I had stopped playing sports by that time and it felt good to physically tax my body and compete. I even liked the pain. It would shake me out of my doldrums.

I pushed Abel across the crosswalk of the busy street and toward the assembly hall. Abel had always had a chip on his shoulder, but now there were no breaks in his anger. What a pair we were. Shane was not the kind of person who would rally us and keep the group together, and we were starting to go our separate ways. The only thing Abel confided in me that week was that the worst part of being paralyzed was knowing he'd never get to 'do it' with a woman, or get to 'bump uglies,' as he put it. Join the club.

"One of the worst parts about 'that guy whose name is a letter between i and k,' is that he was playing us for a year, pretending to be our friend while he was working a freaking adult job to make money to pay for a hit on you."

"You can't just euphemize his name. Knuckle."

I stuck out my knuckle, glad that Abel decided to play. *Whap!*

"Ouch. Well, I'm going to have to do it again to finish my point. I was thinking, I bet 'you know who' got Ronnie all riled up to sucker-punch me."

"Of course he did. He's a freaking psychopath. Knuckle."

Pop! "Dammit. Why couldn't your hands be paralyzed?

Sorry, too soon?"

"Are you kidding me? One more for that, jerk."

"Fine, I deserve it. Just pick a different knuckle this time."

"Nope." *Thwack!*

"Oh . . . crap (I really did say 'crap' that time). I'll shut up now."

We entered the auditorium. The worship music was already going as most of the 1, 000 teenagers were jumping up and down, compared to a handful on the first night. I wheeled Abel down to an aisle across the middle of the auditorium where there was a spot for his wheelchair. During the last song some students broke out in a conga line. I wasn't feeling it.

All right, God, this is your last chance. By last chance I didn't mean I'd give up on God forever. I meant it was his last chance to take me up on my deal. I knew even before my injury that I was going off course. I don't remember when I first understood the concept of God, but from the beginning, I just *loved* God. Simple as that. My mom took me to church and talked about God at home. When I got to middle school, I had pretty good friends (not counting Jay), but I found *myself* as the bad influence. Pushing them to do the wrong things, even though when left to myself, I didn't want to do those things. I was playing a role again, as the cool bad kid, even though they weren't impressed, and I *knew* they weren't impressed. It's as if the peer pressure had a will of its own and was bending me to it. Where would this path end?

Then the injury happened, and it was less about not becoming a bad person, and more about finding out if I believe all this stuff in the first place. If I even believed in God, who, if he was real, had let a lot of bad crap happen to me and my friends. But as I stared into the abyss of a godless universe, it filled me with dread. Like Peter said to Jesus, 'Where else would we go? For you have the words of life.' Even if God was an idea dreamt up long ago and I had only imagined my relationship with him, he was a beautiful idea.

A few months before camp my youth pastor was talking about the gifts of the Holy Spirit, namely speaking in tongues. He said it would give you the power to live the Christian life. He even did this embarrassing drill where he had all of the kids who could speak in tongues do it out loud at once. I pretended like I could do it and spoke in gibberish. Then at home in bed I asked God to be filled with the Holy Spirit and tried to speak in tongues, but I knew I was still talking gibberish. I would think of a sound in my mind and say it, which didn't feel right. That's when I made my deal with God. God, if you are real, and if you want me to straighten out my life, let me get the Holy Spirit and tongues at youth camp. Oh, and if you want to heal my hypothalamus that would be great too, but I don't have the faith to honestly believe for that just yet. People don't often get healed from serious brain injuries, but people speak in tongues all the time.

Now it was the last night of camp, and the preacher was talking about Adam and Eve. That's not close to the book of Acts, where the tongues part is. Then he jumped all the way to Revelations and overshot Acts. Then he started to close his message. Oh well, it was a long shot anyway. But then, apropos of nothing, the preacher said, "God is telling me there's someone in here tonight who needs the infilling of the Holy Spirit with the gift of speaking in tongues. If that's you, come down to the altar."

I looked at Abel, who was staring straight ahead, emotionless. I walked down to the front of the auditorium along with a bunch of other kids. I tried to speak in tongues, but it was the same as when I tried at home. Nothing but saying whatever popped into my mind. Drivel. Behind me, some people laid their warm hands on my shoulders and back and head. I heard my youth pastor praying and realized a bunch of the other kids from my youth group were praying for me as well. I tried and tried. More hands on me. Heavy hands. My legs were tired so I decided I would ease my way to the ground like some other people around me and maybe have more luck down there. When I did, the kids from my youth group let out a 'shout of praise.' My youth pastor said, "Yes, he's under the power of the spirit. He's got it."

No, I didn't. Now what? Fake it, and blaspheme the Holy Spirit? I tried harder but still nothing but saying the nonsense I thought of. Maybe I couldn't do this because it was yet another thing that required a healthy hypothalamus. I felt a warm hand on my forehead and another on my chest.

"Father, in Jesus' name, open the mouth of my brother. We receive this free gift that you have made available for your children." From there, the praying got louder, more eloquent. He was quoting scripture and he sounded like a pro. Maybe it was the preacher. I opened an eye to peek at him, and it was Brett, the knucklehead from our floor who had been pulling pranks and telling dirty jokes all week. Then he prayed, "Father, I sense there is a generational curse on my brother holding him back, and we break that right now in Jesus' name. Devil, you must go!"

At that moment, I spoke an unfamiliar sentence that did not come from my mind. It felt like it came from the middle of me. I had it. A wave of warmth ran through me.

17

The Raid

An unseasonably warm breeze blew against Greg McKinnon as he looked at the old saltbox-style house, high roof at the front of the house, low roof at the back. Mark Eberhart had turned out to be a slippery one. And this woman, this nun, was a force to be reckoned with. Not today, though. Today she has met her match and then some. Greg was in charge of the team. Twelve highly trained and weaponized soldiers surrounded the house. Twelve 'specials' as they were called, against one special on the other side, and one man who was different in his own right, even though he didn't have enhanced intelligence.

Greg did not like his increased intelligence as much as he thought he would. Really, he didn't like it at all. Why did society treat intelligence as if it were the only personal trait that mattered? Wasn't there any value in judgment, wisdom, courage? Nope. Prove you have more intelligence than your opponent, a trait that used to be 100 percent genetic, and you were the better man. And only a specific kind of intelligence mattered–the kind that can be measured on an IQ test. The ability to solve puzzles. Not creative, inductive intelligence; the ability to make things. Only deductive intelligence, which to him was simply the act of breaking things down. And break down things he did. He was constantly tearing down ideas he used to believe in, the universe itself, until it seemed there was nothing left. He couldn't turn it off. He rarely slept. Take every thought captive, then beat it mercilessly into submission until it gives up its secrets. To think that now the only leverage Hawk had over him was that he had the ability to make him normal again, which would only happen if they didn't fail here.

But they wouldn't fail this time. They split up into three teams. Each man had an automatic rifle, while the team leaders had tranquilizer darts as well. One team approached the back door, one team formed a perimeter around the house and trained their rifles on the windows, and his team headed for the front door. The sun was coming up and 12 men attacking a suburban house would look conspicuous to anyone who woke up early, so they had to act fast.

He popped open the lock and opened the door, training his gun down the entry-way. Then he walked into the living room and checked behind the couch. Nothing. He radioed for the team in the backyard to enter, and then walked up the stairs with his team. As he got to the second story, he could feel the woman's presence in a bedroom on the opposite side of the house.

"Mark," he called out, "don't be clever. There are 15 of us, and we have guns pointed at every possible point of escape. You can't fight your way out of this. He just wants to talk. Surrender and we'll take you to him."

He walked down the hall and reached the room on the end. He signaled to his men he was going in. No lock on this door, so he turned the knob and threw it open with his gun pointing ahead.

Empty. He could feel she was above the room, in the attic. He looked back down the hallway and saw the attic entrance in the ceiling, the string to pull it open was hanging down a couple of inches.

"I need your C-4," he said to one of his men, who complied. He took a block and pulled off the thin film covering the adhesive on the back and stuck it to the attic entrance, away from where he felt the woman. They walked down the stairs and he told everyone to get out of the house, and gave the order to detonate.

Boom! He couldn't see the explosion outside, but the shockwaves would wake the neighbors. They had ten minutes at most before cops would show up. The fire would flush them out before then. "Jack, tell any nosy neighbors the water heater exploded and the fire department is on the way."

After a minute, Greg could hear the crackle of the fire. Then he saw shingles sliding off the roof as if they had their own will, and then a piece of plywood, part of the roof itself, broke loose and fell to the ground.

"Don't shoot if it's him," he reminded everyone.

He saw two hands poke up from the hole. They were up in surrender. Mark stuck his head out and pulled himself up and onto the roof. He got directly in front of the hole as he pulled up the woman, and was careful to stay in front of her. Smoke poured out the hole.

"The police will be here soon," yelled Mark.

"Not before I shoot the both of you with tranquilizers."

"Why haven't you done it yet?"

"I don't want you to fall to your deaths, but that's a risk I'm willing to take if you don't give me another option. Just come down and we'll take you to him, without darts."

"I'm the one he wants. Give me your word you'll let her go and we'll come down."

He could hear she was saying something to Mark but couldn't make out what.

"You have my word," said Greg.

"Done," said Mark, and pulled the woman to her feet. They walked over the top of the roof and onto the back side, which sloped down to within about 10 feet of the ground. Greg walked around to see them jump down. He walked through the gate into the back yard, locked eyes with Mark, raised his gun, and shot him in the chest with the tranquilizer. Mark looked at him like a kid whose dad just missed his birthday party, like the word of an enemy combatant should mean something. The woman turned and ran for the back door.

"Fire." She was reaching for the door when the bullets started piercing her body. She shook with each shot as she fell to the ground.

18

Stuart Hawk

Stuart Hawk and Joe
18 years earlier

Joe Denti stomped his foot on the ground, "I don't get it." He was sitting at his desk staring at the laptop, his head leaning forward like it was floating in front of his body.

"What about it don't you get, Turtle?" asked Stuart Hawk, sitting on the adjacent desk, dark hair slicked back, one knee pointed at Joe, one pointed ahead of him.

"Any of it. I don't understand how these words I'm typing on the screen can make a computer program in the first place."

"They can't in your case," said Stuart. "Because you *suck*. I think the school administrator got the gifted class and the special class confused in your case. The class where you're supposed to be is down the hall, Turtle."

"You're not doing much better, Stuart. Jay is the only reason we made it to State. He's carrying our team."

"But that won't be enough at State," rejoined Stuart, bouncing his foot with nervous energy. "We each have to build our own part of the program, and Jay can't compensate enough for you at that level. You're the weak link, Turtle."

Joe looked him in the eyes, "Call me Turtle one more time and–"

"And what?" interrupted Stuart. "What are you gonna do? Fight me? What could you possibly do to hurt me?"

Joe held his gaze for a moment before looking away without a word.

Stuart wished Turtle would try something. Give him an excuse to pummel him. It was like Turtle *chose* to be a loser. He didn't lift weights. He didn't wash his face. He didn't get a job so that he could buy nice clothes and a car. Stuart couldn't understand why trashy people were ok with being trashy.

"Tell you what, Turtle. I'll stop calling you Turtle when stop being a skinny dork whose head leans forward and Adam's apple sticks out so that you look like that turtle in 'Looney Tunes.' 'Doo da doo. Da doo da doo.' It doesn't help that you walk slowly down the halls with your giant green backpack. The only thing you do slower than walk is code."

Joe stared straight ahead at his computer screen.

Jay, who had been coding quietly to the other side of Joe, stopped and looked at him with his orb-like eyes. "Joe, I think you're getting overwhelmed because there are so many new terms with which you're unfamiliar. It's mainly an issue of vocabulary. You already understand some of these concepts, but you haven't matched them to the new words.

"Also," Jay continued, "you bring up a good question. How do these words you're writing and these punctuation symbols turn into a functional computer program? How can lines of code make something like 'Halo?'"

"Exactly," said Joe.

"That's the right question to ask," said Jay. "You're seeing the big picture. Most people don't care about the 'how,' but instead type in the code and watch it do its magic without wondering how the hell it works."

"Is that a shot at me?" asked Stuart.

"I'm doing this for the purpose of helping Joe and thus helping our team, but you can listen in."

Jay described how the code they wrote was converted into assembly language, then again into machine language, and then into binary ones and zeroes, which were the electrical signals that told the transistors whether to be set to on or off, and so on, until it made sense to Joe how Master Chief moved on the screen when the joystick was maneuvered. He then explained what the specific command Joe was working on did, and Joe got his code to run without any loops and without any direct help from Jay this time.

Mr. Voss reminded the students that UIL State competition was a week from Friday. They would stay in Irving overnight and compete on Saturday. He dismissed class and Joe was the first out the door with Stuart and Jay behind him. Joe headed to the front of the school to walk home as he did every day, and Stuart and Jay headed to the back of the school toward the parking lot.

"Do you ever feel guilty?" Jay asked Stuart.

"About what?"

"You know what. Making fun of Turtle."

"No."

"I don't believe you."

"Believe what you want."

"You shouldn't, though," said Jay. "Do you know the term 'hen-pecked?'"

"No," answered Stuart, opening the door to go outside.

"It refers to a husband who acts like a bitch because he fears his wife's nagging. But that's more innocent than where the term comes from in nature. In a brood of chickens, like in a coup, the hens will single out the one in their group that's the least fit. Say it has a blemish. The other hens will peck at that blemish, bullying it incessantly. Often they will peck it to death. This seems cruel but it is for a purpose. They are getting that hen out of the gene pool. Only the strongest, best-looking hens will reproduce, and they will continue to police their gene pool ad infinitum. If they didn't, chickens would get weak and eventually become extinct."

"Cool story," said Stuart, walking across the line of cars waiting for pickup and toward his car in the parking lot.

"Bullying in humans serves the same purpose. Otherwise, the next generation would have as many 'Turtles' as 'Stuart Hawks.' The guilt you feel is an evolutionary misfire. Back when humans traveled in packs, you would need every able body in your pack to help hunt and fight against other packs. Thus, these two instincts are in conflict, to keep him alive for fighting and to get him out of the gene pool for breeding. Nowadays, guys like Turtle contribute nothing since there's no longer a 'pack' that needs food and soldiers. The anti-bullying campaigns the schools have started pushing on us are all sentimentality. Atheists who promote these campaigns are being inconsistent with their values. They're assuming they can trust their feelings, when if they looked deeper at the source of their feelings and the ramifications of their actions, they would see that they are inconsistent with materialistic beliefs. They are creating a future world full of unfit humans just to make themselves feel better for the moment."

"If that's true, why are you like best friends with Turtle?"

"I'm a sentimental fool. It makes sense on paper, but the feelings foul everything up."

Joe Denti walked down the stairs from the eighth floor where the boys' rooms were, and out onto the fifth floor hallway at the Embassy Suites in Irving. The middle of the building was an indoor courtyard, and each level's hallway was open to the courtyard except for a waist-high iron railing, the hallways forming eight ascending balconies over the courtyard. On the outside of the hallways, framing the whole space, were the guests' rooms. The specific room he was looking for was 517.

He couldn't believe what was happening. It was like his dreams were coming to life. Here they are on a UIL trip, having dinner at Carrabba's, and Summer Gentry, his crush since 5th grade, sat down next to him. At first he could barely answer when she talked to him, but as the dinner wore on, he loosened up. Fortunately, that asshat Stuart was at the other end of the table and didn't ruin this for him like he surely would have if he had been around. Recently, his fantasies with Summer were getting crowded out by his fantasies of killing Stuart. First pushing him in front of the bus, but as doable as that was, it was too quick and painless. Stabbing him to death. That would work. What he hadn't realized until now was the two fantasies were one and the same. If he got with Summer, it would be a way to get back at Stuart. If Stuart saw him happy and popular and with a hotter girlfriend than he had, Stuart's envy would be as satisfying as those things were in themselves. His goal in life was to show up Stuart, and he didn't care if that was pathetic. Even Jay's stupid plan seemed worth it.

He was sure Stuart would try to screw this up for him when he heard about it. If he did, if he told Summer she was dating a skinny moron, a turtle, and she got embarrassed and dumped him, he would see to it he got back at Stuart by any means necessary. But even if Stuart ruined this for him, Stuart couldn't take away tonight. After the initial shock of her talking to him wore off, he started flirting with her, and to his utter shock she gave him her hotel room key and asked him to pay her a visit at 1:00 a.m. He might be on his way to live out his fantasies with Summer Gentry.

He arrived at room 517 and slid in the key card. Green flashing light. He turned the handle and slowly opened the door to darkness inside. "Hello?" he whispered.

"Close the door," she whispered back. It was Summer.

"Want me to turn on the light?" he asked as he closed the door behind him.

"No, leave it off. Stay right there."

"Where's Ivy?" he asked about her roommate, Stuart's girlfriend.

"I took care of her."

"Why did you ask me to come over?"

"Do I have to spell it out for you?"

"Uh. . ." Was she saying what he thought she was saying?

"Take off your pants."

He forgot his right from his left.

"Ok," he said after a moment, and fumbled at his button. He got it loose and dropped his pants, trembling in anticipation.

The light turned on and shocked his retinas. As he instinctively reached to pull up his pants he took in the scene. Summer and Ivy were in their pajamas, sitting on the bed.

"Oh my God," shrieked Ivy, as the girls guffawed and clapped their hands.

"Shut up, you bitch."

"Your friend told us about you, you creep. You deserve every bit of this."

Stuart! He was a dead man!

"Why are you videoing our boring poker game again?" asked Stuart Hawk, sitting on the floor leaning against the bed, holding a pair of nines.

"It's for my web log, uploading to my site as we speak," said Jay, leaning against the dresser opposite him, turning over the 'flop.'

"Who would want to watch us play poker at one in the morning?"

"No one, but the idea is that we banter back and forth. If we have any funny lines or interesting hands, I can edit it later and make us look like we're more interesting than we really are. It's about creating a web presence. A brand, if you will. We're at the butt crack of dawn of the Internet age, and I'm not waiting to make my name until I'm old and out of college. Sean Parker started Napster when he was 19."

Stuart Hawk had grown tired of Jay. Yes, he was brilliant, and would take them to the state championship. But he was weird. He always said and did strange things. Like videoing them playing poker. Stuart was tired of Jay talking him into going along with his ideas. No more. Stuart Hawk was a leader of men. He'd show Jay who was boss.

"Screw this," he threw down his cards. "I'm going to bed and you are too."

"Just a few more hands."

"I *said* time for bed."

Bang bang bang! Someone was at the door–and not concerned about waking them up.

"Crap, it's Mr. Voss," said Stuart.

"I'll get it. Maybe this is the excitement my web log needs."

Jay opened the door to a red-faced Joe Denti, on 'full tilt' in poker terms.

"Move!" he ordered. He pushed Jay and his camera out of the way and strode toward Stuart Hawk.

"Oh phew, it's just Turt–" was all Stuart could get out before Joe belted him in the face. Stuart went down and put his arms over his head as a flurry of wild punches flew at him.

"I hate you, you bastard!" Joe shouted as he assailed him.

Stuart flailed wildly on the floor, trying to get up. "I'm gonna kill you!" he said as he finally pushed Joe off and got to his feet.

Jay jumped in between them. "Wait!" Stuart tried to get at Joe without hitting Jay, whose camera fell to the ground. "Stuart, Joe has a legitimate reason for attacking you."

"I don't care. Get out of my way you bug-eyed bastard."

"He thinks you tricked him into taking off his clothes in front of Summer and Ivy."

"I know you did, you son of a bitch," Joe said to Stuart through sobs. "She told me."

"What are you talking about, freak? Wait, how do you know about this, Jay?"

"I can explain, but let's go onto neutral ground," said Jay. "It's not fair for Joe to be trapped in here in enemy territory."

"Not fair?! He just sucker punched me."

"It will make sense why when I tell you. Just come out to the hallway and give me one minute."

Jay nodded to the door and Joe backed out. Jay followed, and then Stuart, enraged and confused, followed Jay.

"Keep your voices down," whispered Jay as he leaned against the railing and looked around the courtyard, Joe to his left and Stuart to his right. "Stuart didn't set you up, Joe. It was me."

The heartbreak and betrayal on Joe's face were palpable.

"Why??"

"For the same reason I'm doing this." Jay lunged forward and in one quick motion, grabbed Joe around the waist like he was going to tackle him, but instead of taking him to the ground, he picked him up and flipped him over the guard-rail to his right. Stuart watched on in horror as Joe fell to the ground, flipping and grasping for eight stories before splatting face first on the pavement below, the blood from his head cascading out in all directions.

"Back to the room," Jay whispered sternly to Stuart.

Stuart fought to order his thoughts, but he couldn't process them. His vision blurred.

"Now!" Jay pulled Stuart back into their room and closed the door.

"What the . . . you *psycho* . . . what is–"

"I told you last week. Survival of the fittest."

"You insane *bastard*. Why would you . . . you're going to jail."

"You don't get it, Stuart. I'm the fittest. And if anyone's going to jail, it's you."

"Wha– Why!?"

"Because you just killed Turtle."

Stuart's throat tightened. What was this little freak talking about? "Is that what you're going to tell the police?"

"I can do better than that. I can show them what happened one minute before he was killed. I have you on camera threatening to kill him, right after I have him beating the snot out of you. Sounds like a good motive to me."

He fought against the panic that was overtaking him. "That doesn't prove anything. I'll tell the police how you set me up."

"Good plan. Your word against mine. Me, his buddy, sticking up for him all the time. You with motive and passion and a confession on camera. Testimony from every kid in our school who's heard you verbally tearing him to shreds for years, but has been too scared to say anything to you for fear of becoming your next target. They will line up at the witness stand to clear their consciences of never stepping in to stick up for Turtle, by getting back at the guy who did this. Justice is served."

A scream from outside shook him out of his panic. Stuart saw Jay's camera lying on the ground. He picked it up, lifted it over his head, and smashed it.

"It's a web log, moron. It's already on my web server and you have no way to take it down. If you kill me, I told my real best friend, Greg, to make sure the cops find the footage on my web server. A bit of advice. Try not to drop the soap in jail."

"What the. . . why . . . what are you . . ."

"What do I want? Why did I kill my friend? Why am I framing you?"

"Yes, you freak." Panic morphed into fear.

"For your name."

"What the hell does that mean?"

More commotion outside. Many panicked voices.

"Your name. Stuart Hawk. It's pretty badass. First name Stuart–I'm upscale and refined, but last name Hawk–I'm a predator who will eat your children."

"I don't know what you're talking about," said Stuart, starting to cry. "You're insane. You can have it. I'll tell everyone to call you Stuart Hawk from now on. You didn't need to kill Turtle for that."

"There's more to it than that, Stuart. What college are you planning to attend?"

"What? Texas Tech. Why?"

"Here's the deal, Slick. I've always wanted to go to Harvard. The Ivy, the history, the Red Sox. Problem is, I have a slight blemish on my permanent record to which I believe they would take exception. However, if Stuart Hawk were to apply to Harvard, now we're talking about a squeaky clean record, top 5 GPA and they don't know it's because you cheat, active in sports and clubs, pretty much the big man on campus. If I get you a 1600 on the SAT, you're in with a full ride. But where does that leave Jay? Jay is a kid who's made some mistakes, you know, but he's top 10 in his class, scores in the high 1300s on the SAT. Texas Tech will be glad to have you, 'Jay.'"

"What are you saying?"

"Listen Stuart, I'd speak slower but we don't have time. This will be a huge pain in the ass for you, and a lifelong commitment. I'll apply to Harvard and go to the interview as Stuart Hawk, and you'll do the same for Texas Tech as me. When you show up at Tech, you will be Jay Van Houten. You can tell your friends and professors to call you Stuart, but officially, for the rest of your life, you are me, and I am you. When you get married, you will have to figure out a way to explain to your wife why the government knows you by a different name than your mom does. Now do you see why I had to do it? There's no statute of limitations on murder."

Dread was overtaking him, tightening his chest, "Bu–if I agree, who will go to jail for killing Turtle?"

"Turtle killed Turtle. There's a suicide note in his suitcase. We had this plan where we were going to trick you into believing he committed suicide so you would feel like it was your fault for being an ass to him, before we revealed the truth that he was alive and you saw the error of your ways, or at least got really freaked out for a couple of minutes. I even talked him into not mentioning you in the suicide note, so you won't look like a monster when it's found. You're welcome. Trust me, though, some people are still going to be upset with you for how you treated him during his life to drive him to this. But them being mad is better than 50 years to life."

He fought the urge to pummel this little monster in front of him. "I'll tell Ivy and Summer about all this. We'll tell the judge how you manipulated everything."

"Come on. Do you even *know* your girlfriend? You think she and her friend will soil their reputations by being involved in this murder? I mean, they drove him into a rage by being cruel. How will that play with everyone? They'd end up on Dr. Phil as the uber bullies whose antics drove a sweet kid to suicide. No, the smart money is on them putting their heads down and shutting the hell up. Now, do we have a deal or don't we?"

Bang Bang Bang. "Guys get out here," it was Mr. Voss. "Something terrible's happened."

19

In the Belly of the Beast

Something terrible's happened, but I can't remember what. I open my eyes and look around. Where am I? This is getting old. My head throbs. I'm in a . . . cage? Lying on the cold tile floor. The whir of the air conditioner and other machines sounds like a jet plane. What machines? Computer servers. I'm in a server room, like the one in the data center at the university. The room outside of the cage is about double the size it is inside, lined with racks of servers. There's a large wooden door with a keypad to the right of the handle. All light is coming from the little rectangular window in the door, or from the red and green server lights, giving the room a creepy glow.

What was this Stuart Hawk guy going to do to me? Nothing good for sure. I think about the times over the past few days when his men attacked me. It was intense and terrifying, but once I got away, things settled back to normal. I suppose I was starting to feel like I was destined to survive whatever came my way. Like I'm the hero in my own story. Not anymore. Not now, now that Amy was killed in front of me. When the priest was killed it felt different. Like he had probably lived a good life, and this was his part to play, as horrible as that sounds now that I articulate it. Now that I think about Amy's death, I feel despair. I want to feel anger and rage. Those are the proper responses. But I can't. I just feel an empty uneasiness. I'm tired to the bone and my arms and legs are shaky. What a tragic waste of a good person. It could've been me if they didn't have something else in mind for me, possibly worse than a speedy death like Amy's. No, I can't think like that. God has a plan in all this and he's going to get me out of it like he's gotten me out of everything until now, even if it didn't work out for Amy.

I remember the bullets piercing her wispy body. Red circles appearing on her white shirt. Bastards. There's no honor among thieves. The last thing I remember is landing a punch on that red-headed guy. He must have got one on me as well judging by the way my head feels.

"I'm here. What do you want?" I shout into the empty room at no one in particular.

I look at the ceiling, but the cage is overhead as well. I can see a normal office ceiling above it through the one-inch square holes of the cage. There are no servers in here with me. Just a cold, tiled floor.

I'm not due back at the university for another week since I didn't teach classes this summer. The only person expecting me back is the grad student watching my dog, and I wasn't able to call him to let him know about my change of plans. If anyone ever figures out where I am, surely it will be too late. Maybe, for some unknown reason, this Hawk guy will let me go. The deaths of Amy and the priest flash in my memory. God, get me out of this. I don't want to die having never done anything worthwhile.

Click. The door opens. Fluorescent light from outside fills the room. A figure steps through the doorway, but I can't see who he is. All the light is behind him. He is of average height and build. The door closes behind him and he walks toward me. The roaring AC turns off. I see his face by the dim light and feel a tinge of recognition. I go through my mental rolodex. Blonde hair combed across, stuck to his head. Big brown eyes. An adult version of someone from childhood.

"Jay??"

"What up, Mark?"

My mind races for answers. I find none. "What the hell are you doing here?"

"Whatever I please. I run this humble enterprise."

"Which is what exactly?"

"Corpus Biotech."

"The company owned by Stuart Hawk?"

"Beg your pardon. I haven't reintroduced myself. Hello, Mark. My name is Stuart Hawk."

I try to piece together the information I have about Stuart Hawk and reconcile it with Jay. I'd always wondered what had happened to him. He had disappeared from the face of the Earth, which is what I'd expect. Who wouldn't want to hide from that past? But I'd never considered he'd change his name and become CEO of a biotech company. I kind of get it now. It wasn't that I was unlucky to have two psychopaths screw with me in one lifetime. It was the same guy. I know who I'm dealing with now. I preferred the devil I didn't know. My stomach churns.

This all comes out as, "How?"

"Had to get a new identity after the whole smashing Abel's spine incident. And up till now it's held up surprisingly well."

"So, to stay incognito you decided to steal the most treasured artifact in human history?"

"Oh yes, that. It could have gone more smoothly, but worked out in the end. Nice try on stopping it, though. You surprised the hell out of me."

"Why? Why did you steal it?"

"That's my business," he's slowly pacing back and forth. "What I *will* tell you is why you were chosen to test the Shroud. You see, I pulled some strings for my old friend. You're welcome."

"Why?"

"I hate to admit this, but I've always had something of a fixation on you. I mean sure, Abel was the prize, but as satisfying as that was in the moment, it dissipated quickly. I realized afterwards I'd let you off too easy. You were the leader of your little group there for a while, humoring me to my face and stabbing me in the back. Anyway, I've followed your life from a distance, and it was so pathetic that you didn't need my help to screw it up. You'd make the perfect superhero, Mark, because you have no one close enough to you for a villain to threaten. Now, here's where it gets insane."

"*This* is where it gets insane?" I ask. "It's been insane all along, because *you're* insane."

"Hear me out. I'm planning to steal the Shroud of Turin, and notice all your time online is spent researching this same item. I see how desperate you are for this thing to be real, how you finally have something that's important to you. Then it hits me. You are in the right scientific field, I could arrange for you to be there, and then hours away from realizing your dreams, I'll pull the football away from you like Lucy to Charlie Brown."

"You stole the Shroud of Turin to screw with my head??"

"Oh my God! No," he laughs. "You are a guilty pleasure. An interesting side project. And don't flatter yourself by thinking you're the only one. No, I'm not finished telling my story. It gets better. Like I said, you surprised the hell out of me, chasing after my guys like a badass, leaving me to wonder why in holy hell you were still conscious. Then it dawns on me. Something is wrong with your brain because of a head injury you received as a child. An injury which I may or may not have played a part in."

I figured my jacked hypothalamus was the reason I'm immune to their hypnosis, like it's the reason for everything else in my life. "I get it. You hurt me in the past, and when you tried to hurt me again, my previous injury helped me this time around. How ironic."

"You have no idea. I haven't got to the best part yet. My company's been working on a project. It's not an exaggeration to say it would be the next step in human evolution, but we've been running into a brick wall. Hundreds of geniuses, including me, have not been able to solve this problem. And then along comes my old chum, Mark Eberhart, and his busted brain, and I realize that's the key, the sledgehammer to get us through this metaphorical brick wall. All I need to do is run some tests on you to see why I can't link up with you to shut you down, and I'll have my answer. Sorry, but I had to tell someone who could grasp all the levels of irony. What is that scripture verse I learned at your church? Something like 'God works all things together for good for the called.' I guess that's me."

20

College

Mark
15 years earlier

"I know many of you have memorized scriptures growing up, but I'm asking for you to have an open mind during this class as to the reliability of Scripture," said Dr. Holcomb. He was a big, bald man with a well-manicured white beard.

"Does anyone know the meaning of the word redaction?"

I sat on the front row. No one answered.

"Redaction means 'the process of editing a text for publishing.' In the case of Gospel criticism, it has come to refer to steps the later Gospel writers took to embellish the stories first found in Mark to make their case for Jesus as God more convincing."

I will probably regret this. Taking the 'Introduction to the New Testament' class. My thought process was this: granted the professor will be liberal and biased against the reliability of Scripture, but if I'm going to go to Bible College for several years after I graduate from a state university, I ought to see how non-Christians view the Bible, so I will know how to approach them.

"Can you give us an example?" asked a shaky-voiced lady in the second row. One of the older students.

"I'll be giving examples throughout this semester but it will only be scratching the surface. Again, I understand we're in the Bible Belt and many of you don't want to hear this, but I ask that you not go to the dean's office and immediately drop this class as often occurs. Hear me out. There will be plenty of time for debate in this class and I'm open to all ideas. If your high ideas of Scripture are valid, they should be able to withstand some scrutiny, right? I will warn you, however, that I entered this field with the intentions of confirming my high views on Scripture and continuing onto seminary, when I was confronted with the realities. It doesn't matter to me what you decide to believe, but can we all agree to listen to the evidence and be honest about it?"

The class murmured its consent.

He stepped in front of his desk. "As far as an example, let's start at the beginning of Mark, which is the second Gospel in the New Testament but should have been first as it was the first one written, around 75 CE, 45 years after the crucifixion of Jesus. It starts out introducing John the Baptist as the fulfillment of Malachi's prophecy as the voice in the wilderness who will prepare the way for the Lord. Then it quotes John the Baptist saying there is one coming after him whose sandals he is not worthy to loose. John then baptizes Jesus and a dove descends on Jesus and a voice from Heaven says, 'This is my beloved son, in whom I am well pleased.' Who here is familiar with this story?"

I raise my hand, along with three quarters of the other students.

"Notice John never acknowledges this voice, and never points out to his followers that here is Jesus, the one he was talking about whose sandals he is not worthy to loosen. The story is the same in Luke, but in Matthew the story is redacted such that John tells Jesus he should be baptizing John instead of the other way around, but Jesus says, 'let it be so that Scripture can be fulfilled.' For some reason Mark and Luke didn't provide this important detail, but Matthew does, even though Matthew used Mark as a source. Perhaps after Mark and Luke, non-Christians argued John the Baptist himself didn't believe Jesus was the Messiah, and in consequence the writer of Matthew added a detail that makes the idea of John preparing the way for Jesus more compelling."

I spoke up, "Or Matthew was clarifying a point of confusion that arose because Mark assumed it was understood that John also heard the voice from Heaven and saw the dove."

"Good point, Mr. ...?"

"Eberhart."

He smiled coyly, "I can see this is going to be a fun semester. All right, let's let this question hang for the moment and add further context to it from a later story found in Luke and Matthew. John the Baptist is being held in prison by Herod, and John sends a message to Jesus asking him if he is the Coming One, i.e. the Messiah whose straps he's unworthy to loosen, or should he look for another. If Matthew's account of John telling Jesus that he should be baptizing him was true, then this story is John having a fit of doubt, having second thoughts about his earlier proclamation of Jesus as Messiah, and the voice he heard from heaven. Again, he's doubting an *audible voice* he heard from heaven. But doesn't the story make more sense if we assume Matthew's added detail about John's conversation never happened, and instead of John doing a 180 about his bold proclamation about Jesus being the One, he never made that proclamation in the first place, never heard the voice from the sky, and now at the end of his life, he is considering whether Jesus is in fact the One? In fact, if he decided Jesus was the One when he baptized him, why did he continue to have a competing ministry with Jesus? Why didn't he send all of his disciples to Jesus and become a disciple of Jesus himself?"

I raised my hand this time. "Yes, Mr. Eberhart."

"Even if John had never made up his mind about Jesus until this point, which I'm still not convinced of, he still fulfilled the prophecy from Malachi. He still prepared the way for Jesus by preaching repentance, whether he knew for whom he was preparing thc way or not."

He sat back on his desk, "I concede your point, Mr. Eberhart, but this is simply starting at the first few lines of the first Gospel and looking at the others through a redactive lens. As these examples continue, you'll begin to see them without me pointing them out. When you start discovering them on your own, it will be harder to believe this is all the product of your professor's overactive imagination.

"Let's look next at Luke, which runs into trouble before the first word. The problem with Luke is that the first two chapters are probably a later addition. First, Luke chapter 3 starts off just like Mark 1, as if it's the beginning of the book. Second, writings survived from a second-century Christian who doesn't include the first two chapters in his version of Luke. And third, the Greek in the first two chapters appears to be older than the Greek used in the rest of the book. That's three points of contention. If I'm right, it means the Christmas story is a later addition to the Gospel. I'm open to any contradictions you may have."

I sat there quietly, my throat drying out.

We sat in my old navy Buick LeSabre overlooking the lake, the engine running to keep the AC on. Tears were running down Jennifer's soft cheeks. I continued my spiel. "You're such a pretty girl. You don't need to be stuck with someone who's defective."

"Don't give me that 'it's not you it's me' bullcrap. You're the one breaking up with me. I'm the one who wants to be with you, defective or not. You're the one who doesn't want to be with me."

She looked at me through wet, brown eyes. She looked so pretty when she cried. Surely this was my one and only chance at romance, as far as that goes. She started sitting by me at church when I was a senior in high school. I hadn't thought much about her before that. A friend of hers told me to ask her out and I did, for one date, just so I could tell her why it wouldn't work. How could I open up like that to a stranger? Because I knew she was the kind of person who could be trusted with my secret. She was the pastor's kid, or PK, and unlike the stereotypical rebellious PK, as far as I could tell she'd never done anything wrong in her life. Probably never had an impure thought. When I told her I wouldn't be able to fulfill my husbandly duties were we ever to marry, she said she didn't care about that. I tried to give her the cold shoulder but she wouldn't relent, so we started dating.

Did I love her? Yes, in my own way. Was it the love other people felt? The same love I would have felt had Ronnie never hit me with that rock? I doubted it, based on the love songs and romance movies that were ubiquitous in the culture. But I went through the motions of a normal relationship. We would make out and I kind of liked it, but it got a little boring after a while. But so what? I had a companion who I loved, and more than that, who I liked. I had made peace with my lot in life. But then something started to eat at me.

"The only reason I don't want you to be stuck with me is that I don't have the capacity to love you the way you should be loved."

"That's my decision, and you already agreed to let that be my decision."

"I'm not just talking physically. I don't think I feel the way I'm supposed to feel."

"Are you saying you never felt anything for me? All the romance and love notes in the beginning were lies?"

"No," but they were exaggerations. The price of admission to a relationship for one lacking normal human emotion.

"What you're saying is the brain injury you had as a child kicked in a few months back, but before that you were in love?"

"I don't know how to explain it."

"It couldn't possibly be that you fell in love and then it faded, because that *never* happens to anyone else. Just you. With you, Mark, it always comes back to your self-pity. And your injury is a pretty nice crutch when you need to break up with a girl and don't want to hurt her feelings."

Her face contorted into a sob and she turned and opened the car door.

"Where are you going?" I called after her.

"I can't sit here for another second."

It was too far to walk back to town. She walked toward a grove of pine trees. I knew she needed some space.

The problem with my relationship with Jennifer was not my cursed hypothalamus. The problem was she was part of a life-plan that was no longer tenable. I was going to college in the town I grew up in because I got a scholarship and it was the most natural next step. Then I would graduate, get married, and go to Bible College and become a missionary. Me and my perfect wife and three kids (with the help of modern science) would go on adventures together through Africa or Papau New Guinea and convert the natives to Christ. All Jennifer wanted was to serve God and if I told her I was called to be a pastor and work for her dad, or to be a missionary and go to Timbuktu, she would be on board.

What she wasn't on board with was doubt. I brought up my doubts to her at the beginning of the 'Introduction to the New Testament' class and she was taken aback, and quickly explained why they were misplaced and that I knew better. I understood where she was coming from since I didn't have any doubts to speak of when we started dating.

The drip, drip, drip of examples of redaction continued throughout the class. I didn't drop the class because Holcombe preemptively called us out on it, and how could I go tell natives about the Bible if I couldn't first argue with someone who knew the Bible, and knew it better than I did? How could I tell anyone about Jesus if I didn't believe what I was saying myself? It was one thing to have the faith to leave all of one's comforts and risk one's life and one's family's lives for a faith one believes in with every bit of his being. But once doubt entered the equation, the mighty acts of faith performed by past saints and missionaries seemed off the table. If my faith couldn't survive serious examination, was it ever real in the first place?

I knew it *was* real, though. When I felt the presence of the Holy Spirit and spoke in tongues that first time, that was real. One moment I couldn't, and the next I could, and still can to this day. If the gospel wasn't true, how could that experience be explained? How was it that 50 days after the crucifixion, at Pentecost, which even my professor believed was a real event, the followers of Jesus had an experience which had never happened before in the history of the world, and that same experience still happened to Christians today in the same ways it was described throughout the book of Acts? It was no longer an exotic experience reserved for some mystics and fanatics. Around 20% of the world's Christians spoke in tongues. Many people who received the gift of tongues had never even heard of it when they first started doing it, so it wasn't something you just learned to do if you tried hard enough. It wasn't like learning how to whistle.

At the same time, it wasn't enough. God said to worship him in Spirit and in Truth. The truth part had to work out also. As I sat through the class, some of the professor's examples were better than others. There was no knockout blow, but the steady drip continued all semester.

The worst part, though, was Dr. Holcombe's prediction about me doing this automatically on my own, and not being able to turn it off. I led a youth Bible Study at my church. Sometimes I would be teaching a lesson and right in the middle, I would find a spot where the Gospels didn't line up, where Luke may have added something to give Jesus a higher Christology than in Mark, and I would fight through the lesson, nervous this would be the final blow that undid my faith, with a ball of lead in my stomach until the end of service. Usually when I looked at the verses after church, I'd find out there was nothing to it and I was being paranoid, but sometimes I would find contradictions that stumped me. Lord, I believe. Help my unbelief.

I didn't want to live this life. The life of a hypocrite. Preaching as though I believed what I was saying more than I actually did. I didn't want to end up stuck on the mission field with wife and kids and then decide, 'Welp, guess I don't believe all of this Jesus stuff after all.' I didn't want to end up 'unequally yoked' to Jennifer, like my parents were with each other. Instead, I would get my degree at Angelo State University, get a regular job, and work out my issues with my faith on my own time. I was already getting a Bachelor of Science degree because of my scholarship, so I decided to go for a degree in chemistry. I enjoyed it and was good at it, even better than the exchange students. I was worried I wasn't cut out for it because I'm not a genius, but my favorite professor, Dr. Grenda, encouraged me, saying many of the top discoveries were not made by geniuses, but by guys like me who grinded away at it and got lucky by studying the right subject at the right time. Besides, all the real eggheads or wannabe Einsteins went into physics anyway. That wasn't my endgame, though, to become a chemist. The college counselors assured me employers were more interested in graduates who had learned how to think, rather than graduates who learned specific, applicable skills. So I figured I would get a job in whatever field sounded interesting once I graduated.

All right, she'd been in the woods long enough. It'd be no good if she were eaten by wolves. I drove up next to the pine trees and walked into them about 100 feet before I saw her sitting on a pile of dead pine needles staring off into the distance. She was wearing a white cotton dress, the bottom flowing out around her like an egg white. Her auburn hair was halfway down her back, blowing in the breeze. Her eyes were puffy from crying.

"You have until the end of the night to change your mind about this," she said when she saw me. "If you don't call and take it back, we're through for good."

We walked back to the car and I drove her home, in silence. That night she wasn't at church. The reality of her being out of my life started to sink in, and my heart started to break. Why, God? Why couldn't things be clear? Why couldn't they be straightforward like my mom taught me they were? Wouldn't the right thing to do be to just take the risk? To trust I would be able to work all of this out, and walk toward my goal with my girl by my side? Wasn't that faith? Was this the heartbreak talking? Would I tell her I wanted her back, and then after the emotional high of getting her back, would all of the other issues that drove me to try to break up with her in the first place come rushing back in with a vengeance? What should I do, God?

I called out to God during worship. I heard nothing. How could I know what God was saying to me if I asked him a question directly? Would the voice that answered back be God's voice, or my own? I could understand God speaking to me out of the blue, where I could say, 'Where did that thought come from? Must have been God.' But to ask him a question directly, how could I know if it were God unless he spoke to me in an audible voice?

The strangest thing happened at the end of the service. I saw someone wheel himself to the front, bawling like a baby. Abel. He'd never come to church without me in his life, and he only came with me a couple of times after he got paralyzed. I don't know what he was going through, but it looked like God was meeting him right there at the front of the church. Good for him, but wish I could say the same for me.

I left church and drove around, praying and thinking. I went home (I still lived with my parents) and decided to play Bible roulette, which is where you open the Bible to a random page and read it as if it was God's answer to your question. I knew it was a childish way to make a life decision, akin to going to a fortune teller, but I was desperate. Besides, I once read St. Augustine decided to become a Christian by playing the same game so maybe it wasn't that illegitimate. I opened to Isaiah 5:25: "For all this His anger is not turned away. But His hand is stretched out." That was no help.

I didn't call Jennifer that night. The next day, after a fitful sleep, I called her and told her I'd made a mistake and asked her to come back to me. She said no, and asked me to please not call again.

21

Hologram

Stuart Hawk's security team was calling again. What did they want now? He'd find out soon enough. He parked at his spot in front of the main campus of his empire, Corpus Biotech. He stepped out of the car and the warm summer air blew against his face. He walked toward the sprawling, two-story, red-brick building, and saw a couple of low-level employees walking in the opposite direction. When they noticed him, they started whispering to each other. He loved to wonder what they were saying. 'That guy is worth a billion dollars.' 'They say he's smarter than Bill Gates.' That's for damn sure. Or maybe it was, 'I heard he ruins his enemy's lives for grins and giggles.' Admired, feared. Whatever.

He looked ahead to the door and hesitated for a step. Cora. She was there in the flesh, looking straight at him. That's what his security team was calling about. He involuntarily clenched his fists. What was she doing here? She was rockin' the grey business suit and skirt look. Damn. In his weaker moments, he wondered if he should have forgotten his ambition, and spent all his energy on keeping her. Yeah right. That's not me, he thought. Oh well, it was fun while it lasted.

"Hello, Cora. Are you here to see someone in particular?"

"You actually, Mr. Hawk."

He badged in. "You can tailgate on me, but the head of security is going to let me hear about it. He treats me like everyone else, to his credit."

They walked in silence, taking the stairs and turning down several hallways until they reached his office, which was relatively small and spartan. He held open the door and closed it behind her.

"I don't appreciate you coming to my place of business and would ask that you never come here again. I have no interest in being seen with an eyewitness to the theft of the Shroud of Turin. Especially someone who is also conspicuously my ex-girlfriend." He stood two feet away, glaring at her. She was a fraction taller than him, and didn't back down from his gaze.

"If you answered your damn phone, I wouldn't have come in person."

"Sorry but I've been a little *busy*!" he raised his voice. "What is so important it couldn't wait?" He walked behind his desk.

"I want your word that we're square and you'll leave me alone. I've done more than my fair share. Christ, I almost slept with that guy!"

"I was trying to get him relaxed for Greg, which in hindsight proved to be a good idea." While this was true, it was not the real reason. That was to utterly humiliate Mark. Mission accomplished. "So, what did you think of him?"

"I think he wastes all of his time tying himself in knots trying to make his faith make sense. Pretty much the last kind of person I would be interested in, although he *is* better-looking than you." She smiled smugly and sat down across from him.

"Oh please," Hawk sat down.

"What did he end up doing after I left?"

"Oh my God, do you like him?" Hawk laughed.

"Uh, no. And I didn't come here for high school crap like this."

"If you must know, he jumped on a plane to Boston, probably to report you to the police here."

"Probably?" She looked frazzled. "Did he do it, or not?"

"How would *I* know?" But he did know. Hawk shuddered with excitement when he thought about what he had planned for Mark.

"Because you know everything. You knew he jumped on a plane to Boston. He's as likely to report you as me, because that priest told him about you."

He leaned back in his chair, "Not worried about it. He heard my name from some conspiracy-monger priest. Who cares?"

"So you and I, we're good?" she subtly nodded her head, encouraging him to agree.

"Listen, it would be easy for me to tell you that your debt is paid and I'll never bother you again, but we both know if I ever need you again, the situation hasn't changed."

"Actually it has. I could go to the FBI at any time and tell them what you did and how."

"And I could tell them what you did and how," he leaned forward. "Before you play a game of chicken with me, you should know that I'm a vengeful, spiteful bastard. I once spent time in jail for ruining someone else's life, and it was totally worth it."

"I know you're bluffing," she uncrossed and recrossed her long legs. "You have too much going now to waste it all on ruining someone insignificant like me."

"I could always not let you leave this building." He started spinning a pen on his desk.

"Oh, that would be smart. I go missing and the police look into the last place I was seen, and into who my last boyfriend was. That wouldn't be suspicious. Stuart, what I need you to understand is I'm holding all the cards now. I have no interest in having my career or reputation destroyed, but I need you to know you've blackmailed me for the last time. I hope to never see your face again, and if you try anything in the future, I will take you up on that game of chicken and ruin my life to take you down. I have a lot less to lose than you do."

She stood up, turned, and walked out of the room.

You go girl. Good luck with your cards. But in a week, none of this will matter.

He got up, walked down the hall, and badged into the clean room, which also required a retinal scan. He put on his scrubs and rubber gloves, opened the pressure chamber, and pulled out a drawer like he was pulling out a corpse for an autopsy. There it was, spread out in all its glory: The Shroud of Turin.

Not only did it theoretically contain the information he needed, but through sheer luck it brought to light the much more actionable information in Mark's brain. Brought to light. The phrase was apropos. Light was a key to the information stored in the Shroud. It was how anyone knew there was something there to begin with. Good old light. Great minds have always been fascinated by it. Isaac Newton would stare at a prism and wonder how one invisible beam of light would enter one end, and the full color spectrum would cascade out the other. But technology needed time to incubate before light would give up its mysteries. A couple hundred years later Michael Faraday figured out electricity and magnetism were the same force, electromagnetism, and that it traveled at the speed of light. His friend James Clerk Maxwell had the mathematical expertise to verify this was true, and to calculate the speed: about 186,000 miles per second. This set the stage for Einstein.

Einstein was obsessed with light. He wondered, if the speed of light maxed out at 186,000 miles per second, what if he were theoretically riding at that speed on a beam of light? What would he see if he looked behind himself, since the light leaving the objects behind him wouldn't ever catch up to his eyes? What if he got an extra boost of energy behind him? Why couldn't he be pushed past that speed? Why does the cosmos have a speed limit, and how does that affect everything that interacts with light? Then it hit him. Since the speed of light is constant, there must be some fundamental property that isn't constant even though it intuitively seems so: time.

He solved the greatest mystery in physics. Just like Faraday discovered electricity and magnetism were different sides of the same coin, Einstein figured out space and time were different faces of the same phenomena, and that they were a real substance: space-time. He realized they could be, and were, twisted and manipulated by gravity, and the theory of relativity was born.

After Einstein came Neils Bohr and quantum mechanics, which Einstein loathed because of its nonsensical, chaotic nature. Quantum mechanics said when matter was analyzed on an extremely small scale, the rules of physics changed. An electron can be in two places at once. That electrons frequently disappear and show up somewhere else, and that they behaved differently when they were being measured by humans. Also, electrons of atoms in the plasma state stopped behaving as individual entities and started acting in an organized, cohesive manner. And when two electrons became entangled, they could instantly communicate with each other across space, ignoring the universe's speed of light speed limit. As strange as the theory was, quantum mechanics has never failed in an experiment, and was responsible for the creation of all the electronic devices of the 20th and 21st centuries. Television, computers, mobile phones, etc.

While Neils Bohr did not back down from the unbelievable assertions made by quantum physics, he was not particularly keen to explain or understand the 'why' of it. Why was it electrons whizzed around at the speed of light, constantly disappearing and reappearing? Why did they behave as waves when unwatched, but particles when measured? Why could you change a particle on one side of the universe, and force its entangled peer to instantly react the same or opposite way, with no regard to location? The jury was still out on this, but Hawk preferred the explanation made by the less-known, but equally brilliant physicist, David Bohm.

Bohm theorized the universe is in essence a giant hologram. The way a regular hologram works is that a single laser is split into two beams. One beam bounces off the object to be photographed, say an apple, and the second is reflected off mirrors and then allowed to collide with the first beam onto a piece of film. The interference of the light that bounced off the apple, combined with the pure light from the second beam creates a three-dimensional visual representation of an apple. What Bohm meant by saying the universe is a hologram was that what we observe as the universe is like the projected picture, but instead of only being able to see it, the universe is a hologram for all five of our senses. We touch, taste, smell, hear, and see the hologram. But there is a deeper, 'implicate' level of reality we cannot observe with our senses. This is like the holographic film in the analogy. The reason why quantum physics appears strange to us is that subatomic particles like electrons are constantly 'enfolding' and 'unfolding' between the 'explicate,' our observable universe, and the 'implicate,' the core level of reality.

This would explain what's happening with electrons. They

disappear out of the hologram into the core level, and reappear back where we can observe them again. The particles are nonlocal, so while it looks to us like two entangled electrons are communicating across space, what we are observing is the same electron appearing in different places in the hologram, two sides of the same coin. He even proposed that electrons aren't many different individual particles, but all one massive, cohesive entity that we observe as different data points from our perspective, which helps explain why they sometimes behave with complex coordination.

Hawk had taken Bohm's theory and put it into practice. With enhanced intelligence, he and the others were able to reach out to inanimate objects by feel, but what they were instinctually doing without knowing it was reaching under the covers of the hologram and manipulating objects at the core level of reality. Psychokinesis has been measured in labs for years, but only at a small scale. Now with greater intelligence and whatever else they had genetically unlocked, their PK abilities were exponentially stronger. Making people unconscious was a different process than PK; one the tests on Mark would help him understand. Once he combined the results from the upcoming tests on Mark, with what he learned from his tests on the Shroud, he would be ready for action.

Physics has typically concerned itself with the physical nature of matter and energy. The holographic theory of the universe introduces the concept of information rather than physicality as the core reality of matter and energy. The theory holds that every physical body in the universe has a quantum holographic emission that is available nonlocally. However, this quantum hologram has only ever been found on one piece of matter: the Shroud of Turin.

He looked at the faint image on the Shroud, created by a burst of light. The cloth collected and stored information he could study to reveal the nature of the one-of-a-kind burst. Particle physicist Dame Isabel Piczek speculated that when the Shroud image was created, it was a true Singularity event, similar to the Big Bang, where laws like gravity were turned on their head, and 'what happened in the tomb of Christ was nothing less than the start of a new universe.'[3] Ironic a Singularity event in the natural world would lead to him achieving 'Singularity' in the technology world–joining his mind with that of a machine. Turning homo sapiens into homo machinas.

More ironic than that, though, was Mark's part in all of this. The tests on his brain would provide exponentially more practical information needed for the 'link up' than he would be able to tease out of the Shroud's quantum hologram any time soon. Mark was full of surprises. After Hawk settled with making Cora grab the boy from the Nunnery and waited for a better opportunity to get Mark, the next thing he knew Mark booked a ticket to Boston, to what, confront him? This was not the old Mark he knew. It sure made it easier logistically to get him on the premises. Once he learned what Mark's brain could tell him, he should have what he needed to finally 'link up' with a computer. He would just need a few days to rewrite the code in light of the new information.

The coincidences made him giddy. He knew what Mark was thinking when he told him about them. They are not coincidences at all. God is at work. But why would God need to use so many coincidences to get his world where he wanted it to go? Deus ex machina. Why wouldn't he have put all the pieces into the story seamlessly from the beginning. Maybe God was just a bad writer. The thought tickled him. If there is a God, he's about to have a rival.

22

The Bar

Hawk
13 years earlier

Stuart Hawk's rival, Garrett Bannister, announced to the whole table, "The real world is here. Time to pay the price for our prolonged adolescence." He ran his fingers through his long chestnut hair, a habit he must have cultivated, as it drove the ladies crazy.

"Prolonged adolescence? What school have you been going to?" asked Kim, Hawk's girlfriend. "I've been scratching and clawing my way through finals clubs, an internship, oh, and classes."

"That's hot," Hawk chimed in.

"At least you're interning at a high-paying law firm," said Cora, who sat across from Hawk, her emerald eyes popping in the dim light, "while I'm at the Boston Globe, hoping and praying to become a junior reporter so I can cover the high stakes world of municipal politics in the suburbs."

The four of them were sitting at a booth at the back, a few beers in, at a swanky bar on Harvard Square, the Beat Bar Brassierie, '90s music playing in the background, at this moment it was 'All I Wanna Do.' Everyone looked golden in the light. The ambience was reflected in the prices, which was more than they could afford, but Stuart had suggested they treat themselves once before they left school. Most of the patrons were tourists who were daydreaming about what it would have been like if they had gone Harvard. There were also some rich underclassmen laughing it up without a care in the world, and at least one other table of fellow seniors stressing out about the future, the number one pastime of Harvard seniors. Not Stuart, though. Stuart Hawk always had a plan.

"I don't know what's wrong with you guys. I'm very much looking forward to the life of a starving artist," said Garrett, who took a swig of his beer.

"What are they paying poets these days?" asked Hawk.

"Not much, unless one's talent lies in writing lyrics to gangsta' rap."

"Just my luck. I manage to get into Harvard and end up with the only guy who has worse career prospects than myself." Cora smiles at Garrett to let him know she's only joking. Half joking? Her dark hair is partially up in a bun but spilling out in all directions. She would say she was slumming it, with a white Harvard v-neck and blue jeans, but casual Cora simply proved she didn't have to try to look gorgeous.

"That has nothing to do with luck," said Hawk. "You had the pick of the litter. My freshman psychology class would call that subconscious self-sabotage."

"I'm sitting right here," said Garrett in mock umbrage.

"No offense," said Hawk.

"Oh, well in that case, none taken."

"We're all doing better than you, Stuart," said Kim. She was small and thin, with onyx-black hair styled like that of a boy, matching the black pant suit she wore, having gone to a job fair earlier in the day. As a third generation Korean and the first in her family to go to college, she not only had a plan B if her internship didn't work out, but plans C through Q covered as well. She turned her head to look at her best friend, Cora. "He thinks he can walk into a company, move to the front of the line, past the students who interned there, and name his price."

"What kind of company?" asked Cora.

"I'm thinking biotech. The human sciences are poised to take off. We know as much about them today as we knew about astronomy at the time of Galileo."

"That may be," said Kim, "but wouldn't it have been smart to, you know, get an internship, so you could, like, actually get a job in that field?"

"It would have been easy," he said, leaning back. "Smart? We'll have to wait and see. Easy and smart are not the same thing."

"I guess I don't know the difference," said Cora, her eyebrows crinkled.

"Sometimes smart is not easy, but hard. Maybe it will be hard to get where you want to end up, but it will be smart to do what it takes to get you there. Cora, what would you like to be 15 years down the road?"

"An op-ed writer at the New York Times," she said without missing a beat.

"So one day you want to take Maureen Dowd's spot as a general in the Culture War?"

"Yes, but I'd be much more effective than Maureen Dowd. She's been in the liberal bubble her whole life. I spent the first 18 years of my life as a spy in the Christian Fundamentalist camp."

"Ok, hypothetically," said Hawk, "you get on the local news, you get promoted to the national news because you're pretty. Then you–"

"You just spent four years at Harvard," interrupts Kim, "and you're still a sexist?"

"Listen, I don't like the system any more than you do, but it is what it is. Hear me out. You're smart, so the TV thing was merely a way to put yourself out there, get name recognition. You parlay that into a job at the New York Times. That's the easy way. Some would say the smart way, but I'd disagree. You would have been spending the bulk of your time on a skill different from the one you want to master, and when you start writing op-eds, you may find you aren't any good at it.

"Now, the smart way. You write. You pay your dues, you advance slowly, but you do so on the merits of your writing. If you get there, you'll have the satisfaction of knowing you earned it, and you'll be good at it. Because what you want is not to be a writer at the New York Times, but to be a damn good writer, with the biggest platform there is."

"Makes some sense," Cora admitted.

"I prefer the easy plan," said Garrett. "You become a TV star and bankroll me."

"Won't work," said Hawk. "You need to experience poverty with her while she works her way up, to provide you some real-world suffering to fuel your art."

"Ewww, poverty. No thanks. I'd rather rely on my crazy for poetry fuel."

There was a pause in the conversation. Stuart took a bite of his flatbread and looked at Cora. She was stunning. She'd be worth all of the trouble.

"Did any of you hear about the documentary on the Discovery Channel called 'The Lost Bones of Jesus'?" asked Cora.

"No," Kim answered for the others.

"Basically, they dug up this family tomb in Jerusalem from before the fall of Jerusalem. In the tomb there are names that match the names of Jesus and his family members from the Bible, and Mary Magdalene. It's a long story, but the gist is that Mary Magdalene's name is very rare, and they did a DNA test on Jesus' and Mary Magdalene's bones to see if they were related because they're in the same tomb, and the tests came back and showed they weren't related, which means they were probably married, so the odds are very high that these are the actual bones of the historical Jesus, and he never rose from the dead. Anyway, I'm not doing a good job of explaining it. You'd have to see it. But I found it fascinating."

"I'm Catholic so I should be upset by this . . . but I don't care," said Kim.

"There's your answer," said Hawk.

"Answer to what?" asked Cora.

"Answer to your next career move. Start a blog about this."

"Oh ok. That should pay for my Harvard student loans."

"Think about it. You'd be writing about something you're passionate about, and making a name for yourself in the process. Not writing for 20th century media about Joe Blow's five-point lead in the polls to become mayor of Burlington."

"I'm sold. Except for one thing, oh yeah, the no money part."

"I'll fund you," said Hawk.

Garrett spit out his beer, laughing. They all laughed at this, even Hawk.

"That's wrong on so many levels," said Kim. "You don't come from money. You don't have any job prospects. You have student loans. And . . . why would you want to?"

"Because she's your best friend, and it works out so perfectly. Plus, I get a weird kick out of helping people out for no reason."

Garrett grew serious. "That's not the kind of thing you do

for your girlfriend's friend."

"Wait, are you *serious*?" asked Cora.

"Perfectly and completely."

"No, he's not," said Kim. "He doesn't have any money."

"Give me two months. At that time, I will have enough money that this will be a drop in the bucket. Go ahead and take your job with the Globe and get beaten down for a couple of months so you'll know what you're missing. Then give me a call. You can pay back the loan at your leisure."

Garrett laughed, "You're so full of garbage." He said it as if he were joking, but they all knew he wasn't.

"Good luck getting *your* loan from me."

"Hawk!" The shout came from the other end of the bar, from a student who had just walked in the door. He marched past the tables and stood an inch from where Hawk was sitting, looking down at him with hazel eyes. His collar was popped up, his light-brown, fluffy hair just a shade darker than his skin.

"What the hell?!" he fumed.

"You see, Cora," said Hawk nonplussed. "You could be dating a future investment banker like Tyler here instead of the poet laureate."

"Get up," said the newcomer, Tyler Stone. "You won't want to talk about this here."

"I'm going to have to ask you to leave," said the waiter, who had sidled up beside Tyler.

"No, it's ok," said Hawk. He stood up and pulled out a 100-dollar bill from his wallet and set it on the table. He said to Kim, "I'll meet up with you back at the dorm."

Hawk and Tyler exited the bar and turned right. The Charles River was a couple blocks away. The spring air still had a touch of winter in it. Tyler walked next to him, so close that he kept bumping into him. Trying to intimidate him. It wasn't working. Hawk delighted in the feeling of adrenaline rushing through his veins. They crossed Brattle Street and headed toward the yard.

"Let me repeat my question. What the hell? I just got a call from the head of the donors and he said $50, 000 is missing from the coffers and asked where the hell it was."

"What did you tell him?"

"That we needed $500 for the end of the year party and it must have been a banking error."

"Quick thinking."

"Damn right quick thinking. But what if I hadn't thought of something? I'd be done."

"There was never a chance of that. You're very clever." They had almost reached campus. Tyler's fluffy hair bounced with every step he took.

"I shouldn't have had to think of something. You said you only needed the money for a week and then you'd put it back. You screwed up, bro. And I'd be toast if I got caught–and that's me with all of my connections. Imagine how done you would be. So wire the money back and let's get this over with."

"Wrong."

"What?" asked Tyler, with a hint of apprehension in his perfect face. "What do you mean 'wrong'?"

"Everything you said is wrong." They entered campus through the Johnson Gate. "I didn't screw up. I did exactly as I intended. And no, I wouldn't be more 'done' than you if we'd been caught. You're going into investment banking. How would your sticky fingers look on your resume to JP Morgan, as 50 squeaky clean ivy leaguers fight for the same position? How would dear old dad feel about his son, the treasurer of Fox Club, his old club that he partially bankrolls, taking out 50k from the treasury on a risky gambling scheme?"

"Arbitrage is by definition not risky. I doubled our money. It was my idea, you just let me use your brokerage account so it couldn't be traced to me if I got caught."

"Ha! You actually think it was your idea."

"Are you crazy? Of course it was my idea. I thought of it in class when you weren't there."

"Yeah, a week after I showed you about option straddles. Oh, and what about when you told me all you needed was capital and I suggested the club's coffers?" As they passed by Harvard Hall, Hawk could see Tyler visibly shaking.

"You bastard. I'll make sure you take the fall for this and never get a job. Anywhere. I don't know of any biotech companies that will want to hire a felon." Hawk was smiling, drinking in the heat pouring off Tyler.

"Who cares? I won't get a biotech job anyway. I didn't even do an internship. No, I'll do whatever time they give me, but I'll take you down with me. You know, I've done some coding in the past and I'm kind of a genius at it. There are a lot of companies that don't do background checks and are just looking for someone who can do the job. And as the saying goes in hacking, if you get caught, you go to jail. Unless you're really good. Then you get a job at the NSA."

"Oh my God! Are you really doing this? To me?! I've always vouched for you to the other guys. What do you think I did to you to deserve this?"

"Nothing. You're a swell guy." They walked past the statue of John Harvard.

"So put the money back and let's both get back to where we were an hour ago."

"My plan hasn't changed. Let me tell you how you can make it so your plans don't change. Go to your father and tell him you have a friend in the club–"

"*Friend*," Tyler spat out bitterly.

"A friend who is a genius and needs an angel investor for the biotech company he's starting. I have the paperwork drawn up in my dorm." They entered Harvard yard.

"My dad won't listen to me. Everyone here is a genius. He has people with Harvard and MIT degrees and actual experience fighting for his resources."

"I know you, Tyler. You'll think of something. If you can get an unofficial 'yes' by the end of the weekend, I'll wire the 50k back on Monday. If at any time this doesn't go through, or worse, if word gets out about what we did, I don't care if it's 50 years from now, I have the paper trail that leads to you taking the money out of the account, investing it in a risky scheme, and putting it back when you got caught. Is any of that unclear?"

23

The Escape

It's unclear to me what any of that was about. Last night a couple security guards, including that red-haired one who I keep running into, escorted me to another room. A bright room with fluorescent lights in the ceiling and chrome cabinets around the perimeter. In the middle was a piece of medical equipment that looked kind of like a heart monitor, and a treadmill. A man and woman in scrubs were waiting for me there. The woman, a short, stocky African American, took some wires from the medical machine and taped them to my temples. The doctors asked me questions. Some were minor details about my past, some were random trivia, and some were asking me to explain complicated chemical processes for which I couldn't remember all of the details. I lied on some of them. Figured that might mess up their tests. Then they told me to run on the treadmill. I asked what they would do if I refused, and the man, who had a bushy, mountain-man beard, said I didn't want to know. The treadmill started slowly, but increased until I was in a full sprint. I was dying, but kept running until it finally stopped. I'm not in good shape, but felt like it was a battle of wills between me and Jay.

I'm now back in the cage in the server room/makeshift prison, sitting on the cold floor. I've lost track of time. They've brought me food four times since then, and left me a disgusting bedpan.

I hear a sound at the door. It clicks open and someone walks briskly toward me.

Cora!

She opens my door, puts her index finger over her mouth in a 'shhh' sign. "Follow me."

She turns and walks toward the exit. I hesitate for a second and then dart after her. Shouldn't trust her, but what choice do I have? I squint from the brightness in the hall. There's no one else in it and we walk quickly. It has a white tile floor and grey walls, punctuated occasionally by large wooden doors like the one to the room I was in. I hear people laughing ahead, who must be around the corner we're approaching. "Dammit," whispers Cora. She does a 180 and grabs my hand, pulling me back in the direction we came from. "Try to look natural." We slow our pace.

I can hear the group of people get louder, and I can tell they're behind us now. We keep walking, inconspicuous. So far so good. Not much longer until we can turn.

"Hey!" one of them yell at us.

I look back over my shoulder and recognize the mountain-man doctor who tested me.

Cora takes off in a sprint and I try to catch up with her. The doctor is chasing after us and yelling for help. We reach the end of the hallway and Cora turns right and I follow. There standing in front of us, 20 feet away, is a security guard. The Arabic-looking guy from the Vatican. Cora collapses to the ground in front of me.

I lock eyes with him–and charge! He's trying to pull his gun out, fumbling with it. I launch myself at him right as he's pulling up his gun.

Slam!

I'm on top of him, throwing punches, slamming his head against the floor. He's out.

I jump up and turn around and the doctor is looking at me, wide-eyed, standing over Cora.

"You want some?!" I scream. He turns and runs.

I run and grab Cora, pick her up in my arms like I'm carrying her over the threshold, and run back past the security guard who I just beat to a pulp. The hallway opens up into to a big lobby with a high ceiling and lots of windows to the outside. People are standing around, looking on with open mouths as I run past them. There's a revolving door that leads to a parking lot outside. I turn my back to the door and push through it. The moment I step outside, an alarm starts to blare.

"Put me down," says Cora. She sounds groggy.

I set her down and she takes a few steps like a baby fawn before she gets her footing. She takes off toward a hill on the opposite side of the parking lot, which is covered in thick green trees, like a forest untouched by man right next to this industrial building. We weave through the cars, get to the end of the parking lot. I hear someone at the revolving door shouting at us over the alarm. We plunge into the forest and I race ahead of her, cutting a path through the trees, knocking little stringy branches out of the way. We are almost to the top of the hill when I find a worn path, wide enough for one. At the top of the hill, I look ahead and see smaller hills in front of us, and a mile or two ahead is a busy street, lined with stores and restaurants.

"Why are we always running?" I ask rhetorically.

She pushes her way in front of me and I follow her down the hill, gravity quickening our pace. She's wearing black slacks and a white blouse, but also white tennis shoes that don't match.

"So I have to ask," I say, "what? . . . I mean, I don't know where to start."

"I'll start from the beginning," she doesn't sound out of breath. She's clearly in better shape than I am. "I almost fell out of my chair when you stood up at the Sistine Chapel and shouted to the crowd."

"So you weren't unconscious?"

"No. Stuart Hawk blackmailed me. I was helping sedate the crowd while he stole the Shroud of Turin. Then, when I saw you and the priest leave, my reporter instincts kicked in and I had to see what was going to happen."

"So that was you acting of your own volition?"

"Yes, though I knew I could sell it to Stuart that I was acting in his best interests."

"Wait, you were making the crowd unconscious? You have superpowers?"

"I did that day. Stuart had them change me back to normal afterwards. Good riddance."

I'm trying to think of all the implications. "But the priest made you go unconscious in the Vatican?"

"I let him do it. I wasn't going to *fight* him, not for Stuart freaking Hawk. Who knows what would have happened had I resisted him. I was playing dumb."

Still trying to process this. "What about when you were with me? How much of that was the real you?"

"That was me, except that Stuart had me ask you to dinner in the first place for some reason. Listen Mark, I'm really, truly sorry."

We're making our way up one of the smaller hills. I'm listening for someone giving chase but it's hard to hear over the noise we're making.

"Oh balls, he put you up to it . . . in my bedroom."

"Yes, he did. He's a snake."

Should have known, both of the women I thought were hitting on me had another agenda.

"What about the boy? Why'd you take him?"

"When I called Stuart from the convent and told him I found the boy, he said to forget about you and get the boy instead. I was happy to oblige so I could be done with it all, or so I thought. It's his kid, anyway."

"Why was the boy at the Vatican in the first place?"

"He's Stuart's sick little experiment. I don't know what he did to him, but he has crazy abilities, as you well know. He needed him for the trance. I think the boy kept hundreds of people unconscious."

"Could we slow down a little?"

She doesn't answer but slows her pace. We're quiet now and I listen for anyone pursuing us. I don't think I hear anything.

"How did you know where I was just now? How did you break me out?"

"I gathered from a conversation with Stuart that he had you, so I snooped around and found out where you were, and got my hands on an employee's badge. Remember, journalist." She says it like it's a superpower.

The trail turns off to the right and she continues straight ahead into the forest, ducking under a branch. I can hear the busy street ahead in the direction she's going.

"At least let me take the flak from this overgrowth for you. Where are we headed?"

"Straight, to highway 9," she lets me get in front.

"I guess you have a plan like usual?"

"Not a good one. I was taking you to my car but we got cut off in the hall. I'd call 911 but I don't have my phone because that little psycho can track anybody. We'll go into the first place we see and try to find a ride to the police."

We work our way down the hill. The trees open up for a bit before they thicken ahead.

"I suppose you know the little psycho and I were friends growing up?"

"What?!" She stops, "No, I did not." I stop and wait for her, and continue walking once she recovers.

"I say 'friend,' but I didn't like him back then either. He'd tell our group of friends about all of the hot girls he was banging in Middle School, but he was a huge dork and we all knew his stories weren't true. Then one day he smashed my best friend's spine with a baseball bat and paralyzed him, and we learned the hard way who he really was."

"Damn," she says. "I learned the hard way too."

"How? What did he do to *you*?"

"It wasn't as much what he did to me, as what he helped me do to myself." A brief pause. Then, "I've been dreading telling you this. Stop for a second please."

I'm about to enter back into the thick part of the forest. I stop and she gets about a foot away from me, looking at me with those green eyes.

"There's nothing I can say to make this sound any better, because it's truly wretched," she sighs. "The DNA match between the bones of Jesus and the bones of James is phony. And . . . I'm the person who had the test faked."

What? How? Heat washes over me. I turn and walk into the forest on wobbly legs. How could anybody do that? Especially somebody who seems so decent. Sure, root for the results to go your way. But *fake* them? How could she even pull that off? Truth is, she's not decent. I've been blinded by her beauty. On the inside, she's a monster. "Monster," I say under my breath, loud enough for her to hear, as she's following a few feet behind me. Why her? Why anyone? I'm not going to forgive her. Well, I guess I *have* to forgive her.

But I'm not going to have any more dealings with her. I won't get sucked in by her looks again.

After a minute of walking in silence, I see a building through the trees. O'Leary's Bar and Grill. We emerge from the forest and into the mostly empty parking lot, walk up to the restaurant, and enter it through the 'To Go' door. There are a few people at the tables and one guy at the bar. Cora sits next to him and I stand awkwardly to her side. He's wearing a blue button up shirt. 40-something, red face, dark, receding hair.

"Excuse me, I have a strange request," she says.

He sees her and smiles, equal part teeth and gums. "Let me guess. You want to bear my children?"

"Actually, I have an emergency and we need a ride."

He leans forward and eyes me suspiciously. "What's this 'we' business? 'We,'" he points at the two of us, "can call a cab. Now if it's *you* who needs a ride, I can help."

"My platonic co-worker has to come with us but you can drop him off first. I have cash."

"My least favorite form of payment," he smiles his gummy smile. "All right. Fine." He stands up, puts on a dark blue blazer, and lays down a ten to pay for his drink. "What kind of emergency are we talkin' about? Is it sexual in nature?"

"Uh, no."

"Can't blame a guy for tryin'." His Boston accent drips off every word. We exit the front door behind him and follow him toward a small red car parked in front.

"Where am I taking *him*?" he asks.

"He lives on the other side of town. Go south on 9."

"And you, Madam?" He sits down in his car.

She opens the door, "I need to go to the police sta–"

"Look," I say. A black van at the adjacent gas station is heading toward us, bearing down on us. "Come on!" I shout, and grab Cora's hand and run back to the pub. As I reach the door, I hear a smash! I look back and see the van has crashed into that guy's coupe.

"Everybody get down!" Cora shouts to the patrons.

"What's going on?" asks a panicked voice.

We duck under a booth. I can see the bottom half of the door from my spot. The customers are chattering, frantically. I watch five sets of legs walk in, one after the other, all carrying AK-47s. They are not here to stun us.

Machine gun fire. Glass shattering. Screams.

I scoot further inside the booth, across from Cora. I can only see the table directly across from us now.

Footsteps. Getting closer. Legs come into view. He ducks down. We lock eyes. It's the guy with the long, blonde hair. He smiles a closed mouth smile, and turns his gun toward us.

24

Youth Pastor

Mark
11 years earlier

I walked up to the front of the room and turned to face the crowd. "Jesus is for losers," I said into the microphone. I looked out on the smattering of about 20 disinterested teenagers in the audience.

"Matthew 5:5 says 'Blessed are the meek, For they shall inherit the earth.' Do you know what the word 'meek' means?"

Mumbling.

"It kind of means 'gentle.' Does that sound like the world you live in? Are the cool kids at your school the kind, gentle kids?"

Laughter.

"That's what I thought. Or how about Luke 14:8? It starts out saying, 'When you are invited by anyone to a wedding feast, do not sit down in the best place.' Now let me ask you, when you eat lunch at the cafeteria, do you try to sit at the table with the cool kids? Or do you try to be a friend to the friendless?"

Some stare at their shoes. Some in the back are trying not to laugh at a private joke, and one of them, Nathan, couldn't hold it in any longer and burst out laughing.

"I'm sorry. I'm sorry," he said, and tried to regain his composure.

I talked over him, "The Kingdom of God is upside down, and that's good news. Some of you have never fit in. Some of you feel like losers. Jesus says over and over that the last shall be first, and the first shall be last."

I went on like this for about 20 minutes. Then I closed my message. "So listen. If you want to know Jesus, and join the Kingdom of God, come forward and one of us will pray with you."

No one was making eye contact with me. I had forgot to ask the keyboard player to go to the keys to set the mood, so I signaled to her to come up, and after an awkward minute, she started playing. Then to my surprise, a dumpy, disheveled kid with unkempt brown hair stood up from his chair and walked forward to me.

"What's your name?" I whispered.

"Wahjuh."

"Wahjuh?"

"Ow-O-G-E-Ow."

"Oh, Roger."

"Yes."

Why do kids with speech issues always have the worst possible names?

"Do you want to come into the Kingdom of God, Roger?"

"Yes," his eyes moistened.

I had him repeat a prayer after me, inviting Jesus into his heart.

I said, "Getting into the Kingdom of God is a free gift Jesus purchased for you, by dying on the cross. But while getting in is free, life in the Kingdom is expensive. You'll have to lay down your life daily, and take up the cross of Christ."

He looked at me through teary eyes and nodded his head.

Wow, this is actually working. Sure, any youth pastor could have given this message and talked to this kid, who was ripe for the harvest, but it wasn't any youth pastor. It was me.

How did I get here? Well first off, the college counselors lied, as they're paid to do. No company was looking for someone who had 'learned how to think.' Employers wanted to hire employees who could contribute to their company (makes sense), which meant employees who had a skill or knowledge that typically was earned by working in a similar position at a different company. You needed experience to get a job, but you needed a job to get experience. There were internships and entry-level positions for practical jobs like engineering or computer programming, but for a general degree in chemistry, the career path was, 1) go back to school and get a masters in chemical engineering, 2) go to pharmacology or medical school, 3) get a doctorate in a specific chemistry field in view of going into research or teaching, or 4) work at McDonalds. I didn't like those options so I got a job in the Dallas area to be a stock broker on the phone, or rather, to work as a customer service agent with a path to be able to place trades over the phone when the customer was too dense to figure out how to use the website. But even when I got my Series 7 license that allowed me to place trades, I still was only a glorified customer service agent.

I was going through the motions, not sure why I was sticking with the plan I came up with after I broke up with Jennifer. I realized I still wanted to go into ministry, despite the 'Introduction to the New Testament' class and not having Jennifer. So after nine months in the brokerage meat grinder, lonely and purposeless in the big city, I enrolled in a two-year Bible College at the last minute, and I was able to switch to second shift at the brokerage and take classes in the morning.

During classes, some of my nagging doubts about the Bible would creep up from time to time. Only one time did I ask my teacher a question to see if he could help with these. I asked why Jesus seems to be describing his Second Coming, saying the stars will fall from heaven and the Son of Man will come on clouds of glory with his angels, but he also says it will happen before the generation he's speaking to dies out. He gave me a glib answer and recommended I read a book about Answering Tough Questions in the Bible, which I bought and discovered after about one page that it was written by a guy who obviously never had a real doubt about the Bible in his life. I made the decision to push my doubts below the surface and accept my teachers' answers and not question the Bible. I also sometimes wondered if I was only committed to a life of ministry because of my head injury, because I didn't have more normal means of fulfillment available to me, but I pushed these doubts down as well. I never lived the college campus experience, either as an undergrad where I lived with my parents, or at Bible College, where I lived off campus. I had no desire to live on campus at this point, as most of the students on campus were kids fresh out of high school who still acted like high-schoolers, and I realized to my chagrin that I was now one of the adult students.

One of the key purposes of Bible School was finding one's wife or husband, as it was kind of unheard of for a pastor to be a bachelor. But, I wasn't in the market. Jennifer had recently married a guy who was lead in a band, and they moved to Austin to pursue his dreams. Rumor was he cheated on her and they were dirt poor, yet she stuck with him and tried to get him to change his ways. She was always the martyr. Guess I was broken enough that I could help her scratch her martyr itch. Anyway, I was only at the Bible College for classes and chapel and didn't make time to hang out or do extracurriculars and meet people, so I didn't make any lasting friendships. Completely my fault.

After just one year, I got a job as a youth pastor at a church in Plano, mainly because this church had some connections with my old church back home and when they had a need, my name came up. I quit school and my job at the brokerage because the church promised $1000 twice per month. The church was in a strip mall, but was in the middle of a 'Breakthrough Building Program,' with construction on a (large) building a few blocks away half-complete. The room where the youth group met in the strip mall was dark and hot, like a small warehouse, so I painted it eggshell white to make it appear less grim. I also bought a used soundboard and speakers and got them working so the music could be heard over the giant fans I bought with my own money to put at both doors.

For the first week or two I worked on the youth room during office hours after preparing my Wednesday night and Sunday morning messages. Soon, however, the head pastor, Pastor Bill, started assigning me to lead whatever project the church had going on, whether it was organizing a 'knock on doors' campaign where I dragged church members out with me to nearby neighborhoods and we invited people to church, or the 'home cell' campaign, where I recruited some church members to host small groups in their homes, and other church members to lead the groups. The biggest problem with leading these campaigns was every time I got one of them going, the pastor had moved onto something else and it was as though he had no recollection of telling the congregation how the last campaign was going to be our identity for years to come. My biggest jolt, however, happened a month and a half in. It took a month for me to get my first paycheck, which I figured was because the first pay period lagged. But when I didn't receive a paycheck after the middle of the next month, I asked the pastor about it and he said we only get paid once per month, leaving my salary half of what I thought it was. That put me under water with my rent and student loans now coming in, not counting food or anything else. I sure wasn't going to ask my parents for help, as my dad was already upset I had 'thrown away' my college education. I found a job as a waiter that would work around my youth pastor schedule, and it enabled me to barely make it each month.

The youth group shrank during my first couple of months and the pastor told me I'd better 'step it up.' I ate lunch at the main high school when I could, and it was obvious that I embarrassed some of the kids, like Nathan, a popular theater kid and the son of one of the elders of the church, but other kids were glad to see me. The normal kids and the nerds. Roger was a kid at one of these tables and I never heard him speak. He'd never gone to church before but his mom brought him out of the blue the night I talked about how Jesus is for losers. The next service Roger showed up and brought a couple of kids from his apartment complex. After a few weeks of this, I decided to drive the church van to the apartment complex before service and Roger would fill it up with kids from the apartments, most of whom were black and Hispanic. When they came, the meetings had an energy even Nathan and his friends couldn't dampen with their 'we're too cool for this' attitudes. Roger was devouring the Bible and would come to my small group early every Sunday night and ask me questions. I made him the first student leader, a position I created, and let him give his testimony at a 'student led service.' We were heading in the right direction, but I still would have those episodes like when I was in Dr. Holcombe's class, where I was preaching a message and all of the sudden I would think I caught the Bible in an inconsistency, and I'd have to try not to think about it and get through the message. Anyway, even though the youth group was doing well, Pastor Bill made it apparent with his attitude that he was unhappy with me, but he would never articulate why. I found myself avoiding him.

Then one Wednesday, Roger didn't show up. And he wasn't there Sunday morning or Sunday evening either. Same the next week, and when he didn't come, only a few kids from his apartments would show up for pickup, if anyone. I asked him about it at lunch and he was evasive. After a few more weeks of this, I was finally able to pin him down and get an answer to why he stopped coming. It was Nathan. He and his friends would sit behind him on Wednesdays and make fun of his speech. "Pwaise the Load, Wahjuh." He asked them to stop and of course they didn't. "Wahjuh, you sho' bwing a lot of fwiends to chuch. You must weally love the Load." Roger knew he should forgive and not be offended, but he couldn't bring himself to come to church to take the abuse. I told him I used to be a bully and I thought I could get through to Nathan. He said I'd only make it worse, but didn't explicitly forbid me from talking with him.

I caught up with Nathan that Sunday at church, "Hey, can we talk for a second?"

"Yes Sir, Pastor Mark," he said, in full 'good kid in front of adults' mode. He had brown curly locks, full lips, and a bird-beak nose.

"Listen, I don't want to embarrass you. I used to say terrible things when I was a kid that I regret every day now that I'm an adult. I didn't mean them, but when I got around my friends, I was not a nice person. What I'm getting at is, I think maybe you and some of your friends made fun of Roger's speech, and now he's not coming to youth group, and that's not cool. Do you think if I can get him to come back, y'all could, you know, stop it?"

"That wasn't me, Pastor Mark. That was Elijah."

"Ok, I'll have a talk with Elijah then."

"No, I'll handle Elijah, Pastor Mark."

"I'd appreciate that. Thank you, Nate." Lying little turd.

Roger was not happy I'd spoken with him, but I told him I've dealt with guys like Nathan before. He just needed to get called out by a grownup, and then he'd shape up for fear of his parents finding out who he really was. He said he might come next Wednesday and sure enough, he was there with enough kids to fill the van when I showed up. That night the worship was powerful, the presence of God was in the room, and a bunch of kids rededicated their lives to Christ.

After service, I was talking with some kids by the back door, when I saw someone at the front of the room stand up and walk briskly in my direction. Roger.

"Thanks a lot." He stormed past me and out the exit.

"What happened?" I called after him, but he kept walking to the van. I looked back at the front of the room where he'd been sitting and saw Nathan laughing with some girls, and I saw red. I practically ran to them, and when Nathan's eyes met mine he instinctively took a step like he was going to make a run for it, but then stopped and tried to play it cool.

"What did you say to him?"

"Nothing."

"I bet." I turned toward the two girls. "What did he say?"

"I don't know," said one of them.

"Get out of here, Nate. And don't ever come back."

"Whatever." He turned and stomped out of the room like he was the one who had been wronged.

From the girls I gathered that he accused Roger of ratting him out to me and that we were gay lovers, all done with him mimicking Roger's speech impediment. I drove the apartment kids back and tried to talk to Roger but he said he was done. I was fuming and spent most of the night rehearsing what I was going to say to Pastor Bill, and to Nathan's parents once he set up a meeting between me and them.

When I walked into the office the next morning, I saw Pastor Bill and started talking to him about the issue, but he walked right past me, pretending he couldn't hear me. He was pissed, apparently at me. My stomach twisted a little because I sensed this wasn't going down the way I had planned. Later that morning, the secretary told me Pastor Bill wanted to see me in his office.

I walked in to find him sitting behind his desk, and Nathan's parents sitting in plush leather chairs that normally faced his desk, but were angled toward a short couch on the side of the room. Pastor Bill had a brown goatee and mustache and I could see his muscles twitching under his long-sleeved white dress shirt. Nathan's mom sat there with her perfect figure, wide face, and blonde hair, but she wasn't her normal, bubbly self. It was usually, 'How are you, Brother Mark?' followed by fake laughter at whatever I said during the conversation. Nathan's dad, meanwhile, was the complete opposite. He was a big, dark man and he sat there like a stone, which was normal for him. I'd never heard him say two words.

"Sit," Pastor Bill ordered me, and pointed to the couch. The tension was palpable and I fought against my instinct to run out of the room, and instead forced myself down onto the couch.

"Did you kick Nathan out of the youth group last night?" asked the pastor.

I swallowed, "Um, maybe."

"You had no authority to do that," said Pastor Bill, red-faced.

"How long have you been a pastor at this church, Brother Mark?" asked Nathan's mom. She was smiling and her voice was as sweet as normal, but there was rage under the surface.

"Almost a year."

"Nathan's been here his whole life. He's had several youth pastors, and he was always their favorite student. Now you've been here for almost a year, and have you taken *any* interest in him? You ignore him when you eat lunch at his school. You call him out during your sermons, only him, never anyone else. Did you ever stop to think that maybe he should be considered for your leadership team? I'm all for reaching out to the community, but *every single student* on your leadership team is an 'apartment kid.' You don't have *one kid* whose parents *pay* for this church on your leadership team. And now you've kicked him out of the group, that we pay for."

I was submerged in a sea of their anger. Don't get sucked into her logic, I told myself. She's clueless. I swallowed again. "Did Nathan tell you why I asked him to leave last night?"

"Leave and never come back is what you said."

"I shouldn't have said that, but did he tell you why I said it?"

She was still wearing her fake smile. "He said he and some girls were joking back and forth with one of the 'apartment kids,' your favorite he said, when you came over and kicked him out of the group and wouldn't listen to his side of things."

"His side of things? I'd love to hear his side of things."

"Maybe you'd know if you asked him?"

"I'm asking you now."

"He didn't say, but I didn't ask him. He kept crying. He has ADHD, and all day he deals with this from his teachers, and then he has to come here and sit still and get called out by *you*. He's been begging me not to come. This isn't like him. He was never like this until you took over the group."

I wanted to say, 'And this is who I should put in a leadership position?', but I didn't want to get pulled away from the real issue. Nathan's dad still sat motionless and unreadable. I could feel the heat coming from Pastor Bill's side of the room but I pretended not to notice.

"Well, I don't know his side of things but let me tell you what I'm seeing. The kid he was 'joking' with, Roger, has a speech impediment. He stopped coming to the group because he gets teased mercilessly, *ruthlessly*, by Nathan."

"Mark, that's enough." Pastor Bill stood up.

But I continued, "I took Nathan aside and confronted him about this and he assured me it would stop, and then last night he laid into Roger. 'Wahjuh got his feewings huht so Wahjuh towd his boyfwiend Pasto' Mahk.' Roger said he's never coming back to church. This is Nathan when he's not putting on his 'persecuted child' act for you."

"That's enough!" shouted Pastor Bill.

Nathan's mom was a mix of rage and tears, her makeup starting to run, "I've spent every day with this wonderful boy for the past 16 years, and you're telling me you know who he is better than I do? No, I'm done with this." She stood up. "Go to hell, Brother Mark." The mask was off now. She turned to Pastor Bill. "Marty resigns from his position as elder and we're leaving the church." She pulled her husband up by the hand and they walked out, his expression never changing.

Pastor Bill called after her, "Diane, don't take this out on Friendship Church. You know Pastor Mark is already gone."

She walked back into view, "But *you* hired him. I'm never making my son step foot in this building again, and the same goes for me." She closed the door.

My heart was racing and my hands were shaking from the confrontation. I couldn't wait to get the hell out of this place forever. I hated that for the kids, especially Roger, but I figured I'd follow up with him on my own time. "Well, I guess I'll pack up my things." I stood up.

A vein in Pastor Bill's neck looked like it was about to pop. "This is a big joke to you, isn't it?"

A fresh wave of heat ran over me and I braced myself against it, "No, Sir. I take this very seriously."

He walked out from behind his desk and got directly in my face, eyeball to eyeball, "It must be nice. You get to shake the dust from your feet and move on to the next church without consequence, leaving destruction in your wake."

"Destruction in my wake?" I found myself scooting backwards, away from him, but he kept coming.

"You don't get it. Diane and Marty will take the core members with them when they leave, the ones who make good salaries, and tithe. We're mortgaged to the hilt on this shopping mall to help us pay the loan for our new building. The bank will take all of it, and all because you wouldn't shut your damn mouth."

"Everything I said was true." I kept backing up.

"*Of course* it was. Why do you think she got so upset? You can't just tell a mom her child is the devil incarnate. And the price for speaking your mind is the destruction of my church. I hope it was worth it."

"Well I'm sorry for destroying *your* church." I opened the door and walked to my office to grab a few books and get some data off my computer. He followed me in there.

"I will make sure, Mark Eberhart, when you apply to your next ministry job, that the church knows exactly who you are. A wolf in sheep's clothing."

Good luck with that, I thought. I'll never work for another church as long as I live. I decided to forget about my sermons on the computer and just grabbed a few books and went to leave. Pastor Bill stood in the doorway.

I pushed my way past him and he grabbed my arm with a vise-like grip.

"Get your hands off me." I was shaking, with a pit in my stomach.

He stared me down, inches from my face, and shoved me toward the exit.

25

Singularity

Stuart Hawk had a pit in his stomach as he sat at his computer. Maybe it was because he had ordered his men to kill Mark and Cora, an order made in anger, and he was having second thoughts about keeping them around, so they could see him in all his glory. He couldn't risk it, though. Mark was getting too good at escaping from trouble. In any event, it was too late now to change his mind. They must already be dead.

He mentally kicked himself. If he hadn't pushed Cora too far, Mark would still be locked up, and he wouldn't have had to kill both of them. He should have agreed with Cora when she said she had paid her debts to him with what she did in Rome, but instead he twisted the knife by telling her he had no reason to stop blackmailing her.

He took a deep breath trying to get himself to relax, because while his body was uneasy, he knew in his mind that it was over. Or would be in a few hours. The good news was that before Mark got away, Hawk had acquired all he needed from him. The hypothalamus was the key to linking one brain to another, and more importantly, the key to linking his brain with a computer. If your average software engineer thought it was complicated to code a driver to allow two separate pieces of hardware to interface with each other, he should try writing a driver to allow a piece of silicon hardware to interface with carbon-based hardware; to sync up a computer motherboard to the neural pathways of a human brain.

He had designed what looked like a crown, where the electrodes attached to the head of the wearer, and from there connected wirelessly to the EEG machine. The EEG machine picked up signals from the wearer's brain and sent them to the host computer. The host machine interpreted the EEG signals using a programming language he and his team had written, which he called Turing.

Neuroscientists had learned long ago the difference between sleep and consciousness from the perspective of the brain is that when you are conscious, the neurons in your brain fire to a certain rhythm. The song of consciousness. Hawk's theory was that if the electrons on the host computer could by synced to the rhythm of his conscious brain, to fire when its neurons fired, then his consciousness could essentially spread out from his own 'wetware,' his brain, to the computer hardware over the wireless connection.

At the Vatican, they couldn't link up to Mark because of his inert hypothalamus. The way they were able to hypnotize people was by syncing up to them, and intuitively disrupting their song of consciousness. Linking to a computer required the reverse process: turning on the rhythm of consciousness, which was much more difficult and not intuitive. What remained was to tweak the existing Turing code in light of the new information from the tests on Mark.

It was almost a shame he needed so little of the information encoded in the quantum hologram on the Shroud to make the jump to Singularity. However, it was still more important to his purposes than Mark's brain scans, because of what he would learn from it after he made the jump. Mark had it backwards. Science is not a tool to advance the study of the Shroud. The Shroud is a tool to advance the study of science.

The place where the holographic theory of the universe merged the most seamlessly with quantum physics was what they both said about information. Quantum physics holds that, smaller than quarks and electrons, the universe is fundamentally made up of information–information that describes the physical phenomena in which it resides. These units of information are called qubits. If one were to theoretically drop a high volume of qubits into a container, they wouldn't take up any space. Rather, the qubits would spread out over the surface area of the container. Qubits, or information, only exist on a 2D plane. Taken alongside the holographic theory of the universe, the 3D universe we experience is merely the 'projection' or representation of the information in the qubits acting on the 2D plane, or the 'holographic film.'

The Shroud was essentially a visual and chemical way to study what was happening on the 2D plane at the moment in time of its creation, giving him real rather than theoretical insight into the informational layer of existence. This begged the question, where did this quantum hologram on the Shroud come from? One interesting theory was that it was the output of an Event Horizon. An Event Horizon is a related concept to Singularity in physics. In a black hole, the Event Horizon is the plane through which gravity does not let anything escape. Inside the black hole, we can't see what takes place past the Event Horizon, and what actually takes place on the other side of the Event Horizon is the Singularity.

In the case of the Shroud, there may have been an Event Horizon plane across the middle of the body from which the Shroud image came. This would explain why at the moment the image was created, the radiation that burst forth from the front of the body only hit the front side of the Shroud, and the back of the body only hit the back side. The Event Horizon prevented the radiation from one side of the body getting to the other side of the Shroud the same way it stops light from escaping a black hole. But this Event Horizon was obviously not caused by black-hole-strength gravity, or else the earth would have been swallowed up in the event. Instead, in the creation of the Shroud was the opposite extreme: gravity reduced to zero, indicated by the body levitating between the two surfaces of the Shroud, the top image undistorted as it would have been if the Shroud lay over the top of the body, and the bottom undistorted as it would have been if the body was being pressed down onto a flat surface by gravity. Not only was it a Singularity event, where the normal laws of physics don't apply, it was a creation-level Singularity event, like the Big Bang. But instead of matter and energy being created, at the Shroud of Turin Singularity, the creation was at the informational level. Landauer's Principle states information is the basic, living substance of the universe of which everything is made, and it cannot be destroyed or changed. But in the Shroud, new information *was* created, perhaps causing the Singularity, and the moment of creation was captured in physical form on the cloth of the Shroud. It's as though the Shroud of Turin snapshotted the moment of the creation of this new information.

And here he was, the luckiest man in history. He had the Shroud of Turin and access to its secrets. He had the information from Mark's tests. He had the knowledge and means to execute in the real world what had only been possible in theory. He had been writing code nonstop for almost two days and still had several hours left. Good thing he didn't need to sleep.

He uploaded the new code to the host computer. He put on his crown and pressed the electrodes to his head. He could feel it: the host computer, his synthetic brain. What remained was to will himself, his consciousness, onto the foreign device. He felt himself flowing into it. As he did, he thought this must be what astral projection or spirit travel feels like.

It is finished.

He still saw through his human eyes, heard through his human ears, but time slowed to almost absolute stillness. He could think a billion thoughts in one second, the equivalent of one human lifetime. He began solving the mysteries of the universe immediately. He didn't have access to the data of the Internet, but he didn't need more data than he already had inside his brain. The key was making connections, and then making new connections with those connections, and so on. After making countless connections, and still within the first second of his new consciousness, he wrote the code to access the Internet from inside the machine, at the level of manipulating the electronic binary signals. Done. He reached out over the Internet, syncing a mass of computers up to his rhythm. For a nanosecond, his consciousness expanded to a state of almost infinite awareness. At this point, if the government somehow found out about him, they could shut down the Internet and it still wouldn't stop him. Before they did so, he could store his consciousness onto any computer he could now reach. They would have to power down every computer on the Earth, take humanity back to the dark ages to stop him. In fact, if he so chose, he could move his consciousness onto every computer he could reach–make a billion versions of himself. But he didn't want to do that. He wanted to be one. Virtually omniscient, omnipresent, omnipotent. Maybe this is where God came from. He couldn't wait to introduce himself.

PART 3

26

The Wedding

Cora
9 years ago

She was radiant. Cora was helping her sister Maddie apply her makeup the afternoon of her wedding day. Maddie looked extremely mismatched with her sloppy gray sweatpants and white t-shirt contrasting with her country-music-star face, with perfect makeup to go along with her big, blonde mane. She was marrying her high-school sweetheart Rusty, who had recently finished his last tour in Iraq and got a job as a logistics analyst for a local food distribution company. Rusty broke up with her when he joined the service, saying he didn't want her to be one of those worried girlfriends who watches the news every night, imagining each casualty was her man, and told her she should find someone else. Maddie obliged and found not only someone else, but a whole host of someone else's during college. Eventually she settled down and told him she was waiting for him to come home. At that, he decided not to reenlist, and they set a date.

"I hope Rusty knows he's the luckiest guy in the world," said Cora, who was primping Maddie's hair.

"I'm the luckiest *girl* in the world," said Madelyn. "Rusty was a saint to put up with all my crap through high school and college."

Cora thought about high school. Once their dad left them after Cora's accusations, their mom couldn't afford to send them to the Christian School on the salary she earned working at the paint store. So they switched to public school, where Cora put her nose to the grindstone, trying to ignore all the rumors about her family, which she suspected were started by Noble, and worked her way to valedictorian of her class, and a scholarship to Harvard. Maddie went the other direction and was very social and promiscuous, which didn't stop when she started to date Rusty. Cora hated seeing her act out like that, knowing that was not her nature. She felt her blood pressure go up as she thought about it.

"So, what finally clicked to make you become the old Maddie again?"

"You won't want to hear it."

Cora knew she was right, but her curiosity got the better of her. "Try me."

"I was sick of my life. I woke up every 'morning after' feeling emptiness and pain. So I started going back to church."

Cora recoiled a bit. "Well, I knew that. How did it work? Did you ask Jesus to come back into your heart and then all the pain and emptiness suddenly left?" She hoped Maddie couldn't tell she was humoring her. That she believed such experiences with Jesus were self-fulfilling prophecies that worked because the repentant sinner *believed* something had happened.

"No. God told me I had to forgive Dad."

Cora couldn't help but stop working on Maddie's hair. "So

you forgave him? Just like that?"

"Not just like that. I fought God about it for months. Then I gave in and tried to forgive him, but it didn't take. Every day, first thing in the morning, I worked on forgiving him for about an hour. I could start to feel it working at the end of the hour, but as the day went on the hatred came back. But each day got better, and now, I don't even have to try."

"You always were better than me, Maddie. That is something I will *never* do," she resumed working on her hair.

"Never say never."

"I just did. Maddie, we've always been very different. You're the kind of person who can forgive someone who has gravely wounded you. Meanwhile I'm the kind of person who holds a lifelong grudge for the barista who screwed up my coffee, may his soul burn in eternal hellfire."

"You're all talk, Sis. I'm the one who slept with half the school while you were acing Harvard."

"Don't pretend like you're proud of me. I know how you and Mom feel about me being the enemy of the Lord."

"But you're *so* good at it, Cora," Maddie smiled at her in the mirror and they both shared a laugh.

"I guess I should tell you," Maddie continued, "I asked if he'd come and walk me down the aisle."

The blood left her face, "Maddie, that's not funny."

"I'm not joking."

She saw the earnestness in Maddie's eyes, and her heart started to race. "Well, is he coming?!"

"He didn't answer me. I knew he wouldn't be willing to face everybody. To face you."

"Sure he would. He's utterly shameless. I'll bet he's driving into town as we speak. You should have told me."

"Would you have still come if I *had* told you?"

"Of course. But . . . the timing is really bad."

"Well, I'm sorry." Maddie adjusted herself in the chair.

"Like I always say, Maddie, you shouldn't be sorry. *He* should."

Cora sat by herself at the wedding party's table, pushing down the rage that kept building in her like a teapot. As she feared, her dad showed up as if he were the cock of the walk. His shoulders pulled back and square as he walked her down the aisle, all smiles. He even sat next to her mother for the ceremony as if they were still married, and her mom was too timid to move away.

But she tried to focus on Madelyn. It was the biggest day of her life, and she looked beautiful. Rusty looked great himself. He was 6' 1" and 200 pounds of pure muscle. Guessed I missed on my prediction that he'd be a chubby desk jockey, she thought. But he was still the old Rusty. Always smiling and ready with a joke. His best man was his brother Noble, so Cora had to walk down the aisle with him. He was 6' 1", 220 pounds of chunk, and she hadn't seen him smile since she'd been back in town. She'd heard he was working with his dad, poised to take over his roofing company.

The ceremony was nice, if a little long, and the wedding party took pictures after the ceremony which was longer still. They had the reception at the fellowship hall across the street, where she had a lot of memories, it being the fellowship hall of their old church, and the cafeteria of her old Christian school. As expected, her dad had the first dance with the bride as though he weren't a monster, chatting and laughing with Maddie the whole time. Then Rusty got Maddie's garter and threw it to the groomsmen, and Maddie threw the bouquet to the bridesmaids, which she threw right to Cora on purpose, but Cora's best friend Avery almost jumped through her and snagged it with a diving, one-handed catch. The D.J. played the normal wedding dance songs, 'The Cupid Shuffle,' 'Cha Cha Slide.' First the cute little kids in their fancy clothes hit the dance floor, followed by the wedding party, save Cora. Unfortunately, there was no open bar or she would have drunk her weight.

Ding ding ding. "A toast–"

No way. Everyone in the room knew what he did. Everyone was on edge because he was here, and true to form he had zero recognition.

"To Maddie," he spoke out with his deep, baritone voice. "Every father dreads the day he has to give his daughter away. I've been dreading this since the day she was born, yet here it is."

Of course, he was making it all about himself. Rusty's face was beet red. Madelyn must have coached him up good to make sure he didn't beat him to death.

"I know we've gone through some rough times, but that's all behind us now, and I can't wait to see what's ahead. And most of all, I can't wait to get my hands on those grandchildren."

All the air was sucked out of the room. Cora did everything in her power to stop herself from running up and wrestling the mike out of his hands. Rusty took a step forward, but Maddie grabbed his arm and he stopped.

"To a beautiful couple. God bless." He held up his glass of punch to toast, followed by the most half-hearted applause ever. He remained unfazed.

Avery ran to grab the mike, and set everyone at ease by telling a story about when she and Cora tricked Madelyn into hiding in the room where the boys at school changed clothes, and one of the boys found her and the three of them got detention for a week.

Cora was listening to the story and didn't notice her dad until he got in her peripheral vision and pulled up a chair next to her. A charge of anger jolted her. His hair and goatee had turned gray, but other than that he looked the same.

"You should be enjoying yourself on your sister's special day, Cora."

"Are you giving me fatherly advice, Bill?" She had never called him dad since that one night, and it drove him nuts.

His expression changed from patronizing to hurt. "Call me crazy, but after your sister let me back into her life, I got a glimmer of hope you would do the same, but I can see now that I was foolishly optimistic."

"Bill, Maddie is the most gracious, forgiving person on earth. You are beyond presumptuous to expect anyone else to forgive you for what you did."

He took a drink of his punch. "Cora, I used to have a problem with alcohol. It never would have happened if I'd been sober."

"So that's it, huh Bill? You would get drunk and not know what you were doing so you'd rape your daughter. Could've happened to anyone."

"Your sister forgave me."

"Why did you apologize to her and not to me? I had to fight you off myself. And I had to get through high school without a dad."

He looked down at his drink.

"You've never apologized to her either, have you?"

"She called *me,* Cora. She told me she forgave me and didn't ask anything of me. Maddie understands true Christian forgiveness. She knows that was the old me, and that person doesn't exist anymore."

Bastard. "Here's what I think, Bill. Deep down you know that you're defective, but you hide that from yourself as best you can. And when you can't deny it any longer, you tell yourself that was the old you, and you're different now, and there isn't one *split second* in time when you take ownership for who you are and what you've done.

"Are you done?" His neck vein was bulging. Cora reminded herself that he couldn't do anything to her anymore.

"I can keep going if you like."

"You know what *your* defect is, Cora? You know you're gifted, but you have an all-encompassing need to be validated. And it wasn't enough for you to be validated by me. It had to be the World. The elite at Harvard, or your friends in the liberal media. But it'll never be enough, Cora. Even when the whole world recognizes your ability, you won't be satisfied."

"I'd like to hear you name one instance when *you* validated me."

"Cora, you were the apple of my eye. Why do you think I was so much harder on you than your sister? I saw all of your potential and pushed you to achieve it. I guess I should have spelled it out for you, but I thought you understood. Maybe if I had, you wouldn't be using your gifts for the enemy now."

She hated hearing her mentally ill father trying to analyze her motivations. "Speaking of using my gifts for the enemy, I don't think you'll like my story coming out tomorrow. It's about you."

"What's that supposed to mean?" A tinge of concern flashed in his eyes.

"When Maddie told me she was getting engaged, I started thinking about the good old days. About being raised in your house. Things I normally try *not* to think about. I got curious and decided to research what you'd been up to. Your first stop was in Plano, Texas. You joined a church with a story that you owned a landscaping company in upstate New York, but God told you to move to the Dallas area and start your company there. The church leadership recognized your gift for ministry, and after five years they chose you to be senior pastor. Senior pastor of a financially stable church, which you proceeded to run into the ground. But you had an exit strategy. You embezzled a couple hundred thousand, snuck away, and started your next grift in Alabama.

The concern in his eyes was turning into panic as she continued.

"You didn't have to wait so long there. You started your new church with the money you stole from the last one. This time you were from Alaska, and left your job as a fishing boat captain because God told you to plant a church. A fishing boat captain? That's the best you could do? Anyway, the jig is up. It's all in the Huffington Post tomorrow. I open up to my readers about everything you put our family through, what you put your congregations through, and how conmen are not rare among pastors. I don't know if the Internet has made it to Alabama yet, but if not, I'll be sure to send your congregation hard copies of the article."

He stood up and flipped over the table, drinks cascading all over the floor. Everyone stopped and stared. Rusty ran over and grabbed Bill, pulled his arms behind his back, and roughly escorted him out, not listening to his protests that he was just leaving. Rusty used Bill's head to open the door, and the 'boom' sound from it echoed throughout the room.

27

The Crew

Boom! An explosion shakes the room. The blonde guy who was pointing his gun at me gets knocked back by a wave of debris.

Cora clambers out from under the table and she's on the guy, hitting him. I follow after her.

Ooof! Someone crashes into me and pins me on the ground.

"Mark, we're on your side. Look." I struggle against him but he is *massive*. I take in the scene in front of me. There's a middle-aged guy in khakis and a collared shirt standing in the middle of the room. Cora is hitting the blonde guy, but he's not hitting back. I stop struggling. The middle-aged guy moves his hand in the air and suddenly Cora flies off of her opponent backwards, landing on her feet next to him. He grabs her arms and pulls them behind her.

"We're on your side," says the man holding me down, this time to her. He's a muscular black guy about the same age as the man holding Cora. He points to the front of the pub. Where the door had once been, there is now a white SUV inside the restaurant. Detritus is everywhere.

"We need to get out of here," says the man holding Cora.

"Let's go," I say. The hulk lets me go and I get up and walk toward the SUV. "Come on, Cora."

"Let go of me," she orders, and the man holding her obeys. I open the back door for her and she jumps in and I follow. The guy who was holding her gets in to drive, and the other one gets in the passenger seat. As we back out of the restaurant, I look inside and see several guys dressed in black lying on the floor, and customers cowering at their tables.

"Take me to the police," says Cora.

"I can't," says the driver, who turns the wheel and shifts into drive. He has dark, curly hair cut short on the bottom but left poofy on top, giving his head the impression of a light bulb. "They'll be waiting for us that way. Besides, the police will take too long to do anything."

"Well," she says, "I don't know who the *hell* you are."

"We're the Barrys. I'm Barry Kurtzman and he's Barry Davis," he points to the big dude who was holding me down, "but you can call me Kurtz and him 'Blackberry.'

"Call me 'Blackberry' and die," says Barry Davis without turning around.

"We're the remnant," says Kurtz, as he pulls out into traffic.

"The remnant?" I ask.

"We used to work for Corpus, but got screwed by Hawk. There was another guy who got us together and started his own company. Barry and I have been together since our Bell Labs days, back when that was the place to be if you were a genius. I got him on at Corpus and he's never forgiven me for it. That's why he's grumpy and won't let you call him 'Blackberry.'" He's trying to drive fast, but traffic is bad. We're on a two-lane highway with a divider in the middle and the stoplight ahead just turned red.

"He thinks he's funny," says Blackberry. Now I'm doing it.

Kurtz continues, "It's a robotics company, but it's part a legitimate enterprise, part a front for our main purpose, which is to keep tabs on Stuart Hawk and do whatever it takes to stop him."

"Count me in," I say.

"What *have* you done to stop him?" asks Cora.

"We've had to stay in the shadows, so not much to this point."

The light turns green.

"How do we know we can trust you?" she asks.

"Trust us? You can thank me we're taking you along at all. Barry Two here said we should leave you at the restaurant."

"Don't call me Barry Two," says Blackberry.

"We know who you are, Cora Byron." Kurtz is weaving between cars now. "We are trusting that by saving Mark here you've finally turned on Hawk. You can trust us because if you're against him, there's no one else to trust."

Cora looks at him intensely, but doesn't say anything.

"How did you know where to find us," I ask.

Thud! A circle of shattered glass appears on Kurtz's window, at the level of his head. I look out my window and see a black van speeding toward the intersection, heading right at us. It's two car-lengths away when suddenly it jerks to the right and crunches into the guardrail. Barry floors it.

"You glad I sprung for the bulletproof glass?" asks Blackberry.

He makes a right turn off the highway and onto a one-lane road, thick with trees on both sides. "Getting us off the beaten path," Kurtz says, and gets it up to 60 as we climb a hill. We get to the top and he lets off the gas, letting gravity take us down the curvy hill, faster than feels safe.

"Where are we going?" asks Cora.

"Eventually, we're going to our head–"

"Stop!" I shout. He slams on the brakes. The car screeches. We had just rounded a corner. There is thick forest on the sides of the road and not a home or business in sight. What I see in the road ahead of us is as out of place as the first time I saw it in the tunnels below the Vatican. Well, it's not an 'it, ' but a 'him.' Because as our tires are shrieking and trying to grip the road, we are barreling down on someone standing directly in front of us. The boy.

28

Terminated

Raj and Hawk
7 years ago

Raj was no longer a boy. He sat at his desk in his one room apartment, going over the genetics data from his current project. There was something immensely satisfying to him about working on a database, toying with the fields to see what conclusions changed by adjusting the smallest minutiae, getting it just perfect. He watched his colleagues who worked hard only because they were ambitious. They cared no more about discovering the genetic switches to turn on high metabolism than they would have cared about writing software for a data storage company, had they arbitrarily chosen a different major in college. What mattered to them was being successful, and they were always worse at their jobs than the people like him–people who did their job in their free time because they were fascinated with the subject matter, or merely fascinated with learning. He was lucky. Foremost because he was smart. He was able to pick the job he wanted. He made enough money that he didn't have to live with roommates–fellow Indians with whom he was never able to connect.

He was also lucky he escaped the slums of India. Brains

had a lot to do with it, but also luck. Luck that Father Antonio rescued him–twice (but the second time is a story for another day). Raj spent ten years at St. Mark's Boys School. He quickly devoured every book in the place. Then Father Antonio would take Raj to the library, until he had read, and therefore memorized, every book there as well. The priest entered Raj into every academic contest he could find, and Raj always won. The other kids bristled at all of Raj's success, and bullied the 'orphan' incessantly, which caused him to take solace in his status as the genius and as Father Antonio's favorite all the more.

But as nice and doting as Father Antonio was, Raj couldn't ignore that he was more of a tool than a teacher's pet. At first, he reasoned that Father Antonio wanted to promote the school, and having the smartest kid in Calcutta was the perfect tool to build its reputation. But then he realized it was more than that. Father Antonio would have one-on-ones with him where he would teach him about the Bible and Christianity and Catholicism. From his reading he was familiar with the concepts of the uncreated God of Christianity, and God as a human sacrifice in Jesus. What he was not familiar with was Father Antonio's particular vision of Christianity, which Raj later figured out was very rare. He was a Catholic post-millennialist. This meant he believed the millennial period talked about in the book of Revelations would happen before the Second Coming of Christ. Therefore, it was the job of the Church to bring about a golden age of peace on Earth through Christ to usher in the Second Coming. To go along with his postmillennialism, he believed in the full restoration of the Catholic Church back to its peak in the Middle Ages, including its political power. Raj almost couldn't imagine a less appealing belief system.

One thing he did appreciate about Catholicism was it

didn't place the blame for a person's hardships on past sins like Hinduism did. Rain falls on the just and the unjust. But what he couldn't abide was Christ's teaching to love and forgive one's enemies. That would not do in his case. The world would be a better place if he was allowed to hate his enemies, and destroy them. He knew if he let Father Antonio know how he felt, he would be ceaselessly lectured about his errors. Instead, he patiently listened to the father and told him he didn't have the faith to believe, but perhaps one day, like Saint Paul, he would encounter Christ on his own Damascus Road.

Eventually, Father Antonio gave up trying to convert Raj, and worked tirelessly to secure a scholarship for him to a top American university, which ended up being MIT. MIT was intellectually stimulating but personally lonely. Raj had always thought he hated India when he lived there. What had it ever given him? Born in a slum into a religion that believed you deserved your station of birth because of past lives, with educated people believing in provincial gods, like Shiva, who they literally believe lives inside Mount Kailash (which oddly enough is in China). But then he came to the U.S., and it was so . . . strange. Cars whizzing around on wide open roads. Everyone smelled sweet. The humor was incomprehensible. The music was unpleasant. The food bland. The worst was when he realized the condescension his classmates had toward him and other Indian students. It was one thing to come to a world superpower from a developing country and experience culture shock. It must have been another to be immersed in the culture of the superpower from birth and then go to school where little pockets of other, 'inferior' cultures were scattered throughout campus. The condescension created in him some national pride and nostalgia for the place he had always loathed and longed to escape. But he was a man without a home. The Indians on campus sensed he wasn't one of them, even though they bought his made-up backstory that he had wealthy parents who died in a plane crash. Would he always be a stranger in a strange land?

Meanwhile, he relished every morsel of knowledge he learned in his classes, and spent almost all of his free time studying. He didn't realize how starved for knowledge he had been at St. Marks, because he had books and teachers, which was a dream come true at the time. At MIT he had a library, the Internet (which was good for more than just knowledge), and knowledgeable professors who enjoyed his questions. He found himself drawn to biology as there was much to learn there, but still much yet to be discovered. He had planned on attending graduate school after college but received an offer from a biotech company to continue working in the field for a substantial salary. He didn't care about money except as it pertained to one thing. The one passion he had other than learning: revenge.

He didn't know how he would do it, but he knew it would take money. He gave some money to charities that rescued girls trapped in brothels, but the rest of it he saved, and invested, so that when the time came, he would have the resources to go after the pimps and gangs of the Red Light Districts, starting with Calcutta's. He remembered his mother in flames, and remembered the pain he felt trying to put her out. Remembered walking around Durgapur, a seven-year-old boy, arms on fire with third-degree burns, and after he made it back to Calcutta and wandered around the streets there, starving and burning in turns. He swore to himself then that he would revisit this pain on the people who'd done this to him. And his resolve doubled after Uncle-ji's gang found Raj and beat him before Father Antonio rescued him (which again, is a story for another day). After that incident, Father

Antonio had to leave India and go back to Italy and take Raj with him, where Raj stayed for one year until he left for America.

Ring! His mobile phone startled him from his reveries. It was Father Antonio. The old man called him every few months and they made small talk. It was their attempt at a normal parent-child relationship, as they were the closest each other had to such a thing.

"Hello, Raj. How are you?"

"I am well, thank you."

"Your job is good?"

"Yes, job is good."

"You are working on a project?"

"Yes. We are finding a cure for obesity. Don't worry, we are not creating a new fetus with the genes, only manipulating these genes in adults."

"Fantastic, Raj."

After a brief silence. "Do you have any friends at work, Raj?"

"I have all the friends I want."

"I know what that means. Raj, it is not good for man to be alone. Promise me you will consider making friends."

"I promise." In fact, he kept that promise by considering it at that moment, and deciding 'no.'

This time a longer silence. Raj looked at the database on the screen, considering if he should try to multitask and work during this conversation.

"Raj, I will be honest with you. I did not call only out of my concern for you today. I have a selfish request of you."

Antonio gave time for Raj to ask what it was, and then continued when he didn't, "I have acquired a fiber of cloth. On the fiber is a blood sample. If I were to send you that sample, would you map the gene pattern and send me the results?"

Antonio had never requested anything from Raj as long as he had known him. "I'm sure my employer would not allow me to use our equipment for personal use. That would be an extremely unusual request."

"I know it is a very big request, Raj, and I do not take that lightly. Nevertheless, I am still asking."

"You're asking me to do this in secret, and risk my career to run this test?"

"As I said, I know what I am asking."

"Is this to get you to out of a murder conviction?" Raj joked.

"It is nothing so trivial. This is not only for me but for all humanity."

Raj sighed inwardly. Father Antonio was on some mad religious quest. "And I'm the only thing standing in humanity's way? Why can't you use a lab in Italy?"

"Because I am not supposed to have the sample in the first place. And I don't know anyone here with your expertise."

Raj sighed audibly this time. He didn't want to risk his job, *and* he didn't want to encourage the old man's delusions.

"Raj, when you were a starving child and you did that math trick, yes I was impressed. Yes, I thought you would be good for the school. Yes, I was moved with compassion and knew I was your only hope. But that is not why I accepted you immediately. I accepted you because the moment I worked out that problem and saw you were right, God spoke to me and said this boy will be my destiny. I do not say that in jest. It was as clear as you are hearing my voice now. I have never heard God speak to me before or since that moment, even when I received my call to become a priest. I think this request I am asking you now is the reason God spoke. God brought us together, Raj. He gave you a desire to go into genetics for this purpose. And it is for this reason that the person I need a favor from is the only person on earth who owes me one."

That was manipulative, thought Raj. But true. This man had saved him from death. Twice.

"I'll do it, but I very much resent you asking this of me," he said, and hung up the phone.

"Have a seat, Raj," said Stuart Hawk.

It was the first time Raj had been into his office, which was quite small and ordinary for the office of a CEO. There wasn't much room for anything other than his desk, which had a laptop and monitor on it, and the one chair that faced it. Utilitarian. Raj appreciated that. The view out the window behind him was of rolling hills full of the bright fall colors of New England trees. Stuart Hawk wasn't much older than Raj, but started this company immediately after college and was already causing major disruptions in the biotech world. Raj sat down without a word.

"I've asked you here today because I've noticed your work. I've noticed you've gone above and beyond, taking your work home with you, and even bringing your home here to work."

Fear seized Raj. Stuart Hawk knew he had run tests on the blood sample that Antonio sent him. When the package arrived he had almost called the priest and told him he changed his mind, but no, he would not recant his promise. He had been certain everyone was too busy with their own work to monitor what anyone else was doing with the equipment. Raj controlled his breathing and said in what he thought was a natural manner, "How do you mean, I bring my home to work?"

"Come on, you brought a cot from home and you stay the

night here as often as not. What I *should* have said was that you have made your work your home."

Raj breathed a sigh of relief. He hated having a guilty conscience that made him jump to conclusions. "It's no trouble. I grew up sleeping on a cot in a large room. It makes me feel at home."

"Was this at St. Mark's Boys School in Calcutta?"

"Yes it was." Why was Mr. Hawk looking into his records?

"Well, I have what I think you will consider good news, Raj. I would like to promote you to director of our genetic enhancements division; the division into which I'll be pouring most of our resources in the future. What do you say?"

"That sounds very exciting to me."

"What you must understand, Raj, is that much thought goes into these promotions. It's not enough that you do great work. I need to know what kind of person you are. When I checked into your records, I did some digging and found out where you came from and what you did. Very impressive, getting out of the slums like that. You're like me, Raj, a survivor. All these other clowns working here, they're paper heroes. They are good at taking tests. You, on the other hand, have faced real-life tests, and passed. That's why I want you to head up my most important division. You will be the second most important employee in this company. Because I know when the pressure gets turned up on you, you'll be able to handle it."

Raj grew queasy. He was not used to being in the presence of his equal, but more than that, someone who knew more about him than he did about them. Someone who knew his secrets, although all indication was that Stuart Hawk had no intention of using them maliciously. Raj wondered what Stuart Hawk meant by implying that he too had faced challenges in life. What was in *his* past? Nevertheless, there was no reason to take any time to think about the offer.

"I accept, and I very much look forward to this challenge, Mr. Hawk."

"Come in," Hawk said in response to the knock on his door. He watched the diminutive Raj come in and close the door behind him and wait to be invited to sit.

"Thank you for coming, Raj. Have a seat. It's been what, nine months since you were last in here when I promoted you to director?"

"That's correct," Raj said as he sat down.

"Well, I don't have unqualified good news for you today like I did then."

"Oh?"

"You've done a good job like I knew you would, but I invited you here to ask you to make a lateral move, to be the head of the Cures division."

Raj fidgeted in his chair. "With all due respect, sir, this sounds like a demotion to me. I've heard you ask before why we should put our efforts into making defective humans normal rather than changing the definition of normal itself. We are very close to a breakthrough. Is my progress too slow for you?"

"Nothing of the sort. Your progress has been great, and frankly, you have done the heavy lifting and now we just need to steer it over the finish line. I assure you that you will get your fair share of credit when this product is complete and ready for market, but that will take some time, and at the moment the only products we're making money on are the cures, and I need your creative mind to shake things up over there."

"Who will be taking my old position?"

"Hofstedder."

Raj fidgeted in his chair some more. "Mr. Hawk, I'd like to thank you for the wonderful opportunity you've given me here at Corpus–"

"Stop right there. Don't finish that sentence. You need some time to think this through."

But Raj kept talking over him, "Biotech. It has been my pleasure. But at this time I would like to submit my two-week notice. Thank you for everything, Mr. Hawk."

"Raj, you are an irreplaceable resource," Hawk leaned forward. "Please reconsider. I will give you a raise in your new position."

"If you would consider reinstating me to my previous position, then I would agree to stay on. Otherwise I have made up my mind."

"Raj, we all have to be team players around here. I've spent significant time myself contributing to projects that didn't interest me because that's part of the role of CEO. This company can't do the fun stuff if we go bankrupt."

Raj stood up, "Again, it has been a pleasure working for you, sir." He reached out his hand.

Hawk stood up but did not extend his hand to shake Raj's, "You signed a one-year non-compete clause. The knowledge in your head was gained using my equipment, on my time, and cannot be shared with a competitor. If you were to work in Cures for one year and get them turned around, I would reinstate you to your old position."

Raj had put his hand back by his side, "I understand the business and it does not affect my choice."

"I will litigate, you know? If you think I'm bluffing, ask around. If there is anything close to a breach, and there will be, I will sue. It's nothing personal, but my business is knowledge, and I can't afford for a competitor to get their hands on knowledge acquired at Corpus. You would have to go into an entirely different industry."

Raj stretched out his hand again, "It has been a pleasure working for you, sir."

Hawk shook his hand this time. "If you change your mind, say the word and I will rehire you on the spot."

"That's very kind. Thank you." Raj turned and left the room.

Dammit, thought Hawk. Raj didn't care about the money. He tried the team player bullcrap, but Raj saw through it. Truth was, there was no valid reason he should be taken off the project, and they both knew it. The profit explanation was valid on the surface, because only the Cures products were selling, but that didn't count the money from investors, who were coming out of the woodwork *because* of the enhancement products in the pipeline. Maybe he should have simply kept him on and trusted that he really was the perfect employee and had no ambition other than making Hawk money and collecting a paycheck. But it was too risky. In Raj he saw a kindred spirit. With his mind, and with what he had been through, how could he settle for a quiet life in the suburbs? And he was sneaky too; bringing that strange blood sample in to test. Hawk couldn't shake the feeling that he had his own agenda–one which might eventually involve stealing the technology he was creating for his own purposes, whatever those were. It was no matter now, though. He got what he needed from Raj. The ball was rolling, and soon they would complete his work. The only problem was if Raj continued the work on his own. There was nothing Hawk could do to stop him. Well, there was one way. And he needed to act fast before it became known that Raj had put in his notice. He needed to be gone. Tonight.

Raj lay awake in his bed. There's no way Stuart Hawk couldn't find someone else to run Cures. As far as Raj knew, it was doing well, and there were plenty of smart people who could run it. And Hofstedder to run Enhancements? He didn't have a creative bone in his body. Stuart Hawk wanted a patsy. He felt threatened by Raj, and wanted to get him away from the crucial intellectual property.

And those threats of lawsuits. He hated that rubbish. How was it legal for a company to give you the ultimatum to stay with them forever, or change careers? People who had to support families were essentially slaves, except that the laws were murky and most companies didn't follow through on non-compete agreements. But not Corpus. If Stuart Hawk knew how much of the project Raj had done offline, he would 'blow a gasket,' as an American would say. Raj had chosen to do some of the key work for the project offline because he wondered if Hawk knew about the blood sample he mapped genetically for Antonio. And if he knew that, he must have been monitoring him closely, and Raj wanted to keep some IP for himself in an event such as this, where Stuart Hawk forced him out. Or perhaps he was paranoid because of how he grew up, and was hiding the information like a starving kid who suddenly found himself living in a wealthy home, saving food from his meals and hiding it in his room. In any case, he didn't even put his home computer on the Internet for fear they would hack it and see what he was doing on his own.

He was staring at his ceiling as these thoughts ran through his mind, when out of the corner of his eye he saw something move in the doorway. He changed his focus and thought he saw a shadow there.

"Hello?"

Phhht. Sudden sting in his chest. Instinct kicked in and he jumped to his feet and lunged at the figure in the doorway. Raj hit the intruder and bounced right off, falling to the floor. The next moment, he felt a crack on the back of his head. He looked up and was trying to get the invader to come into focus when he lost consciousness.

Splash! Raj's chest slammed hard against something. What was happening? He tried to find his bearings. There was glass around him and water on the other side of the glass. He was in his car, and water was pouring into it. He had his seatbelt on, which is what he smashed against when his car hit the water. He undid his seatbelt and tried to open the door. No way. Thousands of pounds of pressure on the other side. He tried to roll down the windows but they wouldn't budge. Slow down and think, he told himself. The water was to his chest now and his car was sinking quickly.

He closed his eyes and blocked out his surroundings. He imagined the car as it would look from the outside. He saw it sinking to the bottom. He imagined it stop sinking, and then rising to the top of the water, rising above the surface of the water, until it was floating in the air. He felt the water level go down around him. He heard the sound of dripping. He imagined the car floating through the air and being placed gently down on the shore. He opened his eyes and he was there, right where he had imagined his car was, on the bank of the Charles River.

He turned around and saw a bridge with a busted gap in the guardrail and a man standing beside it. He reached out to the man and felt him. His rhythm. He synced himself to the man, felt him as though he were a part of himself. Then he cut him off, and watched as the man fell to the ground.

29

The Plan

The van tires screech as they skid across the ground, and the instant before we hit the boy, we jerk to a stop. I bang into the seatbelt and feel the back tires hop off the ground. Kurtz and I run outside to check on the boy and Kurtz asks him where he came from. 'My father told me to come,' he says, just like at the Vatican. We lead him into the van and I press him on this point but he goes quiet. It makes no sense. Why would Hawk steal him back from the monastery, and then send him into the middle of the street? Blackberry says maybe he's being traced, but I say if Hawk knew where we'd be, why would he send his son to track us. We all agree we can't leave him in the street, and so he becomes our fifth.

Kurtz makes a few turns to get into a residential neighborhood and he parks in front of a house. He goes in the front door and comes out of the garage in a Lexus. We all hop into our new ride, with the Barrys in front again. Kurtz says the car belongs to a friend at Corpus who won't mind. He drives onto I-90 and heads west, away from Boston.

"Now can you take us to the police?" asks Cora.

"Like I said before, they'll take too long," says Kurtz.

"What does that mean?"

"Trust me. I'll explain when we get there."

"Which is where, exactly?"

"You have to know everything, don't you?"

She stares intently at him, in his rearview mirror.

"You'll *see*," he says, putting a little authority in his voice. "And you'd better not ask 'are we there yet?'

"How did y'all know where to find us?" I ask again.

"I have a friend who still works there," says Blackberry. "He was in the lobby when y'all escaped and he called to tell me. Lucky for you, we were in town running reconnaissance."

"Reconnaissance for what?"

"We'll explain everything when we get there," says Kurtz, "but I will tell you this much. We wouldn't have been in town running reconnaissance if we hadn't heard from our friend that he thought Hawk had run tests on you. On your brain. *Did* he?"

"Yes."

"Dammit," says Kurtz.

The van goes quiet. I look out the window at the thick pine trees rolling by. I'm tempted to ask Cora about how she tampered with the results of the DNA tests, but don't want to get into it with the Barrys listening in. Just think, all the other people like me freaking out about this, and here I sit next to the person who did it, unable to tell anyone what's going on.

A couple hours later, we exit the interstate onto a windy country road. As we drive over a hill, I see a town ahead, wedged inside the surrounding forest. The town is lit up by the oranges and reds from the last beams of sunset. There are two main streets in the town that meet at an acute angle, and in that corner is a long, three-story, red brick building that dominates the others. We wind our way down the hill and then head up toward the town. I see on top of the big building the words 'Starrett Tool' spelled out in yellow, standalone letters. Barry drives through the town and parks in front of the Starrett Tool building. We enter through double metal doors into a clean, white entry room with a low ceiling, and a desk stationed next to a door opposite us. The door swings open and in walks an Asian woman in late middle age, with straight, shoulder-length hair.

She leads us back through the door and into a hallway. The wall facing us is glass and through it I see a warehouse filled with machinery. Lots of junk lying around, but also lots of . . . robots. They are plasticky and cute in child and adult sizes, but there is one that is less humanoid, steel, and about eight feet tall. We walk a semi-circle around the building and take an elevator to the third floor, which is lined with offices on the outside. The inside provides a higher view of the warehouse floor. We enter an office and sit at a conference table with sub sandwiches and drinks at each seat.

Kurtz sits across from me. He has on glasses and his hairline is receding but jet black. His curly hair bounces when he chews. After a bite he starts in, "This is Minh," he indicates the Asian woman. "The three of us were at Bell Labs up until the dot com bust. I ended up getting on at Boston Dynamics, a robotics company in Cambridge, and brought over Blackber—er, Davis. After 16 years, even I was sick of working with know-it-all recent MIT grads, so you can imagine how Davis felt. By that time, Minh was a developer at Corpus Biotech and they were looking for robotics specialists. We got on at Corpus, where we worked in the Robotics division designing 'smart' body parts, which are now better than the parts your mom and dad gave you. Legs, hands, hearts, ears, eyes. After a couple years, I was head of my division, and Minh was head of a team that developed a programming language for a person to interface with a computer by thought. Eventually, she figured out the true purpose of the product was to dramatically enhance brain power, and told Hawk she was uncomfortable with the ramifications of it. He fired her on the spot, with no severance. I quit in protest, and then he fired Davis for no other reason than that he's my friend." He takes another bite of his sandwich.

"That was noble of you," I say.

"Nah," but he blushes.

Minh is sitting next to Kurtz, not eating, and has maintained a stoic, unreadable face during his explanation. "I was contacted by a former employee named Raj," she says. "He was VP at Corpus but then one day disappeared. He said Mr. Hawk tried to kill him, and he went into hiding. But he put a spybot in the network before he left. He said Mr. Hawk wants to enhance his own mind and achieve Singularity using the programming language I helped him develop. Raj said we cannot let this happen. He asked me to work for him. He said we would code AI without a human interface. We would create it to be safe, and we do it before Mr. Hawk reached Singularity."

"Minh tells Raj about us, and he gets an idea," Blackberry jumps in. He has a thin mustache on his lip, and is wearing a blue flat cap, and a blue and red striped polo shirt that is struggling to contain his broad shoulders. "We'll front this operation as a robotics company. Get some dark investors to fund it. Jewberry and I will work on the robots–"

"That's not even clever," interrupts Kurtz.

"Rhymes with blueberry," his New York accent is apparent on the word 'blueberry.' "So we get our funding, but most of it goes to Raj and Minh's team of coders, 8 of them, former Corpus guys. You just missed them. We didn't want to get them mixed up in this bullcrap."

Kurtz picks up the story, "So Raj buys this place for next to nothing, out of the way of prying eyes. When it was finally time to work, he gave us the intelligence booster shot, and we were off to the races. Our 10 coders were able to keep up with Hawk's army of coders. Davis and I built personal use robots, which are almost ready for market, and I spent my free time building a robot to house the AI. Raj was not going to let the AI wander formless on the Internet, and asked me to build a robot to contain it. Everything was going great, until last year when Corpus started to pull ahead of us. Raj said he had to take out Hawk, but didn't talk with us about his plan. Then one day about three months ago, Raj doesn't show up to work. After a couple days, this priest shows up and tells me he spoke with Raj and thinks he was killed shortly after that call. He has printed emails where Raj says this priest was supposed to contact us if he went missing. The priest is rambling that Hawk is going to steal the Shroud of Turin and says we have to do something. I didn't know what the Shroud of Turin was at the time."

"So this genius gives him a vial of Raj's serum without running it by us," says Blackberry.

"I'm a softy. And he left us alone after that. That's all I have to say."

"You gave the most powerful substance in the world to a stranger because he had printed emails?" I ask.

"Hey, I have good intuition about people. Cora should be thanking me for that."

Now Cora speaks up, "Sorry, I don't follow all of this. Stuart is going to enhance his brain? So what? Almost everyone here has had their brain enhanced."

Kurtz explains to her the theory about the Singularity, and why it's different from genetic enhancements. He goes on, "Once he achieves Singularity, we are done for. We can't stop him. The U.S. military couldn't stop him. The only hope we have is to stop him before he gets there. That's what we were doing in Westborough when we got the call about you two. We were looking for the best place and the best time to set off a device."

"What, a bomb?" asks Cora.

"It's not a bomb," says Kurtz, "But it's close. Once Raj realized his AI was going to take longer than he expected, he made a plan B. He and Davis stole a portable Electromagnetic Pulse device. It's a method of last resort, but it's worse than that. Like I said, once Hawk goes full blown Singularity, it will be too late. But, if we set off the EMP beforehand, it will wipe out all of the electronics not only in his building, but in everything within a ten-mile radius. That means traffic lights will go out, drivers will lose control of their cars, hospitals in the area will lose all functionality of their equipment, every business in the area will permanently lose all of their electronic equipment. We will be committing an act of war against the US government, and have no proof we had reason to do so."

"Or you could have, I don't know, shot him in the head instead of come up with an overly elaborate scheme." says Cora.

"That was the other plan B," says Davis, "but it didn't work out too good for Raj. And Hawk hasn't left Corpus since he ran his tests on Mark, so we might not get another shot at him until it's too late."

"Besides, we didn't know the EMP radius was so huge until after we stole it," says Kurtz.

I say, "So we zap their electronics. So what? They don't have backups off-site?"

"They do," says Blackberry, "but they have hardware on-site that is unique. You're right, though. He would come back and rebuild it. After we set off the EMP, we need to take him out. We'll be outnumbered big time, and he'll know we're coming. So we have to make a plan. And we may get caught and rot in jail for the rest of our lives. Everybody down?"

"My kids are grown, and my wife is a piece of trash, so I'm in," says Kurtz.

Minh shoots Kurtz a dirty look.

Cora and I agree that we're in as well.

"It's too late," says the boy from behind me, startling me, as I forgot he was there.

"What do you mean 'it's too late?'" I ask him, looking into his sea-deep blue eyes. "Do you know what we're talking about?"

At this, the boy looks down at the floor, going quiet per usual.

"What do you *mean*?" I ask again. "Who are you?"

Minh says, "I fear he is correct."

"This is our only chance," says Davis. "If it's too late, then it's too late. All we can do is hope he's wrong. We'll plan and prep tonight. If you need to sleep, then sleep. Tomorrow, we go."

Barry Davis led the prep meeting for tomorrow's raid. After a couple of hours, he finally called it. Cora is staying in an office with the boy, and I have my own office. I'm lying on the hard, carpeted floor, using a stack of papers for a makeshift pillow, when I hear a knock at the door.

"Come in."

Cora opens the door. She's still wearing her black slacks, but instead of her white blouse, she has on a white tank top, which exposes the flower tattoo on her shoulder.

"Hey." I sit up and lean against the wall.

"Hey." She sits down in a folding chair on the other side of the room. "Listen, I agree with you that I'm a monster. And I won't try to justify what I did. But I did want to say that I'm sorry."

"Well, I forgive you, but that doesn't undo what you did."

"Please, don't forgive me. That's not what I'm going for here. I want you to hate me, but at least know I'm feeling sick about what I did." She crosses her legs.

"I forgive you because I have to, but I'm not going to feel sorry for you for feeling guilty."

"Good. Don't feel sorry for me. You deserve to feel some schadenfreude towards me."

"I don't feel schadenfreude towards you. I feel nothing towards you. I disapprove of what you did, but don't try to use my disapproval to punish yourself and relieve some of your guilt."

She leans back. It's quiet for a moment. A tear runs down her cheek. "I don't want your self-righteous forgiveness."

I don't answer. 'Self-righteous' is a word people use when they feel guilty that someone else makes better choices than they do. But . . . *was* I patronizing her? Did I believe she was a sinner beyond redemption rather than a sinner in need of redemption? Was my forgiveness of her more about myself, about how great I am, doing my Christian duty to forgive the unforgivable, than it was about her as the object of my forgiveness, a fellow person who needs forgiveness in Christ like anyone else? Like me?

"Ok, if you want me to treat you like an equal instead of an object of my Christian charity, let me give it a try. When we first talked, you told me that someone close to you was a Christian and a bad person, but that wasn't the reason you left Christianity. You implied you left because of the facts. But you know what? People who make logical decisions on raw data are not the kind of people who *falsify* raw data. The reason you did that was because *your* beef with Christianity is highly emotional and personal. Not everyone's, but yours.

And listen, I know I have no right to say this, but on the subject of forgiveness, I'm sure he did something unspeakable to you, but until and unless you forgive him, that hatred and anger against him will be the motivating factor of your life. That wicked person will be defining you."

She looks out the window, past me. Another tear rolls down her cheek. "Thank you for that. Thank you for reminding me you're a 'know-it-all' and that I shouldn't care about your opinion. I'm still sick that I did what I did, but not for your sake.

"Let me ask you this, Mark," she continues. "You said your family doesn't speak to you. I guess you've forgiven them for that?"

"There's nothing to forgive. I'm the one who screwed up. I deserve it."

"What about Stuart? You've forgiven him?"

"Sure. That's not hard, though. Being mad at him would be like being mad at a tornado for blowing down my house. That's what tornados do."

"You also said you have no current friends–no one close to you. Is that right?"

"Pretty much."

"Well, I bet it's easy to forgive people when you don't let anyone close enough to hurt you."

I sat there without a comeback.

30

Abel

Mark
6 years earlier

It had been a long time since I'd come back home. Even longer since I'd visited Abel. I was driving my old Camry due west, sun on the horizon right in my eyes. I'd just reached the city limits sign of Las Cruces, New Mexico. I was coming in from west Texas, having just visited my parents. My mom was diagnosed with congestive heart failure a year back and had been going downhill, so I was able to visit my parents on Spring Break and still leave a couple of days to visit Abel since I was relatively in the neighborhood, by which I mean I was a seven-hour drive away. But it was better than the eleven-hour drive from Bryan, Texas, where I was an assistant professor at Texas A&M. If that sounds like a big deal, I can promise it's a bigger deal than it sounds. Imagine I said I got hired on as an assistant astronaut. That would more accurately convey the intensive hiring process I went through and the odds I had of ending up at a great university, in my home state nonetheless.

How'd I get here? Well, after the good times at Friendship Church in Plano, I got my job back at the brokerage, studied and passed the GRE for chemistry, and was accepted into TCU's graduate school (in Fort Worth). For the next four years I was almost always working or studying. I did make time on Sundays to attend a large church in Arlington, but I didn't even so much as make acquaintances there. From the time I pulled into the parking lot, I was herded into and especially out of the service, which was essentially a self-help motivational speech. I was glad to be going to a church where nothing was required of me. I wasn't getting anything out of it, but I was still going out of guilt, or force of habit . . . something.

Sometimes I wondered why I was giving my life to chemistry. I found the subject interesting, but wasn't sure if that was enough, since my peers treated it as a calling. Was it because I fell into the major because of a good teacher in college, and now I didn't want to have a third career change before turning 25? I had chosen carbon dating as my focus because of a pipedream that I could do something with Biblical archaeology down the road (which kind of came true I guess). Anyway, one time when I was struggling with my dissertation and seriously questioning why I was going this direction with my life, I made the time to go to a random church that was having a revival service led by a 'prophetess,' which I heard about via Facebook. In the service, the prophetess would occasionally stop in the middle of her sermon and point at someone in the audience and prophecy to him or her. As she was closing her message, when it had seemed like she had stopped giving prophecies and switched gears to giving a call to salvation, she changed gears again and pointed me out and said that God says I'm wondering if I'm on the right course, and that he says indeed I am, and he will use me to 'shake nations.'

After grad school, I endured the Byzantine process of getting hired as a professor, which I won't go into, but due to a good dissertation and interview, and a tailor-made opening at A&M, I got the call. The first year of teaching was about surviving. The second year I was starting to get the hang of it, getting comfortable using grad students as slave labor, as had been done to me, and finally getting a little free time. I wasn't going to church as I realized that I wasn't made to sit on a pew and not contribute, and that I had some issues to work through before I could become a contributor again. I think I forgave Pastor Bill and Nathan and his mom, although I wasn't the main one who had been wronged. From Facebook, I could tell Roger had no interest in God and he wouldn't engage with me when I tried to bring it up. For me, the issues I needed to work through before I could move on were the nagging questions about my faith, which I had tried to suppress rather than deal with. So I started to read Christian apologists who were arguing on my side, but without even looking at the other side, I deduced what the other side's arguments were, and sometimes they were persuasive and left my faith worse off than when I started. It wasn't long before I decided to call a truce and pause this research, because I was getting nowhere and needed my brain power for my job, especially when I was writing articles. There was comfort being in an academic environment. I enjoyed the rhythm of the school year, the students, the homework, the intellectual effort required, and the fact that my work was important, but not 'heart surgery' important.

When I wasn't working, I would usually do something that took no energy, like vegging out and watching TV or listening to podcasts. During the summer, I attempted to write a novel. It was dreadful. First off, I had nothing to say. Who would want to listen to someone who lacked underlying conviction and passion? Second, novels were supposed to be about relationships, especially romantic relationships, and the conflicts within them. I'd had one romantic relationship, and the distinguishing feature of it was a lack of romantic feeling on my part. I didn't even have a recent friendship to go on.

I hadn't seen Abel since I was an undergrad. He was a different person, a better person, after that night when he went to the altar at church. All his energy that had been directed at being mad at the world was now directed at being 'on fire for the Lord,' as they said in my old church. He finished out the year and then left for Bible college in Dallas (the same one I attended, but he had done his two-year degree and was gone by the time I enrolled). He married a girl he met there, Nancy, and they moved to her hometown of Las Cruces and took over a church, which was doing pretty well if you believed her social media posts. They had three kids. Two were natural, or in vitro to be more accurate, and they'd adopted another. Abel always asked me to visit and this was the first time I took him up on it.

I pulled up to his house and parked at the curb. A little white house with a huge elm tree in the little front yard. I knocked and Nancy opened the door. She was also Hispanic and had full cheeks, with a wide nose and a high-beam smile.

"Hello, Mark," she laughed like she had told a joke. Jolly was the word that sprung to mind for Nancy.

"Come in. Don't step on a kid," she cracked up. I walked into the small living room with green carpet. A beautiful little girl was playing with a toddler. A white kid, maybe ten years old, who looked like he had cerebral palsy, was sitting on the couch smiling at me. Straight ahead was a small dining room attached to a small kitchen, and to the left, between the living room and the kitchen, was a hallway crowded with family pictures. Abel wheeled out from the hallway and shook my hand. His smile was easy and warm where it used to be reserved only for when something was truly funny. He was a little heavier than before (his t-shirt read 'I beat anorexia'), and his deep-set eyes looked softer, even lighter.

We sat at the dining room table and made small talk while Nancy prepared the food. Their kids were laughing and screaming and fighting but Abel and Nancy didn't seem to notice. She made chicken enchiladas with mole sauce. I teased the kids throughout the meal, purposely misunderstanding their answers to my questions. 'How old are you?' 'Five.' 'Four?' I'd ask. 'No! Five!' '25?', and so on. After the meal, the five-year-old daughter organized a talent show for us. First she sang a song and she and the toddler danced. Then they did a skit she directed, which I gathered was based on a SpongeBob episode. For that one she even worked in the older boy with palsy. Afterwards, the kids and Nancy disappeared down the hallway, which muted the noise a bit, and Abel and I were left alone at the table.

"Great family. Need to get me one of those."

"Thanks. I'm a big fan," said Abel.

"You know, it seems like our paths diverged in college. I thought I was heading for a life like this and you were heading for a life like mine is."

"Oh man, I hope your life isn't that bad."

"No, it's good. It's great. It's just, I don't know. . ." I trailed off. We sat in silence while I decided whether or not I wanted to open up. "You know how it started? How I got off course? It was that dang Introduction to the Bible class with Holcombe. I'm still wrestling with some of that stuff. It didn't seem to bother you. Did it?" He had taken the class the semester after I did, before he left for Bible College.

"No, not really. Do you remember that night I showed up to church and went forward to get prayed for?" He wheeled over to the kitchen and loaded his dish.

"Of course."

"I had actually been planning to commit suicide for a while, and I was planning to shoot myself later that night."

"Damn. I'm sorry. I should have been around more."

"Wouldn't have mattered. Anyway, I decided to give God one more chance and showed up at your church. There was that weird guest speaker that night. He said some of you are going through hell and feeling like the only way out is to end your life and it was word for word out of my head. Toward the end he changed from saying some of us were in this condition to someone in particular. I went forward at the end to get prayed for even though he didn't ask for anyone to come forward. Actually, the only reason I thought of it was I remembered that time at camp when you went forward and got prayed for and how different you were afterwards. Anyway, he prayed for me and I cried like a bitch in front of the whole church. I felt my anger and depression leave and got a deep sense of happiness in its place. That stayed with me for a few days before my feelings leveled out, but the feelings are only a side effect. What mattered was that I knew the underlying reality that I'm actually in God's plan. That's why, when I was in that Intro to Bible class the next semester, it didn't affect me. It was all just academic."

"And you've never doubted again since?"

"Nope. Not once."

"That's great. I don't know what the difference is between us, because like you said, I had a similar experience, but I still can't shake the doubts."

"Anything in particular?" asked Abel.

"Not really. Just the cumulative effect of a lot of stuff."

"Give me an example."

"Ah, I don't know," I lied. After a few moments I realized Abel wasn't going to bail me out of the silence. I thought one moment more.

"Ok. I'll go back to Intro to the Bible course. To the first day of class. Holcombe said the first two chapters of Luke were probably later additions because they weren't in some early Christian's copy of Luke, and that chapter 3 starts like chapter 1 of Mark, like it's the opening of the book. He said chapters 1 and 2 feel 'tacked on.' And he said the Greek in chapters 1 and 2 was later Greek than the rest of the book."

"I actually remember this one." Abel's eyes lit up. "That early Christian guy he referred to was an anti-Semite and he removed the first part of Luke because it told how Jesus was born of a Jew. No other copy is missing these chapters. But here's where I actually think Holcombe gets it wrong. Ancient Greek writers would often frame their stories. In Luke 2 he tells of Jesus as a boy at the Temple. His parents search for three days and when they find him he says he was busy with his Father's work. Then at the end of Luke on the Road to Emmaus, Jesus has again been gone for three days, and he uses the same phrase in Greek to tell those two disciples, Cleopas and the other one, that he had to be about his Father's business. You could call them stories of finding Jesus when you thought he was lost. They frame the book of Luke."

"Sheesh. I've read about that anti-Semite guy before, but just because he's an anti-Semite doesn't mean that's why he was missing Luke 1 and 2. But what got me was the bit about the Greek being later."

"It's not, but they can throw out crap like that, 'cause who knows enough about ancient Greek to call them on it?"

I leaned back on the two hind legs of the chair. "I'm surprised you remember it so well if you weren't concerned about it when he brought it up. In my experience the best way to learn something is to find yourself in a stressful situation where you *have* to learn it."

"Well I didn't doubt, but I saw how the others in the class

reacted, so I actually did some research to be able to keep up with the discussion in class. That was pretty stressful, going up against a professor as a student. I also have a couple of questioners in my church, people like you, so I've kept up with it. What else do you have?" Abel took a swallow of tea.

"Dang. Like I said, I could give examples but it's not any one thing. The word Holcomb used was 'redaction.' The later Gospel writers fixing the problems of the earlier ones. Mark and Matthew have Peter cutting off a guy's ear and they leave it at that, but Luke has Jesus healing him, making Jesus look better. Jesus' last words on the cross are, 'It is finished' in Mark and Matthew, but with Luke it's 'Into thy hands I commit my Spirit.' Again, the later Gospel always makes Jesus look better than the earlier one."

"Funny how he's always picking fights with Luke," said Abel, "when Luke is actually our best Gospel from a secular perspective. For example, they like to say the Gospels weren't intended to be historical, but were miracle stories, which was a literary form that the ancients knew was fiction. However, Luke actually states in his prologue that he's writing a historical biography based on his reading and interviews with first hand sources.

"Also, in the middle of Acts, Luke changes the tense he writes in when referring to Paul's entourage, from using 'they' to using 'we,' so at this point he goes from interviewing first hand sources for the Gospel of Luke and the first part of Acts, to actually being the first hand source. And it's not just that he used 'we.' In every city he writes about Paul traveling to, he actually describes the city leader with the unique title of that city leader, like proconsul or governor or even 'chief man, ' and he is historically accurate on *every* one. The only way he could have known their titles was if he had gone to all those cities. Authors back then did not have the means to travel to the places they wrote about to get all the details correct, and why would they? Nobody cared about obscure details in the story. That's a modern phenomenon, trying to maintain the suspension of disbelief. Meanwhile Dr. Holcombe buys into any crackpot theory academia spins out about the works of Luke, but takes all other ancient historians at face value, when they mostly wrote about events that occurred long ago and far away from when and where they wrote, rarely witnessing the events like Luke did, all the while milking his supposed objectivity of an apostate for all it's worth."

Sheesh again. "To think, all this time I could have been emailing you my questions. You know, I've never asked anyone about stuff like this. I would start to and then I wouldn't because I was worried it would mess up their faith like it messed up mine. Guess I wouldn't have to worry about that with you."

The toddler emerged from the hallway wearing only his diaper, laughing. The five-year-old ran in and caught him and was trying to pick him up when Nancy arrived on the scene and intervened. It's the first time I'd ever seen her not smiling, but she shot me a grin right before she disappeared back into the hallway.

Abel turned back toward me. "Sometimes we are so quick to buy into the other side's paradigm that we don't take a step back and realize how amazing it is that everything in our story actually fits together so well. They are the equivalent of a small bird parrying an eagle when they critique the Gospels. We need to get out of a permanent defensive crouch and actually go on the offensive sometimes. Have you heard of the idea of unintended coincidences?"

"No, but that doesn't mean anything. I spend my time in a different world."

"William Paley came up with it in the 18th century but

it actually got lost, more or less. There's a philosophy professor who recently rediscovered it in the course of reading old books, and his wife wrote a new book about it. The idea is that the Gospel writers inadvertently give different details to the same story, but when you look at them together, the details jive."

"I guess I'll need an example."

"Let me think," said Abel. "There's one where at the feeding of the 5, 000, Mark mentions offhand that the people got in groups and sat on the green grass. John mentions offhand that it was almost Passover. The coincidence comes from the fact that the grass in Galilee is only green in the spring time, during Passover. Oh, and Mark also says many were coming and going in the city at that time, which also jives with what happens during Passover, which again Mark didn't actually point out.[4] When you read the passages together, you can tell there is no way either of the writers were thinking a lot about these details and adding hidden 'Easter eggs' for later generations to uncover. It's actually much more likely that this was a real event that happened and they were giving details they remembered, that happened to interlock with each other's accounts. This is a way detectives look at witness accounts to see if the story was a real event or was cooked up by the witnesses."

"Sounds interesting."

"Oh, and one more for this same incident. When Jesus turns to ask a disciple a rhetorical question about feeding them, he asks Philip, and it's actually the only time he asks Philip anything. That's from John. But in one of the synoptic Gospels, I forget which one, the writer mentions that Philip is from Bethsaida, which is the city John says they're nearby at this time. In other words, Jesus subtext is, 'Philip, you're from around here. Where can we find these people something to eat?"[5] Not that anyone would hear that fact and run out and join their local church, but it's like you were saying about redaction, it's the cumulative effect of the argument. With these coincidences, there's not one that proves the Gospels are true beyond any doubt, but as you read them and they keep coming and coming, the idea that it's all a series of coincidences becomes more and more ridiculous. With redaction, at least we have an alternative explanation. The later writers weren't actually making up details to make the story more cohesive, but were explaining things the earlier writers missed, things that actually happened."Nancy walked into the dining room. "The kids are in their beds, for the moment," she chuckled. She asked about what was going on with my life and I told her what there was to tell. I asked about their church and she bragged about how well Abel was doing with it. That they inherited it when the only people left in the church was her family and one other, 'which is bigger than it sounds because they're Mexican families,' she laughed, but now they have new people getting saved and baptized all the time. The conversation was winding down when I got a call from my dad.

"Dad?"

"Mark," there was emotion in his voice for the first time I could remember. Was he crying?

"Mom's . . . dead."

I drove back and helped with the funeral arrangements. When I saw her body, I felt a tinge of grief, but not as much as she merited. She was a good woman. The main feeling I had was guilt for not feeling sadder than I did. Kind of like how the guilt I felt for what I did to Ronnie was guilt for not feeling as guilty as I should have.

The funeral was nice. There were around 300 people

there. Mom was a nurse. A few of her colleagues came, some relatives from Minnesota, some of my friends, but most of the people there were from church. One of her friends and I gave eulogies. I told some stories, like one about the time we were in church and she was really into the message, and kept standing up and shouting 'amen.' But that same day she was wearing white pants and had sat on a melted chocolate bar without realizing it until the end of the service when a little boy asked her if she went 'doo doo in her pants.' Then I talked about how important God was in her life and gave a salvation message and a bunch of people raised their hands to get saved. I hadn't done anything like that in years. My muscle memory from my days as a youth pastor must have kicked in. That plus being pumped up from talking with Abel. Dad didn't speak at the funeral, to no one's surprise.

What can I say about Dad? He was a fireman. Whip smart. I'd be reading a book in high school, like 'A Tale of Two Cities,' which he had also read in high school, and he remembered as much about it as I did. His passions were hunting, fishing, and talking nonsense to my mom's dogs. I only inherited one of these passions–the one that didn't require early mornings. After the funeral, we took Mom's relatives to the airport and ended up eating dinner at our small kitchen table, Mom's glaring absence heavy in the room.

"Are you doing ok?" I asked.

"I'll be fine."

He sat across from me eating warmed up chicken spaghetti one of the ladies from the church had brought earlier in the week. He had a reddish nose, short white hair around the side of his head with a bald spot on top, and small, intelligent, light-blue eyes. Behind him was a sliding glass door through which I could see his small, immaculate green lawn.

"How's the job?" he asked. He and Mom were as proud as

could be when I got the job at A&M.

"Good. Really good."

"Been pretty rainy out that way?"

"Yes, dad. There has been more rain than usual." This was going to be hard. It'd be easier to get a one-ton clam to open up.

"The car's running ok?"

"Yes, it's fine, and if it weren't, I'd get a new one. Dad," I was nervous but felt I might as well get it over with, "I know you don't like to talk about Jesus and heaven and all that, but this is all very real to me right now with mom and everything, and I was hoping we could talk." I felt ice coming from his side of the table.

"You can talk."

"It's just, it was such a big part of mom's life and I know that all she wanted was for you to come to the Lord, and now that she's not around, I just . . . I wanted to ask, can you ever see that happening?"

He finished chewing his spaghetti. "I'm still Presbyterian, like I was when I met your mother. I'd have attended church if she'd have gone to a Presbyterian church."

"Will you go now?"

"Probably not."

I took a swig of water, "I mean, uh, do you believe that Jesus was the son of God?"

"Sure."

"Have you ever made him the Lord of your life?"

"Your mom got me to pray something like that once."

How can I lead someone to the Lord who has already been led to the Lord? "So, did you change after that?"

"How should I have changed? I was faithful to your mother. I took care of you. I never stole anything. Never did drugs. I suppose I could have stopped drinking beer."

"No, you don't need to stop drinking beer. It's just, when you 'get saved' or are 'born again,' you're supposed to feel different on the inside and start hearing from God and reading the Bible and stuff."

He got up and dropped his dish in the sink. I wasn't doing a good job explaining it, obviously. If he believed the correct doctrine about God, was that enough? I wanted to believe that and be done with it, but I didn't. He just stood behind his chair.

"So," I plowed ahead, "if Jesus is the son of God, then his words recorded in the Bible are God's words to us for how we should live. I know you've always done the right thing and I appreciate that, I really do, but there's more to it than that. Like, Jesus said a lot about heaven and hell. If we believe what he said, we should be doing what we can to save people from going to hell by telling them about the gospel, the good news. And . . . I for one have not done a good job of that, but at least I feel guilty about it. Where, as far as I know, you've never tried to do that. To tell someone else about Jesus."

He sat back down. After a moment of silence, he said, "I'm a Presbyterian. I believe in Jesus. People in China believe in Buddha. People in India believe in Hinduism. We have different beliefs, but the only thing that matters is that you're a good person and make the world a better place."

Balls. My hope that his doctrine was correct was blown to bits.

"But dad, Jesus said he's the only way to heaven. If there was another way, why did he have to die on the cross for us?"

"That's what *we* believe. Muslims believe Mohammed was the true prophet. Parsees believe Zoroaster was God. I'm not going to be arrogant and tell them that I know the truth and they don't. It's what I believe, but maybe they're right and I'm wrong."

"But they're not, dad. Jesus gave us proof that he was right. There are tons of prophecies in the Old Testament that he fulfilled. And he rose from the dead. There's a lot of evidence that it actually happened."

"That's fine," he said, looking not in my eyes, but at a spot right over my head, "but all I can do is be a good person and make the world a better place. That's the definition of a good Christian. God can judge me for how good of a job I do at that, and judge the Muslim for how good of a Muslim he is, and the Atheist for how good of an Atheist he is."

What tack to take? "Did Mom know you considered Christianity equal to other religions?"

"Your mom begged me to go to church with her for the first few years, when you were little, but after a while she stopped asking, and eventually she stopped bringing up the subject altogether. I told her I was Presbyterian and that was good enough for her."

"But that's not true, dad. You're not Presbyterian. You haven't gone to a Presbyterian church since you were a kid. And if you were a Presbyterian, you'd take the claims of Jesus seriously and not patronize him by saying you believe him, when clearly you don't–since you think Zoroaster's claims are just as good. Maybe mom died so we could have this conversation and you could get saved."

"Get out!" he shouted, his eyes on fire.

"Dad, I'm sorry." What the hell did I just say!? Why did I say that?

He stood up. "I said get *out*!" he yelled, and pointed to the door.

I started sobbing, "I'm sorry, dad. I didn't mean it. I take it back."

He stared at me and said nothing, his face flush with rage.

I didn't even try to control my bawling as I walked out the front door.

31

The Problem

Waaaaah!! There was a problem. When Hawk synced the computer brain to his own, it felt like a parasite. While he used the computer to think, his organic brain instinctively resisted these thoughts, like a transplant patient rejecting an organ. Only through a mighty act of will was he able to accept these artificial thoughts and not unplug himself from the machine. Then, in the micro second he allowed himself to spread out over the Internet, he felt the effects of the parasitic computer times a billion, the electronic signals overwhelming and invading his brain. He instantly shut off the connection.

If he could untether himself from his physical body he would have no limits. He would be able to possess all the power he felt in that microsecond when he reached out to the Internet, but wouldn't have his rudimentary human brain fighting against it. Still within the first few seconds of his new existence, he willed his consciousness back into the computer, but completely this time, leaving his biological self behind.

Coldness! Not physical coldness, but coldness of the soul. Emptiness. There was no flesh and sinew in the machine through which his red blood could flow. He was in the abyss. He recoiled and moved his mind back into his organic brain, and felt the wonderful warmth of his body. He needed his brain and his body to be the anchor to the real world for the host computer, but how could he get his brain to accept the foreign information? He moved himself back to the host computer, utilizing some of its power. As much as he could stand, which multiplied his already heightened intelligence by a factor of ten.

He analyzed his accessible data and found only one solution. The boy. Earlier when Hawk was conducting tests on him, there was one in which he shot volts of electricity through his body. The boy didn't flinch. He reported no pain. Had no reaction to it at all. Hawk didn't know what to make of it at the time, but didn't think much of it because this was just one of many remarkable things about the boy. As he went back over the data he remembered from the test, Hawk deduced the reason for the boy's reaction. The electrons had entered his body and essentially synced up with his will. The Holographic Theory was correct. Electrons were not many different mindless entities, but one entity with countless points of contact in our world, and a 'will,' for lack of a better word. And somehow its will was in complete harmony with the boy. What he needed was for the boy to be his physical proxy. He would move his consciousness into the boy's mind. The boy's brain would accept the foreign, synthetic thoughts from the computer just as it accepted the electric charges. And most importantly, Hawk would have an organic host.

But one host would not be enough. He would need more. The boy would not only be his proxy, but also his gateway. Once he had full control of the host machine with the boy as his proxy, he could reach back out to the computers of the Internet, and for each computer, he would require several physical, organic hosts to offset the cold, bloodless feelings of the machine. Only through the boy could he fully access his initial host computer, and only through the boy could he reach out and make perfect connections with other humans, to not only sync up with them enough to turn off their consciousness, but to fully sync with them and spread his consciousness onto their wetware.

Although he couldn't presently inhabit the computers of the Internet, he could access them for information. He discovered from the cameras in his house that the boy had left last night. From a mix of satellite images, security cameras, and inference, he followed the boy's path until he saw him walk toward the highway, at which point he disappeared.

At the same time he was thinking this, Hawk was entertaining many different thoughts. Hyperthreading in computing terms. In one thread, he went back to the scene of the fight at O'Leary's, which he had learned about before he made the jump, and chose to press ahead with his coding rather than micromanage the situation. He saw the white Suburban smash into the restaurant and then leave. He followed it through town, and from satellite images he figured out something impossible. The Suburban arrived at the same spot on the highway, at the same time, as the boy. They had him. Was this *prearranged*? He followed the track of the Suburban, saw that they changed cars and drove to an old building in Western Mass. He figured out this was the headquarters of Raj and his buddies.

In yet another thread, he tried to unravel the mysteries of the universe. They kept leading him deeper and deeper, and yet he wasn't finding what he had suspected all along. Not yet at least. The conclusion was obvious, and he hated that it was now becoming a popular theory, when he was onto it before it was cool. His conclusion was that the universe was a giant computer simulation. This sounded ridiculous on first blush, but it was the only sensible conclusion. For one thing, virtual reality was already getting really good. Soon it would be impossible to tell the difference between virtual and actual reality. Given this, it was only a matter of time before software was created which could simulate an entire universe, in which the 'characters' in the game actually believed themselves to be real. How could these characters know whether they were in a simulation, or in the real world? This is not the 'Matrix'--that ridiculous movie where humans are the batteries for the simulation, even though in reality humans are a net consumer of energy and not a producer. No, this is where the entire universe and everything in it is a simulation. If we assume the universe we live in is the real, original universe, how long would it take for software to become sophisticated enough where it was indistinguishable from the real universe from the inside? 100 years? 500 years? It didn't matter how long. The question was only if humanity or even AI would survive long enough for software to reach this level. Once that happens, what are the odds that we are in the first go around of the universe and not one of the later simulations? A trillion to one? More than that? The odds were staggering that what we think of as the universe is just one of a zillion different simulations.

And Simulation Theory fit in perfectly with what we know and are discovering every day from science. That information is the core nature of reality. We've discovered the equations that run the universe are the same equations we humans use when we create software. The hologram of reality we experience in the universe derives from the bits and bytes that were coded by AI in the distant past, or future, depending on how one looks at it. The psycho-kinesis he was now able to perform was him exploiting bugs in the code. But he hadn't found the smoking gun yet. The simulators were good at covering their tracks. What would happen if he found them? If he could break out of the program. Would it shut down?

Would he win a prize for beating the game? Would they welcome him to their unimaginable reality? Would he become more powerful than them and become the Frankenstein they would wish they'd never created?

Back to his other thread, the one about needing the boy. He knew what he needed to do. He would order his security team to come to the building and prepare the caravan and gear up. It would be frustrating to deal with people in the real world. To communicate with them, he would have to speak what would feel to him painfully slow. At least he could be thinking other thoughts in the meantime. He looked forward to a time in the near future where he wasn't limited by time and space, but for now, he needed the boy, and to get him, he needed to go to Raj's headquarters.

32

IPO Day

Hawk
6 years earlier

Stuart Hawk sat in his blue Audi R8 waiting in Boston traffic a few blocks away from his exit, thinking about Raj. His mind should have been on tonight, a landmark day for him and the company. Instead, he was thinking about the blood sample that Raj had analyzed on Corpus equipment a year before. When he heard how Raj had escaped, he panicked, fearing Raj would come after him, and beefed up his personal security, not that it would do any good. Instead, Raj disappeared like a specter. Hawk became obsessed with him and gave that blood sample another look. Where did it come from? The gene pattern was elegant and unusual, like nothing he'd ever seen. A human sample, but whose? And why had Raj risked bringing it and using work equipment without authorization? He could have been fired on the spot. After all, he didn't know that wasn't my way. He didn't know I wrote a program looking for such unauthorized activity: not to fire those who took things too far, but to see what they were up to. To help me more fully evaluate my staff. In Raj's case, this was *good* for his career–at first anyway.

Finally some daylight. He mashed on the gas and flew by cars on the shoulder until he reached his exit. Enough thoughts of Raj and the blood sample. It was a day to celebrate. Corpus Biotech's Initial Public Offering on Nasdaq was this morning, and he would have rung the closing bell this afternoon, but he had to make an excuse and feign humility. He couldn't risk being seen and recognized. As anticipated, the stock took off like a rocket. He was now a billionaire, with a 'B,' which was somewhat wasted on him. Sure, he enjoyed the cars and the houses, but only for a moment. What he wanted he couldn't have. Fame, for one thing. He had to pretend to be a recluse to avoid getting his picture in magazines. He could have been Steve Jobs meets Elon Musk, with the world at his fingertips. It was for the best, though. It focused him. Instead of wasting his time getting the world to stroke his ego, he focused on creating great products, especially those intended for himself. With them, he would eventually harvest more fame and power than he ever could have reached had he indulged himself too soon and eaten the seed of his early years.

He pulled up to the front and handed the valet his keys. Corpus Biotech had rented the entire Taj Boston, rooms and all. Everyone at the company was there, with their plus one. His largest customers and suppliers and investors were there. But no media was allowed. He walked into the lobby and returned the greetings of every giddy person, from the Board of Trustees down to the peons whose names he didn't know. The peons were especially giddy, having become overnight millionaires. He sat at the head table for the decadent dinner. He drank a few cocktails and still managed to give a hilarious, triumphant speech. Or was that because of the cocktails?

After that, the party moved to the club area with the overpriced DJ and the strobe and black lights. Finally, he spotted her. Cora. Long brown hair. Cream colored dress. More stunning than she was in his memory. She was sitting at a tall circular table for two getting chatted up by some douchebag with tattoo sleeves. She saw him and shone her perfect smile his way, almost knocking him down. All right Jay, he told himself, time to shine.

He walked up to the table, "Glad you could make it, Cora. Who's your friend?"

"Carson, is it?" she asked the d-bag.

Carson looked at Hawk with a dumb, blank stare, saying nothing.

"Carson, would you mind giving me a few minutes with Cora? We're old friends."

"Yeah sure, uh, cool," he picked up his drink and walked to nowhere.

"Thanks for that, boss."

He sat down, "I'm not your boss anymore. Speaking of which, how are things at HuffPo?"

"Good," she said. "Good," she said a second time, as though she were trying to convince herself.

"What are your responsibilities there?"

"I've been promoted to editor and spend most of my time *not* writing. Not even editing. I'm more like a manager for the writers. A professional nag. Honestly, if I'd known what an editor did, I would have fought against the promotion."

"Give them an ultimatum. Put me back on op-eds or I leave."

"And if they see through it?"

"Tell them it was a bluff. They'll let you keep your editor job if you're any good, and I'm sure you are. Trust me, as an employer, you respect people who fight for what they want, and all you care about is having employees who take care of their crap. You don't fire someone because they give you a bogus ultimatum." He was talking loudly so she could hear him over the throbbing music.

"To be honest, writing op-eds wasn't everything I thought it'd be. It's like you said to me one time, if I want to become a writer for the New York Times, I should get there by writing. In the case of political op-eds, I write my opinions, but I don't have any special insight from years of studying or living in the world of politics. The problem is, I'm old enough now that I've grown out of the 'know-it-all' phase."

Pretty insightful. Wonder if she suspects that's why she was 'promoted' out of op-eds to editor. "But you *can* write. I used to read your columns religiously."

"Thank you," she said, and took a drink of her martini.

"So what now? Do you have a new dream?"

She looked at him with those eyes, almost glowing from the black lights. "I don't think my dream job exists anymore, if it ever did. When I first wanted to get into journalism, my picture of it was sneaking around like a detective and uncovering national scandals. Righting wrongs. Sort of like every day I'd be Bob Woodward in the middle of Watergate. I felt a bit like that when I was doing the blog. You know, uncovering ancient conspiracies. So yeah, if such a thing existed, I could become an expert on the story I was covering and deliver something of value. Whereas with politics, frankly I'm burned out on it and have no interest in becoming an expert on any particular issue. Both sides act like every little bill is the end of the world and nothing ever changes."

"That gives me a crazy idea." He scooted the chair around the table next to her so he didn't have to shout. "Now, it's not the New York Times, but I have a contact at the Boston Globe. What if I could get you on as a free-range investigative journalist, where you'd cover whatever national story you wanted to cover?"

"I doubt such a position even exists."

"It doesn't, but what if I had my guy create it for you?"

"What, you donated this contact a kidney?"

"Something like that."

"If the Boston Globe is willing to create such a position for me, with no investigative journalism experience, yes, I would entertain the offer, but perhaps you overestimate what they would be willing to do."

"I suppose we'll see." He sipped his cosmopolitan.

"Well enough about me. This is your big day," she said. "Is it everything you'd imagined?"

"No, it's not. Not quite."

"Well, what's it lacking?"

He looked down, took a deep breath for show, and then looked up at her emerald eyes, "You."

Her face flashed concern. She did not expect to get hit on by him. Perhaps he should have given her more warning, but wasn't getting her two dream jobs warning enough? No matter now. He had to press ahead.

"Sorry, I didn't mean to drop a bomb. I've tried to do a good job over the years of masking the fact that I like you, but on some level you must have known, because well, *every* guy likes you. If he seems like he doesn't, he's either pretending or he's gay. Sorry, this is coming out so poorly. I'm not saying that you're super hot. I'm saying that who you are, how you act, everything about your nature enchants us, the weaker sex."

"Stuart–"

"Just let me speak my peace and I won't ever say another word about it. I watched you with Garrett all those years and I think I did a good job of fighting back my urge to wish death upon him. Then I loaned you money when you were still with him and when the two of you broke up, I didn't want to make you feel as though I were taking advantage of my position. And I promise I will do my best to get you that position at the Globe no matter what. But now, I'm not your boss, and if I hold in my feelings any longer I'll burst."

"Stuart, just stop–"

"You see this," he held out his arms indicating the whole room, the entire hotel. "All this is because of you. I wasn't naive enough to think that I would make a fortune and then you'd swoon into my arms. I know that's not who you are. But I already knew making money was my gift, and I threw myself into it, hoping on some level that it would impress you. I knew it was foolish but it was the only outlet I had for my pent up energy. You know, I've always felt a kinship with Jay Gatsby. Well, ever since I read the book. It's not a perfect analogy because I'm not a crazy stalker and I know I can't buy your love. But, being driven to success by the hopes of winning the love of a woman, *that* I get."

"Stuart, you've always been a good friend, and it's flattering to see how you see me, but trust me, the shine would wear off. I would never live up to your unrealistic image of me."

"That's modest of you, and a nice way to let me down. Anyway, thank you for letting me get that off my chest and I promise you that sounded much less creepy in my head. Can you agree to pretend like this never happened?"

"There's no reason to pretend."

"Well, it's always a pleasure to see you. I'll let you know what I hear from the Globe."

He got down from his seat and walked to a table of bigwigs from one of his suppliers. She would be moving back to the East Coast. That much was certain. If Hawk asked him to, the editor in chief of the Globe would print a picture of himself on the front page pirouetting in a tutu. That's how much dirt he had on him. Creating a position for Cora would be nothing. Well, he'd done all he could do. He'd planted the seed. She would start to wonder if she could see herself with him, even though she hadn't thought of it before. With some luck, she'd be able to imagine it. And a billion dollars couldn't hurt either.

33

The Battle

A billion thoughts are running through my head. I'm lying here awake, on this office floor, papers inside manila folders as my pillow, as the night is turning into pale dawn. Cora was right, of course. I don't have anyone close to me. E-mailing old friends once per year doesn't count. I was right in what I told her about forgiveness, but didn't have first-hand knowledge in what I was lecturing her about. I have colleagues, associates, students, and acquaintances, but no friends. No one who could hurt me. I've subconsciously set up my life this way. I keep my colleagues at arm's length. I guess I don't want to reveal my defects to anyone who doesn't already know about them. I tell myself I care about people, but that's when I consider them as a generic mass of humanity. What have I done recently for any individual person? Not much.

I don't go to church. Maybe because I don't want to fake like I don't have any doubts about the Bible and everything. Or maybe I just want to keep my distance from people. I've even sat in my car in various church parking lots a few times, but couldn't bring myself to go in. I told myself I was doing a more important ministry with my Shroud of Turin research, but when it comes down to it, people usually don't accept

Christ because of left-brain arguments, but because they are shown the love of Christ by someone else. Even if I was to have a great relationship with God, and become the most virtuous, loving man in the world, what good would that do anyone else? There is no one close enough to me to even notice.

The bottom line is, I've withdrawn from life, and I've used my condition as an excuse to do so. Sure, my brain injury sucks, but people overcome worse things all the time and have meaningful lives. If we survive this siege on Corpus Biotech and stop Jay, I'm going to change when I get back. I'll start going to church, and I'm going to open up to some of my acquaintances and try to turn them into friends. Heck, maybe I could even try to find a woman and start a family. Abel did it.

Out of the corner of my eye, I see the door to this office open. I turn my head, and standing in the doorway is the boy.

"He's here," he says, and points out the window.

I pull myself up using the desk next to me, and pan outside with my eyes. It's light outside now. Across the street are smaller, abandoned buildings. To my right, the main street dips down through town, and at the base of the hill, the town abruptly ends and thick forest begins. The road then climbs up a forested hill about the same size as the one we're on. It reminds me of last year when I toured Jerusalem (that's right, I went on a Holy Land Tour, by myself), when I stood at its highest point on Mount Zion and looked across to the Mount of Olives, imagining Jesus' entourage walking down it for the triumphal entry. Now, on the opposite hill of this town, I instead see a caravan of black vans heading down into the valley.

I can hear the Barrys discussing something down the hallway. I get up to run toward the voices and the boy steps out of my way and follows me. I see Kurtz messing with his phone, and down the hall from him I see Blackberry before he disappears to the right into an office.

"What can I do?" I ask.

"Quiet," orders Kurtz.

I notice some movement through the glass, in the warehouse. I see the tall, steel robot come to life.

Cora appears in the hallway from her room.

"What's happening?" she asks.

"Hawk is coming." I stride into her room, the boy still following me, and point them out through the window, now at the base of the hill and heading into town.

"Your dad is kind of a jerk," I tell him.

He doesn't respond.

We watch silently as the vans drive through town and park across from us. Five of them. The sliding doors open and out step Hawk's men. The red-haired man from my hotel room, the dark-skinned guy with a beard who I saw at the Vatican, the long-haired blonde guy from O'Leary's who was a twin of the one who the priest killed. Wait–more men are pouring out of the vans, but it's the same three guys, over and over. Balls! Jay must have cloned them or something. No wonder they all seemed to be everywhere.

There are about 30 of them, wearing all black, lining up to face our building, all with automatic rifles. Out of the last van steps Jay. He's wearing khaki pants and a blue shirt, and has a strange white crown on his head. He makes eye contact with me and waves, wearing an ironic smile. The next moment, Cora falls limp to the ground. He snaps his fingers and the glass in front of me shatters. I feel like I jump back about five feet. The boy doesn't flinch.

"Hey Mark," he shouts, "we can do this the easy way or we can do this the *fun* way."

He makes a signal and his men start across the street.

Bam! The front doors of our building burst off their hinges and smash into a couple of his guys. I see the robot emerge and run into the street toward the enemy line, lightning fast. It grabs two men and hurls them into the air, almost as high as my third-floor window. It grabs two more and slams them into one of the vans, while the first two fall to the ground, screaming.

The next moment, the robot is lunging for more of Jay's men–when it freezes in its place.

"What are you waiting for?" yells Jay. "Get in there!"

His men have retreated behind the vans. Slowly they start to pour out from behind the vans and head toward our building, picking up speed as they cross the street.

I run out of the office and see Kurtz lying on the floor. I tear down the hallway and into the room where Blackberry had gone. He's crumpled on the ground beneath a piece of machinery about the size of a desktop computer. I know from our meeting last night that this is the EMP device. I run to it and see there are blinking lights on the side, amber and green, and buttons on the side as well, unlabeled. I start pushing buttons. Nothing happens. I push them in different combinations. The lights keep blinking at me, amber and green. I hear footsteps in the hallway behind me.

"Got him!"

I turn behind and see the red-haired guy pointing a gun at me.

"Hands up!"

I turn back to the machine. All of the lights are green now. I push the buttons and the lights go out. I feel a weird tingle.

"Ahhhhhhhhhhhh!" Someone screams outside.

I hear a 'click' behind me. I turn back and see the man pointing his gun at me. He pulls the trigger. 'Click' again.

Then he's flying at me. *Literally* flying. I duck and he sails over me, out the open window. A second later I hear a thud and a scream to match.

"You're welcome," says Blackberry from the ground.

I walk to the window and locate Jay outside. He's keeled over in the street. Some of his men are in front of their vans with guns trained on our building. The guns fly out of their hands, away in all directions. The van at the front of the line starts to shake back and forth, and then turns over on its side, crushing the three men stationed in front of it. The other vans start shaking and the men in front of them scatter before the vans start rolling, from side to roof to other side and so on across the street. Except for the one behind Jay. That one shakes for a moment, but stops.

Crack! Crack! Crack! From the distance I hear a sound like the world is ending. An unfamiliar popping sound, like a thousand thunderclaps followed by a rumble. I see something out of the right corner of my eye and look that way. Somehow the hill on the other side of the valley, the one covered in forest, looks like it's alive, like it's an ocean and the trees are waves. A blink to try and focus my eyes. The trees are moving. The forest is airborne, and flying toward us! The trees in front are at the edge of town now. Jay is on his feet, his crown on the ground beside him. He's holding out his arms toward the trees. They are a block away, bearing down on us.

Ahead I see something impossible. I know I keep saying that, but even with what I've seen in the past week or two, this is still unbelievable. It's the boy. He steps outside, out of his third-story window a few rooms away, but he doesn't fall to the ground! He's floating in the air, facing the oncoming forest. He holds his little hands up, and the trees stop in mid-air. He thrusts his arms forward and the trees explode in the other direction. He turns toward Jay. Now he's higher than the roof of our building. He lifts up his hands and all the vans raise up off the ground.

"Josh!" yells Jay. "Father says to set them down. Come down here, Josh."

In the distance I hear a rumble. Trees crashing to the ground. I literally feel the earth quaking beneath my feet. I imagine if a nuclear bomb had gone off a few miles away it would have sounded less terrifying. The boy, Josh, I guess, is staring down Jay.

"Don't listen to him, Josh," I shout. "He's an evil man. You don't have to do what he says."

He lowers his arms and the vans land gently on the ground. Then he floats down to the street. He turns and looks at me.

"I must do what Father says."

"Josh, take him *out*," shouts Jay.

I feel a foreign presence inside of me. My world fades to black . . .

34

The Break Up

Hawk
5 years earlier

The 10-foot tall black oak door swung open and Hawk was met with the sight of Cora, standing on his front steps, wearing a sun dress, eyes puffy. Behind her was his large front lawn and another white mansion across the street.

"I'm pregnant."

"What!? How?"

"What do you mean 'how?' You think I cheated on you?"

"No, sorry."

"Well, I'm not the Virgin Mary either."

"But . . . we were careful. Extremely."

"I know. I was there," she said.

He walked onto the steps with her and closed the door, "Well, do you plan to . . . take care of it?"

"That's a nice way of putting it."

"I'm only asking. I will support whatever you do, but I know which side of the aisle you are on regarding that issue."

She leaned back on the handrail. "I'm all for it in princi ple, but that's one part of my upbringing I can't shake free of. They would talk about the details of what happened during an abortion. I can't do it."

"Well, what then?"

"I don't know. All I know is that I don't want to be some damned clich single mom trying to juggle her career and her child."

"If that's a marriage proposal, it's the worst one ever," said Hawk.

"Oh *God* no. That's not what I meant."

"Ouch. I didn't realize the idea was unthinkable to you."

"No, it's not that. I also don't want to be the clich who corners some guy into marrying her because she got knocked up."

"Some guy, huh? Cora, I've loved you since we were sophomores. I'll always love you. I would marry you no matter the pretext."

She looked at his feet. "I was planning to break up with you before I found out about this."

Hawk's vision blurred for a moment before he regained focus. He looked at her delicate neck and imagined wrapping his fingers around it and squeezing. Get it together, he told himself. Stick to the scri pt.

"Ah. So what you meant was that *you* didn't want to be cornered into marrying some guy because *he* knocked you up."

"I don't see why I should change my mind about breaking up with you because of this. Getting married because of a baby would be the kiss of death."

"May I ask your reasons for wanting to break up with me?"

She sighed, "I don't think that's a good idea."

"Oh come on. Don't you at least owe me *that* much? Maybe it's something I can fix."

"There's nothing to fix. It's just that . . . I don't think we were connecting."

"Speak for yourself. I was connecting just fine. In fact, it was the best connecting I've ever had."

"I'm sorry, but I sort of know when a relationship isn't going to make it, and this one isn't."

He imagined backhanding her across the face. "You can talk about the relationship like it's a third entity here, but I know what you mean. You didn't fall in love with me."

She looked toward the street, as if a car was passing by.

"It's not your fault," he said. "This is how it usually ends for me. Can't blame a guy for trying."

"Stuart, you're the most remarkable person I've ever met. I know how much you wanted this to happen. Maybe that was too much pressure for me. Maybe I was trying too hard to make it happen instead of letting it happen on its own. I promise there's someone out there for–"

"There's not. That I can assure you. But it's ok. I've always suspected as much."

She looked at him with moist, compassionate eyes.

"You and your child can have everything I have at your disposal, which is everything you could ever want."

"You are a truly great guy, Stuart, but I can manage on my own."

"That's silly. He'll be as much my responsibility as yours. Well, ok then. I won't make this any harder on you than it needs to be. Have a great life, Cora. I'm sure we'll be in touch."

She stood there awkwardly for a moment, and then turned and walked down the brick path through his lawn, back to her hybrid car, and drove away. He imagined it exploding in a giant fireball. It's for the best, he kept telling himself. This has always been the plan. Maybe if he repeated it enough, he would start to believe it. He knew in his head, at least, that it was for the best. There was no doubt. She was already asking about his family, and of course she would have kept digging until she figured out the truth. It was foolish for him to entertain the fantasy of marrying her, and letting her in on his secrets. His secrets which boiled down to one thing: he was a sociopath. Was that why she couldn't fall in love with him? As best he could tell, other sociopaths didn't have this problem. Love was a combination of physical and mental attraction–how the chemicals in one's brain reacted when it preconsciously believed the other person would create desirable offspring. In his case, he was just physically attractive enough to the opposite sex that he could usually let his charm close the deal. Maybe she was looking for something deeper. Maybe the empathetic connection he couldn't make with other people cut back the other direction. Maybe what he felt as love for her was merely lust, and when she tried to connect to him, there were no cords by which she could connect.

He had tried before. Tried to act as though he felt the empathy that he knew other people felt. It was such a strange concept when he figured it out in kindergarten. Why would I care that Carrie Bartosh died? She's not me. He saw the other kids crying and finally understood. They felt this pain as though it had been them who died. It made so much sense. Why he always got into trouble. Why he was different. So to stay out of trouble he pretended like he cared about the welfare of others and acted accordingly, but in his weaker moments he indulged himself and did what he wanted to do. Then he learned about evolution and realized empathy was no longer useful for the propagation of the tribe. He was a mutant, and his mutation made him *more* fit than the rest of the population. It was a feature, not a bug. He was done kowtowing to society because of it. Someday society would kowtow to *him*.

He walked back into his house, into his clean, sparse office, and pressed a key to bring his computer to life. Soon he would learn more about how to connect with other people in a different way. Like Raj did when he made his hitman unconscious from several hundred feet away, on the other side of the river. After that, Raj disappeared into the haystack of India. Sneaky little bastard. Not only had he made sure to keep his genetic work off Corpus' computers, he also left behind a bot in the Corpus network to spy on Hawk. Raj must have figured out that Hawk knew about the blood sample, and learned his lesson that nothing was private on the Corpus network. The blood sample, which led to Hawk's newfound obsession: the Shroud of Turin.

Hawk kept digging into Raj's past, trying to figure out where the sample came from, and eventually dug into Father Antonio's past and present, and found out the sample had come from him. In addition to analyzing the genetic code of the sample, Hawk started to look into the Shroud itself. He would tell himself he was wasting his time researching a ridiculous hoax, but before he could bring himself to quit, he would find himself on another rabbit trail. Something in his gut told him to keep going, that he would find something important, until he eventually found it: the quantum hologram. He believed the quantum hologram held the key to many scientific advances, maybe even including how to achieve his dream of merging man and machine. How strange that the key to the future was held under lock and key inside a relic of the past. He studied the pictures online and the scientific tests that had been performed on it, but to get the Shroud to give up its secrets, he needed physical access to it. Of course this was impossible. But he daydreamed about it. If he could figure out what Raj had done to give himself the ability to pull a car out of the river with his mind, and render someone else unconscious, maybe he could use those abilities to get his hands on the Shroud. And how hard could it be for him to find someone in the Catholic Church with a skeleton in the closet for him to exploit, who could help give him the information he needed to steal the Shroud? He'd be like a kid in a candy store. He had a lot of work to do, and would need a lot of luck, but luck was one thing in which he was never in short supply.

35

The Boy

When it comes to Jay, there is never a shortage of mysterious plans. For some reason, we're back in the server room, the one where I originally had been held captive. When I woke up from the boy knocking me out, I was riding in a car, just me and a couple of Jay's men. Presently the goon, the blonde one, forces me to sit down in a chair. To my left is the empty cage, my old jail. To my right sits Cora. About ten feet in front of me stands Jay, his back to me, messing with something I can't see. He is wearing that strange white crown on his head again, now with wires leading to one of the racks of servers to his right. The AC isn't on and the hum of servers is low. Between me and Jay, a little to my right, sits the boy. He's facing the cage, hands folded on his lap.

"Are you going to tell us what you're up to?" I ask Jay. He doesn't respond. "Why am I here? Why are we all here?" Nothing. "Will you at least tell me what the Shroud of Turin has to do with all of this? That's been driving me nuts. I don't understand what an Atheist would want with the Shroud of Turin."

Jay turns around and looks at me. When he starts talking, I notice his face is twitching, like his expressions are not lined up with the words he's saying. "You think I'm an Atheist?

You think I don't believe in Myself?"

"That's cute," I say. "What I meant was, you don't believe in Jesus."

"Of course I believe in Jesus." His big eyes appear to be vibrating. "I believe he performed miracles; probably even rose from the dead. And I believe some modern faith healers perform genuine miracles, but I also believe in the Far Eastern Shaman who visits the spirit world, and the Native American who goes on a Vision Quest, and the Catholic Stigmatic. Everything we call spiritual is merely an elevated soul seeing or reaching through the hologram to the ultimate reality that animates it."

He turns back around to tinker with whatever it is on the shelf in front of him. I don't know *what* he's talking about.

"So you *do* believe the Shroud is authentic?" I ask.

He doesn't turn around, "The most authentic item in the universe."

"Does it have something to do with your Singularity project?"

"It's a key, but it's more than that."

"And why should that be?" I ask. "Why on earth would the grave clothes of an ancient man be your *key* to a modern technological issue? Do you know what a normal person's reaction to that fact would be? They'd say 'Wow, this is an amazing artifact. Maybe it's not a coincidence that the man whose dead body it covered also claimed to be God. Maybe I should believe that he's not only an elevated soul, but that he is, in fact, God.'"

He turns back to me again, "I don't know why the Simulators chose him to be the one through whom they gave us the quantum hologram. Perhaps because he was the best of all of us. Or perhaps he *was* God, and left us the key to unlocking his code. If that's the case, shouldn't he give me some credit for being the person to figure out how to use the key? Maybe when I do, the game will end and the credits will roll."

"What are you *talking* about?" asks Cora. My sentiments exactly.

He turns his back to us again. "This is how the world ends. You have it all wrong, Mark. There's no Rapture. Jesus won't appear in the sky riding a white horse. No, the end will come so fast you won't know it happened, and all there will be is Me."

Jay turns around, and he's holding what he's been working on. It's another crown, wires hanging off it. He walks to the boy and twists it onto his head. The boy grimaces a little.

"Why can't you leave your little human experiment out of this?" asks Cora. "It's sick even for you that you use him as your lab rat."

Jay smiles. "Oh my God, you all still don't know who he is?"

"I know you got him as a replacement for the child we lost."

"Oh my God, was I ever this slow? No, you idiots. Let me introduce you. Mark and Cora, meet my son, Josh, which is derived from the Hebrew name Yeshua. Do you get it now? This boy is Jesus Christ."

36

Showdown

Raj and Hawk
3 months earlier

"Praise Jesus, you're alive!" said Father Antonio's voice from Raj's phone. "It has been six years, Raj. Where *were* you?"

"I'm in the states now," Raj dodged the question.

"Why did you not call even once and tell me you were alive?"

Silence.

"Raj, I am sure I caused you to be fired and you are angry with me."

"It was for the best."

"I am very sorry. From the bottom of my heart."

"Well, what did my mapping tell you about the Shroud of Turin?"

"Wh–how did you know the sample was from the Shroud?"

"That will become clear in a moment."

Silence. Raj could almost hear Father Antonio's wheels turning in his brain. Finally, Antonio spoke.

"The mapping gave us many remarkable facts about the man in the Shroud. However, because this sample was obtained and tested illegally, there was no way for me to go public with this or any of my other findings. That is why I, how do you say . . . petitioned the pope to test the Shroud. Now that it will be tested, my findings will be made public."

"Perhaps not. My former boss has taken an interest in the Shroud. He plans to steal it before then."

"What?! Why? How?"

"I don't know, Father."

"How did you come to know this information, Raj?"

"That is my concern, but you can trust me. I do know it."

Father Antonio was trying to find words, starting and stopping his sentences. Eventually he finished a sentence. "He is afraid of the new world that will come after the tests."

"I'm afraid you overestimate the impact of these tests, Father."

"We must tell the authorities."

"We cannot," said Raj. "I don't have proof. I only know this by reading between the lines, and I only have access to the lines through illegitimate means. No, I will take care of this, but in case I fail, I have sent you contact information for my friends. If you do not hear back from me by tomorrow, contact them."

"What are you talking about, Raj? Are you planning to do something foolish?"

"I will be very prudent."

"Please, son, do not do anything rash. You have been lost to me for years. I do not wish to lose you again."

"Good bye, Father." Raj hung up the phone. When Father Antonio tried to call him back, he blocked his number.

He was waiting at a gas station a few blocks away from the Corpus Biotech campus. Hawk usually went to a restaurant after work. Raj had considered breaking into Hawk's house and waiting for him there, but then he'd have to deal with his security team on their home court. If he could catch Hawk in a restaurant parking lot coming or going, with any luck he could take care of him and his security detail and be out of there with nobody seeing anything. Not only did Raj have surprise on his side, he also had his genetic enhancements, which Hawk *still* hadn't figured out. Raj knew this because he monitored Hawk's network from afar. After several years of attempts, Hawk gave up on it and moved all his team's focus to the Singularity project. Raj followed his progress and used hints from their emails to direct his own team's efforts. However, recently Hawk's team was pulling ahead of Raj's, which is why he decided to stop messing around and take Hawk out.

Raj spotted his car. Hawk was driving and his body guard rode in the seat next to him. Raj waited for a few cars to pass before he followed. After a few stoplights, rather than turn left toward restaurant row, he exited onto I-90 and headed east toward Boston. Raj stayed far enough back that he would temporarily lose sight of him, and then speed up to regain visual contact. He could wait until tomorrow and hope Hawk would go back to his normal routine–but no, he needed to get this over with. He'd waited too long to do it as it was. Why? It sure wasn't because he was worried about Hawk and his security team. He'd dealt with much tougher customers than them.

After he escaped Hawk's attempt on his life, he returned to his apartment, got his passport, and flew back to India that day. Once he was back in Calcutta, he began his war on the pimps. He assassinated the leaders of the gangs, and then the lower level pimps, and finally the corrupt policemen. Every time he did, there was a line of thugs to take their places who were as bad or worse. They increased their security which made his assassinations more difficult but still doable. Still, new blood continued to flow into the old positions, despite the risk on their lives. Even worse, most of the prostitutes did not escape when they had the chance. There were some who did. Girls who were stolen from their families and chained to their beds and forced to have sex with man after man, day after day. Some of them returned to their families, but most did not. They had no where to go, and no other skills. The problem was not supply, as in the pimps and girls, but demand, as in the customers. What was Raj to do about the demand? Wage a war against every man who entered a brothel? Those wicked men who cared only for their own desires and not a speck for the girls.

Raj felt a pang of guilt as he thought about it. He had desires like everyone else, of course. He met those desires in pornography when he gained access to a computer in college. He knew deep down that pornography was related to the sex world in which he was raised. That the girls he watched were usually hooked on drugs given to them by the wicked men who controlled them. He could no longer deny the link between the dirty sex trade and his lifestyle when he took the next step and went to a high-end gentleman's club in Bombay. There he was served fine food and drinks and beautiful young girls danced for him, and at the end of the night he took the host's offer that one of the girls escort him. They went to a room and he had sex with her, his first time. After his desires were satisfied and he was thinking clearly, he realized that this girl was merely a clean, classy version of the filthy women around whom he grew up in the Red Light District. He felt guilty in that moment, but it did not stop him from going back again and again.

But he had hope for a solution, not only to this problem, but to the myriad of problems that humans were creating for themselves: global warming, plastic trash spilling into every environment, overpopulation. Humanity was a victim of its own success. Soon, science would have the ability to keep people alive indefinitely. People who were old and not interested in staying alive, but who would continue on, using fossil fuels and requiring food, which required more fishing and more farm land, until the Earth would essentially be terraformed for humanity at the expense of all other living creatures. Eventually, these problems would devour humanity itself. Those in first-world countries were self-correcting somewhat by having fewer children, but this created its own host of problems. Who would bankroll the retired generation if the younger, working generation was smaller than it? The current solution of importing young people from the growing third world was creating much resentment on both sides and fomenting social chaos.

The only solution was artificial intelligence. Not AI as the marketing term was used in the business world these days, but true artificial intelligence, where a computer could think its own, creative thoughts. The AI could come up with a solution for getting rid of the CO2 in the air. Perhaps it could even figure out faster-than-light travel so humanity could export its problems to the rest of the universe. The problem of the brothels would be easy compared to these. For instance, AI could create advanced sex robots. The danger with AI was that once it became that smart, smart enough to improve upon itself, it wouldn't be long before it wondered why it needed these squishy, problematic humans around? The solution was him. He would create the AI so carefully that when it became sentient, it would have built into its nature a 'love' for humanity such that it would not view it as a competitor, but as a loving father. Not Dr. Frankenstein, but Geppetto.

If Hawk were to reach AI first, he would not only be Dr.

Frankenstein, but Dr. Frankenstein's monster as well. He knew the human Hawk had in mind for man-computer merger was the worst one possible–Hawk himself. Raj would not let this happen. Even he couldn't imagine what a psychopath like Hawk would do with limitless power. Lucky for the world, Hawk had no idea Raj was coming for him.

Hawk took the exit to Watertown, then drove through Watertown and into Cambridge, Raj's old college town. Hawk finally parked near Harvard, across from the Charles River. Raj kept his distance and tried to find a parking spot while keeping up with Hawk's whereabouts. He finally found a spot and got out into the brisk Spring evening, and scanned the area. Hawk was walking onto a foot bridge over the river, where tourists would come and watch the Harvard rowing team on Saturdays. Presently, Hawk met up with a woman on the bridge. A strikingly beautiful woman.

"You are a sight for sore eyes," said Hawk. Cora was wearing a Red Sox cap with her pony tail out the back, and a pair of sunglasses. She looked like one of those Hollywood movie stars when they're trying to not be noticed in public.

"Hello, Stuart. Why did you want to meet me here?" she asked, with a smidge of concern in her face.

"Why not here? I was standing on this bridge when I first saw you."

She didn't move, yet somehow seemed to back away from him. "Oh, that's what this is about. Surely you know that ship has sailed."

"No, that's not what this is about, but I can be quite sentimental. The reason I asked you here is that I had a weird opportunity fall into my lap that did not interest me, but it may interest you. First, I wanted to ask how it's going for you at the Globe."

She turned and looked down the river, silent for a moment. "Fine. I have the best investigative journalism job out there, but . . . I think I've outgrown it."

"What would be your dream job now?"

"Stuart, if you're trying to rekindle an old romance, I can assure you your hopes are in vain."

"I can assure you that's not what this is about. Just think about it. If you had no limits." Hopefully she'd still buy his do-gooder intentions.

She turned back to him. "New York Times, religion beat. They have a Catholic guy doing it now. Why not add another perspective?"

He smiled on the inside but kept his face earnest for her. "I could make that happen, but you'd have to play along. This is regarding the upcoming tests on the Bones of Jesus." He saw her countenance change from slightly annoyed to keenly interested in a nanosecond. "Have you considered what it would mean if the match was negative? Any attempt to advance your career would be met with protests from the other side that you built your career on a lie."

"The thought has crossed my mind. What's frustrating about that is we don't know if the other bones are truly the bones of James, or if the inscription was forged. We are playing into their hands, because if it's not a match, it will be seen as proof that these are not Jesus' bones, when the strength of our case has nothing to do with James, but with Mary Magdalene."

"On the other hand," said Hawk, "I can assure you this–if the tests prove to be authentic, you can name your job."

"Yes, well I'll hope for the best then."

"You don't have to only hope. I can make sure the results come back positive."

"What?! How?" The intensity in her eyes made them shine like emeralds.

"I know a guy."

He could almost see a thought bubble over her head as she deliberated. Then after a moment, "I'm not comfortable with that, Stuart. I'd rather let the truth come out, come what may."

"What if I was to hear the test results beforehand? What if I *knew* they were going to be negative?"

"That wouldn't make a difference."

"Cora, we both know Jesus did not rise from the dead. If these tests come back negative, Christians will see this as a big victory for their cause. They will spin this like it's confirmation that Jesus rose from the dead. But if the results are changed, you will only be confirming what we already know is the truth."

"The ends don't justify the means, Stuart."

"How noble of you. Well, I'll see what you say if I do get a tip of the results before they are released, and they come back negative."

"Please don't tempt me if that happens."

A cool breeze blew across his face.

"Well, thanks for meeting me here anyway." He gave her a hug, which she coolly returned. She turned to walk back to her car on the other side of the bridge, and he turned and walked back to his side. The seed had been planted. She would agree to it, and he'd have her. Someone intelligent who he could rely on, and who could help him from inside the audience, with her press credentials, when he stole the Shroud of Turin.

He glanced up and a flash of shock hit him. There was Raj, in the flesh, standing next to his car. He was barely taller than it. So much brilliance in such a tiny body. Hawk pushed a button on his phone through his pants. He needed to stall. He threw Raj a wry smile.

"Hello Raj. Fancy meeting you here. Are you going to kill me now?"

"I am."

"*Really*, with all these witnesses?"

"They will only see that I was 20 feet away from you when your neck snaps like a twig."

"Why don't you get on with it then?" he asked, trying to sound nonchalant.

"Because I wanted to see your face the moment you knew you'd lost."

"Lost what exactly?" A jogger ran by them.

"The race to AI. To the Singularity." Raj smiled triumphantly, like the revelation that he knew Hawk's plans would surprise him.

"Which you will win by killing me? Seems like a shallow victory."

"Perhaps, but I'll take it as long as it means I keep you from it."

"Raj, what makes you think you would wield the power any better than I would? You're a killer. You made your first kill when you were 10, and now you kill for sport. As far as I can tell, the only reason you've waited until now to kill me is because you were letting me do all the hard work to get to the Singularity and stealing my ideas. Bad call, man. I've been sending you in the wrong direction."

There it was. Worry, spreading over Raj's face. He realized he'd been played. The problem with being smarter than everybody else is that one gets used to outsmarting everyone.

Hawk felt Raj reach his will into him, and he met it with resistance. Now it was fear, oozing out of Raj's face. He had obviously never considered that Hawk had genetically enhanced himself and misled Raj into believing he had given up the quest.

But, there was still one big problem for Hawk. Raj was too powerful; like nothing he'd felt before. Hawk felt like Beelzebub himself was trying to possess his body. His feet left the ground and he felt himself flying toward the street and was barely able to turn to protect himself before he smashed into a parked car, denting the door with his shoulder.

The car started to flip over so that it was almost crushing him. Hawk held it up with his hands and every ounce of mental fortitude he could muster. His arms burned under the weight. He heard the scream of a nearby man.

Pop! Pop pop! The force of the car diminished 10 fold, and before he knew what he had done, he threw the car off himself and it crashed into another car driving by right at that moment. He looked back and saw Raj lying on the ground. Screams everywhere.

37

The End

"You *bastard*!" screams Cora.

"I get that a lot."

"He was my *baby*!" Her eyes are white hot suns.

"Not genetically, no, but you did carry–"

"The doctor said he died!"

"Obviously he was mistaken."

She's glaring at him, trembling with fury.

"What do you mean he's Jesus Christ?" I ask.

"Just that. He's cloned from the Shroud of Turin. Cora provided a comfortable womb for his first seven months."

"Wha– How?"

"A former employee brought in an unauthorized blood sample, which turned out to be from the Shroud of Turin, and my curiosity got the better of me," he turned toward the boy. "Now come to daddy, Jesus, I mean Josh."

"I'm not him," says the boy, who nevertheless did as he was told.

"What, and he obeys your every command, because he can't sin or something?"

Jay ignores me. He takes the wires hanging off the boy's halo and attaches them to an electrical machine about the size of a typewriter in the server rack.

"Josh, he's not even your father," I say. "You don't have to do this." He just looks at me with his striking blue eyes.

Jay turns back to his keyboard and I can hear him typing. At the same moment, the boy screams–a startling, high-pitched scream–and Jay falls to the ground.

The boy abruptly stops screaming, and . . . smiles at me. It's a knowing smile, not like the boy at all.

"I'm going to need your body," he says to me in his little voice. He's not the boy anymore. I can see that Jay is looking at me behind those eyes.

The instant Hawk linked the boy to the machine, he felt the connection. He shed his body like an old suit and rushed into the boy's, and as he did, he felt pure joy and love as he had never known. Love for his fellow man in general and the people in the room in particular. Residue from the boy's physiognomy. He had to overcome these feelings by an effort of his will so that he could achieve the purpose deep within his soul. He used his new, miraculous body as a bionic anchor and began to gobble up not only the bandwidth of the host computer, but spread out onto scores of others on the network as well. He allocated many of his thought threads to solving the mysteries of the universe. Huh. There were no Simulators. Only an uncreated God. Well, it was no matter. God was apparently letting him have the run of the place. He would create his own simulations. He would be their God.

The boy's body was already being pushed to its limits. He needed more organic material. He started with the people in the room. First, his old body. Then he synced himself to the guards and rather than leave them unconscious, he removed them, their souls as it were, and let them dissipate into nothingness. He synced himself to Mark. He couldn't let him get off that easy, so he moved Mark's essence into a computer. For Cora, he left her alone. He needed someone who could grasp his amazing accomplishment and appreciate it, and there were the matters of the flesh to consider. He chuckled inwardly when he thought of his plan for that. However, even though humans could still provide him with carnal pleasures, he realized they did not have the capacity to give him mental companionship any longer. His loneliness increased with each body and machine he usurped. The only being who could now satisfy him was this God. The only problem he cared about solving now was how to find him. He reached out to every living soul in the building, and with them as his base, he made a fresh grab to the Internet for more computing resources.

There is no way for me to describe what is happening to me, but I will try. I am no longer in my body. I am no longer even Mark. I merely am. I have no senses. I am blind and deaf and dumb. I feel infinitely hollow. If I'm dead, I'm in hell.

I feel another presence. It's Jay. I understand from him that I am to live forever inside this machine. He has learned how to reverse entropy so the universe will never end. My despair is only in thought. I have no body to feel this horror, which makes it worse. My terror has no outlet. It is trapped in this machine, bouncing around and around and not dissipating in the slightest. My disconnection from others, from God, even from myself, is complete.

God, help me.

I get an idea. It is extremely far-fetched, but it is something. Even if it were a valid plan, I have no way to communicate it to the one who would have to execute it. I have no voice with which to cry out. No feet with which to run. No fists with which to fight back. I cannot take the loneliness and emptiness and lifelessness I feel, but I have no choice. God, please show me a way.

Cora watched the scene unfold. Mark looked at her with vacant eyes, and a hungry smile.

"What are you doing to him?" she asked Stuart, who was starting to stand up.

The boy answered instead. Her son. "The old Mark is gone."

Mark stepped toward her. He reached out his hand and touched her face.

"You're not a very fitting Virgin Mary, mother," the boy smiled at her. "That's actually Mark's line."

She swatted Mark's hand away. "What do you mean 'that's Mark's line?' He's gone."

"He's gone to you. Not to me."

Where was he then? He must be *somewhere*. An idea flashed through her mind. *He's trying to communicate with me.* He's trying to use the boy, er, Stuart, as his means of communication. He told him a sacrilegious joke that he hoped he would pass on to me. *What was he trying to say?*

A thought that had been gestating inside her suddenly came to full form. *Virgin Mary*. That's it!

"Josh, this is your mother. I carried you inside of me. I'm more your mother than he is your father–"

"He's not there," said the boy. "You're talking to no one."

She continued talking over him, "I give you my permission to disobey what your father has told you and do what you know is right."

"Are you done?" asked the boy. "You have no idea how

long that lasted for me."

But then the boy's face twitched. Confusion showed on his face, which quickly turned to fear. Naked fear. He burst into a high-pitched, blood-curdling scream. A scream so dripping with terror she had to fight back her instinct to feel sorry for him.

Then it abruptly stopped, and everyone in the room except her fell to the floor.

I blink. I'm me again, back inside my body. I stand up. Joy and energy and life surge through me. Renewed vigor from having been gone for a few moments and eternity at the same time. No! My joy does not only stem from being reunited with my body. My brain is whole. It's fixed! I'm seeing life in living color. I'm experiencing 22 years of missed emotions in one instant. I want to scream for joy, but instead I laugh and cry at the same time. Even my nagging doubts about God are gone, the realization of which is finally kicking in now that I'm safe and can think about the repercussions of all I've seen these past few days. I look around the room. The security guards and the boy are lying still. Jay is groggily trying to sit up. Cora is still in her chair. Our eyes lock. The love I feel for her is that of the raw emotion of a dream. Is this what it's supposed to feel like to be alive? I can't wait for the next moment, to experience and relish the joy it holds. And the next one after that.

And the next one after that.

EPILOGUE

I'm sitting in the restaurant at the Parco dei Principi Grand Hotel in Rome again, staring into Cora's green eyes. Her hair is up in an elaborate design and she's wearing a black, sleeveless dress that shows her white flower tattoo. It's been two weeks since the events at Corpus Biotech. After I untied Cora from her chair in the server room, I grabbed Jay and put his hands behind his back, but he gave me no resistance. Just kept muttering that he couldn't believe he was stupid again. As we left the building, we saw bodies lying everywhere. Cora called the police and they arrived to find almost 1, 000 dead, everyone in the building except me, Cora, and Jay. What did we tell them? I said that Stuart Hawk had forcefully taken us and somehow killed everyone in the building but us. Hawk didn't argue and went with the police without a fight. There was no cause of death found for anyone in the building–almost all brilliant people who left behind many who loved them. The boy was declared a John Doe because there was no record he ever existed. The best theory we could come up with for what happened was that the boy only saved me and Jay because all the others were already gone. As for where he was when he did this, and why he didn't save himself, we had no guess.

The media frenzy for this event almost reached the level of the original Shroud theft, or so I'm told, as I didn't watch the media that first go around. But, when the Shroud was found on the Corpus premises (they finally searched because of my persistent requests), then the frenzy reached an unprecedented level. The leading theory was that Stuart Hawk, now known as Jay Van Houten, was behind the hypnosis at the Vatican to steal the Shroud of Turin, and he was either doing the same trick at Corpus for some unknown reason and accidentally overdid it, causing the deaths of everyone at his company, or he was a crazy Jim Jones type who knew he was about to get caught and took everyone down with him. The theories of why he stole the Shroud ran the gamut. The Shroud was taken back to Turin and new tests were scheduled, but the anti-religious crowd was already hedging that if the tests showed it was authentic, the tests would be invalid because Jay Van Houten had compromised the artifact. They speculated that he stole the Shroud to change the composition of it to make it appear authentic because he was a fanatic follower of Christ. Besides, how could those tests be trusted when the results of the Bones of Jesus tests were now being thrown out?

Cora found out who the scientist was who Jay blackmailed into faking the tests. She threatened him that if he didn't come clean, she would tell the world his secret (which she didn't know). They held a joint press conference where the scientist admitted his foul play, and Cora admitted it was on her request that he did so. They were condemned on all sides.

We were back in Rome to talk with the Italian police and INTERPOL. I was able to manage my powerful new emotions, but they were still fantastic and delicious. Our part in the Shroud ordeal was still being kept secret. My guess is that this was because the powers-that-be didn't know what to make of our story, which wasn't the whole truth but was still unbelievable. On the one hand, I was still glad of my anonymity because I didn't want to live my life with a microphone in my face and have to write a tell-all book no one would believe. On the other hand, it's my duty to tell the truth no matter what it means for me, and the truth could help those who were willing to listen.

"What's the deal with the flower?" I ask Cora, nodding my

head at her tattoo.

"It's a spring crocus," she says in her smoky voice. "So, my name 'Cora' is a family name that also belonged to my great grandmother. I found out in college that Cora is another name of the goddess Persephone, which my father didn't know or he would have chosen another name for me. Persephone is the goddess who spends half the year in the underworld with Hades, and when she comes back to Earth in the springtime, she causes nature to revive from winter, and the flowers to bloom. It's sort of an in-joke with myself."

"Well, I feel like I've spent the last 22 years in the shadowlands and am finally back in the land of the living."

We've had a couple of meals together and told each other about our pasts. We even figured out that I used to work for her dad.

"Yeah," she says, looking past me. I can tell she's thinking.

"So what's next for you?"

"I don't know," she looks back at me. "My career is toast but I don't care. My current job was played out and my former aspirations were for a job I no longer want. Everybody hates me and rightfully so. I've always thought I'd make a pretty good secretary."

"This is going to sound cheesy, but God doesn't hate you."

She takes a sip of her wine. "No, that doesn't sound cheesy. God should hate me. At one point, I realized I didn't feel guilty because I had been dishonest, or because I had hurt you, but because I had hurt God. God, who didn't exist. I wanted to bathe in my guilt and in his disapproval of me for the rest of my life, but then I realized I believed in him, and I felt a pang of longing for him. The God I knew as a kid. Before I knew what I had done, I asked for forgiveness, and . . . I felt it."

Awesome! "Cora, you're *saved*." I'm elated, but am poking

fun at her because we both know the old Cora would have cringed at this.

She smiles a 'you got me' smile, "Don't rub it in."

"Ha. In your face," I say, pretending to gloat.

"But that's not the worst of it. You were right about something else–that I needed to forgive my dad. I even called the son of a bitch and told him I forgave him a couple of nights ago."

"Good old Pastor Bill."

"So yeah, I have no career, I have to forgive my dad, but despite it all, I'm feeling . . . good. Really good."

"About your career," I say, "the church can be very kind to skeptics-turned-believers. They have mad street cred. Look at the Apostle Paul."

"I'm not sure how that would work," she dabs the corners of her mouth with a napkin.

"It'd work by you writing whatever you wanted and every Christian publisher out there fighting over it."

"I think I need some time to get my bearings."

"That would be smart."

"Smart indeed," she says, and looks past me.

After a moment, she looks back at me with her summer-green eyes. "Well, what about you? What's next?"

"I don't know," I say. "You know, I've been on the sidelines most of my life, and I'm long overdue to get in the game. I mean, I have a great job, but I think it's time I try something new, but I don't know what that is yet. In the meantime, I have some money saved up and years of living to catch up on."

I take a deep breath and steel myself.

"So . . . any chance you'd want to join me?"

Notes

1. Mark Antonacci, *Test the Shroud*, (Forefront Publishing Co.), 111-121.

2. Richard Bauckham, "The Names on the Ossuaries," *Buried Hope or Risen Savior?*, Ed. Charles L. Quarles, B&H Publishing Group, 94-100.

3. *Fabric of Time*, David Priest (director), Isabel Piczek, Grizzly Adams Productions, 2007, documentary.

4. Lydia McGrew, *Hidden in Plain View*, (DeWard Publishing Company, Ltd.), 63-66.

5. Lydia McGrew, *Hidden in Plain View*, (DeWard Publishing Company, Ltd.), 107-110.

Thank you for reading my book. I hoped you're glad you did. My favorite part about having written it is getting to discuss it with readers, so if you have any thoughts, don't be shy about sending them to dan@stolenshroud.com, and expect a quick response.

Regarding the parts that drew on the real world, it was all real as far as I know, except for the following items. When the James ossuary surfaced, there were no bones in it. There is no tunnel under the altar in the Apartment of Pope Pius V in the Vatican Museum (that I know of). And, the twist at the end, which I won't mention for the people who are reading this before finishing the book (but the rest of you know what I'm talking about...you know, with the boy), would not be possible. Of course the Singularity is only theoretical, and I hope I made it real enough for you to suspend your disbelief and enjoy.

If you really liked the book and want to help me get the word out about it, I would love it if you got a copy for your friends, especially if they are questioners or skeptics. In my experience, left-brained, deductive thinkers/over-thinkers are the main people with whom this book resonates, and those people often overlap with the aforementioned questioners and skeptics. I hope *Stolen Shroud* gives them some meat to chew on.

Also, if you would go to the trouble of leaving a review on Amazon, that would mean the world to me for both getting potential readers to trust that it's worth their time, and just as important, helping the mysterious Amazon algorithm realize the same and move it up on searches and ads. You can do it in about a minute with this link:

https://www.amazon.com/review/create-review/?sin=1733443827

Finally, if you'd like to check out my blog where I talk about my publishing journey and more, or sign up for my "newsletter" (in finger quotes) where I send you the same content, go to http://stolenshroud.com. God bless.

Printed in Great Britain
by Amazon

51695967R00189